BOOK ONE

The Illumination Paradox

BOOK ONE

Jacqueline Garlick

SKYSCAPE

Text copyright © 2015 Jacqueline Garlick

Published by Skyscape, New York

www.apub.com

Amazon, the Amazon logo, and Skyscape are trademarks of Amazon.com, Inc., or its affiliates.

ISBN-13: 9781503944558
ISBN-10: 1503944557

Cover design by Kevin C. W. Wong & Mae I Design and Photography

Printed in the United States of America

For my brother, Brad, for obvious reasons.
Always a force in the face of adversity.

For my father, Jack, for whom I was named, and whose
imagination and sense of humor I thankfully inherited.
Thank you for always encouraging me to chase my dreams
and stretch my imagination, and for showing me how.
You are missed.

Oh, and I know this won't make you happy, but . . .
I quit my day job.

Prologue

Eyelet—age eight

A brass mechanical elephant strides toward me, glinting gold in the amber setting sun. Its trunk is raised; steam clouds chug from its nostrils. The carny at its controls peeks out from behind the breastplate, shouting for me to move out of the way.

But I don't.

I stand frozen in the midway, staring up at the elephant's jewel-plated armour and sparkling gemstone eyes, imagining I'm one of the lucky children riding aboard its copper saddle, beneath the bright-pink parasol that shades its back.

Frantic, the carny pulls back a tusk, and the mechanical beauty trumpets, sounding a little bit tinny, yet magically—*elephant!* Its mouth opens wide, showing off a ruby-crested tongue and a row of splendid ivory teeth.

Oh, how I *love* this machine. The way its gears work inside its head so perfectly, unlike the gears inside my own.

"Out of the *way, kid!*" the carny shouts again.

I hear him, but still I don't move.

"Eyelet!" My mother's hand bites down hard on my shoulder, snatching me out of the way. A house-sized plume of dust rises under the elephant's foot, marking the spot where I used to be.

"You could have been killed!" She shakes me by the shoulders. "What were you thinking?" She drops to her knees. "Was it a day-dream? Or was it one of your episodes?" Her eyes are wide and fearful.

I shake my head, but the truth is I don't know. Could it have been an episode and not just my curiosity that held me there? I've been slipping in and out of episodes so much more lately—it's getting harder and harder to tell.

"Oh, Eyelet." Mother's face sours. "What am I to do with you?" She crushes me hard to her chest.

Nothing, I think. It's not up to *you*. Father's promised to fix me. And he will. As soon as he perfects the machine.

I push back in protest, too big for such coddling at nearly nine. "Oh, Mother," I say. "You needn't worry so much. My condition is only temporary. Remember what Father said?"

She blinks at me through glistening green-and-blue-flecked eyes, and for a moment I don't think she believes in Father as much as I do.

"Besides," I say, changing the subject. "Did you see him? The ele-phant, I mean. Did you see how positively *delicious* he was?"

"That I did," she says, the lines softening on her face.

"The way he moved. It was absolutely *perfect*." I turn, watching the elephant clatter up the midway. "And his trunk." I turn back. "It even blew steam! And they have a Ferris wheel, over there"—I point—"made out of a *gigantical* gear! They're giving people rides in its teeth, if you can believe it."

"I can't," she says.

"I *know*!"

She grins.

"And there's long-legged clowns—oodles of them, everywhere." I put a hand to my mouth and whisper in her ear, "*Well*, they're not actually long legged, they're short legged walking around on stilts, but I don't want to spoil it for the other kids."

Mum laughs.

"And one of the clowns, a short one, flew right up and *over* my head." I show her with my arms. "He shot right out of the mouth of a cannon, he did. Greasepainted face all smudged with soot, wearing one of the biggest grins I've ever seen!"

"You're enjoying yourself, then? Carnival is a success?"

"Brilliant." My chin snaps toward my chest. "Only thing that would make it better is if Father were here." I look back at the gates. "He's supposed to be coming, isn't he?"

Her eyes linger on the horizon a little longer than they should. "I'm sure he'll be here soon." She bites her lip, which makes me not believe it. "Until then"—she looks back at me, mustering a smile—"how about some toffee to fill the void?" She pulls three gleaming jewelets from her purse, and my eyes widen.

"Three jewelets," I say. "That's a *lot* of money."

She leans in close, her voice a teasing whisper. "Dad would think it spent on a good cause, don't you agree?"

I grin. "Most certainly."

"All right, then." She stands. "We best go and get in the queue, before they've sold all the sweets."

I frown and cross my arms over my chest. "But I want to watch the elephant until he disappears. I won't be able to see him from the queue."

She glances toward the elephant and back, and I see worry settle in on her face again.

"Please, Mum, I'm afraid I'll never get to see anything like it again."

"All right," she says, reading my disappointment. "But promise me you'll stay put."

"I promise I won't move from this very spot."

She drifts off across the fairgrounds, looking back over her shoulder from time to time to make sure I'm still standing where I should be.

I am.

The midway crackles with the sounds of whistling dynamite, creaky gears, and children's screams. The air tastes dipped in sugar. The elephant saunters toward the back gates, flicking its ears at make-believe flies. I do hope Father makes it in time to see it. Where could he be, I wonder? I gaze at the gates. He promised he'd come. And he never breaks his promises. Even the ones he can't possibly keep.

I close my eyes, and his face comes to me this morning in the kitchen. I hear the soothing sound of his voice in my ears. Smell the lingering scent of pipe tobacco on his neck as he pulls me in for a hug.

"You will be there, won't you?" I fall back and stare at him through serious eyes. He's been working an awful lot lately, and later than ever, too. Mum says it's because of the demotion. Father says it's because he's so smart they can't get along without him.

He leans in, staring back at me just as seriously through sparkling caramel eyes. A match to my very own. "How much do you trust me?" he whispers, and I smile.

I know this game and exactly how to play it. "As much as the stars and the moon and the pesky ol' sun," I say, doing the hand signs—first crossing my fingers, then curling them into a C, then pinching together my finger and thumb to form a circle. My other three fingers wave behind, like the glistening rays of the sun.

It's our little ritual whenever I have to face something hard that I don't like. His promise to me that everything'll be fine.

He pulls me in for one more hug and I melt against him, breathing his smoky aroma deep into my lungs. I could hold on forever, but I don't.

"I'll be a little late." He stands and kisses Mum, whispering into the back of her hair. "I've business to attend to out in the Follies," he adds.

"The Follies?" Mum draws back, looking singed. Her green-blue eyes turn watery grey. *"What's out in the Follies that's important enough for you to leave the safety of Brethren?"*

"Don't worry." Dad smooths her cheeks with his hands and kisses her again. *"I'll be back in time to join you both before sunset. I promise."* He presses something bright and shiny into Mum's hand. *"Until then, keep this safe for me, will you?"* he says, then whispers in her ear, *"Or rather, for Eyelet—for her future."*

He doesn't think I hear him, but I do.

Mum stares at the object lighting up in her hand, closing her fingers over it before I've had the chance to see. *"What is it?"* she asks.

"I'll explain later." Father's eyes flick from her to me and back again. *"For now, just promise me you won't let it out of your sight?"*

Mum nods and he slips away. And I forget to say *"I love you."*

*

Honk! A clown flits past, his horn blasting my thoughts back to the present.

"Witness the magic of the Great Illuminator! Watch photographs come to life before your very eyes!" A man's voice barks from inside the carnival tent behind me. "Gaze through a sheet of metal! See beyond a block of wood! Count the coins inside your purse!"

The Great Illuminator? The coins inside your purse? It can't be, can it? *Father?* I can't help myself. I must see. I'll only be gone a second.

Bolting across the midway, I fall to my knees and duck my head beneath the flap of the red–and–white candy-cane-striped tent. But to my dismay, it's not Father at all, just a carny, dressed up to look like a professor in a pinstriped suit and bowler hat.

"You, sir!" the carny shouts. "Don't you want to know what your wife carries round in that carpet bag of hers?"

The crowd chuckles as the couple blush.

"You're not the least bit curious to know how much she's worth?" The carny's voice lilts. The crowd's heads swing, curious. The young woman's cheeks start to glow. She turns to her husband and grins.

"Come on, now, don't be shy. I won't bite." The carny waves the young woman to the front. He's balding and thin as a communion wafer, with kippers for lips, they're so scaly. I can't help but wonder what's happened for his skin to look so weathered. If I didn't know better, I'd swear he was part crocodile.

He glares out over the crowd through a set of dead lark's eyes, all dried and dull, standing atop a soapbox like he's some sort of king.

"Come, now," he prods the couple, eyeing the man. "You can't tell me you're not a little bit curious?"

The crowd stirs like a herd of hungry cattle impatient to be fed, their lolly eyes flicking backward and forward. The husband finally nods and shrugs the young woman from his arm. She grins, dancing to the stage through the hum of the crowd.

"That's right," the carny instructs her. "Stand up straight, right there, over that X."

The woman skips up the stairs, takes her place.

"What's your name?"

"Mrs. Benson." The young woman blushes. "*Soon-to-be* Mrs. Reginald Benson." She raises her chin proudly, gazing dreamily at the man she's left in the crowd. A chorus of "ahhhh" floats about the tent.

"Very well, then"—the carny tips his hat—"Mrs. Soon-to-Be-Benson. Shall we get started?"

She nods, holding her purse out to one side.

"No, no, like this." The carny steps in to adjust it. "Right in front of you, please. Up tight to your chest. That's it. Just like that. Now hold it." He races from the stage, taking safety behind a short wall erected next to a cabinet-style box that sits on a table. He stuffs a crankshaft into the pinhole and begins turning it. Two large glass plates inside the cabinet start to spin in opposite directions. The noise is incredible.

"Hold it. Hold it," he crows to the woman with the purse as the plates begin to whir, louder and louder. Her eyes are big as saucers themselves. Electrical currents pop and sizzle along the wires. Several in the crowd place their hands over their ears.

My heart races with excitement. I leap into action, forcing my way through the tangle of legs to the front of the crowd. I don't want to miss a thing. The whir of the spinning disks throws the hair back from my shoulders, but I'm not afraid. Unlike everyone else here, I know what's going to happen.

"In a moment!" the carny shouts above the racket. "Lightning will pass between the two brass bolts you see mounted there, on either side of the front of the cabinet!" The crowd gasps. "Don't worry!" the carny assures them. "Everything's fine! No one will be hurt!"

Even the woman with the purse looks scared.

I lean closer to get a better look, my hair streaming wildly about my shoulders. Electricity starts to fly, jumping snakelike between the two brass bolts. I'm both anxious and exhilarated. It's just as I remember.

Women scream. People flee. One woman nearly passes out. But not me. I smile at the familiar whirl of blood that races through my veins, the way my heart jiggles in my chest.

"Wait!" the carny shouts. "The magic has only just started!"

The crowd settles down.

The apparatus picks up speed, and my skin begins to prickle. The hairs on my arms stand straight on end as if some spirit pinched me. It's suddenly far too hot. It's as though I'm getting sunburned—but I can't be, my arms and legs are completely covered by clothing. I don't remember feeling burned before, but then again, it was a long time ago.

An eerie glow begins to fester, streaming out, forming a halo around the machine. I don't remember this, either. My heart says to run. But my brain says to stick. After all, Father insists there's nothing to fear.

I raise a hand to shield my eyes, squinting as the waves of electricity grow until their heat is almost unbearable, the flesh rippling beneath my skin. I consider turning away, when at last it happens—lightning leaps from the bars at the front of the wooden cabinet, up a set of snaggled wires, over to a tube of glass that rests in a stand hovering above the young woman's head. In the blink of an eye there comes a flash, so big and bold it's blinding. It sizzles down the long, thin pointed nose of the tube aimed at the woman's chest, before *zap!* It's gone.

The young woman turns completely green. The outline of her body radiates luminously before the crowd. Her eyes distort, their centres turning red. She looks up, glaring demon-like out into the crowd.

People gasp and fall backward. One woman faints. Others flee. Screaming. My stomach falls to my knees. I think to run, but I'm stuck in place. It's as though my shoes anchor me to the ground. I suck in a breath, my heart pounding in time with the whirl of the machine, the jolt of the current pulsing through me, until at last the demon leaves her eyes and the green glow begins to fade. The lightning bolts between the brass bars dissolve into little puffs of stinky smoke, zapping and twitching as they simmer. The glass plates inside the cabinet whirl slowly to a stop, and I gasp, relieved, as my heart stops whirling with them.

"And there it is!" The carny spins around, pulling a slate-coloured screen from the back of the machine. He holds it up, its image still glowing the most horrid shade of green. "The contents of her purse. Two jewelets, one juniper, and a key!" He points to the skeleton of each object photographed inside the purse's ghoulish green outline. Even the young woman looks amazed. A collective "ahhhh" drifts up from the crowd again. Jaws dangle.

The young woman is quick to dump her purse and hold up each item, proving the photograph correct.

"There, you see!" The carny waves his arms as if to part the sea. "And that's just *one* of the many magical uses for the Great Illuminator!" He grins, and my stomach feels sick. What is he talking about?

"What else can it do?" someone hollers from the crowd.

"It might be easier for me to tell you what it *can't* do!" the carny chuckles. The crowd joins in as he paces the stage, his finger wagging as he shouts. "Suffer from migraines? No more! Unwanted hair? Gone in a flash! Unsightly scars, pits, birthmarks?" He snaps his fingers. "Consider them zapped! Why, this young woman had a moustache when we started"—the carny points back to the woman with the purse—"and just look at her now!"

The crowd laughs.

The young woman looks confused as the carny takes her hand and helps her navigate from the stage. "Bring an end to facial tics, headaches, moodiness, depression—".

"It can do all that?" a plump woman shouts.

The carny turns to face her. "All that is just the beginning!" He leans into the crowd, placing the back of his hand beside his mouth like he's about to tell a secret. "Expose yourself enough times"—he shouts in a half whisper—"and it'll even lighten your skin."

The crowd gasps.

"That's right, my friends. Now, who among you will be the first to own one?" The carny waves his arms as the young woman flashes the price on a sign over her head. "That's it! Step right up! Don't be shy! Get your own, personal, party-sized Great Illuminator, today!" He lifts his arms and the crowd applauds.

All but me.

The carny's eyes settle on me in the crowd. "For you." He grins and steps down from his soapbox, awarding me the photograph like it's some sort of prize.

I look down at it in disgust. At the jewelets, the juniper, and the key. "It's not yours," I whisper.

"I beg your pardon?" he says.

"It's not yours to be selling," I say.

The crowd falls hushed.

"Whatever are you talking about, child?" His dead-lark eyes flicker, worried, and he sort of laughs.

"The machine." I point. "It belongs to me—"

"*Eyelet!*"

My head swings around. My mother stands at the back of the crowd, looking frazzled. A week's worth of toffee sags in her hand. She weaves her way to the front, apologizing, seizing me by the arm.

"But Mother—"

"Not now, Eyelet!" she hisses, urging me to keep silent, and drags me to the back of the tent.

"But it's *not* his. It's mine!" I shout. "Father made it for me. To look inside my head. Not for *him* to take photographs of women's purses with!"

Heads swing round. Mother gasps. The carny's eyes grow wide. Throwing back the flap of the tent, Mother yanks me through, hauling me stumbling out into the centre of the midway.

"Where are we going?" I protest. "Didn't you hear me? That man has my machine!"

"Not here, Eyelet." She glances nervously back over her shoulder. "We can't talk about this here."

"Why not?"

She pulls me forward, but I yank her to a stop. Frustrated, she falls to her knees. Her eyes are wet, like she's about to cry. The corners of her lips are trembling.

She runs her hands down the sides of my hair and cups my cheeks in her palms. I can tell by the look in her eyes she's about to tell me something bad. Something I don't want to hear. "I'm afraid the world is not always as it should be, Eyelet." She swallows, and the water in her eyes seeps over the edges of her lids. "Sometimes we have to do things we don't want to do."

I turn away, staring over her shoulders at the back of the red-and-white-striped tent. Hot tears prick my eyes. "He sold it, didn't he?" I say. "The machine he promised he'd fix me with. Father sold that man my machine—"

"There they are!"

The carny's voice rings out across the midway like the crack of an elephant trainer's whip. "There!" He's emerged from under the tent flap, pointing. The thug standing next to him gives chase.

Mother grabs me by the arm and hurls me onto her hip, though I'm much too big to carry, and bursts through the crowd, bouncing off the backs of patrons as she heads for the gates. My heart leaps in my chest. I bob along, clinging to her, hands clasped tight around her neck. "Why is he chasing us? What does he want?"

"I'm not sure," she shouts.

"Mother?" I say, looking back over her shoulder, my eyes catching on something strange. *"Mother!"* A ghoulish green glow rises up from the horizon, engulfing the whole sky behind us. "Mother!" I shout. *"Look!"*

She turns just in time to see it. A flash so big, so bold, so bright, it fills my head, my heart . . . the whole universe.

Eclipsing all that came before it.

And all that is to come.

Part One

Part One

One

Eyelet—age seventeen

Living in eternal twilight might sound romantic, but it's not. It's simply depressing. No one in the city of Brethren has seen the sun since the Night of the Great Illumination. I close my eyes and try hard to remember what life was like before the flash. But I can't.

It's been nine long years since golden rays have warmed my skin. Nine long years of grey skies and continuous rolling cloud cover, living under a hood of darkness and gloom. Some say the flash knocked out the sun forever. But I refuse to believe it.

Personally, I believe it's up there still, stuck behind all that cumulonimbus. I raise a hand, squinting through the layers of cloud. Perhaps it's gone to shine over Limpidious—the utopian world beyond the clouds that my father always dreamed existed. Or perhaps the flash just shorted it out, and it'll be coming back on soon.

Whatever the case, I'm tired of waiting. So until it reappears, I've created my own personal dash of sunshine. I pop open my latest invention: the skeleton of a bumbershoot stripped clean of its canvas, its remaining ribs and divers wound tight with wires and tiny, hissing aether bulbs of hope. My own engineered solution to the gloom.

Slowly the bumbershoot blooms, wreathing my head in a mushroom cap of light, its warmth seeping through me, dissolving the chill from my bones. I flit around beneath it like a child, enjoying the presence of my uncustomary shadow stretching dark and lanky through the grey mist out over the cobblestones, re-creating a longer, thinner me.

A puff of smoke spoils the moment, followed by a vulgar zap. The bumbershoot fizzles out.

"*Ooooo!* You ornery thing!" I shake the apparatus in disgust.

If my father were here, *you'd* be glowing.

If my father were here, a *lot* of things would still be glowing.

I stare dreamily into the clouds.

Even *I'd* be fixed by now.

But he's not.

I snap the bumbershoot shut.

Enough jiggering about with this silly contraption; I've far more important things to accomplish today, like returning this *useless* paper journal to the archives unnoticed. Preferably before the start of class.

I look at the thin notebook in my hands, at the word *Lumière* etched across the front. And I was so sure this was the one.

I flip it open one last time, running a finger over the endless columns of data, collections of random samples and their subsequent findings, not at all what I'd expected to find.

What does all this mean? And why did he record it?

—*particulate matter, subject 521, 10 parts per million*—
excessively abundant.

I flip the notebook shut and hug it to my chest. Whatever it is, it's of no use to me. What I need are directions on how to run the machine. And a map to where it is would be useful, too.

One of these days, I will find the right book. And when I do, it'll lead me to my father's machine. And then I'll fire up the Great Illuminator and use it to cure myself of these hideous seizures once and for all, making good on the promise my father broke. Then at last I'll be safe. No more fear of public persecution. No more threat of being found out and deemed insane. I'll no longer have to fear falling into an episode and being locked away in an asylum for the rest of my life, over an illness that the world just doesn't understand.

I look down at my chrono-cuff, realizing the time. Half past—I'd better get moving. Parting a mare's tail of trolling fog, I push on toward the Academy, taking the shortcut through Piglingham Square, though I know I shouldn't. I gasp at the sight of bodies still dangling from the gallows at the centre, and I throw a hand over my eyes. Cantationers, no doubt, sentenced to death for the practice of Wickedry. Their bodies dipped in vats of scalding wax and left to hang as examples to the rest of us.

There are two things you don't want to be found guilty of in this post-flash modern world. The first is Wickedry—the practice of magic, black or otherwise. And the second is Madness. I shudder at the thought of the second one, knowing how fragile my existence is. *"They must never know,"* I hear Father say. *"You must never give up your secret. Seizures are considered an incurable form of Madness in the Commonwealth. If anyone were to know, you'd most certainly be locked away."*

A chill runs the length of my spine, my eyes trailing off toward the horizon, settling on Madhouse Brink—the mental asylum that looms over the edge of the city, where all the Mad are sent. I remember the looks on their faces in the windows, the bone-jarring pitch of their screams.

I shake off the image and race for the school, arriving breathless at the gates moments later. Impenetrable gates for an impenetrable fortress, where educators seek to create impenetrable minds.

I step up to the rampart of twisted, heavy, iron ivy, greeted by two mechanical ravens sitting atop newel-post perches, guarding either side of the gate. Their heads bob robotically, tilting left to right. Their eyes, spurred by a hiss of methane, light up into pairs of beaming cathode rays. Slowly, they scan my likeness, head to toe, systematically comparing my image to the vast library of metal-stamped images housed inside their memory banks.

My father's work, the two of them. "Security Sorcerers," they're called. The first of their kind in the Commonwealth.

The last of their kind.

"What's the matter?" I say when the bird on the right hesitates. "Don't tell me you don't recognize me, Simon?" I fold my arms over my chest, annoyed by his antics. I should easily have been approved by now.

"Don't make me come over there and tighten your springs," I threaten. What on earth can be the matter?

The bird's eyes stall on the word on the front of the notebook I've pressed to my chest, its eyes tracing out the cursive letters.

L . . . u . . . m . . . i . . . è . . .

My stomach cramps. Quickly, I move my hand to block the remainder of the word. This can't be happening. He can't possibly know what it is. Can he?

The bird's wings flutter, and the cramp in my stomach tightens.

"You can't be serious, Simon." The bird's nickel-plated beak creaks ajar. "It's me"—I touch my chest—"Eyelet. Remember? I'm the one who named you!"

None of that seems to matter. Father warned me it would be so. The pulse in my wrist rolls like thunder. What am I to do?

The mechanical raven spreads its wings, preparing to report me. My heart beats wild in my chest. Above my head, the air fills with voices of real ravens feverishly fussing on approach. "The flock," I say as my chin snaps up to see them swirling. "What are they doing here?"

Enamored with my mother, they are drawn to me—black moths to a human flame, often trailing me about the city, cloaked about my head and shoulders, whispering portents of caution in my ears. But lately they trail me less often, a request I've made of my mother to have them sent away. I'm far too old at seventeen to need to be escorted to school, not to mention what the Commoners say.

"What is it, Archie?" I say to the largest of the flock, waving him off. "What's the matter? Why have you come?"

He drops down in front of me, severing the connection between mechanical Simon and me. The mechanical bird's beam falters, bouncing off Archie's feathers, blinding the machine temporarily. Simon blinks his steely lids as his program resets. His wings retract. He tips his head, and the gates fall open behind me.

I've been approved.

"I must say"—I turn to Archie, sucking in a relieved breath—"I've never been so glad to see *you!*"

I smooth my skirts and turn to enter, and Archie swoops down again.

"Enough already," I say, my head twisted backward, my mind distracted by how Simon's left wing has clanked awkwardly down, not quite into place. Perhaps Father didn't have time to perfect the fold? I ponder. Maybe if he'd used a ball-and-socket assembly instead of a hinge?

Archie swoops in again, interrupting my thought, cawing ridiculously loudly in my face. "For goodness' sake." I push him away. "What is it? What is the matter with you?" I notice then that Pan, my mother's raven, is not among the group. "Is it Pan? Where is she, Archie? What's happened to her? Where's Pan?"

"Pan?"

The voice is sadly familiar. I swing around to find Professor Smrt skulking toward me through the front gates. His eyes flick to the raven above my head. "Surely you don't expect that creature to answer, do you?"

"Of course I don't." I pull myself up straight.

"Of course." He grins and rolls his hands. "That would make you appear . . . Mad, now wouldn't it?"

I swallow. Professor Smrt's lips remind me of a snake's. Nothing but a sharply drawn line with a too-thin tongue flicking out between.

"*Straaange*, isn't it?" The word *strange* fizzles off his tongue like newly shaken cola. "How drawn those birds are to you?" He cranes in uncomfortably close. "Why is that, I wonder?" He swats at one, cuffing it on the bottom, sending it sputtering about, nattering in jagged flight. "Could there be truth to the rumours?"

"What rumours, sir?" Blood rushes to my face. I know perfectly well what he's talking about. Lately, the locals have grown suspicious, making accusations about my mother being a Valkyrie. A shape-shifter, capable of changing forms from raven to human and back. Some even claim she's a carrier of messages from the world of the living to that of the dead. Preposterous, really. But that's what they've been saying. All because of the birds.

The all-too-familiar throb of fear pulses in my neck. How many times have I warned her, insisting she sever her association with birds? I don't care that Pan *has* been her companion since birth. Or that Mother's the one who taught Pan to speak. I'd prefer not to end up a wax candle in the square.

I glare at the sky, trying to signal the birds to leave, but for some reason they continue to circle and squawk.

"You expect me to believe you haven't heard the rumours?"

"That's correct," I whisper, ducking my chin, hoping he doesn't recognize the lie in my cheeks. "Now, if you'll excuse me, sir, I've come early to work." Lifting the hem of my cloak, I turn and push past him up the front stairs, raven entourage still in tow.

"About that." His words catch my step. "There's been a complaint." I swallow. My heart thumps in my chest.

"Professor Rapture has informed me that she has reason to believe someone's been entering the archives unauthorized." I squeeze my father's stolen notebook closer to my chest, my hands trembling. The heels of Smrt's shoes snap against the stone walk as he stalks toward me. "Do you know anything about that?" His voice lifts. His shoes creak to a halt.

I ball my fists and slowly turn, picking through the thoughts that swarm my brain. I dare not volunteer the truth; I'd face immediate expulsion. But then again, I dare not lie to him, either.

"I only ask because I've noticed you about the grounds earlier than usual of late." His chin juts out at me over the stones. "Not that a student as astute as yourself would engage in such criminal activity. Or would she?"

I say nothing, just glower into Smrt's beady black eyes, which, without their tiny white rims, could easily belong to any of the ravens still swirling about my head.

"Don't tell me I've rendered you speechless?" He laughs. "I thought that only happened to you in class." I bite my lip, choosing again not to grace him with an answer, worried about where this line of questioning might go.

He slithers up the stairs, quickly closing the space between us. "Tell me"—he leans and whispers in my ear, the stench of his digesting kipper breakfast on his breath—"what happens to you in those glazed-eye moments, when you sit stuck in a stare, gazing lifelessly out the window, unable to form an answer in class? Is it fear that consumes you"—he moves in even closer—"or is there something deeper that disturbs you, Eyelet? Something that might reek of . . . Madness?"

A jolt of terror bursts in my veins. I pull back, trying hard to collect my breath. He doesn't know. How could he? I've never had a full seizure in class. He's just fishing. Trying to bait me. I mustn't crack. I turn and take to the stairs in a whirlpool of black flight and dark chatter, feathers striking softly against my cheeks.

"That's it, then? You've nothing to say in your defense?"

"I have plenty to say." I whirl about.

The professor's brows twinge.

I swallow hard and settle back on my heels, realizing what I've done.

Confrontation with faculty members is prohibited at Brethren's Academy of Scientific Delves and Discoveries. Immediate grounds for expulsion at the discretion of any faculty member, should the need arise. Not to mention, I've just challenged male authority in a world where women have no right to do so. Participating in a dangerous display of sudden broken temperament. I attend this school solely on the good graces of my deceased father's reputation, one of only a handful of girls in the Commonwealth to be granted such a gift. And now, I fear I may have thrown it all away—with one thoughtless lash of the tongue.

The professor *tsks*, his left eye twitching the way it does when he reaches for relief from his palsy puffer in class. He circles me, his eyes worrying the hair on the back of my head, before appearing again, purse-lipped, in front of me. "Caught consorting with ravens, followed by a clear break in temperament. You know what this means, don't you?" He reaches into his breast pocket.

"No, sir, *please*." I cringe.

Sudden breaks in temperament are considered the first diagnosable sign of Madness within the Commonwealth. Especially in women, the *supposedly* more mentally plagued gender.

He produces pencil and notebook from his pocket and flips the book open, my future dancing in his coldhearted hands.

I gasp. "I'm sorry, sir," I sputter. "I don't know what got into me. I promise you, it won't happen again—"

"But alas, it already has." He grins and licks the end of the pencil, then begins scrawling a note in the tiny book. "Such a pity, really." He glances at me, his bare brows lurched. "I knew your father well. How he'd *roll* in his grave to know what's become of *you*."

The last word rolls off his tongue like poison infecting every fiber of my soul. I purse my lips, trying to keep my words from coming, but they seep out anyway, harsh and crisp and curt. "You haven't enough proof. The Council won't believe you. My academic record here at the school is impeccable. They'll never believe Madness could coexist with such brilliance. You'll lose. And then you'll look like a *fool*."

Smrt's eyes reduce to mere pinpoints. He glides toward me, his lips nearly brushing the lobe of my ear as he whispers, "If not bound by the contractual agreement arranged by members of the Academy upon your father's untimely death, I'd see to it you were *tossed* from these grounds *immediately*! And locked away in the asylum where we *both* know you *belong*!"

"Smrt!"

A voice calls across the courtyard, but Smrt ignores it. I shudder, falling back. "What's that?" he says. His eyes lock on the notebook pressed to my chest. My hand bolts up to cover the lettering.

"Where did you find that?" He lurches toward me, trying to snatch the book from my hands. The birds move in, squawking. Archie dives at his head.

"Professor Smrt!" The voice calls again.

My head cranks around to see the full-figured silhouette of Professor Rapture trundling down the steps of Brackishbee Hall, her image swiftly cutting through the fog.

"Come quick!" Her hair is as frazzled and prickly as her voice. "It's a matter of public emergency!" In her hand she holds a paper. It flaps about her head. Smrt jerks back, putting proper distance between the two of us.

Quickly, I stuff the notebook down the side of my boot, rolling it just slightly to achieve the task. The ravens overhead flap and jitter, providing me cover, their wings snapping like sheets in the wind.

"Smrt!" Rapture shouts again, racing to join us, her gait checking to a staggered halt when at last I come clearly into view. Peering at me through her pickle-jar lenses, her eyes grow thrice their normal size. "Back away from her, Irving!" she says, clutching her crucifix. "Back away from that girl at once!"

"What?" Smrt's head swings. "What's the matter with you, Penelope? Have you taken leave of your senses?"

"No, but you might if you don't do as I say. Now for the love of God, Irving, back away!" She pulls a handkerchief from her pocket and covers her mouth.

Smrt squirrels up his face. "I demand to know what is going on here!"

"You're standing in the presence of a living demon, that's what," Rapture says. Her eyes cut to me. "By decree of the Council"—she holds out a message in her hand—"her mother has just been declared a Valkyrie! Guilty of the practice of Wickedry in the presence of mankind, through which she's just ended the prince's life!"

"She what?" Smrt jumps away.

The pulse quickens in my wrists.

"She used her wicked powers to still the babe's lungs." Rapture narrows her eyes. "The sole heir to the Commonwealth, entrusted to her care, is dead."

"No." I shake my head. "That's not true. I just saw him. Before I left for school. He had a fever. That's all. My mother was up all night with him, she never left his side—"

"And now he lies lifeless in her arms."

"No!" I step back. "It's a lie! They're lying! My mother's done nothing! She's not a Valkyrie! She's not a Cantationer! She's nothing! Just my mother!"

The ravens rise, screeching off through the trees.

Rapture's eyes grow wide.

I should have known there was something wrong when the ravens came to get me. I should have known when I didn't see Pan among them.

"She's to be dipped and hung this morning in Piglingham Square," Rapture continues. My stomach pulls up into my chest. "Along with her suspected Valkyrie daughter—"

"What?" I shiver. "But I've done nothing—"

"Trip the gates," Rapture sneers through her handkerchief. "Irving!" She glares. "I said to trip the gates!"

Smrt stumbles backward up the stairs and lunges at the controls.

I turn and hurl myself down the front step, squeezing through the last sliver of gate before it closes, mechanical ravens squawking overhead.

"Stop her!" Rapture's words lap at my heels as I flee. "We're not to let her get away!"

Two

Eyelet

I race up the street toward my home at the palace, my feet slamming hard against the cobblestones. My heart roars in my chest like a runaway steamplough thundering off the tracks. Breath steams from my nostrils.

How can this be happening? How can they think Mother would harm that child? She's always treated that babe as if he were her own. How could they think she could kill him? Kill anything? *Oh Mother, hang on . . . I'm coming!*

I race on, heaving in the breaths, the cold air stinging my lungs. Tears burn my eyes and then fall away, torn from my cheeks by the wind. I must reach her before they do. Before they've had the chance. *Oh, please Lord, let me get there in time.*

I arrive at the gates, gasping and breathless, a crowd already forming, angrily strumming and shaking the bars.

The word is out. The Commoners have come to seek revenge for the death of their Ruler's only heir. They want blood. My mother's. And mine.

"She's a Cantationer," a woman hisses. "Using the powers of Wickedry, she's conjured a plague to still his lungs."

A plague? My head whips in her direction. *She can't be serious—*

"She's a no-good, filthy Valkyrie, that's what she is," snorts another. "Likely contracted some fatal disease while in her alternate form. She must be bled and dipped immediately—both her and her *wretched* offspring—before they cause the death of all of us!"

"Hear! Hear!" The crowd thrusts their fists in the air, shouting.

I gasp, trembling, and fall away. Throwing my hood over my head to conceal my identity, I double back up the street. Boxed in at the end by a row of Brigsmen, steamrifles at the ready, I lower my head and dart down the narrow alley at the foot of the palace road. I run until I reach the livery, then turn and dash through its centre, my boots echoing off the walls. Startled horses snap back their long, broad faces and whinny out of fright. I twist my head around, shushing them, afraid they'll give me away.

Sliding to a stop, I thread myself through a pair of warped bars in the massive iron gate at the end of the livery. Only the children of the palace know this hole exists. I pop out the other side into Piglingham Square, thankful for the escape, planning to cut through the centre of the grounds and enter the palace from the back, when—

I see her.

"Mother?" My chest heaves. I nearly crumble to my knees.

Strung from the gallows, next to the two petrified wax souls I passed this morning on my way to school, hangs my mother. A weave of rope forms a figure eight around her shoulders and neck. Her head hangs slumped to the left.

Pan circles above her head, screeching endlessly.

"Mother!" I break into a run, stumbling forward, unable to feel my feet strike the ground beneath me. My heart thrashes in my ears. I am cold and numb and I cannot swallow. Tears burst from my eyes.

I'm too late. I've arrived too late. I suck in a hollow breath. No, I shake the desperate thought from my head and will myself forward, knowing it's only a matter of time before the crowd shifts. Soon they'll be upon us, clattering at the ten-foot gates that surround the square, insisting that the Brigsmen—willing and ready with keys to burst the locks—let them in to witness my mother's death.

I must get her out of here before they arrive. I've got to somehow save my mother!

I lunge forward, throwing myself at the base of her stake when I finally reach it, my hands grasping at her ropes. "Mother!" I shudder as she falls into my arms, her neck slit and gushing blood. She's been cut and left to bleed. A practice performed only on those thought to be Cantationers, out of the fear they may use their magic to escape their eventual wax-dipping fate.

"Oh, Mother!" I cry, driven to the ground under the force of her weight, my knees buckling. Instinctively, I press a hand to her throat to try and stop the flow. Velvet blood laps through my fingers and soaks my palm.

It's no use. I can't stop it.

"You must go." Her voice reaches for me, raspy and weak. "You must leave me. And *run*."

"I can't!" I shake my head, my tears falling and mingling with her blood.

"You must," she gasps.

"No! I refuse to leave without you."

"Listen to me, child." She reaches up, stroking the tears from my cheeks. "This is my end and your beginning—"

"No—"

"It is the universe's will."

"Pan!" I shout at the sky. "Pan, please, help me!"

"No!" Mother rasps, and the bird retreats.

Voices arrive at the gates. I look up, panicked.

"You, there!" a Brigsman shouts, fumbling for his keys in his pocket. "Get away from her!"

"Hurry," Mother swallows, blood purging from her lips. "Take this." She fumbles in the folds of her blouse and pulls out a pendant. An hourglass vial containing a jumping bolt of what appears to be emerald-coloured lightning swimming in a pool of glowing plasma, sheathed within a filigreed brass case. Emerald, ebony, and diamond jewels adorn its pewter chain.

"Keep this with you always." She drops the vial in my hand. "Never lose it. Never give it up to anyone, for any reason. Do you understand?"

"But—"

"Your father asked me to keep it for him. Do you remember?" My mind shoots back to the morning of the carnival. *Father whispers in the kitchen.* "You must keep it safe now."

"What is it?"

"The key to your future," she rasps. "To everyone's future."

Her eyes roll to the back of her head, the life from them swiftly draining.

"Mother?" I roll her up in my arms.

"Get away from that prisoner!" the Brigsman shouts.

My chin snaps up from my chest.

Casting the lock aside, he loosens the chains. They slither like metal snakes clattering through the rails as they drop to the ground. My shoulders bounce with the fall of every link. The air inside the square blooms with the sound of voices spewing hateful chants as the gate swings open, propelled by the force of the oncoming crowd. Brigsman in front, his rifle ready. The snout of it pointed at my head.

"Go," Mother rasps. "Quickly!"

I stare at her, unwilling to leave. How am I to abandon my mother to this fate?

She stares into my eyes, her own eyes pleading. "How much do you trust me?" she whispers.

Not since the morning of the carnival have I heard those words spoken. The last words my father ever said to me. "Now, go," she begs, her eyes waxing with death. "Run. Hide. *Live.*"

Clutching the pendant, I lean forward and press a kiss to my mother's forehead, grab my bumbershoot, and scramble to my feet. The sweet scent of lavender perfume and the sour scent of blood twist through my veins as I bolt back across the square, slipping between the warped bars of the livery, ahead of the Brigsman, leaving him to cuss from the other side.

"Please, Lord," I beg the sky as I burst off through the streets of Brethren. "Please take her now. Don't wait."

*

I lunge forward, my mother's blood cooling on my skin, cocooned in breath and heartbeats, unsure if my feet still carry me or if my ankles have somehow sprouted wings. I head for the outskirts of Brethren, knowing not what else to do, worried every step might bring on an episode, as other times when I've overexerted myself. *Please*, I beg the sky. *Don't let it happen to me. Don't let the darkness take me over.*

"After her!" I hear Professor Smrt shout. "Do not let her get away!" I glance over my shoulder to see him charging through the gates, Brigsmen flanking his either side.

I race on, winding through backstreets, the blood in my body running cold, my head twisting left to right, considering direction. I've no idea, really, which way to go. With no one left to protect me, no one left to help me keep my secret, what will become of me now? Wherever I go, suspicion will surely follow. Madness or Wickedry, take your pick. I could easily be convicted of either now.

I suck in a breath, trying to quiet the panic in my chest, and push on toward the limits of Gears—the working-class city beyond my own, where life is hard, money is scarce, and women are considered the property of men. Without a chaperone to protect my virtue, any man will be able to pluck me from the streets and claim me as his own. But it's either chance the uncivilized wiles of the working class or face the wrath of the Council, here. I loop the chain of the pendant over my head as I run, terror rising in my cheeks.

I've no other choice. There's nowhere else to go.

Boots pummel up the stone road behind me. A band of Brigsmen closes in.

I turn, racing up an alley through a backstreet, only to hear boots again. I slow, breath loping in my chest, hearing the shriek of ravens overhead. "Pan!" I scream out, seeing her sift through the trees, her tone much louder than the rest.

She swoops, pecking at the arms and legs of my pursuers, giving me a loophole to get away. I rush through it and off up the cobblestones into another street. Smrt closes in behind, his bumbershoot brandished over his head.

Pan swoops. Smrt swings.

"Pan!" I shout, but it's too late. Smrt connects, knocking Pan from the sky. She falls to the ground, a tiny tuft of twisted feathers rolling lifelessly against the base of a lamppost.

I gasp, pulling to a stop behind a tree to hide myself, peering out around the bark. "Get up, Pan," I whisper. "Please, get up."

But she doesn't. She doesn't so much as breathe.

Smrt moves in, bumbershoot poised again to strike, waving it like a billy stick over his head.

"No!" I shout, stepping out from behind the tree. The handle of Smrt's bumbershoot slams into the cobblestones, narrowly missing Pan's head.

He turns and peers at me through shrunken lids.

I meet his gaze. For a moment we stand, frozen in a silent stare—as if the two of us were captured inside one of my episodes. Then one of the Brigsmen sees me.

He lunges forward, his voice calling out to the rest.

I turn and fling myself up the road, the soles of my boots grinding the stones beneath them, my arms pumping determined circles at my sides.

Rounding the corner, I thunder down the face of Bayberry Street toward the city's edge, pendant clapping hard against the bones of my chest. Partway, I ditch off onto Derbyshire, then flank the length of Pickerton until I reach the mouth of the dragon topiary maze at the base of Lankshire Street and Wells.

Made of hedges cut into the shape of a dragon, the maze was created for the Ruler by my father in his capacity as Royal Science Ambassador. It once served as a sanctuary where the Ruler's children played, but it secretly doubled as a weapon—a deterrent to all who dared enter the city through the north end without the Ruler's consent. A lethal lure for the deceitful, Father used to say—a ruthless trap set to catch lawbreakers.

Lawful citizens applied for work cards and passed through the gates at a checkpoint just a few hundred metres beyond the hedge. But these days, there are no work cards issued. Those born in Gears must face their fate. They live their lives as low-paid laborers in factories owned by the rich of Brethren, subject to air tainted by the Vapours.

I swallow down the thought and bolt across the intersection's grassy knoll up into the dragon's mouth, past its teeth, down its throat, into its gullet, battling overgrown branches as I go. The once-ominous-and-majestic ten-foot dragon hedge has now fallen to neglect. Serving as the wall that marks the end of civilized life, it's become uncivilized itself.

I dart left, then right, then left again, making quick, careful decisions, twisting through the creature's belly on my way to its left hind leg. I need to find the dragon's claw—the Mother Root—the place where my father planted the two original hedges used to form the maze. As they grew, he braided their trunks, creating a gnarled and knotted staircase, leaving loophole steps inside each knot, leading up and out of the maze—a secret escape route through the centre of the hedge, just in case anyone were to become lost inside. My father showed me where to find it when I was a little girl, along with how to trip the maze's mechanical defense mechanism, buried deep beneath the ground: a series of metal spikes designed to spring up at the turn of a crank, deterring intruders—or killing them, depending where they stood.

I fall to my knees at the dragon's hind leg, raking my fingers through the dirt. *If only I could remember exactly where it is* . . . I push aside a broken branch and prick my hand on something sharp. The tip of a nail. *"The claw."* The word pushes out with my breath. "It must be." I dig a little farther and expose the rest.

My father sculpted a claw at the base of the Mother Root to indicate its whereabouts. He then fitted the dragon's three toes with a mechanism that, when tripped, activates the maze's arsenal of defense. I reach for the toes, gently clearing away a pile of soggy, decayed leaves, my hand retracting at the cold chill of metal, and the stink of worn, weathered copper. *I've found it.* The mechanism. It's still here. Triumphant, I suck in a quick breath—startled by the sound of boots advancing up the row behind me.

My head swings around. *Brigsmen.* They're closing in, their breath heavy. I'm out of time.

Swallowing down the fear that floods my throat, I stand, abandon the claw, and slip inside the hedge. Using the handle of my bumbershoot, I propel myself up through the centre, digging my toes into the knots of the Mother Root staircase, climbing my way to the top of the hedge.

Before I reach it, something rises within me . . . sharp and dark and slow. I heave in a breath, my body trembling. *No. Not now. I can't do this now.*

The all-too-familiar silver twinge slinks bitterly through my veins. The feeling I get just before I fall into an episode. A migrating metallic feeling that turns my blood cold, my saliva sour, and my entire world—black.

Oh, please, not now. I cling to the branches. *I need all my wits about me.* I struggle hard to fight the feeling as it feeds toward my brain. A blinding arc of light begins to burn behind my eyes.

Closing my lids, I push through the feeling, willing it to be a small one, just a gentle lapse in time, a tiny break in consciousness, not one of the long, gyrating episodes of absence filled with nothingness, where I'm thrown to the ground and left drooling like a beast. I've never gone through one of those without the assistance of my mother. If it strikes, I don't know what will become of me. I've learned to manage the small ones on my own over the years—but a large one, without her—I fear I may never wake up from.

The twinge surges again, my body slackens, and I start to lose my grip. I hang from the branches, praying I'm not revealed, as my world darkens to nothing but shadows. Soon it will all go black. Just as I'm about to submit to the feeling, abruptly it shatters as if crushed beneath a hammer's head. The monster that seized me suddenly frees me, and I gasp in relief. The silver twinge has shown me mercy.

At least for now.

I open my eyes, feeling lost and confused; in the first moments back from an episode, I'm never quite sure where I am. I hate that feeling. Like I've left my skin, and then suddenly been stuffed back in.

And worst of all, I know it's not over. My episodes come in waves of two. Always a mild one, followed by something worse. And then a reprieve of a month, maybe two.

The strength restored to my limbs, I resume my climb—freezing midway up the trunk inside the hedge at the sound of approaching boots. They stop parallel to me on the path. Hot, jagged breaths part the leaves. A set of piercing eyes peers through the branches. My clammy hands slip a bit. I suck in a breath, heart pounding, as the snout of a steamrifle pokes in between the branches, grazing first my arm and then my chin. It's all I can do not to scream out, feeling the cold, smooth barrel of his gun resting along the side of my cheek.

Please move on. Please move on.

"Over here!" A voice calls from the next row. The snout of the rifle retreats.

I release my breath as his boots thunder away, and I quickly descend the trunk through the leaves. Jamming the tip of my bumbershoot into the claw at the base, I activate the maze's defense mechanism. Ten-foot solid metal spikes rip through the earth, piercing anything in their way.

Brigsmen cry out, their voices screeching. Metal gnashes through bone and tears away flesh. I throw hands to my ears to block out the sound, but it's no good—I hear everything. The shouts, the screams, the crash of boots fleeing. Random gunshots ring through the air.

I bite my lip and count to thirty before resuming my climb, then crawl out over the top of the hedge when I reach it. Balancing myself on its stiff, sturdy branches, I scour the horizon through the fog in search of Gears. The checkpoint is at least two hundred metres from here. I'll have to run through an open field, under the windmills, past the purification booms to the edge of the city—without getting caught by the searchlights.

I watch for a minute, seeing them sweep over the grounds like a giant eye.

Please, let me make it.

It's a good two-metre jump to the ground, maybe more, from where I sit. But I've no choice. I've got to do it. Closing my eyes, I leap from the top of the bush, landing, much to my surprise, squarely on both feet. So far, so good.

"Off to Gears, are we, Eyelet?" There's breath at my back. The words curl around me. Professor Smrt's beady eyes bear down on me, mere slits in the shrinking twilight.

He stands, Brigsmen at his sides, their steamrifles clutched and ready. I shudder, knowing I don't stand a chance. I make a move and they could shoot me.

"Funny, in all the years I knew your father, he never shared the secret of his maze design with me. Yet clearly, you knew not only where to find the Mother Root, but how to activate the impalement devices. Which makes me wonder . . ." Smrt grits his teeth. "What other secrets do you harbour, Eyelet? What other *classified* information do you know?"

I swallow, squirreling backward, trying to distance myself as he closes in, bringing a hand to my chest to cover my pendant. "Hand over the notebook."

"What notebook?"

"Don't act like you don't know what I'm talking about. I know you have your father's notes."

"I lost them," I say, dropping my eyes.

"Liar!" He signals for the nearest Brigsman to raise his steamrifle. I shudder as he presses it to my temple. "Now hand it over, or prepare to join your mother and father."

I reach down, slowly pulling the notebook from its hiding place in my boot.

Smrt snatches it away, my hand refusing to let go. A tug-of-war ensues. The cover of the journal strains and then tears in half, revealing a secret flap. A small ticket of paper flutters loose out onto the wind. A storage ticket marked *Confidential*, written in my father's hand.

It feathers down, coming to rest at my feet. I stamp on its edge and read the rest.

1460 Wortley Rd., Warehouse #47, Gears.
Item stored—The Illuminator.

I can't believe my eyes.

Lumière. I gasp. Of course—code for the Illuminator.

Smrt's gaze drops to the ticket under my boot. His hands release the journal. Each of us swoops to collect the ticket first, nearly clacking heads, but I prevail as winner.

"Give me that!" Smrt shouts as I throw up my hand, the wind trying to pry the ticket from my fingers. The look in his eyes tells me he knows what it is—a treasure, apparently, to us both. What could he possibly want with this ticket? What does he want with my father's machine? "Hand that over immediately, you rogue little imp!"

I stand firm and stare coldly at him. Has this been what he's wanted all along? All the time, following my every move about the Academy— was he just waiting for me to uncover this secret? "Never!" I shout.

I turn and fling myself at the hillside, racing away as fast as I can.

"Stop her!" I hear him shout over the readying of the Brigsmen's guns. "No! Don't shoot. I want her alive. Now go! Return her to me immediately!"

Skirts clutched high, I twist through the rocks and down the hill, my heart alive with my new mission. "Fourteen-sixty Wortley Road, Gears, Warehouse Forty-Seven," I chant, sprinting across the open field toward the fence that divides the two cities. "The Illuminator! I've found it!"

Three

Eyelet

I must make it to the warehouse before Smrt. But first I need to shake loose these Brigsmen.

I *cannot* risk entry through the checkpoint gates. I'll be spotted there for sure. Besides, I have no work card, no papers with me. I'll be arrested immediately. I've no choice; I have to cross illegally through the forest at the back of the city.

Looking over my shoulder, I see the Brigsmen closing in, their eyes those of circling wolves. I swallow, head twisting, and burst from the woods, veering sideways through a bank of trees. My move confuses some but challenges others, their shouts mingling with the snap of twigs under their boots as they thunder after me.

Inside the trees, I dash through a brook, then take a wicked turn, snaking through a grove of bramble-twisted saplings, hearing the Brigsmen curse as they get caught up in the spiny fingers. I've bought myself a small pocket of time, but not much. I need a plan, and fast.

I reach the boundary of the city and skid to a stop, heaving in breath and clutching my knees, astonished at what I see. I expected some sort of barrier dividing the two cities . . . but I never expected anything like this.

So tall and brutally ominous.

A tumbleweed of mechanical barbed-wire fencing as high as the windmills jiggers back and forth in front me, separating Brethren from Gears. Its thorny, spiraled curls loop in and around one another, like a massive thrasher separating chaff from wheat. It marches side to side, tracking me like a giant soldier stricken with rickets, mimicking my every move. Shifting left when I move left and right when I move right. I don't understand how it's possible. How it even knows I'm here.

I suck in a breath and hold very still. The fence line stands still, too. Squinting, I scan its length, searching for clues, my eyes locking on the answer. Hidden in a bank of quills just beyond the limit of the fence on the opposite side, built into the face of a man-made ridge: heat sensors. Just like the ones my father used in the eyes of the Security Sorcerers, the mechanical-gate ravens back at the Academy. I guess I was wrong— they *weren't* the last of their kind in the Commonwealth.

Looking around, I spot a hole dug by a small animal at the base of the fence, about half a metre away. Tufts of fur dangle from the tips of the wire's barbs there. A gopher, I reason. It doesn't look big enough for me to squeeze through. But there isn't any other way.

I turn back to the fence and stare hard into its bright-red sensors. The piercing light sears my retinas. I squint against the pain, holding my gaze just long enough to confuse the sensor into thinking I'm a stationary object, then thrust a quick hand before my face to sever the connection, just as Archie did with Simon at the Academy gates earlier.

Confused, the mechanism scans the fence line, jerking noisily left to right, until at last its beams cross, canceling each other out.

I seize the moment, throw my hood over my head for protection, jam my bumbershoot into the fence's mechanical guts, and dive head-long into the hole. Kicking and squirming, I claw my way through the tiny space, catching the button of my cloak on a barb. I look back, breath spiraling through the misty air as the fence holds me hostage.

The Brigsmen. They're racing through the field toward the fence line, gaining on me. They've broken free of the woods.

I yank on my cloak, sacrificing the button, and heave forward with all my might. The barbs seize me several more times, tearing holes in my clothes, before at last I'm released. Retrieving my bumbershoot, I run at the city, sirens sounding off behind me as I zigzag my way through the back city streets in the heart of Gears.

"Wortley. Wortley. Fourteen-sixty Wortley Road, Warehouse Forty-Seven," I chant, finding myself in the centre of the market-place—the city's square. I must not stay here long.

My eyes dash quickly over the street options on the main post. Blenheim right. Chatham left. Louisville straight on. *Wortley. Wortley. Where do I find Wortley?* The wooden board points confusingly into the middle of the market. I turn and race headlong into the square's busy centre, hoping I've interpreted the sign correctly. Over my shoulder I spy the throng of Brigsmen who broke through the forest, charging through the main gate, forcing their way past the guards. Soon they'll be upon me.

I slip through a hole in the crowd and stumble along, acting as casual as possible as I weave toward the crowd's perimeter, scanning the building numbers as I go: 1290, 1330, 1421. At the end of the street, the breastplate armour of three Brigsmen glints. A metal cart trundles noisily through the silvery fog, catching one of the Brigsmen off guard.

I lower my gaze and dash across the street, throwing myself into a second crowd, realizing almost instantly that I've made a grave mistake. I've thrown myself into a crowd of leery-eyed and boozy-breathed men letting out of a tavern. Or being thrown out, I'm not sure which. Their voices are loud and throaty, their comments grand and lewd.

"Fancy this bit of luck!" A stranger grabs me, his fist full of my behind.

I gasp as I'm pulled away by a second; his arms wrap tight about my middle as he reels me in, my back thrown up against his chest.

"Please," I cringe. "Let go of me!" The heels of my boots climb his shins.

He laughs, unaffected, hissing in my ear. "Where d'you think you're going, anyway?"

I struggle to free myself, but it's no use. His hands are everywhere. Groping me, pinching me, sifting through the layers of my skirts. His hot liquored breath falls heavily over my chest and I recoil. "Please," I beg. "Please, don't do this."

"Come on, sweet'eart." He nuzzles close. "Give us some fun." He scratches the contours of my neck with his scraggly chin. I jerk my head to the side as he kisses me, his rough, hungry lips dragging across my cheek.

"Please," I say as he pulls me in closer. "My father waits for me."

"Your father, eh?" He laughs in my ear, his fingers fondling me from behind, slowly making their way to my breasts. "What father? I don't see any!" He throws his head back in a laugh and I seize the moment, raising my heel sharply between his legs.

"Oh!" He gasps, clutching his groin, releasing me in the exchange.

I throw him off and push my way up the street, slapping down the hands of the others. "Don't you dare touch me," I spit. "Or I'll cut you, I swear!" I swing around, producing a blade from my boot. A special one, masked inside a seam. I back my way out of the crowd, flip my hood up over my head to disguise myself, and race up the road through their howls, unsure if the men will tolerate what I've just done.

I race down the centre of the street, keeping watch out of the corner of my eye for them as well as Brigsmen, buildings blurring past me.

Thirty-three, thirty-five, thirty-seven . . .

"Stop!" someone shouts.

Turning, I see the drunkard from before stumbling along behind me, clutching the centre of his drawers. "Come back 'ere, or I'll call the Peelers! You belong to ol' Barnaby now!"

I thrust myself forward, boots charging after me. *Thirty-nine. Forty-three. Forty-five . . . Forty-seven.* I slide to a stop, hurling open the wooden barn doors, pigeons taking flight. Red chips of paint flake in my hands as they rattle across the tracks. Electricity runs through my blood as I slip inside, closing myself in. Laying my back to the door, I wait for the man to pass, hearing the shouts of others gathering close by. I bend, gasping for breath, pinching a stitch from my side, my eyes straining to adjust to the darkness.

A dark, empty, dirt-floored room spills out before me. Nothing but cedar rafters held up by cedar posts. No metal. No machine. Nothing.

"This can't be. It has to be here," I chant, rushing forward. "It just has to be."

A low-pitched squeal draws my head around, the rumble of train wheels over tracks. I dash behind a beam for cover and hold my breath, squinting toward the opening revealed after the noise. At the opposite end of the warehouse stands the illuminated shadow of a man pushing something out through the now-open door. A heavy red-velvet drape hangs over it. Concealing it.

The Illuminator. It has to be. Whoever this man is, he's stealing it. My father's machine, right before my eyes! Or perhaps not, perhaps he owns it. Perhaps *this* is whom my father sold it to.

Whatever the case, I can't let him have it. Not after all this.

I don't even think. I race across the warehouse floor, following the man out into the street. Only then do I fall back against the jut in the building, realizing it could be Smrt. Twisting my face around the bricks, I'm relieved to see it's not him but a young man, dressed in top hat and tails. He stands with his back to me, next to a peculiar-looking horse-drawn vehicle that looks more like a box on wheels than a carriage.

Try as I might, I can't get a glimpse of his face. It's as if he's hiding it on purpose. He can't possibly know I'm here, can he? I lean out, staring at the carriage, constructed of solid sheets of black metal. Ink-stained rivets freckle its gurney. A thick circular lens serves as the only window in back, blown from what appears to be blackened glass.

What sort of person travels in such a creation? Why, it doesn't even appear to have seats.

I crane my neck a little farther as he throws open the side door, fighting to load up the machine. I can't let him do it. I can't let him take it from me. Not after all this.

My eyes fall on a needle-nosed tube resting up against the side of the window. Memories flash like lightning through my brain. The carny. From the carnival. The one who demonstrated the Illuminator all those years ago. That tube. It's a Crookes tube—like the one that hovered over Mrs. Benson's head. That's the Illuminator. It has to be. That man. *He's stealing it.*

I step forward just as an angry crowd rounds the corner, pressing in on the young man, hollering and slinging obscenities his way. They call him a pillager, a vagrant, a thief, rocking his carriage, trying to steal the contents within it. They pound on the doors, even try to jimmy the wheels loose from their axles. The young man fights them off, throws the doors shut, and hauls himself up onto the driver's mount. Something falls to the ground. He takes the reins, slaps them hard over the horse's neck.

The horse rears up, driving the crowd back, creating an opening for the carriage to thread through.

"Wait!" I shout, pressing ahead, shouldering my way through the angry crowd. "Wait!" I pound at the doors. "Please! I need to speak to you!"

A second crack of the whip and the horse surges forward.

I hoist my skirts and start to run. *"Wait!"* I shout again, struggling to keep up at the side of the carriage. "Wait!" I pound. "Please, wait!"

The stranger brings his whip down hard over his horse's back. I dig in, thrusting on, stretching my legs out farther than they've ever been stretched before. "Please," I shout, losing ground. "Please, I beg you, *stop the coach!*"

If I lose him, I've lost everything.

I can't let that happen.

Won't let that happen.

I've no hope without my father's machine.

I lunge, throwing myself at the back of the carriage, barely catching a toe on the edge of the running boards, embedding my nails into the carriage's seams, and hang on with everything I've got. The carriage surges forward, the streets of Gears fast becoming a memory.

"Stop!" I plead. My boot slips from the running boards. I swing out to the side of the carriage, dangling by one arm, struggling, trying to kick my way back up onto the platform, slowly losing my grip. "Stop, please!"

The stranger at the mount turns his head. "What are you doing?" he shouts. "Get off!"

I hang by the tips of my fingers, shocked, staring at him. I don't know whether to scream or cry. The face of a monster stares back at me, framed in a mop of curls darker than a raven's wing. His skin is ghostly white, marred by raised and purpled bruises. One, in the shape of an open-mouthed snake, devours his face—while the other, a purple hand, wrings his neck. He stares back at me through eyes as pink as a rabbit's. A strange and single lock of pure-white hair cascades down over his left eye. I've never seen anything like it. Not even in a book. It's as though he's escaped a freak show.

"I said, get off!" he shouts again.

I purse my lips, trying not to cry. "I won't!" I shout, hoisting myself up higher onto the back of the coach, my eyes still shamefully glued to his startling face.

My foot slips again and I sink beneath the rooftop, striking my chin hard on the way down. Grasping for a seam, I try to pull myself up, only to lose my grip with the other hand. My heart lodges in my throat as I swing off again to the opposite side, the toes of my boots burrowing twisted trenches through the dirt behind.

The stranger's face appears over the top of the cab. His eyes are lit like flares. "For the love of God," he cusses, teetering on hand and knee, then disappears, only to reappear a second later, the reins clenched between his teeth. "Give me your hand!" He reaches out for me.

My heart staggers in my chest. "I can't," I shout up at him. "I won't!"

"You *won't*?" His brows fold. "Are you mad?"

My fingers slowly begin to slip from the seam; my heart spirals into my throat.

"You are in *no* position to be negotiating—now take my hand!" the stranger insists.

"But—"

"Take it!" he shouts. When I still don't, he clamps his hand around my arm. "Now," he says, "on the count of three, I'm going to pull you up—"

"Oh *no*, you're not!" I clench my teeth.

"Then I'm going to let you down, which is it?"

I drop my chin, surveying the speed of the terrain rolling beneath my feet. "Up," I say, turning my chin toward him.

"Rational choice," the stranger says. "On the count of three. Ready?"

The carriage hits a bump, tossing him haphazardly off to one side. *"Confounded!"* He struggles. The horse spooks, picking up speed, ripping the reins loose from the stranger's teeth.

My stomach sinks as his grip slips and then retightens around my knuckles, his legs floundering dangerously over the edge of the coach.

He's sprawled on his back, kicking and flailing until at last he thrusts into a roll, flopping onto his belly again.

"Three!" he shouts, not yanking me up but swinging me out and around the end of the carriage, kicking the side door open with his boot. Before I've had the chance to object, he casts me deep inside the dark belly of the coach, slamming and locking the door behind me.

Four

Eyelet

I land hard. My head strikes the object that fills the seat next to me, hidden behind the red-velvet curtain. A trickle of blood snakes its way from my temple down my cheek, and I reach up to tend to the gash when the stranger cracks the whip. I'm thrown backward as the carriage jolts forward, carpets dropped down over the glass. The sound of hooves galloping over the cobblestones fills my ears as we rumble away from the city, out into the country, into the unknown.

Where are we going? Where is he taking me? My head cranks around. *Good Lord, what have I done?*

I rest my chin on the back of the seat, face pressed to the window glass, trembling as I peer out from beneath the flapping carpet at the last sliver of Gears. The horizon fades into the rolling cloud, and my stomach drops like a stone. My eyes warm at the thought of the stranger, and I release a terrified breath. Who is he? *What* is he? I swallow. *What was I thinking?*

I spin around and throw my head against the cushioned seat. Whatever happens now, I must be brave. Mother would want that from me. I must get through this on my own. I must not reveal who I am or why I've come. I must stay solely focused on the machine. I've come all this way to use it, and use it I shall. I'll let *no one* stop me.

Once I've used it, things will be different. I will no longer be the leper I've been, but a lamb, with a new life just beginning.

The light in my pendant catches my eye. The pulsing emerald light bathes the dark carriage in an eerie green glow. Something sparks, like a bolt of lightning within, and I gasp. I roll the vial over in my fingers, and the light sparks again. It's a charge—no, a tiny, bottled, candescent arc.

The vial starts to pulse more quickly. The power of it warms my skin. How can the key to my future—to everyone's future—be held here, in this tiny glass vessel? And why does it contain an arc?

Mother would have told me if she knew, wouldn't she?

She must not have known. But why wouldn't Father have told her? I move my eyes to the ceiling, remembering.

Perhaps there wasn't time.

Or perhaps it was too dangerous for her to know.

I think about Father's notebook—which I swiped and tucked safely down the side of my boot before I ran—about how Father had used *Lumière* as code to hide the Illuminator's whereabouts from Smrt.

Could this vial be code for something, as well?

I turn to the heap of metal sitting next to me, concealed behind the drape. Just as I'm poised to pull back the curtain, a surge of silver prickles in my veins. A lightning bolt of it this time, rising steadily, yanking at my breath. *Burning bread.* I smell burning bread. My warning, the only warning I ever get before the silver drags me under. It's a grand mal seizure this time, not just a petit one like the one that struck me back at the hedges. I'll not escape its venomous strike.

No. Please. No. I clutch the seat, trying to quell my fear. I've never gone through a grand mal seizure alone. My mother's always been there. The petit ones I can handle, I've trained myself how—but a full-blown seizure without assistance, or anyone to hide the fact . . .

I may not even survive it.

I start to tremble, the silver invading first my lips, then my entire jaw. It won't be long now. I can feel it, the heaviness inside my organs, the softening of my limbs. I can try to fight it, but it's no use. The demon that lurks within me controls me now.

Clinging to the last fragments of my consciousness, I panic, clawing at the seat. What if the stranger overhears me moaning and stops, only to discover me collapsed and gyrating about on the floor of his carriage, mouth agape, tongue exposed—frothing?

What then?

What if he thinks I'm Mad—or worse? What if he deems me a Cantationer possessed of demonic thought, and hands me over to the authorities for the practice of Wickedry, before I've even had the chance to wake up?

I can't let that happen. He can't see me. He must not *hear*.

With the last shred of my strength, I tear my gloves from my hands, ball them, and stuff them in my mouth just as the silver pulls me under. My body quakes. I writhe down the seat onto the floorboards, my face mashed against the red-velvet cushion, buttons etching lines into my cheeks.

Inside the heavy smoke that muddles my brain I see him—my father—standing next to my machine.

The Illuminator.

The one he invented solely for me. To try to put an end to this madness that plagues me. To save me from a life locked up in an asylum.

The one he sold . . .

Before he bothered to fix me.

Then *died* . . .

And left me here . . .

Still defective.

To fight this demon.

All alone.

The smoke in my mind turns from grey to black, the world around me erasing . . . slowly . . .

I wish you'd never invented it.

Never sought a solution.

Never let me believe there was hope . . .

I wish I'd never been born defective.

I wish I'd never been born *at all.*

I wish I could reverse *everything—everything* that's happened.

Part Two

Part Two

Five

Urlick

I squint, guiding the carriage through the dark, dank, criminal woods, drifting through fog as thick as pudding in spots. Nothing but the clomp of Clementine's hooves and the jingle of her tack to keep me company. Not so much as a whimper out of the stowaway cargo in back.

I hope she's still alive.

I look over my shoulder at the silent carriage bobbing along behind, seeing the girl's face as she clung to the roof—the sheer grit and determination in her eyes. What kind of a girl acts like that? Forcing her way up onto the property of a total stranger, hiking up her skirts and running at the speed of a broke-rhythm racehorse? Better still, what kind of a girl dares to wander the markets of Gears without a chaperone? Clearly, one who doesn't know any better.

I wonder where she's from. Certainly not Gears. It has to be Brethren, there's no other choice. What could she be running from, a waif like that? What could she possibly have done to drive her to flee the safety of her world for the likes of *this* one? I look around. No one in his or her right mind would intentionally do that.

"Oh, good Lord," I gasp. "Please don't tell me." Clementine whinnies. "I haven't just kidnapped a girl, have I?"

Clementine swings her long, sad face around and sighs heavily.

"You're right," I say. "She came of her own volition, didn't she? Didn't she? You'll vouch for me, won't you, old girl?"

Clementine snorts.

"Good, as long as we're in agreement." I pull on the reins, bringing her to a stop in front of the barn outside the house, feeling the rush of worried heat subside from my cheeks. I don't think I've ever been so glad to be home. Then it dawns on me. What am I going to do with the girl now? I can't possibly let her in the house.

I swing down from the coach box into a pool of swirling fog, patting Clementine on the haunches. Evening mist hangs thick from her nostrils. Vapours crowd the summit of the escarpment on the horizon.

"It won't be long now before they spill down over the hillside, eh, girl?" I stare up at the swirling clouds, willing them away. "Wretched things, contaminating everything in their path." I tug at her laces. "Blasted Vapours. *And* their deathly tentacles."

Clementine snorts again.

My eyes drift onto the handle of the carriage. "You don't suppose she's died back there? She hasn't made a sound in clicks." Clementine whinnies, stretching her lips back toward the door. "I know, I know. I'll let her out, don't worry"—I pull on a strap—"as soon as I figure out the best way to go about it."

The stowaway stirs inside the carriage, sending me shuffling backward, my spine slapping up against Clementine's withers. My heart rattles like a bag full of snakes. Never in all my life have I been this nervous.

What's the matter with me? What do I care what this stranger thinks? Besides, it's not like she's in any position to judge. She's the one who forced her way into *my* carriage, I've not invited her here. I tug at the tails of my waistcoat. Who is she, I wonder? Who sent her to infiltrate? *Don't be silly, she's just a girl. They don't send girls to do men's dirty work. Do they?*

Clementine reaches around, nudges me with her muzzle. "Don't push me." I shove her off. "I'm getting to it." I drop the reins, suck in a breath, and head for the carriage door, my hands wet inside my gloves.

The buggy wobbles side to side. I hesitate just outside the door. Shivering in the damp morning light, low mist curling about my feet, my hand hovers centimetres above the handle.

Perhaps it'd be best if I just *throw* it open. Expose her to my ugliness straight away. Or will that be too much? I turn and pace. Will she die of fright at the sight of me? I turn again. Oh, good Lord, get on with it, will you? She's not a monster. She's just a girl.

Besides, it's not like she hasn't already seen me. She looked me straight in the eyes. That much I know. Even so, has she *really* seen me? Had the chance to take me all in? And if she has, what must she think?

Clementine shuffles her feet, growing impatient. The carriage lurches again.

I close my eyes and fling open the door.

The stranger gasps.

I look to see her staring at me through eyes round and full as a harvest moon. She peeps, a startled fledgling in a nest of darkness.

"I'm sorry," I say, and throw out my hand. "May I?"

She lunges backward. "May you what?"

"Help you from the carriage, of course."

Long black lashes bat over caramel-coloured eyes so striking I can hardly pull mine away.

"No, thank you." She slides forward, averting her gaze. "I'll be fine."

Creamy white hands grip the sides of the door, with nails as round and delicate as rosebuds. She exits toe first, followed by a lanky leg covered in a stretch of thigh-high spat-style stocking. The kind sophisticates wear. A ruse of buttons runs up the stocking's side. Lace trims its top. A plume of emerald-green skirts follows, billowing out from the mouth of the carriage, featuring a centre skirt cut so shockingly short, a flash of bare leg winks between the finished edge and the top of her stocking—*not that I'm noticing*. I can't help but wonder, do all Brethren girls wear their skirts so scandalously short?

She turns and swipes her lavish cranberry bustle out the door. It falls, adorning her bottom in layers of velvet so rich, so plush, it looks as though she's stepped straight out of the palace court. Granted, I don't know much about women's clothing, but I know no one in all of Gears or the Follies dresses so.

Good God. I gulp. Don't tell me I've kidnapped royalty. I'm both a kidnapper *and* a thief.

Don't be silly. I've kidnapped no one. She came of her own volition. Didn't she?

My eyes fall to her mud-caked hems, the lace on her sleeves stained in what appears to be . . .

Good Lord, is that blood?

She straightens, her bosoms bubbling up against the border of her low-cut chemise—*not that I'm noticing*. A tinge of heat rises in my cheeks. I tug down the tips of my waistcoat and avert my eyes. That's when I notice it. The necklace she wears around her neck. A vial of something pulsing green, on an emerald-and-ebony-beaded chain. I've never seen anything like it. I must ask her what that is. The vial rolls, lodging low between her breasts. Embarrassed, I dash my eyes away. Later, of course. Not now. I swallow. That would be ridiculous.

Wouldn't it?

"What's happened to your gloves?" I say, noticing them balled in her fist.

"They've become soiled, I'm afraid," she says, hiding them in her skirts. "Where are we?" she demands, turning her attention to the escarpment, her gaze tracing it from mount to base and back again. Wisps of nutmeg and crimson hair frame her face, where her upsweep has become all unswept. She brushes a rouge strand from her eyes and I'm rendered breathless.

"Home," I say, pulling myself back into the moment.

"Home?" she repeats, sounding a mite frazzled. "And where might *home* be, specifically?"

"Ramshackle Follies—"

"Ramshackle Follies!" Her head swings around. "*The* Ramshackle Follies?" Her mouth falls agape.

"Yes."

"The Follies that lie beyond the limits of the Commonwealth, where—?"

"Those would be the ones."

She falls back on her heels and twists her hands together. "I see." She exhales. "Very well, then." She narrows her eyes and addresses me firmly. "It seems I've made a grave mistake. I'll need you to return me to the marketplace immediately." She raises her skirts and tromps back toward the carriage, the heel of her right boot wobbling. She mumbles, *"Perhaps I can hire someone to fetch the machine for me . . ."*

"What was that?"

"I said, I need to be getting back to the city."

I chuckle, which sharpens her copper eyes even more.

"Do you find my plight amusing?"

"No, it's just—" I stammer.

"Fine, then." She starts away. "If you won't take me, I guess I'll just have to walk."

I laugh. "You'll not get far in those." I point to her wobbly heel. "And then there's always the criminals." I turn my back.

"Criminals?" She falters, halting midstep.

"The woods are full of them," I say, loosening Clementine's tack. "Not to mention the Infirmed." She turns, her eyes wide and lily white

57

through the grey trolling fog. "You know, those mentally incapacitated creatures even the asylums won't accept?" She swallows. "The discards of your society deposited here by your beloved Commonwealth. Thrown from passing steamploughs in the night, or strung up by their necks in the trees and left for dead." I slip the harness from Clementine's back. "Trouble is, some die . . . and others *don't*."

Her eyes grow wide as saucers under tea.

"And if the criminals don't get you, the Vapours will."

"The Vapours?"

I gesture behind me at the roiling dark mist that hovers over the escarpment's mount. "Random clouds of gas that roll the hillsides out here, asphyxiating all in their path. Surely you've heard of them," I jest, knowing full well Brethren's Ruler erected giant scrubbers, known as booms, years ago to filtrate the air around the entire perimeter of Brethren, protecting its people from the toxic effects of the Vapours—leaving the citizens of Gears and the Follies to fend for themselves. "The Vapours are particularly lethal in late summer"—I lean toward her—"which it currently is. And *especially* severe during half-to-full-moon phases"—I whisper—"which are due now, any day."

She scuttles closer.

"But don't let me deter you." I loosen Clementine's halter and let it drop from her face. "If you really need to get back to Gears, you'd best get going."

Her face prunes.

I grin as I turn my back to her.

"Perhaps it would be best, then, if I stayed."

Her words catch me. "Who said anything about staying?" I whirl back around.

"What did you say your name was again?"

"I didn't—"

"And why not?"

I crinkle my brows. "Considering you basically shanghaied my carriage, I think perhaps you should divulge *your* name first."

Her lips pull into a firm, thin line.

"Fine." I loosen another strap on Clementine's back. "What do you say we both reveal on the count of three? Ready? One. Two. Thr—"

"Eyelet Emiline Elsworth!" she blurts.

I grin, saying nothing.

She scowls. "A man of your word, I see." She turns on her heel and starts away.

"Now, where are you going?" I call after her.

"Well, you can't expect me to accept the hospitality of a person I can't even trust."

"What hospitality? Who said anything about hospitality?"

"Are you denying me shelter?" She swings back around.

"Denying you? I haven't even offered—"

"I cannot believe you'd drag me all the way out here and then refuse to keep me—"

"Me? Drag *you?*"

"What kind of a monster does that?"

I stiffen.

"Brute, I mean." She blushes.

I purse my lips, eyeing her hard over Clementine's withers. My blood bubbles under my skin. And to think, I thought she was pretty! "Is there somewhere you'd like to be delivered? A relative's house, a friend, an acquaintance, maybe? Perhaps there's someone I can summon to come pick you up?"

"You're not serious—"

"Very." I turn, hauling the rest of Clementine's gear off to the barn.

She steams after me. "You can't just leave me alone in this terrible place."

"I could." I turn. "But then you'd die. And I'd be the monster you just accused me of being." I stiff-arm my way past her gape-mouthed face, making my way back to Clementine.

"I demand you give me shelter." She stamps her foot.

"You what?"

"I demand you take me in and keep me for as long as I need."

I stare at her, shocked, unbelieving.

"Look, for reasons I'd rather not discuss, I can't keep you here. Now, there must be somewhere else you can go. Surely you had a plan."

Her face falls.

She didn't. I sigh. What kind of girl shanghais a carriage out into the middle of nowhere without concern for her own well-being? What's the matter with this girl?

I scratch my head. "Do you do windows?" I say.

Her chin snaps up. "Do I do *what*?"

"What about the dishes? Would you prefer to do the dishes?"

"I beg your pardon?"

"Well, surely you don't expect me to keep you for free?"

Her lips clench tight as a pair of pliers, and it almost makes me laugh.

"What about the privy?"

She scowls.

"The floors?"

She gasps.

"All right, then. Dishes it is." I extend a hand to seal the deal.

She hesitates, her lip in a pout. Finally she drops her hand into mine. I shake it firmly, jumping at the sparks that light between us.

"But absolutely *no* laundry." She grins.

"Damn." I drop her hand. "I forgot that one."

She smiles, then traipses after me, circling. "But don't go thinking just because I've accepted your *strained* offer of hospitality that I've agreed in any way to become your property or your slave." She juts out her bony chin. "Have I made myself clear?"

"Sparkling." I push past her and mutter, "Lucky for you, I don't believe in slavery."

"What was that?"

"Nothing." I turn. "You're welcome to stay until the Vapours have cleared"—I grow serious—"but after that I must insist you find another place."

"How long before the Vapours clear?"

"Couple of weeks maybe, could be a month."

"A *month*!"

I reach back and slap Clementine on the arse, sending her off into the underground stable, trying not to laugh as Eyelet jumps.

"What then?" she says, primping away her ruffled look.

"Then"—I tilt my head toward the escarpment—"we're good for another three to six months before they rear their ugly head again."

"I see." She stares off over the horizon. "And where is it that you live, exactly, Master . . ." She looks around.

"Babbit," I mumble. "Urlick Babbit."

The words struggle from my mouth. It's been years since I formally introduced myself. I lower my eyes to the ground.

"Urlick." She rolls the word around on her tongue, her eyes shining. "Is there a house?"

I point to the base of the landscape behind her, to the weathered, brass porthole door, burrowed into the side of the escarpment's base, beyond the belly of the moat. Gutter water runs past the entrance beneath a wooden pallet porch. A swing bridge made of planks and twine fixed to a pair of old trees connects the dwelling to the side of the earth. Her eyes slowly drink in the scene.

"You live there?" She points. "In that hole, in the rock?"

"That's correct."

She looks as though she's drunk a vat of poison.

"Rather the perfect hiding place, don't you think?" I lower my voice, flitting past her toward the carriage. "For someone who's on the run."

She darts backward as if she's been singed. "I take it you live alone?"

"No. I live with my father." I pick up the forks of the buggy.

"Really. What does he do?"

"He's a scientist."

"How interesting."

"Not really."

She drops her hands.

I yank on the forks, wincing under the weight of the carriage, pushing it parallel with the barn. "Have you forgotten something?" I say, catching her eyeing the carriage door.

"No." She drags her hands down her skirts.

I drop the forks, pull myself up on the coach box, and yank a lever, sparking the fifth-wheel running gears into motion. The axles on either side of the carriage pivot a full 180 degrees. From there, the whole carriage sets into motion, drifting sideways, parallel parking itself in the barn. Eyelet's eyes grow wide at the sight.

She's never laid eyes on a self-parking coach before. But of course not; I've only just invented it. They don't have *everything* in Brethren.

"How did you do that?"

"It's a secret," I say, jumping down next to her, slapping the dust from my hands. I pause, reaching for the gash at the side of her temple. "What's happened to your head?"

"Nothing." She ducks away. "I've just grazed it, is all."

"On what?"

"On the machine that rode next to me in the carriage."

I swallow.

How does she know about the machine? Was she watching me? Did she see me steal it? Who is this girl? Has she been sent?

"I'm afraid I don't know what you're talking about," I say, altogether too quickly.

"Nonsense," she scoffs. "You're the one who stole it from—" She stops herself.

I twist my brows and stare at her sternly. My hands begin to sweat.

She purses her lips and stares back. For a long moment there is nothing but silence. Then, before I can stop her, she turns and bolts toward the carriage. *I can't let her open the door. I can't let her see it.* I lurch forward, catching her hard by the wrists. "That machine is none of your business," I seethe through clenched teeth.

"Really?" She yanks herself free and rubs her wrists. "I'll have to try to remember that."

Six

Eyelet

I follow Urlick out over the makeshift bridge that leads to the portal door to his home. The bridge swings, and I grab for the handrail made of dried, twisted vine, pulling back at the prick of thorns.

"Everything all right?" Urlick's head turns.

"Peachy," I grin, sucking the blood from my finger. Truth is, I'm cold and more than a bit afraid of heights, though I'm not about to admit it to the likes of him.

"How old is this thing, anyway?" I reestablish my gait, trying my best not to look down.

"Old as the house, I suppose. Why?"

"No reason."

I scowl at the stench of sewer water gushing past beneath the bridge. A vulture pecks the flesh of a dead rat nearby. I turn my head and bite my lip—partly to keep my teeth from chattering, but mostly to hold down what threatens to come up—and wobble my way across the rest of the bridge.

"Are you sure you've got the right place?" I jest and fold my arms, seeing Urlick struggle to open the combination lock.

He scowls at me over his shoulder and spins the lock again. "Are you always this clever?"

"No, usually I'm more."

The vulture plucks the rat's eye from its head. I cover my mouth and look away. I can feel Urlick smiling. What have I got myself into? When Mother insisted I run and hide, I'm sure she didn't mean in the underground lair of a total stranger at the edge of the civilized world.

Mother.

I close my eyes, imagining my mother's wax-coated body hanging from the gallows in the square. My heart races. My eyes pop back open. I blink away the tears that come, ashamed to have left her alone. I turn and stare out into the rolling mist.

My father died out here. His body was found somewhere along the road between the Follies and Gears. His hands were scorched, and the right side of his face was blackened as if he'd been burned. His gas mask was stripped from the cords around his neck. In one hand he held a lab report. The officials in attendance ruled he'd been overcome by the Vapours. But I never believed it to be so. Mother never believed it, either, though she remained silent; I know she didn't, I could see it in her eyes.

I stare up at the Vapours pooling in the distance, over the top of the ridge. There was never any evidence found to suggest Father was asphyxiated. And he died in early spring, not late summer.

"There we are." Urlick's voice breaks my train of thought, followed by a startling *clunk.* A clangor of gears churns inside the lock until the door finally pops open. A blinding ejection of steam gives way to a dimly lit corridor. Butane-dipped torches dot the sides of mud walls. Grease-lacquered puddles spot the floors.

"This is it?"

Urlick smiles, says nothing, and my heart jerks in my chest. I can't see myself living in such a place, even if it is only temporary. I'm a girl, not a worm.

Urlick reaches inside, plucks a torch from the wall, and with his other hand summons me to follow. I gulp down the clump of anxiety that's just rushed to my throat, and I follow reluctantly. I shiver, my pupils blooming as I step across the threshold into a puddle, cold water flooding through the stitches of my boot.

Urlick sloshes his way gingerly up the dark corridor in front of me, his head wreathed in a halo of torchlight. I follow close behind, ducking and darting, hurdling new puddles, fending off spiderwebs. I know it sounds silly, but I long to take his hand, to feel the warmth of something familiar, though I barely know him.

I'm not sure which I find more disturbing: the cramped state of this chamber, its lack of light, or the abundance of millipedes dropping into my hair. Moments later we come to another door, and I can say I've never been so glad to see one. Hopefully it will lead somewhere more civilized than this. It's round and made of metal like the one outside, only this one glows green and smells like aged copper.

Urlick swings his torchlight past the cogs on the lock, revealing a thick coating of rust. "Hold this," he says, passing me the torch. He peels off his coat, tossing it to me as well. I can't help but notice his coat smells strangely like rosewood and cinnamon, though by the look of it, I'd expect it to smell more of tobacco and chimney soot.

He rolls up his sleeves, sets his stocky legs shoulder-width apart, and throws his full weight onto the crank, biceps bulging, quads straining, ropes of muscle rippling beneath his forearm skin. His milky hands glow pink against the rusty crankshaft, his long, dark locks dampening with sweat. At last the gear begins to creak, jittering slowly at first, then racing wildly around. Urlick falls forward, choking on the waft of steam that pours from the opening door. If getting *in* is this much trouble, I can't imagine how difficult it is to get *out*.

Urlick pushes aside the door, his pink eyes shimmering in the tiny column of light that floods through the opening. "After you." He motions for me to enter, backhanding the sweat from his brow.

I bite my lip and peek around him into the stiflingly tiny room beyond. A sour taste invades my mouth. This room is in no way more civilized.

"You all right?" he asks, his mouth pulled tight with concern.

"Quite. Thank you," I lie.

Turning sideways, I thread past him, careful not to catch my drapery afire on the torch now burning again in his hand. Gooseflesh blossoms on the back of my neck as my shoulder blades brush across the front of him.

The room is small, all right, incredibly small; I could easily reach all four walls from where I stand. A scaffold of cedar braces and pillars, held together by massive bolts, supports the earth from collapsing in at the sides. It appears to be an elevator shaft, if I'm not mistaken, much like that found in old abandoned coal mines. Above my head, the ceiling climbs endlessly. Below, a plank platform masks a bottomless pit.

Urlick joins me seconds later, his back pressed up tight against my front. The platform shimmies under his weight, and my hands fly up at my sides, finding Urlick's sleeves.

"You're sure you're all right?" He almost laughs.

I let go, blushing. My breath races as though my lungs have suddenly grown too large for my chest.

"Hang on," he says. *To what?*

He releases a lever, and the platform jumps. Bits of sour spittle launch up into my throat. I work hard to swallow them back down as the enormous steel ropes at the sides of the pillars begin to coil, screeching and straining through sets of giant pulleys. I close my eyes, clasping the pendant at my chest like a crucifix, overcome by the smell of earthworms, moldy cedar, and grease rising through the trembling, brittle timber structure.

Partway up, the pulley slips, sending the platform skittering off balance. My hands again fill themselves with Urlick's sleeves, this time not retreating. Steel ropes whir recklessly, spiraling down through the shaft until finally catching on the pulley's worn teeth, jerking the platform upright. Our hearts strum thankful concertos—well, at least mine does—as we again begin to evenly rise.

We continue for what seems like hours, until at last the platform comes to a fluttery stop in front of a large, wooden, windowless door, resting on a track. The kind found on the side of a steamplough boxcar. The ones used to cart lunatics off to the asylum.

Where am I? Where has he taken me? Did he hear me in the throes of an episode in the back of his coach and decide to have me put away?

Before I can form a question, Urlick steps forward and hurls back the door. It rattles wildly over the track.

I suck in a breath and close my eyes, bringing my hands to my mouth to stifle my scream.

"What?" Urlick laughs, and I open my eyes. "Not what you were expecting?"

Beyond the door stands an ordinary kitchen. Decorated in the most modern shades: red, mustard, terracotta. The walls are dressed in expensive, flat-patterned paper. Exotic orchids and lilies make up the print. Hardwood kitchen cupboards stand lined with the newest lin-seed-oil countertops. Fashionable red-and-white-chequered linoleum tiles gleam from the floor.

"No." I let go of my breath and smooth my skirts. "Not exactly."

Seven

Eyelet

"Tea?" Urlick crosses the kitchen floor in just a few swift strides, his movements so lissome, so graceful for a man.

I stumble forward, and the boxcar door rumbles to a mysterious close behind me, triggering a short siren and a lock when it meets the wall.

I jump at the sound of clattering turbines, followed by an ominous *clunk*.

"Is that the only way in or out of here?"

"The only way you need know about," Urlick mumbles, scouring the shelves for a tin of tea to honour his proposal. "Please"—he gestures with a hand toward the dining-room table in the centre of the room—"have a seat."

Gliding toward it, I run my fingers over the tabletop's grain before dropping into a seat. Oak, I believe, which is strange. Oak hasn't grown in these parts for over a century. Perhaps I'm wrong. Perhaps it's just thick-ringed pine?

I look up, further perplexed by the presence of a darkened porthole window over the sink. Why would anyone go to the expense of glass to cover a hole from which nothing can be seen? "Is that real?" I flick my chin toward the window.

Urlick turns. His piercing pink eyes startle me at first. I gasp and then feel instantly guilty. Those are certainly going to take some getting used to, that's for sure. Though I do find them strangely intriguing—in a rather morbid, yet alluring sort of way.

"If you're wondering if it's operable, then the answer is no. But if you're talking aesthetics, then yes."

"Oh." I swallow, still lost in his eyes. "Of course." I twist my hair nervously. Though I'm more uncomfortable than nervous. "Why is it so dark, then?" I push. "If it's intended for aesthetics."

His brow furrows. "Why, to keep the birds from crashing into it, of course."

Of course.

I'm not sure if he's intentionally trying to make me feel daft, or if he's just always this wonderfully insolent. If this keeps up I'll be in dire need of a mood barometer soon. Perhaps I'll have to build one.

"The loo's over there."

"Pardon?"

"The loo." He glances across the room. "The *water closet*."

Again with the insolent thing.

"I thought you might want to freshen up a little." His eyes traipse the length of my frame.

I look down at the stains on my lace, my muddied skirts. "Oh . . . *yes* . . . ," I gasp, popping from the chair. It's the first time I've even thought about my appearance. My reflection in the tabletop tells me it's far from good. Mud-spattered cheeks, a squirrel's nest of hair, dried blood smeared from my nose to my chin. How utterly charming. What must he think? Oh, goodness, what *must* he think? I swallow, creeping across the floor toward the loo, embarrassed.

"You'll find fresh clothes on a chair in the corner."

Fresh clothes?

"I messaged ahead to have some set out for you."

Just as I'm about to ask how, I throw open the door and the thought evaporates. I've never seen such a lavishly decorated *water closet* in all my life. The delicate porcelain sink, the granite-veined floors, a crystal aether chandelier? I touch it and it tinkles. How can this be? Such fine accessories out here in the middle of no-man's-land. I run my fingers over the shiny brass taps.

"Did you find the clothes all right?"

"Yes," I shout, turning my eyes to the neatly folded pile of clothes on a chair in the corner. A formal day suit—I pick it up—featuring modest peplum-style hip draperies, with velvet bustle in back. Not bad. The centre skirt is far too long for my liking, nearly floor length compared to my usual midthigh, but I suppose it'll have to do. I hold up the jacket. The shoulders are far too wide, grotesquely too wide. Oh well, those who commandeer their way into others' worlds can't be choosers, now can they?

I pick through the undergarments, wondering to whom they might belong. Urlick's mother, perhaps? Though he's not mentioned a mother. I give the skirt a shake and start to undress.

"There are a few house rules I need to go over with you," Urlick hollers through the door.

House rules? The authority in his voice sharpens my quills.

"Breakfast is at six thirty sharp. Lights out at nine o'clock."

Nine o'clock! I step from my old skirt and yank on the new one, wrestling it up over my hips. I reach for the chemise, afraid to bend over too deeply. *That's unusually snug.*

"No one is allowed to roam about the house at night; it's strictly forbidden," Urlick continues.

Forbidden? Really. "What do you mean, no one?" I holler back. "I thought it was just your father, me, and you?"

He ignores the question altogether, barking still more rules. "You are never to leave the Compound."

I tighten the strings on the corset, fasten the buttons of the bodice, dry my face, and restack my hair. "Compound?" I say, emerging from the room still fussing with my skirt.

"Yes, *Compound.*" He turns, indicating the rooms of the house with his hands. "You are never to leave here without a chaperone. It's simply too dangerous. Do so and you risk being attacked by roaming criminals or the Infirmed. No one leaves the buildings at all during half-moon-to-full-moon phases, when the Vapours are at their worst. It's too deadly, for obvious reasons." I swallow. "And *if* and *when* you ever see my father, which will be rare"—he eyes me hard—"you are never to bother him, *never* speak to him for any reason. Is that clear?"

"Why?"

"Why?" He turns, tugging at the points of his waistcoat. "Because it is the *rule*, that's why."

That's the second time he's done that strange little movement— once outside at the carriage and now again. I'm not sure if it's his way of emphasizing his point or just a nervous habit, but before I've had the chance to figure it out, his back is turned, and he's heavy into his tea preparations again. Plucking the tea service off the shelf, he slams it down onto the countertop: first the pots, then the creamers, followed by the sugars and lids.

I wince, trying not to look disturbed by his behaviour, though, truth be known, I am. But no more than I am by staying in a house with blackened windows.

"You are *never* to climb the stairs to my father's third-floor laboratory," he continues, before I can utter a single word. "No matter *what* sounds you hear."

Sounds? What does that mean? What kinds of sounds does one emit from a laboratory? Dread curdles in my belly. What kind of laboratory *is* this?

"We live here alone, my father and I, except for Iris, who prepares our meals and does light housekeeping. They're her clothes you're wearing"—he eyes me warily—"but you needn't thank her. She prefers to be left *alone*."

Alone?

"She has her own apartment on the second floor, below my father's laboratory"—he hesitates, pouring the water from the stove into pots—"which you are *never to enter*. Do you understand?"

I look up, drinking in his ominous expression. Dread seeps from my gut to my bones. Why all the secrecy? Why such dire instructions? I nod silently, wondering what's really going on.

Then, as if there's been a shift of the wind in the kitchen, his mood lifts. "Sugar?" He sort of smiles, as much of a smile as I've seen pass his lips in the two short hours that I've known him. What on earth is wrong with him?

I nod and he clatters toward the table, still dark and broody about the edges, tea service rattling loudly in his hands. He places things down, a little confused about their order, changing things twice before settling, offering me endless lumps of sugar and loads of cream.

"Care for a humbug?" He flips his coattails out behind him, joining me for tea.

"A hum-*what*?"

"A *candy*?" His brows rise. He shakes the candy bowl in my direction.

Forget the mood barometer. I may need a full psychoanalyst kit to decipher the rapid mood swings of this man.

Reluctantly, I accept the sweet, examining it before popping it in my mouth. It tastes of butter and cocoa and fiery peppermint, mixed with something bitterly unexplainable. I spit it out and examine it again, peering through its clear coating for a bug. God only knows what one might serve in a home with blackened windows.

Urlick laughs. Then clears his throat to cover it up. His eyes fall to the pendant at my neck. "Tell me about that necklace," he blurts.

"There's nothing to tell," I snap.

"Surely, there's a story behind something so unusual—"

"A connoisseur of women's jewelry, are we?" I tip my head.

"I wouldn't say that," he answers slowly.

"Then how would you know?"

"Know *what*?"

"If it's unusual."

"I guess I wouldn't."

"*Well*, there we have it." I cross my hands and look away.

Urlick clears his throat again, and for a long time we sip our tea in steeped silence—me pondering why he's asked me such a thing. What interest could he have in my jewelry?

It takes a while, but finally—heads fixed forward, hands warming round our cups—snatches of actual conversation begin to pass again between us, rising through wisps of Earl Grey steam.

"Is that a bruise?" I pause. "On your face, I mean?"

Urlick looks up from his cup. "A birthmark. What were you running from?"

"Trouble. Has it always been that colour?"

"Worse. What kind of trouble?"

"The worst kind. How did it happen, exactly?"

"I got stuck. What do you mean by 'the worst kind'?" He grimaces. "Is there any other?"

"No. What do you mean, you got stuck?"

"In the birth canal. Why is it you're getting more information out of me than I am you?"

"Practice. And your mother?"

He looks away. "Died, giving birth to me. Yours?"

"Passed." I run a sad finger around the lip of my cup. "Most recently."

"I'm sorry." Urlick's head drops.

"So am I." The room fills with the sound of my spoon grating the bottom of my cup.

"What is that about your neck?"

"A necklace. Are they painful?"

"Pardon?" He looks up.

"The marks on your face. Are you in pain?"

"No." He glances at the gash on my temple. "Are you?"

"No."

I take a sip of tea, slurping, not meaning to, but slurping just the same.

"You're not dangerous, are you?" He raises his cup to his purpled lips. "An escaped criminal? Mentally imbalanced? Certifiably insane?"

"No." I take offense. "Are you?"

"No." His gaze drifts away from me across the room. "I just look a fright."

"Interesting."

He whirls around, scorching me with a look.

"I'd call it interesting, not frightful," I clarify.

"Then you'd be the only one." He stands. "More tea?"

Eight

Eyelet

"No, thank you." I decline Urlick's offer, my teeth still stinging sweet from the last over-sugared cup.

"In that case, I'll see you later." He stands. "I'm sorry, but I've work to do."

"Wait," I say, popping to my feet. "I'll come with you—"

"You most certainly will *not*!" He tugs on the points of his waist-coat again. "I mean—" His pale cheek turns a lovely shade of crimson, almost matching the purpled one. "It's man's work. Too taxing for a lady. You'll get *dirty*. And you've only just got yourself . . . *clean*."

His lips pull into a tight and serious line. This can mean only one thing. The machine. He must be planning to move it inside. Elsewise, why would he care if I shadowed him?

He can't possibly be willing to leave me alone with the run of the house and no one to watch me, can he? Not after so many rules. Something's up. He can't be that dim. Or that trusting? Can he? Oh my goodness, he is.

"So." I raise a brow. "What am I to do until your return?" I tilt my head, playing stupid. I know exactly what it is I'll be doing.

He stares at me and hesitates. "I don't know. Whatever a girl of your fragile nature does with her day, I suppose. Paint. Sculpt. Read."

My eyes shrink beneath their lids. How dare he assume me *fragile*! On what grounds? I've certainly not appeared fragile since the moment I arrived. Dread rises in my throat again. Please say he didn't overhear me in the back of his coach.

"The study is over there." He points to an archway off the side of the kitchen, opposite where he stands. My head swings around, taking note of it. That makes doorway number four. For such a small space, this kitchen seems to be filled with opportunity for escape. The main-entry boxcar door is behind me; another wooden one, painted red, stands opposite, leading to the bedrooms upstairs; the archway he's just pointed out, to the right, opens onto a study; and behind him is a heavily carved walnut one, which, I can only presume, leads to some sort of back kitchen.

"I take it you can keep yourself busy in there until lunch is served?" Urlick continues, glaring at me, all hoity-toity-like, and I've the urge to pinch the smug from his face. How does he keep doing that, switching from nice to nauseous, in so few breaths? Such talent this man possesses.

"Certainly." I grit my teeth.

"Until noon, then." He nods.

I return the gesture, slipping him a smirk-tinged grin.

He slinks across the room and throws open the mystery door, exposing a back kitchen—*I was right*—and off the back of it another door, slightly opened, leading to a long, narrow, darkened hallway. All my senses alight.

He slips through the first door, the curls at the back of my neck tousling as he yanks it firmly shut, abandoning me in the kitchen. Or so he thinks. My blood bubbles with rebellion.

Closing my eyes, I count to thirty—*one thousand one, one thousand two* . . . Then I sprint across the room and sling back the door—

"Can I help you?" Urlick's eyes burn like red rays through the darkness.

"Uhhhh!" My hand flies to my chest as I gulp in a breath. "I, *uh* . . ." My brain wobbles, searching for a worthy excuse for my presence, spotting tea towels drying on a rack behind his head. "I . . . was just looking for a tea towel. Thought I might do up a few dishes. You know"—I smooth a curl next to my cheek—"hold up my end of our deal."

For a moment he just stares at me like one would a lying child. "Very well," he finally says, grabbing a towel from the rack and tossing it onto my head. "You'll find the drying rack under the sink."

"Thank you," I say from beneath the towel.

"Don't mention it." He slams the door again. This time he trips the lock, turbines churning, followed by the clunk of a dead bolt.

I stand there, humiliated, listening to his shoes clatter up the narrow hallway and then down a set of stairs. *"Oooooh!"* I shriek, yanking the towel from my head. "Who does he think he is? Locking me up like this? My keeper?" I stomp my way backward into the study, snapping the tea towel to rest over the back of a chair. "Keep myself amused until lunch is served, eh? Well, we'll just see about *thaaaaaaaaaa*—"

Something sharp jabs me hard in the back. A shiver ripples down my spine. I lift my arm to find a giant beak peeking out from under my armpit with nostril holes the size of jewelets. Raising my arm a little higher reveals a giant head, streaming down from one of the longest necks I've ever seen.

I turn around to find myself in the company of a giant stuffed ostrich, standing nearly floor to ceiling, tucked in behind the entrance to the study. And not just any ostrich, either: a two-headed, double-winged, four-legged specimen, stuffed and mounted on a dirt-covered plinth, its wings perched midflap, legs flailing. One head juts upward while the other juts down. On each head, four giant marble eyes peer from under a total of four sets of feather-long lashes. I shudder at the thought of coming face-to-face with such a creature in the wild. I imagine the look on the face of the hunter who did.

Who stuffs such a hideous thing to put on display? Better still, who keeps it in their study? I look around. Taxidermy trophies sit everywhere. The room is full of them. And not one of them is normal. A two-headed goat bleats from a tabletop. The heads of double-fanged boars peer down from the walls. A disturbing-looking three-eyed wolf stares at me from over the fireplace, while a snarling grizzly, baring rows of teeth like a shark, hovers in the opposite corner. What kind of people collect such horrid things? And where did they find so many?

I lurk about, soft-footed, searching for an alternate door to the kitchen, worried at every turn I'll find something new and even more frightening. But I find nothing. There appears to be only one way in and out of this room—the way I came in, past the oversized guard-chicken. The room has only one window, and it's been painted black. The room is oddly triangular, with one wall shorter than the other two. Honestly? An isosceles study? Who builds an isosceles study? I push on the shortest wall, shocked when it pushes back.

Must everything here be a mystery?

The room smells of old fur, stale cigars, and formaldehyde. Dust layers every inch of the woodwork. Clearly no one has cleaned this study in quite some time, and by *some time*, I mean a century. I drag a finger over the bookshelves, regretting it instantly. What lurks underneath the room's woolly grey coating? I rub my fingers together. I wish I had a petri dish.

I take in a breath and blow it out, clearing the dust from the top of the credenza, nearly becoming winded in the process. Corsets allow only so much space for breathing on a good day, let alone on days when lungs are required for cleaning.

A delicious assortment of household gadgets reveals itself beneath the dusty mess. Extremely unusual-looking household gadgets. In fact, I'm not even sure they're gadgets at all.

One by one I pick them up, examining each carefully, a little afraid of what I might find. Some sort of grater? I turn the first one over. Or perhaps a coffee grinder? I jump when the handle cranks around on the side and a set of cutters mash together like teeth. I've never seen a coffee grinder with teeth before. I set it down. I don't think I should like to see another, either. I let go and it flops around on the top of the credenza, clunking around in a circle, using the handle as a leg. A possessed coffee grinder, at that. How apropos.

I pick up the next item. An apple corer, I believe. I crank the handle on its side, and a pair of vertical blades springs into action, slicing the air. A second horizontal wheel snaps up into place, skinning the edge of a pedestal where seven needle-sharp prongs bob up and down.

"Whatever this is, it looks utterly lethal," I say, tapping the tips of the prongs and drawing blood instantly.

I put the apple corer down and suck my finger, picking up what looks to be a pair of harmless sheep shears. I clip them together, jerking back as the shears spin around in a tight cone instead of snapping together, thrusting back open a moment later, spinning in the opposite direction, like the razor-sharp petals of a deathly flower. I put them down, thinking how easily someone could be sheared of his or her own skin.

What *are* these? And why are they kept in here?

I select another item—a harmless-looking rod-type thing, long and thin like a cigarette holder—turning it up on its end. The object hisses, then bursts into a breath of fire, igniting the trim on the dusty curtains nearby.

I rush over, grabbing a pillow from a chair on the way, to swat the fire out. "Good Lord in Heaven, have mercy," I say, swiping the hair from my damp forehead. I place the smouldering rod carefully back on the credenza in its holder, noticing several similar burn marks about the carpet. Guess it's not the first time that's happened.

I straighten my skirts and return the pillow—singed side down—to the chair, patting it and waving away the smoke. There, I'm sure no one will notice.

I'm just about to abandon my gadget investigation, thinking it best I get on with trying to find my way after Urlick and the machine, when something on the mantelpiece catches my eye. Something so unusual I must know what it is.

I fly across the room, hand outstretched, running my fingers over the hood of what appears to be a bell-shaped glass jar. It sits perched on a plinth on top of the mantelpiece. Both are coated in dodgy black grime.

Smutch, I determine, rubbing the dark, greasy substance between my finger and thumb. Oily to the touch, it's made of soot and ashes spat up from the mouth of the fireplace below. My eyes traipse over the other items on the mantel. The smutch seems to have covered only the jar and its plinth. *And nothing else?* I cock my head. "How very strange," I whisper.

Curiosity overcomes me. I must know what's in the jar. Snatching a doily from the arm of a chair, I intend to polish off the rest of the glass, when a sharp crash in the kitchen sends me whirling around. My heart breaks its stride at the sound of footsteps. Clearly, I'm no longer by myself.

Turning, I toss the doily back, snatch the apple corer up off the credenza, and stalk slowly toward the entrance to the kitchen, holding the corer out in front of me like a weapon. At the doorway, I throw my back against the wall and peer carefully around the corner. I find the room suspiciously empty.

What on earth is going on?

Two clean teacups dry along the edge of the countertop. Fresh bubbles drizzle down their sides. A nest of soiled cups hisses from a bucket placed in the sink. Someone's done up the dishes we left. It wasn't Urlick. And it certainly wasn't me.

I gasp, drawing back, as someone appears, scuttling in and out of the shadows like a confused beetle exposing itself timidly to the light. A girl. Not much older than I. She's of modest height, but not modest size. Her shoulders are much, much broader than my own. From there her physique slims to nearly half its size by the hips, her torso forming the perfect triangle. *That explains my trouble with the skirt.* Her eyes are a collaboration of hazel and grey, hanging droopy and sad as a dog's, half-masked under a pair of lazy lids. Her hair, an undesirable shade of mousy brown, is twisted like tumbleweed and held by a comb at the nape of her neck. Frizzy curls line the edges, sticking out around the sides of her face. She wears a traditional floor-length day dress, sewn of the most modest fabric, although the colour is, surprisingly, dark cherry red. A stiff, white ruffled collar, which she yanks on from time to time, chokes her off at the neck.

Iris. Hands in the dishwater, sleeves rolled back, cherry-coloured-dress-wearing, stuffy-collared Iris.

I look down at the screaming side seams of my borrowed skirt, at the extra space in the shoulders of the jacket. That explains a lot. I clutch the side of the jamb, waiting for just the right moment to reveal myself, not wanting to burst out and frighten her.

She scuttles off into the pantry and just as swiftly back out, carrying a couple of unmarked tins. I step forward into the light, startling her a bit. She pulls back, nearly dropping the tins, which she quickly hides behind.

"I'm sorry." I offer my hand. "I didn't mean to give you a start."

She stares at my hand, bewildered, bottom lip trembling.

"Eyelet. Eyelet Elsworth." I push my hand toward her. "The new houseguest."

She squirms backward as if I were holding out a handful of worms rather than fingers.

"Urlick did mention me to you, didn't he?"

She drops the tins and turns her back, plunging her hands into the dishwater.

"Iris, isn't it?" I step closer.

She nods, clenching her teeth as if it were agony to be in my company, shoulders folded forward around a sunken chest.

What's wrong with this girl? I can't be that repulsive. I've only just arrived. She doesn't even know me yet.

I drop my hand, feeling silly with it hanging there empty in the air. "It must be awfully lonely living here." I click heel-toe around to the other side of her and try again, leaning closer. "Being the only girl, I mean." Her eyes get big. They pepper me in nervous glances. "I was thinking, since I'll be here a while and since we're the only two girls in the house"—she begins to slosh her hands around in the dishwater, drowning me out—"what I'm trying to say is, I should like it if we could become friends!" I shout.

As if scorched by the suggestion, she withdraws her hands from the water, towels them off, and scurries into the other room. She disappears into the depths of the pantry, clanging tins and clattering pans.

It appears I've upset her, though I can't imagine how.

She reappears seconds later carrying a loaf of crusty French bread and a knife as big as my foot. Thrusting both down on the table, she cuts the bread with such enthusiasm you'd think her hands had been set ablaze.

"I understand Mr. Babbit Senior is somewhat of a recluse, is that right?" I start again.

Her eyes jump a little in their sockets.

"I only ask because I wonder what to expect of him when we meet."

She drops the knife, her feet again clattering over the floorboards. This time she makes her way to the icebox and back. I follow, nearly stepping in her footsteps before she's made them. "Surely you've seen him?"

She spins around; worry lines bunch in the corners of her eyes.

"You haven't? Have you?"

She sidesteps me and heads back to the table, a block of cheese in hand.

"How is that possible?" I chase close behind. "How can you live here and never see the master of the house?"

She averts her gaze, making short order of the cheese, her knife falling hard against the tabletop.

"He does live here, doesn't he?"

She looks up at me, swallows, then just as quickly looks away.

What's going on here? Why won't she answer me? She can't be deaf, or I wouldn't have startled her. She can't be daft or she wouldn't look so alarmed at the things I'm saying. Which leaves only stubborn, or unwilling to befriend me. Which is completely unacceptable.

Especially when I've been so perfectly lovely.

"Perhaps you can tell me what this is?" I change the subject, revealing the strange gadget I've held hidden behind my back.

Her eyes move nervously over it as if I'd just pulled out a gun, not some sort of mixer.

"What's the matter?" I say, sticking it up under her nose. "Should I be afraid of this?"

She looks away.

"What about these?" I say, dashing back to the study to retrieve the rest. "What can you tell me about them?" I whirl the apple-coring thingy around in the air, and her eyes grow wide as plates. Her gaze shifts nervously between the blades and a mysterious button on the handle. "What is it? What happens if I touch this?"

The tiniest shriek departs her lips as I move my finger, accidentally triggering the device.

A miniature arrow launches from a secret compartment in the handle, nearly clipping the vein in my wrist. My jaw drops as the arrow whisks across the room, sticking with a crisp *swick* into the wall on the opposite side of the kitchen. Iris's knife misses the cheese altogether, slicing off a generous portion of pink skin from her thumb instead.

"Oh God!" I shout, flinging myself at her, seeing her blood trickling through the holes of the yellow cheese. "I'm so sorry, I didn't mean to—"

She lunges away from me, teeth clamped together.

"You didn't mean to what?" Urlick's eyes catch me hard as he enters the room. His gaze swings from me to Iris. "What have you done?" He bursts across the kitchen to her aid. Producing a handkerchief, he binds her thumb.

"I—"

"I thought I told you Iris was to be left *alone*!"

"I'm sorry." I gulp. "I didn't mean to hurt her . . . I just wanted to know what this was."

His eyes move to the object in my hand, and from there to the ones on the table.

"I found them, in the study," I offer stupidly, "and I was just curious to know—"

"To know what?" He rises slowly, and I step back, afraid. "Something that's none of your business." He gnashes his teeth.

I wince as he darts past. One by one he picks up the objects off the table, shaking them and slamming them back down, naming each. "Coffee grinder! Lemon zester! Cork shaver! And this!" I cower as he wields the cigarette holder up in front of my face. "*This* is a meringue torch! If you must know!"

He's standing so close, the rage in his heart burns through his shirt. "From now on you are *not* to touch anything in this house that doesn't belong to you. *Do you understand?*" He straightens.

"But *nothing* here belongs to me—"

"Precisely!" He storms from the room.

Nine

Eyelet

That night I dream of Iris's thumb, her skin slicing away smooth as butter, Urlick's words as he scolded me: "I thought I told you Iris was to be left *alone!*"

Why wouldn't she speak to me? Was she ordered not to? Why is Urlick so desperate to keep us apart? I toss in my sleep, my mind reeling. I've never so much as hurled an insult at another person, let alone injured one.

I shouldn't have bothered the poor girl. I should have listened to Urlick. He's right; sometimes I *do* need to learn to mind my own business—just as my mother used to say.

I wake in a cold sweat, hot tears stinging my cheeks, bolting upright in the centre of the heavy walnut four-poster bed where I sleep. The huge circular window of the turret room I've been assigned stares across the room at me like a giant eye. To better monitor the advancing Vapours as they pour down over the escarpment, Urlick's father had the windows of the turret only slightly tinted. They are the only windows of the Compound through which things are barely visible,

Urlick explained, which at first I found comforting, but now, watching the Vapours' ghostly black figures twist atop the not-so-far-away ridge, I find it nothing but disturbing.

I blink away my tears, heart racing, sheets clenched in my fists, longing for the thick, velvet window coverings of my former palace home.

Mother. My head fills with her image, her body dangling from the gallows in the square. I sob. If only I'd reached her sooner. If only I'd gone back, immediately, with the birds. I might have got to her before the authorities. And perhaps she'd be with me now.

I bow my head, heavy with the grief of the day, and of the day before that, never having allowed myself a moment to deal with my mother's death. But here, now, in the silence of a stranger's room, the notion of her loss overwhelms me. My shoulders heave under the weight of it. My sobs turn to cries.

I touch the necklace—my last link to my mother, the only thing I have left of my family. I thought the loss of my father was too much for me to bear, but I fear the loss of my mother will be the complete end of me.

"*Run. Hide. Live,*" I hear her say. *But how do I do that without you?* I turn my chin to the heavens. *What is there left for me to live for in this world? You and Father were the only ones who could ever love me unconditionally. The rest of the world seeks to have me put away.*

Even if I do successfully recover Father's machine and use it to cure my affliction, underneath I'll always bear the scars of its emotional pain. The years of exclusion, of living in fear, under the constant threat of being locked away, never able to trust that anyone could ever accept me, knowing only my parents could ever love a thing such as me.

A branch slaps the window, severing the thought. I pull the covers to my chin, shaken. The light of my necklace pulses through the bared threads of the sheets, breaking the darkness of the room. Through its dim haze I see something fluttering on the opposite side of the window, a dark shadow rapping at the bubble-speckled glass.

I hurl back the sheet, worried at first that the Vapours may be shifting, seeing their ghostly figures still dancing on the ridge.

The shadow again comes slamming into the glass, a black puppet cast aside by the force of the wind.

"Pan?" I say into the air, squinting. "Pan, was that you?"

She appears again, this time shrieking, and I fly from the bed across the room, falling to my knees on the window seat.

"Oh, Pan!" I stroke the glass. "It's you, you're not dead! How on earth did you find me? Oh, Pan, you have no idea how glad I am to see you!"

She nestles in close to the glass as if trying to absorb the warmth of my hand, her head tucked close to her chest.

"I'm so sorry," I say, pressing my cheek to the window. "I should have listened to Archie. I should have followed him home." I drop my head in shame. "Oh, Pan, what ever are we going to do without Mother?" I look up. Tears have filled her eyes, too. "How are we supposed to go on?"

I stare through the slightly darkened window, thinking my eyes are playing tricks on me, realizing her beak shimmers crimson, the colour of blood. "What's happened? Why is your beak red? Has someone marked you, Pan?"

She turns her head as if to hide it from me.

"Who did this to you? Was it Smrt?"

She lowers her eyes.

"What is it? What's wrong? Why won't you speak to me?"

The wind tosses her feathers aside, revealing a fresh scar at the base of her neck. "It was Smrt, wasn't it? Did he harm you after I left?"

The wind sucks her down, away from the window.

"Pan!" I leap forward, seeing her descend deep into the fog-filled cavern below. Located at the back of the Compound and the only piece of the building that projects from the rock, the turret offers the only natural view of the surrounding landscape. My head swims; I note that the footing rests half on and half over the lip of the ravine. I've never seen a sheerer drop. There's nothing beyond it. No forest. No valley. No trees. Just a pit.

A bottomless swell of swirling black froth.

Pan fights against the downward spiral, finally breaking free of the gust, emerging up through the darkness. She returns to the window and digs at it with her claws. I fling myself at the seal, trying to open it. "It's no use. It's stuck." I shake my head. "Wait!" I say, and I burst across the room for the door, rattling the handle, slamming my shoulder into it. "It won't budge!" I shout, bouncing back into the room. "I'm locked in! He's locked me in!"

The winds pick up again, sucking Pan down into the pit.

"Pan!" I scream, flying back to the window. "Pan! Come back! Please, come back!"

I press my forehead to the window, seeing her disappear into the roiling froth below. My eyes move to the ridge. The Vapours crest the escarpment.

Unlike the swirling, docile clouds I'd feared when I first stepped from the carriage, these Vapours are rearing their venomous heads, threatening at any moment to spill down over the hillside and into the forest, and devour us in their wake. Just as Urlick warned. *It won't be long now*, I hear him say. *A day or two, maybe a week.*

Pan reappears on a gust of wind outside my window. "Go!" I shout, slamming my palms against the glass. "Get out of here, Pan! The Vapours! You must go!"

Her head twists forward and back.

"Please, Pan!" I urge her. "Don't worry about me! Just go!"

She hesitates, then bends her head and breaks away, breaking my heart as she goes.

"Be safe," I whisper, fearing I'll never see her again. She wings off over the treetops, a dark blotch in an ever-darkening sky, and I dissolve, hug-kneed, to the turret floor, and sob.

Ten

Eyelet

I wake, a frazzled mess, to the stench of phosphorus being struck and the sound of the spinning chimes on the candle carousel in the corner striking six.

The Vapours did not break over the ridge, as I had feared. But the night was not peaceful. It was filled with racking, restless winds. Stronger winds than I've ever experienced in my life before, continuously flogging the sides of the Compound. Between the onslaught of the winds and my mounting grief, I was up most of the night.

I blink open my weary eyes to the sound of the lock on my door mysteriously giving way. The handle turns and the door falls ajar.

Lights out at nine. Breakfast at six thirty. What am I, his prisoner?

I'm up and dressed in seconds, racing down the stairs. How dare he lock me in my room. I am a guest, not a threat. I sprint from the bottom stair through the doorway of the kitchen, prepared to confront Urlick, a barbed tongue my weapon.

Iris looks up at me from the eggs she's preparing and quickly looks away.

I stalk past her to where Urlick stands stretched out over the pantry, failing miserably to look innocent, while he selects his morning tea.

"I demand to know why I was locked in my room last night," I say, hands on hips.

"You do, do you?" Urlick almost laughs as he turns his back.

Iris's whisk picks up speed.

"That's right," I say, scuttling around to the front of him, skirts swinging. "I have the right to know why I'm being held captive."

"Captive." He guffaws. "Don't be silly."

He turns and makes his way across the kitchen, apparently abandoning his thoughts of tea.

"I couldn't open my window, either." I chase after him. "Do you care to explain why?"

"Simple," Urlick answers matter-of-factly. "They're sealed."

"And why would anybody do such a thing?" I pinch my face up close to his face.

"To keep the Vapours from ravishing the house, that's why. *All* the windows of the house are sealed." He turns to me. "Not just yours, Princess. But I can certainly have yours *unsealed* if you'd prefer." He leans in close, his breath beating a moist path across the hollow of my neck.

I snap back, disgusted.

Disgusted with him. Disgusted with myself for not thinking of it. Of course they'd be sealed. What's the matter with me? What's the matter with him, staring at me like that? All googly-eyed and silly. If I didn't know better, I'd think he was enjoying this.

"And the door." I wag my head cockily in front of his. "Do the Vapours threaten to seep under *there* as well?"

Urlick purses his lips into a hard, thin line.

Iris whips her eggs into a froth behind me.

He says nothing, tugs on his waistcoat, and breezes past, his quick, lithe movements prickling my skin.

"All the locks of the Compound are designed to keep things from getting *in*, not out," he says at last, clutching the doorknob in one hand. Letting the other hover just above the keyhole, he drags it slowly down the length of the brass plate. Turbines churn beneath his palm, and the lock shifts out of place. "They operate on sensors, activated by the molecular chemistry of the human hand. You see?" he explains, applying slight pressure to the brass plate, then releasing it. Magically, the latch releases. The door falls open, creaking on its hinge. "You can escape at any time."

I take a breath, feeling stupid. His goal again, I suspect.

"As long as you are human," Urlick says, turning slowly around, "you will never be denied passage to any room in this house. Unless, of course, the dead bolt's been tripped."

"Yes, of course, unless that." My arms cross over my chest. "What are you trying to keep from getting in?"

He crosses his arms as well. "The roaming criminals, the cannibalistic Infirmed, and other undesirables of the woods."

"Human? You said human." I breathe. "But what of the touch of the criminals, or the Infirmed? Are they not humans?"

Urlick grimaces. "Once exposed to the Vapours, a person is forever changed. Right down to their molecular core."

I stare past him out the blackened window at the shadows of Vapours still forming on the ridge. Pan. I close my eyes. Please let her be safe . . .

"Now if you're through with your interrogation, perhaps we could get on with breakfast?"

He again tugs the points of his infernal waistcoat, then plops down in a chair at the opposite end of the table from me. A span of three feet of polished oak and a plume of unyielding silence grow fat between us. Iris finishes whipping the eggs.

She pours them on the griddle, and I stare at him through the sizzling mist that chokes the kitchen. How can one person be so incredibly tolerant one moment and so hard-hearted the next?

A few moments later, Iris serves us, then scuttles off to her apartment to eat alone. Her eyes avoid me, as they've done all morning, though I'm so desperate to extend her a heartfelt apology over what happened yesterday.

She leaves us with a plate of bacon piled high—a favourite of Urlick's, apparently—and two plates full of slightly overcooked eggs, some toast, two glasses of milk, and no tea.

Urlick groans at her oversight, hesitating a moment before he stands. Fetching two strange-looking mechanical teapot apparatuses, he plops them down, one in front of each of us, along with two cups and two saucers.

I long to ask about the strange teapots but think better of it after what happened yesterday.

"I call them Teasmaids," he says as he sits, flipping his coattails out behind him.

"Your creation?" I ask, sneaking a piece of bacon.

He nods, eyeing me hard. "They're individual automated tea services." His brows rise. "For when your hostess has been maimed by your guest."

"How clever." I gnaw the strip of bacon, imagining it's his head.

He drops a lump of sugar into the bottom of his dry cup, and my shoulders bounce at the sound. A shrill whistle sounds, and the Teasmaids go off, Urlick's features growing soft behind a flux of steam. I watch as the hinge at the side of the contraption activates, tilting the tiny copper pot up on its end.

"Push your cup beneath it." He demonstrates. "The spout, like this. Hurry!" he barks. "Before it pours out!" Like I'm some sort of idiot.

I move just in time to collect the stream and am rewarded with a full cup of Earl Grey for my trouble, give or take a bit of sloshing. Pushing the Teasmaid back, I reach for the sugar, and Urlick pounces, snatching the bowl from under my grasp.

"Sit." He motions to me like I'm a dog. *How dare he!*

I narrow my eyes and sink slowly into my seat, annoyed. Doubly annoyed by the thought that he'd serve himself first.

He stares down the length of the table, squeezing his right eye shut, working to square the handle of the sugar bowl with my cup.

What on earth?

Cocking the handle back like a medieval catapult, he lets it go, ejecting a cube of sugar skyward. End over end, it lopes across the table, landing in my cup with a splat. Tea spittoons upward like a geyser, soiling the tea doily, my sleeve, and a nearby chair.

"One lump or two?" He grins.

"One will do, thank you," I say, blotting up the mess. "Dare I ask for cream?"

He punches a button on the side of the creamer, and a tiny set of wheels pops out of the sides. Drawing the bowl back, he releases it as I wince in fear. The dish shoots forward, scuttling noisily down the length of the tabletop, then slows and parks itself directly in front of my cup. A bell pings, and the whole system lifts up off its wheelbase, delivering the perfect spot of cream before slithering back down into its carriage again.

Urlick leans onto his elbows, all puffed up and grinning. "Impressive, don't you think?"

"I . . ."

Something burps.

I drop my eyes to the creamer, astonished.

"Excuse me!" Urlick blurts.

I look across the table, puzzled. I'm sure the noise did not come from him.

The wheels on the creamer disappear, sucked into the sides of the carriage in one spring-loaded motion, and I jump.

"Watch out for the handle!" Urlick warns, nearly jumping across the table. "Eyelet! Your hand!"

I glance down, pulling my hand back just as the handle on the creamer swings, guillotine-like, and snaps into place. Had I not moved when I did, I could quite easily be missing a finger. I gasp, trying to appear unmoved, though the speed of my heart indicates otherwise.

"Should I expect to be similarly surprised by everything in this house?"

Urlick furrows his brows. "I should think you should expect no further surprises at all, considering you're not to touch anything. *Remember?*"

I narrow my eyes and reach for more bacon.

"Ah ah ah ah . . ." He shoos me away. Reaching into his pocket, he produces what looks to be a telescope and leans back in his chair. The next thing I know, he's cast the strange object out over the table like a fly fisherman would his line. The pole shoots forward, length after length appearing, each segment thinner than the last. A small mechanical hand appears at the end of the rod, a set of fingers wiggling above the bacon as they hover over the plate.

"Crispy or not?"

"Not," I reply.

"Not it is." He pinches a clamp at his end of the rod, and the fingers fly. He pinches the clamp again, and the fingers close around a slightly soggy strip of bacon. "Good enough?" he grins, and I nod. The fingers swing forward, tossing the bacon onto my plate.

I jump back, trying to avoid the spray of grease, but unfortunately it finds me, striping the front of my corset and chemise.

"Would you like a second?" He smiles cheekily.

"No, thank you." I cross my arms.

Cranking the side of the handle, he retracts the device, wiping the fingers clean with a napkin before dropping the gadget back into his pocket.

I stare at him and he stares at me, neither of us relenting.

Picking up a piece of toast, he sinks his teeth into it dramatically, as if challenging me, lopping off a healthy-sized bite.

I accept the challenge, picking up a slice of my own. I do the same, mimicking his bite, only doubling the size.

Not to be outdone, he ratchets up the competition, this time devouring nearly a quarter of his toast in one bite.

I stare at him, smirking, as he struggles to chew what's in his mouth. Opening wider, I stuff nearly half my toast into my mouth—at which his falls open, a rather disturbing sight.

He races to chew and swallow what's in his mouth as I chew beastly fast, scarfing down the other half of my toast before he has the chance to swallow his, throwing open my jaw and sticking out my tongue to prove myself victorious.

He concedes, midswallow, and reaches for a glass of milk to help wash it down—challenging me again with his eyes as he gulps.

I reach for my milk and gulp right along with him, draining my glass and slamming it down mere seconds before his meets the table.

"I win!" I stand.

"You what?"

"Do you deny it?"

"No," he snorts, struggling not to laugh. "Of course not—"

"What's so funny?"

"Nothing." He smiles, his eyes fixed on my cream-coated upper lip. "Clearly you wear the mark of the victor." He motions as he snorts again.

"Very well, then." I turn, exiting the kitchen along with my moustache. "As long as we've got that straight."

I grab a tea towel from the rack in the back kitchen to wipe the moustache from my face, eyeing the door. *"You'll never be denied passage to any room in this house. Unless, of course, the dead bolt's been tripped."*

Yes, of course, unless—

I reach for the lock, tripping the bolt, staring at the slender, nickel-coated bar that protrudes from the middle, the matching hole carved into the doorjamb on the opposite side. Gazing through the doorway at Urlick, I tear a small corner of fabric from the tea towel with my teeth and cram it up inside the hole.

Eleven

Eyelet

"I trust you can find something to keep yourself occupied this morning?" Urlick glances at me as I return to the room.

"Yes," I say, eyeing the lock on the rear kitchen door as I slide back into my seat. "As a matter of fact, I've already got something planned."

"Excellent." He scarfs down his tea and rises to his feet. "Then I'll see you for lunch at noon, before my tutor arrives."

"Tutor?" I stand, not really meaning to but rather out of reaction. "A tutor? Here? In the bowels of the Earth at the farthest recesses of the Commonwealth?" It just comes out before I've the chance to think about it, but honestly, who would be insane enough to take a job like that? It was Urlick who said this was the perfect place to hide a fugitive. And now he's gone and invited in a visitor.

"Yes, *tutor*." He looks angry.

My heart trembles in my chest. What if this tutor is from Brethren? What if it's someone who'll recognize me? What then? What do I do then? "Would this be someone from the Academy?" I squeak, breathless.

"No." He tugs at his waistcoat points. "She's an itinerant. Living locally. But every bit as good as any employed behind the gates of your beloved Academy, I can assure you *that*! Why?" His brows twist in that ugly way they do when I've frustrated him. Which is most of the time, I'm afraid.

"No reason," I say, my voice meek.

He stares at me through narrowed eyes.

"I'm sure she's wonderful," I gulp, trying to restore the nerve I've just obviously stomped on.

Urlick's lips grow pursed. He clenches his fists at his sides. His white cheek flushes red. "You are really something, you know that?" He turns and grips the door handle and gives it a twist, like a bear would the neck of a fragile rabbit. "Oh . . . I almost forgot." He hesitates. "Iris would like her clothes back. You'll find yours hanging on the back of the door of the loo off the kitchen there." He flips his head. "All clean and pressed."

My head swivels to the door and back again.

"You can leave hers folded on the chair. She'll be down shortly to collect them." He whisks through the door.

"How shortly?" I blurt without thinking.

Urlick turns back, tossing me a dagger of a look. "What does it matter how long she takes? Do you have plans to go somewhere?"

"Don't be so silly," I stammer, "of course not." I roll the sweat from my hands onto my skirts. "It's just that I wouldn't want to be tardy and hold up her day. Especially after what's already happened between us." I lilt my voice at the end of the sentence, but it doesn't seem to have worked.

Urlick lowers his brows and stares at me. Perspiration curls the hairs at the back of my neck. "How considerate of you," he finally says, then disappears through the doorway.

I lean, calling after him. "I'll be sure to thank her."

Why can't I just shut up?

My voice halts his step. He juts his chin back through the door. "No thanks necessary," he snaps.

He closes the door with extra force. Turbines churn under his hand. He shuffles away—then shuffles back, tripping the dead bolt.

I grin as the hammer slides only partway into the hole, falling silently as it jams into the cloth.

I turn and race for the loo, snag my clothes from the hanger, and dress as fast as I can, discarding Iris's clothing onto the chair in the corner, and bolt for the door, rattling the handle and jimmying the lock until at last the door falls open.

Twelve

Urlick

I lock the door and charge the length of the underground corridor, agitation driving my step. The clomp of my heels thunders off the walls. My pulse echoes in my ears.

Why must she always be so difficult? Why can't she just follow instructions? Is it too much to ask for her to know her place?

I drag a heavy hand through my hair.

I would have thought she'd been taught basic manners, having been reared in Brethren. *Huh!* I yank at my waistcoat. And I thought *myself* uncivilized.

I swipe a torch from the wall and swing it in front of me. Water splotches from the roof threaten to douse it out as I round the corner and clatter down the stairs.

"A tutor?" she'd said in that innocent voice. Clearly she was mocking me. A tutor. Of course! Why *not* a tutor? Am I that undeserving?

My chin snaps up. What must she think of me?

What do I *care* what she thinks of me?

I should put her out. That's what I should do. See how she likes it out there with the Vapours. Perhaps then she'd follow my rules!

What are you thinking? I gasp. *You can't put her out. She'd die in a matter of days.*

Are you that angry, you want her dead?

Urlick Babbit, you animal, you.

I swallow.

I storm up the corridor, turning left at the forks. All right, so I don't want her dead. I just want her to stop asking so many *blessed* questions. All that fuss this morning over windows and doors. Must she know absolutely everything?

What about that necklace of hers? Why is she allowed to evade that subject? Yet I'm expected to be an open book when it comes to anything about me?

I round the corner and nearly slip in the wet. My eyes squint to slits.

What goes on in that *silly* head of hers, I wonder?

Why is she really here?

Surely it wasn't a mistake, her jumping on my coach.

Why can she hold secrets and I can't?

I reach for the switch on the door when I get to it, using my night-vision monocle to dial in the combination.

Why must women be so puzzling? Why can't they be straightforward like men? Why can't she just stay put and mind her own business? Is that so much to ask?

The breaker sounds and the door swings open. I duck, entering the final stage of the tunnel, and traipse down the dim, narrow hall.

What's most puzzling about all of this is that, despite how much she annoys me . . . I find myself strangely drawn to her.

Something clunks behind me and I swing around, sweeping the torchlight back and forth across the mouth of the tunnel.

"Iris?" I call into the darkness. "Is that you?"

Nothing, just the hiss of the torchlight in my hand.
I turn and carry on.

Thirteen

Eyelet

I snake down the back stairs and along the corridor, chasing the tiny ball of torchlight swinging in Urlick's hand—trying my best to keep enough distance between us so I'm not discovered, listening to the beat of his shoes as they fall hard against the stone. My breath forms crystals in the mist. Water drips from the ceiling, plunking cold on my head. An icy draft tunnels at my back. It's damp down here and getting darker by the minute. An old cavern carved deep into rock.

I put out my hands, feeling my way along the slimy lining of the cavern's belly, shoulders shivering, feeling rather lost. I come across a fork in the tunnel and I don't know which way to go. "Urlick," I whisper, having lost sight of him. A tiny white cloud precipitates from my lips, turning into a clot of frozen mist.

I stand still, rubbing my arms, listening for the stride of his shoes striking stone. But I hear nothing, only the drip of the water leaking through the cracks in the rock overhead. What have I done? I shiver. Where do I go from here? I bite my lip as I look around. Left or right, which is correct?

I was so convinced he'd lead to my father's machine, I lost all sense in the matter. I've gone and followed a stranger down the throat of a dark, ugly cave, only to become lost—without even so much as a lantern in hand.

I reach up to find a spider traipsing through my hair. A quiver of nerves shoots up my spine. I strip the spider away, running in place to keep myself from screaming. My hands flail at my sides.

For a fragment of a moment, I think about turning back, but then the stubborn part of me refuses. The machine *has* to be down here. Somewhere. I *know* it is. Why else would Urlick journey into the depths of such a place? What could he be doing down here that required such secrecy, if not reassembling my father's machine?

I step forward, choosing left over right, praying my instincts are correct, when a glimmer of light catches my eye up the corridor. Collecting my skirts, I chase after it, bursting up the puddle-dotted floor. It's not yellow like the torchlight, but rather a glistening shade of silvery-black, flickering in and out through the darkness. I move quickly but softly enough for my boots not to be heard, hoping to reach the glimmer before it flickers, then fades to black. The corridor once again falls dark.

I gasp, arriving at the spot where I last saw the light, and run my hand over the wall. It's cool to the touch, damp and sweaty, just like the others—only as I move farther along, my fingers catch on the lip of what feels like a rail of steel. I follow it up the wall, surprised when it curves around in a giant circle. Jumping my fingers over the rail, I run my hands across the inside. The surface is rough and scaly, like the bottom of a cast-iron pot. At the centre of it there's a handle.

I've found a door, a huge one—more like a hatch on a boat, but a door nonetheless—embedded into the side of the stone wall.

I look up to see two large metal springs hovering over my head in the darkness, flanked on either side by a scaffold of pulley-fed gears. Metal ropes feed between the two structures, up and over a giant support beam mounted above the middle of the door. Attached to the top is some sort of chronometred device. I brace a boot against the wall and pull myself up. It's ticking. The device is ticking—measuring time right down to the nanosecond, in a backward countdown from one hundred.

Just forty-three seconds and twenty-nine nanoseconds left.

I drop down and reach for the handle on the door. If I'm going to pass through, I'd better hurry.

I just hope I find Urlick on the other side.

I swallow hard and pull on the lever. Turbines click, then the hatch glides slowly open, emitting a waft of white, curling steam. I wave it away and lunge across the threshold, gasping as the chronometred device overhead signals zero. Before I have the chance to turn around, the massive metal door swings shut, threading itself back into the hole in the wall behind me like a giant screw. Two metal arms fly out of the sides of the walls and I duck. They clamp down over either side of the door, like a giant spider would its prey. I throw my hands over my ears at the tremendous *gong* sound, and pad my way up the corridor.

The corridor gradually narrows the farther I go, closing in over-head, until at the end of the hall, coming up from the floor, there's a blast of light followed by a sharp hiss.

It's as if someone's just lit a match.

I chase after the light, throwing my back up against the wall when I reach the source. A second hole.

Craning my neck out around the corner, I'm astonished to see—

A laboratory. Urlick's laboratory. In a dungeon-like room below.

Urlick stands centre stage, torchlight in his hand, his wavy black hair aglow.

A metal staircase extends from the lip of the hole beside me, folded up like a set of bellows. Rusty chains form a handrail. Metal treads serve as steps. The whole thing hangs suspended midair from a set of cables anchored to the stone-slab ceiling.

That must be how he got down there. The steps must extend.

Urlick drops his head into a crib of tools and starts digging. I make my move. With the stealth of a cat, I edge carefully out onto the top of the suspended staircase.

Urlick lifts his head and I lower mine. His eyes slowly scan the room.

I suck in a breath and keep very still.

He stalks across the floor, lighting a sconce on the wall with the new gaslight in his hand, then he walks around the perimeter lighting the rest. Slowly the room hisses to life, revealing the most beguiling inventions I've ever seen.

Strange-looking mechanical bugs of every shape and size cling to row upon row of automated flowers—a garden full of them. A rustic-looking millipede serves as a conveyor belt twisting through the middle, and in the centre sits what must be the prized possession, hidden beneath a black-velvet drape. *The Illuminator*, I'm hoping.

Something deep inside me stirs.

Though it doesn't look big enough to be the Illuminator.

He drops the torch and reaches for the drape. I can hardly breathe as he yanks it away—and I'm struck by shock a second later. He's revealed *not* the Illuminator, but the strangest-looking motorized, double-seat bicycle one could ever imagine.

What on earth *is* that?

It has an aerodynamic frame that looks like the skeleton of a bird. A giant one. From a time we've never seen. Its skeleton head hovers over a fat, white-walled balloon tire with wooden spokes. A matching wheel is at the back. Two lamplights fill its empty eye sockets. Pedals hang below the ribs. Two seats straddle the tailbone, one behind the other. All that's missing are the feathers.

Urlick picks up a wrench, tinkers a moment, then exits the room, muttering about finding something better.

I can't help myself; I must get a better look. I lean forward, accidentally activating the staircase. With a jerk it unfolds, accordion-like, from its perch. I gasp as it strikes the floor with a thud and expels me. I tumble from the stairs to the centre of the room—a disheveled, gape-mouthed heap.

The staircase retracts, rattling treads and quivering chains ascending toward the ceiling as I scramble for cover and dive beneath a tarp thrown across a wooden horse. "What was that?" I whisper, hearing a sigh.

Clutching my chest, I stick my head out from under the tarp. No sign of Urlick anywhere. No sign of anyone, for that matter. *Strange.*

Bravely, I step out into the open and move toward the cycle, examining it more closely, running a cautious hand over its smooth, white frame. Feels like bone. I rap. Sounds like it, too. Gasping, I pull my hand back. It can't be! Can it? Not even people as eccentric as the Babbits would harvest bone for their creations, would they?

My eyes zero in on a strange-looking box wedged between the frame and the second seat. Is that a coffer box? I touch it. Good God, it is. First bones, now a coffer box? I swallow. What lurks within *that*, I wonder?

I reach out again, only to be blinded by a gust of steam. I fall back. My hand meets the handlebar, triggering some sort of mechanism. The lid of the coffer box slides eerily back. Yellow flames burst from its sides like fire from the nostrils of a dragon. A pair of wings spring forth from the sides of the coffer box like two black bumbershoots, expanding at least fifteen metres in either direction over the floor. I scramble backward, gasping as they nearly cast me off my feet. It can't be. I stare. Can it?

Gracefully, *unbelievably*, the cycle appears to *breathe*, as if alive—its wings pulsing gently in and out as they lower themselves to rest on the ground.

I've never seen anything like it. I mean, I've seen winged contraptions before, don't get me wrong. In books and photographs, even once at the fair, but never anything quite like this. This seems to be alive and capable of movement. "Was that you who sighed?" I reach out to stroke its wing, and it jerks back.

It's alive. I swear to God it's alive.

I stare at the wings' soft, thin, delicate webbing, which appears to be made of some sort of—*skin*. I creep toward them, throat closing tighter with every step.

Please, God, not human.

The cycle winces again, as if sensing my presence.

"It's okay," I whisper to it, crazily. "I promise not to hurt you."

Fourteen

Eyelet

"What do you think you're doing?" Urlick's voice slaps me cold in the back.

I swing around to find him stalking across the room, wrench in hand.

"Nothing," I say, backing up.

His eyes find the wings and then my face. "How did you get in here?"

"I—*uh*—I . . ."

"Was it Iris?"

"No!"

"Then *how*?"

He stands so close I smell peppermint tea on his breath, feel the heat of frustration rising off his shirt.

"I followed you," I volunteer—*stupidly*.

"You did what? How?"

"I jammed the lock with a bit of cloth. Yesterday when you weren't looking."

His expression darkens. He pushes past me across the room.

"I'm sorry." I trot after him. "I was just curious—"

"Curious!" He jerks around. "So, curiosity gives you the right to impose on my privacy, does it? Tell me," he says, jutting toward me, "is it customary where you're from to force yourself into people's private spaces, without invitation?"

"Of course not!"

"*Ooooh!* Well, forgive me, then! I thought perhaps it was a cultural difference, not just an Eyelet one!" He throws a fist to the switch on the handlebar, and I jump as the wings contract, snapping briskly back into place within the coffer box—all but the tiny tip of one. Then he turns and stalks away without speaking.

"I don't know why you're so upset." I give chase. "It's not like I caught you with your pants down in the privy." He turns and glares at me. "Well, it isn't!"

A tense beat or two skips between us, during which I worry he's going to order me back to the kitchen. I can't let him send me away now. I've come all this way to search for my father's machine, and search for it I *will.*

Flattery. That should do it. Flattery always works on men, doesn't it?

"Besides," I say, settling back on my heels. "It's incredible, really—"

"What is?" Urlick snarls.

"The cycle, of course." I gesture to it, letting my hand brush his arm. He moves away. "I've never seen anything quite like it," I continue. "Especially the wings." I tip my head so the light catches me; I feel it sparkle in my eyes. I play with the curl next to my cheek, like I've seen so many other girls do. "They're truly ingenious," I add.

His brows crinkle. He clears his throat. The wine-coloured blotch on his cheek flushes even redder.

It's working. He has no idea how to respond. How precious. Has he never been flattered before?

"What are they made of, exactly?" I step toward the bike, letting my gaze float from his face. I scan the room, skimming over several things before my eyes land on a drape. Suspended from the ceiling on a set of rods and rings at the back of the room hangs the perfect red-velvet square.

But I bet I know what its secret is.

I keep walking and talking, hoping to close the gap between us—the drape and myself, that is. "The veins in the wings. Are they bone?" I stare at the drape. Urlick catches me, so I turn to face him.

"Bamboo," he says. His eyes are wary, his voice thin.

"Bamboo?" I tilt my head, acting stupid.

Urlick drops back down onto a trolley, slips beneath the cycle, and sets to work. "It's a reed," he humours me. "Indigenous to the East. Reeds are hollow in the centre, better to simulate the bones of a bird."

"Really." I shuffle sideways. "How clever. And the joints"—I inch toward the drape—"what are they made of?"

"The bleached backbones of an ox, if you must know." He looks up between the spokes at me.

"Oh." I make a face. "Dare I ask about the webbing?"

"Tanned animal hide." He returns to his work, ratcheting a nut in and then out of place.

"What kind?" I lean. My fingertips brush the curtain's tassel fringe. Urlick looks up and I yank my hand back, folding it innocently inside the other.

"Dinosaur," he says, scowling at his work.

"Dinosaur?" I scrunch my brow. Could they have possibly resur-rected a dinosaur intact among that collection of stuffed oddities in the study?

A cheeky smile floods over Urlick's lips.

"Oh, you *cad*. What is it really?"

"Elephant."

"Elephant?"

He grins.

"Why, of course," I play along.

Seriously, what kind of a fool does he think I am? I might never have seen an elephant in the flesh, but I'm smart enough to know they don't come in black.

Urlick returns to his work, a grin still plastered on his lips. I take advantage, shuffling ever closer to my target. I lean, my hand connecting with the drape. Gathering a handful, I prepare to sling it back. "And the rest of the cycle," I say. "Is that ox bone as well?" I'm just about to yank when Urlick's head swings around, his eyes shifting wildly between the drape and my hand.

"Would you be so kind as to hand me that wrench over there?" he stammers. He flicks his gaze in the direction of a wrench on the ground a good ten metres away. I consider his proposal a moment, watching his expression grow even more feverish. "I could get up," he starts again. His Adam's apple twitches. "But you're already standing." He sort of laughs. Perspiration beads his brow.

I glance at the drape, then drop my hand. Clearly this will have to wait. I thunder across the room, heels clicking, stoop to pick up the wrench, and click back, twirling the wrench in my hand. "So, tell me," I say when I reach him, falling into a crouch at Urlick's side. "How does it breathe?"

"What?" He jolts up, smashing his skull on the chain guard.

She noticed? his face screams.

That's right, I did. Explain your way out of this one.

"You heard me. I asked how the cycle breathes."

His lips part. His good cheek turns red. "I don't know what you're talking about," he says.

"Really?" I say, plopping the wrench into his outstretched hand. "You mean to tell me, you've never heard it draw air in and out like a set of bellows being pumped over a fire?"

"No." His lips quiver. "I can't say that I have."

The sounds of our heartbeats fill the room, pulsing off the walls.

"Well, then." I close his fingers over the wrench and hold mine there. "I guess I must have imagined it." I stand, tapping a toe against a tank on the side of the cycle. "What's this?"

"Blooming heck!" Urlick lunges sideways.

"What? What is it?"

"If you're not careful, you'll blow us both to bits. That's a hydrogen tank you're kicking."

"As in the gas?"

"That's correct."

"Really?" I bend to get a better look. "I've never heard of anything being powered by hydrogen gas. Especially not in the form of a motor—"

"Of course not, it's only just been invented."

"By whom?"

"By me!" he scowls. "I refurbished a conventional steam engine to accept gas, then reconfigured it to activate on the buildup of steam."

"And it works?"

Of course it works, his eyes shout at me.

"What about the wings? Can it really fly?"

Urlick's expression sours. He picks up his wrench.

"Don't tell me you've created a winged creature that can't get off the ground?"

"Why are you here again?" He sits up, catching his forehead on the cycle's chain. "I believe I specifically left you in the kitchen, telling you I'd see you later?" He wags his wrench. "In fact, I believe I told you never, under *no* circumstances, were you *ever* allowed to enter my laboratory."

"That was your father's."

He grits his teeth.

"That's it!" He kicks away the trolley and leaps to his feet. "You think you're so smart? Go on!" He points. "Find your own way back to the kitchen!"

"What?"

"You heard me, get moving! Go on! Get out of here!" He presses a button, causing the stairs to lower, then chases me across the room.

"But—" I leap on the moving platform. "I don't know the way!"

"You're a smart girl," Urlick hollers over the motor as he retracts the stairs. "I'm sure you'll figure it out. If worse comes to worst, let your curiosity lead you!"

Fifteen

Urlick

I return to work on the hydrocycle as soon as she's gone, her image still weighing heavy on my mind. That's the way it's been since the moment I laid eyes on her, white-knuckled and clinging to the back of my coach. For some reason, I can't push the thought of that girl out of my head.

I've no idea why she vexes me so. Especially when I find her so very irritating. I drop the wrench I'm holding into the bin and select another, spinning it off the end of a finger. Eyelet in the kitchen. Eyelet in the study. Eyelet at the table, sitting inappropriately close to me. The shape of her face, the lines of her lips, that tongue of hers—incessantly wagging.

The wrench falls, smarting my toe. Cursing, I bend to pick it up.

"The nerve of her, following me down here like that. She's so stubborn, so pretentious and meddlesome, so . . . *beautiful*."

The hydrocycle sighs.

"Oh, shut up, Bertie." I wag my wrench at him. "This is all your fault, you know, revealing yourself like you did." Hands on hips, I stalk toward him. "What were you thinking?"

The cycle cowers.

"Yeah, I know. You weren't. I've the same trouble when she's around." I clutch my forehead, clunking it with the wrench. "What is it, do you think? A mind trick? A sickness?" I whirl around. "Perhaps a spell. Do you think it's a spell?"

Bertie chortles.

"No. You're right." I shake my head. "It can't be a spell. She'd have done away with us both by now if that were true." I pace. "I just don't understand it." I scratch my head. "Iris doesn't make me feel this way. And Flossie certainly never has."

Bertie groans.

"That's enough out of you." I wag the wrench again. "Flossie's an excellent tutor, and don't you forget it. I don't care if you fancy her or not, she's the only one crazy enough to brave these woods. And I'm thankful that she does." I turn, squinting in the cycle's direction. "What *is* that?"

Bertie cringes, trying again to retract the tip of his ornery wing. But it just won't disappear.

"Blasted fold!"

I stride over, grab hold of the webbing and stretch it out, then let go. The wing snaps back like a whip. This time it disappears beneath the lid of the coffer box as it should. "Some day I'll figure out how to fix that."

Bertie shudders.

"Don't look at me like that, I will."

I turn and pick up my wrench again, pacing even more furiously around the floor. "I tell you, that girl is going to be the end of all of us, always mucking about, getting into things that don't belong to her." I turn. "Do you know I caught her yesterday, holding Iris hostage with a weapon in the kitchen?"

Bertie gasps.

"I know, unbelievable, isn't it? Poor Iris nearly lost the end of her finger over Eyelet's antics. And you know how Iris is about blood."

Bertie coos.

"I just don't understand what's wrong with that girl. Why she can't just leave things alone." I tug at my chin. "What on earth could she be looking for?"

Bertie groans.

"Don't be silly, what would she want with a machine? No." I scratch my head. "There must be another reason. Or perhaps she's just naturally that annoying." I lean. "You know she barely knew me an hour yesterday before quizzing me about my face?"

Bertie rattles.

"Yeah, I know. Then she turns right around and persists in acting so enamored with me, when I know she can't be. What's *that* all about?"

Bertie skitters, flushed.

"That's not possible. *Is* it?" My face flushes red. "Of course not. What are you thinking?" I fling myself around again, startling Bertie. "Why would someone like her be interested in a creature like me?" I bend, staring at my marred reflection in the side of Bertie's nickel-plated gas tank, dragging a finger down the fang of the open-mouthed snake mark on my cheek. *You're an abomination*, I hear my father say. *An error. A defect. A disgrace.*

I snap up. A spear of rage rises between my ribs. "She can't be. No one could. Even my own father couldn't stand the sight of me."

I cast the wrench across the room at the wall, where it sticks. "She must have another motive."

Bertie shudders.

"Whatever's going on in that pretty little head of hers, mark my words: things will be different soon. Once I find a way to get that *blasted* machine working"—I point the wrench—"I'll be able to transform myself from the monster of this house to the master of it, and then everything—absolutely *everything*—will be different."

Sixteen

Eyelet

I step from the dark tunnel into the equally gloomy corridor, race up
the stairs, and swing open the back kitchen door. Luckily the tea-towel
plug is still in place. I slip through, panther-quiet, unnerved at having
been so close to what I hoped was my father's machine and yet missing
out on the opportunity to unveil it. I vow to return at my first chance.

I turn around and run smack into Iris.

She jumps back, looking alarmed. Her eyes scan the hallway
behind me in search of Urlick.

"It's all right," I say, sweeping the cobwebs from my hair. "No need
to alert him. He already knows. He's the one who sent me packing."

She smirks, and I swear I hear her laugh as she turns her prissy little
self back to her dishes.

"If it's all right with you, I'm going to retire into the study for
a while," I say, smacking the dust from my skirts. "I think I've had
enough adventure for one day."

Iris glares at me as I pass.

"Don't worry, I promise I won't get into anything." *Much.* I cross my fingers behind my back so I don't have to feel guilty over what I'm about to do. I left some unfinished business in the study yesterday. And there's just enough time before lunch for me to complete it. I pat the ostrich on both its heads as I enter, then fall into a chair in the mote-swizzled room.

Iris snorts, eyeing an unfolded basket of laundry on a chair. When I don't move, she takes up the basket and stomps up the stairs. Precisely what I wanted her to do.

I wait until I hear the click of the lock at the top before I leap to my feet and race across the room to the mantel, snatching a doily up off the armchair on the way. Aether light crackles, dancing in streaks like a storm across the ceiling. Eyes peer down on me from every wall.

I don't think I'll ever get used to these heads.

I swallow, doing my best to ignore them, and reach for the jar, using the doily to clean off the remaining smutch, gasping at what I see.

Inside the glass churns the strangest bit of stygian weather: a writhing, twisting, wisp-like cloud, black as the Mariah that comes to collect the dead, and just about as frightening. Like someone's captured and bottled a wretched storm. I stand there, captivated by its eerie presence, monitoring the twist and turn of its endless journey, running a finger over the glass, and pull back when I realize it's following.

Why on earth would it do that? I lean in a little closer, seeing bits of cloud break off. Like dark fingers they pry at the seal at the base of the glass. I swallow, horrified at the thought of any of it escaping.

My gaze drops to the plinth, still covered in smutch. Using the remainder of the doily, I quickly clean it off. A square of dark-veined marble appears, the colour of a twilight sky. Screwed to the front of it is a tiny, square brass plaque, some sort of identification marker, but instead of words it's engraved, strangely, with a string of numbers—*4690073*—followed by the letters *H.H.B.*

I straighten; my eyes are drawn to the peculiar-looking picture hanging on the wall directly behind the jar. I don't remember that being there yesterday, but perhaps I was too preoccupied with all the heads. I stare at the picture, running a finger over its frame, cut from the same marble as the plinth. The glass is coated in a thick layer of dust. I reach up, quickly scouring a tiny hole through which I spot a drawing. The paper it's on is very yellow, and the ink is smudged here and there, as if it's been water damaged over the years, but still the overall image is clear: it's a map. I've found a map of the Follies. I scour the hole bigger and bigger, confirming that, in fact, a drawing of the Ramshackle Follies does lie beneath, in its entirety, from the edge of Gears forward to the end of the escarpment.

My heart jumps as my eyes soak it in. Every detail, every river, every creek, every bend in every road, painstakingly rendered. And then, mysteriously—there's *nothing*. The upper-left corner of the map has been left completely empty. The last quarter is simply blank. Nothing but a span of yellow paper. No label. No explanation. It's as if the world *is* flat and this is the end of it, the jagged cliffs of Ramshackle's escarpment the last known destination.

I scrub the glass again and again to be sure my eyes aren't playing tricks on me. But there's nothing. There's absolutely nothing there. Perhaps the cartographer forgot to finish . . . or perhaps he *died* before he was able. What other reason could there be for leaving a formal map unfinished?

I remove all the dust, right to the corners, thinking perhaps I've missed something—an inlet, an island, maybe another piece of land— when my eyes catch on a tiny line of writing that stretches across the bottom-right corner of the map. It's cursive. Ancient lettering. Slightly water-smudged and loopy, hard to read, but I squint and manage it.

The Village of Ramshackle Follies, the 17th of September, 1892.

I pull back. Just six months after my father's death.

In the county of Kenton, in the borough of Fluxshire (formerly of the borough of Brethren).

"Brethren?" I gasp. Ramshackle Follies was once a part of the Commonwealth? How is that possible? Hasn't it always been just a discarded piece of contaminated land?

Annexed in the year 1891.

1891? The year prior to the flash. Why the need to annex just Ramshackle from the Commonwealth, I wonder? And why then? Whose decision was that?

My eyes drift over the boundaries, imagining the land as seamless. Imagining all of us under one Commonwealth. All of us equal. All people the same.

I sigh and look again at the map, discovering something else at the end of the writing. A number, in even tinier script.

4690073 HHB.

It can't be—my eyes shift from the map to the pedestal and back again.

It *is*—the exact number that's on the jar. I blink to make sure I'm seeing clearly. There's no mistaking it. It's the same.

What *is* this? I run my finger over the hood of the glass again, and the storm inside switches direction. And what does it have to do with an unfinished map?

"That's poisonous, you know."

I fly back at the sound of a voice in the room, nearly elbowing the jar from the mantelpiece. I throw a hand overtop to keep it from falling, and turn to find a girl, not more than a year or two older than me, draped over one of the ostrich's necks. Her eyes look oddly familiar, grey as the stone on the Academy walls, back in Brethren. She smirks as if she's proud she's startled me. "Good job, you caught that," she says. "Don't want something like that getting loose."

"Like what?" I say, assessing her from head to toe.

"Bottled Vapours." She steps briskly into the room. She's dressed all in black, as if in mourning, yet she wears no veil. She has a harelip and mean eyes, and a dark-brown, oval-shaped mole, covered in thick brown hair, which takes up most of her right cheek. A bloodred line extends from the bottom of the mole, like a tail, curling into a circle at the base of her throat. I can't help but think it looks like a small rat has taken to squatting on her face. She smiles again, and its fat belly wrinkles. Her putty-pink lip strains over snaggled teeth. "Or at least that's what they say is inside," she continues.

"Who're *they*?" I ask as she strips her hands of her gloves in one fluid motion.

"Just people." She hinges at the waist and taps the glass. "I hear they sell them as novelty gifts at the gypsy freak shows on the outskirts of town. Makes one wonder, doesn't it?" She turns to me, her eyes electric. "What sort of person bottles such a thing? Not to mention what sort of person purchases one for display in their home?" She grins again, and I'm fascinated by how her pink-putty lip doesn't split in two.

"You're sure that's what's inside there?" I say.

Her gaze lopes over my features, assessing me. She holds her tongue as if harbouring some sort of secret. "What else would it be?" she finally says.

Bottled Vapours, my bonnie arse.

"You must be the cousin." She extends a hand.

Cousin?

"Urlick sent word I'd be meeting you."

Word? How? I take her hand and it falls to mush like a cold serving of oatmeal in my palm. I shudder, smelling weakness and the lack of a warm heart.

"Flossie," she says. "I'm Urlick's tutor."

Or course, the tutor. I'd almost forgotten. That explains the sudden intrusion and the lack of interference by Iris, the watchdog of the house.

"It's Priscilla, isn't it?" she asks.

"Priscilla?"

"Or do you prefer *Prissy?*" The word hisses through her snaggled teeth.

This must be Urlick's idea of preserving my identity. And a bad one at that. "Priscilla will be fine, thank you." I narrow my eyes.

"Prissy it is, then," she smirks. She turns to walk away, then turns back. "You're an awfully pretty thing." She eyes me sternly. "Too pretty to be any cousin of Urlick's."

I swallow.

"Distant?" Her bushy brows beg the question.

"Quite," I answer, smiling.

"I see . . ." She hesitates and cocks her head. "Well, then . . . It's been a pleasure, but I'm afraid I must go and prepare for the lesson." She nods her head. "I'm sure our paths will cross again."

Not if I have any say.

She turns, carelessly lassoing the jar with her sleeve. My hand snaps out and catches it before it crashes to the floor.

"Oops." She grins, bringing a hand to her mouth. "How careless of me."

I set the jar up straight on the mantel as I stare her down.

What a diabolical pepsin salt *she* is.

She turns, brittle shoes snapping over the hardwood, making her way across the room toward the kitchen, hesitating in the doorway. She leers at me from across the study. "Forgive me, where are my manners?"

she starts. "We'll be studying advanced mathematics today, the principles of quantum physics. You're welcome to join us, if you like." She pulls her gloves through her hands. "Unless, of course . . . that's beyond your capabilities."

"Thank you, but no." I smile, biting my tongue for fear it will lash out and slap her. "I've already received an A in that area of study. Wouldn't want me showing Urlick up, now would we?"

Flossie's sassy expression sours.

She whirls around and disappears into the belly of the kitchen as I fall, relieved, against the mantelpiece—clumsily knocking the jar from its stand.

The pedestal bounces, then snaps. Glass splinters everywhere. The hood of the dome falls away. The mysterious grey cloud within slowly seeps from the wreckage. I back up, coughing, and cover my mouth, worried Flossie is right and it is poisonous.

I blink in disbelief as the cloud expands, then rises, steam-like, above the mantelpiece . . . filling in the unfinished portion of the map. I stand astounded, staring at the fog-like diorama forming before my very eyes. Three-dimensional plots of land float above the map like a series of islands in the sky, hovering and bobbing, strung together by a collection of tiny wooden bridges and rope. Below them, a word slowly begins to appear, scrawled in the same loopy, old-fashioned cursive as the rest of the map . . .

Limpidious

Followed by the word . . .

Groves

"It can't be." I gasp, bringing a quick hand to my mouth. "Limpidious! My father's utopian world! It does exist!"

Seventeen

Eyelet

"Is everything all right in there?" Flossie's voice bounces off the kitchen cupboards. My heart rolls in my chest.

I burst into action, waving my hands through the steamy cloud to erase its details. I lunge at the floor to scoop up the glass, deposit the shards in a nearby potted plant, and kick the remains of the pedestal under the settee just as Flossie's face graces the doorway, her brows woven tight.

"Is everything all right in here?" She glares at me, her eyes two grey pebbles peering out from under a thunderstorm of suspicion.

It's only then I realize I've cut myself. Quickly I throw my hands behind my back, pinching the cut with my other hand to stop the bleeding.

"I thought I heard something," she goes on. "Like a crash."

Her eyes scan the room, and I doctor my position. Stepping to one side just enough to block the empty space on the mantelpiece, I bend my arm and lean my head into my hand playfully to further hide it. "It was nothing, really," I stammer. "I just tripped over this." I kick the cast-iron fireplace ornament standing next to me. The poker falls from the stand. "You see." I bite my lip.

"Really?" She breathes, bringing a hand to her chest, her eyes narrowing to slits. "I could have sworn I heard something shatter."

"Really?" I say, blood dripping through my fingertips.

"Eyelet!" Urlick's voice bursts into the room, causing us both to jump. *"Eyelet! Are you there?"* He appears in the doorway short of breath, cobwebs in his hair, his expression—formidably priceless.

"Eyelet?" Flossie whirls around. "I thought you said your cousin's name was Priscilla."

Urlick pulls a hand through his sweaty curls. "It—it is!" He swallows.

Flossie's eyes land hot on me.

The pulse triples in my wrists.

"It's a family thing." I step forward bravely, looping my good hand through Urlick's arm. "Eyelet is my—*pet* name," I say, thinking quickly. "It's silly, really," I chortle. "But it seems my father thought me as pretty as the trim that edged my dress on the day of my christening. And so I was renamed . . . and it's stuck ever since."

Flossie twists her hands.

"Isn't that right, Urlick?" I turn to him and swallow.

"Right." He nods and pats my hand.

"Now that I've grown up, I've asked everyone to address me by my proper name, but from time to time, Urlick slips. We spent a lot of time together as children. Old habits die hard, I guess."

Flossie's expression stiffens. "I had no idea you were that close, Urlick." Her head cranks around, catching Urlick up in a venomous stare. "You've never mentioned having a cousin *before*. Especially not one you address by a pet name." She turns her eyes on me. "I would have thought I'd have heard of her at some point over the past two years." She floats forward, touching Urlick's other arm, running her fingers lightly down his sleeve. "Considering how close we've been."

Urlick flinches under the weight of her touch, bolting backward as if he's been scorched by fire. His eyes are as wide as a cornered rat's. I can't help but laugh inside.

She folds her hand over his, and the hairs on the back of my neck sizzle. Though I'm not sure why. I couldn't care less that she's touched him.

She gazes into Urlick's eyes, her eyes dancing flirtatiously beneath painted lashes. Running her fingers in provocative lines across her chest, she glances at me to see if I've noticed.

I noticed.

Not that I care.

I don't.

Do I?

"Well, shall we get started, then?" Flossie tips her chin toward Urlick. "I see Iris has lunch prepared." She raises a hand to primp her hair, staring me down out of the corner of her eye. "After all, we've only so much time together." She tightens her grip on his hand.

"Are you coming?" Urlick asks me, looking back over his shoulder as Flossie drags him through the archway into the kitchen.

"I'm not really hungry," I lie, trying to steal some time to figure out what to do about my finger, shifting my boot over the puddle on the carpet.

Looking past Urlick, my eyes fix on a stranger standing with his back to the wall on the opposite side of the kitchen. He's smoking a cigarette, and his left eye is covered in a leather patch, just like the one the Brigsman—

I gasp.

Flossie's eyes track my gaze. "Forgive me—again with my manners. I've forgotten to introduce my new driver, haven't I? Cryderman . . ." She turns, unfurling a hand in his direction. The stranger lifts his gaze.

It's *him.* Smrt's henchman. The one who chased me from my mother's side the day she lay dying in the street. What is he doing *here?* I avert my eyes, trembling. I've got to get out of here. If I stay, he'll surely recognize me. "No introduction necessary," I blurt. "Now if you'll excuse me."

I push past Flossie and dash up the stairs to my room. "Enjoy your studies," I call to Urlick over my shoulder.

"What was *that* all about?" I hear Urlick say.

"I've no idea," Flossie says. "Flighty little thing, your cousin."

Eighteen

Eyelet

I bury my head in my pillow, terrified by the idea of my captor's hench-man lunching downstairs with Urlick at the kitchen table.

What if he *has* come for me? What if he tells Urlick? What if Urlick agrees to hand me over to him? He wouldn't do that, would he?

How did one of Smrt's henchmen suddenly surface as a common-er's driver? I thought Urlick said Flossie lived out here in the Follies. That she had no connection to Brethren.

What am I going to do? How will I avoid him, when she's due here twice a week to deliver his lessons? Every Tuesday and Thursday. That leaves me two days to uncover my father's machine, use it, and figure out a way to flee this place, before Flossie and her henchman return.

I stare out the window into the forest, thinking of the criminals and the Infirmed. I've no choice. I've got to leave. Immediately. I can't risk his discovering me.

My eyes drift to the top of the escarpment where the Vapours hover, coiling among the trees. Where will I go? What will I do? How will I overcome the Vapours?

I can't possibly go back to Brethren. And I dare not return to Gears.

I have no choice. I'll have to stay in the Follies.

I've nowhere else to go.

Nowhere else in the world.

Unless . . .

I hug my pillow across my chest. Yes. Of course, that's it.

I sit up.

Limpidious!

The hydrocycle. I could ride it there. I could fly my way to Limpidious!

Nineteen

Eyelet

Only after I'm sure Flossie and her driver have gone for the day do I make an appearance, sliding into place next to Urlick at the dinner table. After all, I need answers and I need them now. Starting with what he knows about the mysterious land beyond the map in his study.

"Everything all right?" he asks as I sit. His hand swings out to pull back my chair.

I stare at him hard, and he drops his grip. I pull the chair out for myself.

"Was it Flossie?" he tries again. "Because if she said something that upset you . . ."

"She didn't—"

"It's just that . . . I know she can be a real—"

"It was nothing." I raise my hand.

Urlick falls hushed beside me, his eyes wide and blinking.

"What's happened to your hand?"

"Oh, that." I look down at my bandaged finger. "I nicked it helping Iris peel potatoes earlier."

"Potatoes?" Urlick frowns. "But we're not even having potatoes this evening."

"They're for tomorrow," I blurt.

Iris appears out of nowhere, as she tends to do, a dash on the thinnest of air, and I'm grateful for the chance to change the subject, to get Urlick's prying mind off me.

"Oh, my, what have we here?" I say, straightening my back and craning my neck to see as she flits past, steaming bowls in hand, and lays them out on the table. "Spanish yams, spiced okra, quail?" I look up at her, perplexed. "Where on earth did you ever find quail?"

"The market," Urlick blurts, lurching up from his seat before Iris has the chance to answer. "In Gears," he stammers on, adjusting the collar at his neck. "The other day when I found you." The two of them share a curious look, like they've both swallowed a canary.

Quail in the common marketplace? In a laborer town like Gears? *Not bloody likely, that's what I say.* Quail hasn't been readily available in these parts since the Night of the Great Illumination. In fact, it's become rather a delicacy. Raised in private pens, behind locked gates, no longer found in the wild. You're a terrible liar, Urlick Babbit.

Among other things.

"You fancy quail, don't you?" He looks worried.

"Very much," I say.

He takes his seat, looking relieved.

The timer goes off on my Teasmaid, saving him from further explanation—for the moment, anyway. This time I'm ready, slipping my cup beneath its spout before it has the chance to christen the cloth.

Urlick glances up, pleased.

Iris excuses herself as usual—a curtsy for me, a bow for Urlick—then she's off. I can't help but wonder what she does up there all day, alone in her room. How she can spend so many days not talking to anyone? I, for one, would go crazy.

And then there's Urlick.

I look his way and he drops his head, fork and knife busily dismantling his bird. Talking with Urlick is like pulling rusty nails from tarred wood: both frustrating and laborious. It's as though he's allergic to conversation.

I watch as he spins his fork around his plate. Something about the way he holds his silver bewitches me. Index finger pressed firmly down over top of his knife. Fork cradled in his other hand, so delicately. It's as though he's dined with kings, though I'm sure he has not. He looks up, and I pull my eyes away.

"So," I start, trying to make my voice sound light and unassuming. Small talk first, I figure, then on to the gritty bits. I need answers, yes, but past experience tells me if I don't start out slow, I'll get nothing from him. Which is pretty much all I've got so far. And goodness knows, if I lead with the question I'm itching to ask, I'll surely raise his suspicions. Besides, if I'm to be treated as a ward of this prison, I'm entitled to know a little something about the warden, aren't I?

"Have you always lived out here in the Follies?" I say, pushing a bit of okra around on my plate.

"No," he answers flatly, never looking up from his meal.

"Where else have you lived?"

"Away," he says.

This isn't going to be easy.

"Where, specifically?" I try again.

"In Gears." He levels his gaze.

"How old were you when you moved here, then?"

"Nine." He swallows, as if he's suddenly remembered he shouldn't speak with his mouth full.

"So you were born in Gears, then?"

"No, I was born here—"

"But I thought you said—"

"I *did*." He glares.

I strip the quail from my fork with my teeth, and he cringes. Something my mother always hated, too.

"Look, if you must know, I was sent to live with a nursemaid the day after I was born, and I remained there until I was nine years old."

"But why?"

"Because my father couldn't stand the sight of me, that's why." He drops his silver to the plate. "The night I was born, I lay wedged in the birth canal for over an hour, struggling, my mother too weak to assist me. My father, thinking me a demon—birthing face up, staring at him with eyes as red as Satan's—refused to assist her, until finally he could take her screams no longer and stepped in. He wrapped a hand around my throat and yanked me free, but it was too late—she was already dead. According to my father I wear the scars of her death as my punishment."

"That's horrible."

"Yes, well . . . that's the way it is." He lowers his head. "The nurse-maid tried, but she couldn't get the colour to leave my face. Nor could she remove the mark of my father's hand from my neck. If only he'd stepped in sooner, he might have been able to save my mother. But he didn't." He looks to me. "And he's never forgiven me for that."

"*You?* Why should you be to blame?"

"Afterward, he couldn't stand the sight of me—so he gave me away. His only child." The muscles at the side of his jaw churn. "I was quite happy until the nursemaid died and I had to be returned to him."

I swallow down the glob of heartache that's formed in my throat. How could a father do such a thing? What kind of a man blames a baby for his wife's death?

"Is that why he's so seldom seen? Why he remains such a recluse in his own home?"

Urlick lowers his head. "My father and I will be forever estranged."

"Why do you stay here, then? Why don't you leave?"

Urlick glares up at me through burning pink eyes. "Look at me," he says. "Where would I go?"

Iris breezes in, startling me. My back snaps straight in the chair. She rushes to the oven, where apparently she's been harbouring a secret dessert, and plops it down in front of me. It's wrapped in a blue-and-white gingham cloth.

"What is this?" I say, looking up at her.

She brings her hands to her chest like a giddy child.

"Go ahead, open it," Urlick says, coaxing me with his fingers.

I look up and smile, feeling sorry for pushing him into conversation.

Slowly, I unwrap the gingham cloth, unveiling, of all things . . . a pie. And not just any pie: an olallieberry pie! In all its brown-baked glory. It's been years since I've had pie, longer still since I've tasted the sweetness of olallieberries. They've been extinct for years. How is this possible? Where did they find them? First the quail, now the pie. I screw up my face and look at him.

"It's your favourite, isn't it?" Urlick panics.

"Yes," I say. "My absolute. But how did you—"

"Splendid." He slurps his tea with a twisted grin.

I turn to Iris, remembering my attempt at conversation yesterday—me going over culinary likes and dislikes, and her not answering. "This was your idea, was it?"

She shakes her head.

"Yours?" I turn to Urlick.

He looks up, kissed by a bit of blush.

"Better eat it before it gets cold," he says and drops his chin.

I can't believe it. Only this morning he put me out in the darkness without a care, yet all the while, he'd arranged for kindness to be bubbling up in the oven in the form of my favourite pie.

I glance over at him and catch him looking at me. My cheeks begin to heat. Why would he do such a thing? I thought he detested me.

Iris cuts the pie into pieces, serves one to Urlick and one to me, then retires with hers to the back kitchen.

Urlick takes a bite and the olallieberries stain his lips red. He looks funny to me with lips the right colour, having grown so accustomed to his purplish ones. "Can I ask you another question?" I say.

"Would it matter if I were to say no?"

"What lies beyond the Follies? In that empty space on the map in the study?"

Urlick's eyes shoot up from his plate.

"Nothing. Only death. Eat your pie."

Twenty

Eyelet

That night I do the unthinkable.

I unlock my bedroom door and creep, catlike, down the corridor and down the stairs, holding my boots in my hand. When I reach the landing, I scoot through the back kitchen and out through the door, pausing only to pull on my boots before venturing into the dark caverns that lead to Urlick's laboratory.

I hate the thought of being down here alone, especially at night.

The locks are designed to keep things out, not in, I hear Urlick say. I only hope he's right.

Swallowing down the fear in my throat, I push on, imagining any number of bad things that could happen to me—the least of which is that no one even knows I'm down here, should I suddenly go missing.

It's particularly cold in these hallways at night. If only I'd brought a sweater. I rub my arms, the beat of my heart striking in time with the heels of my boots as I race up the stone corridor toward the opening to the main cavern.

Torchlight in hand, I duck my head and enter, letting the door swing shut behind me.

Something scurries across the path. I gasp and throw my back up against the wall, pulling a hand to my chest to conceal the light of my necklace. Curls of breath escape my lips.

Slowly I lean out around the corner, heart racing, daring to take another look. The creature scampers past in a draft of light, and I suck in a quick breath. Larger than a small animal, it appears it could be human. Whatever it is, it's moving too quickly for me to distinguish any features except for feet.

It dashes again and I squint to see, making out, to my horror, a hunched back and a severely crooked neck. No arms dangle at its sides. The shape of its shadow doesn't appear human. I don't know *what* it is.

I pull back again, aghast and trembling, pressing my shoulder blades even tighter to the stones. Sliding sideways, I search for a place to hide but find nothing as the slap of bare feet draws nearer.

Panicked, I douse my torch in a nearby puddle, and curse myself over the billow of smoke that rises. I race down the corridor the opposite way, groping the wall as I go, trying to find some way to escape the corridor, delighted when my hands come across a handle. Even more delighted when I twist it and it gives way. Slipping over the threshold, I plaster myself against the adjacent wall.

Footsteps approach. Blood thumps in my ears. Silhouettes of bare toes darken the sill.

I close my eyes, shaking, as the door creaks slowly open. *No.* This can't be happening. Go away, *please*, go away.

I put a hand over my mouth and hold my breath, counting the heartbeats in my ears. Slowly the door shuffles open, then slowly back. The lock falls into place.

Feet race up the corridor, then up a set of stairs, disappearing into the din.

I let out my breath and slide down the wall. I've never been so relieved. For a long time I just sit, gasping, thanking God for sparing me. When at last I'm brave enough to open my eyes, the most amazing sight spills out before me.

Through the dim light of the room, I see trees. Everywhere. Trees. And plants of every kind. Pushing up from earth so rich and black it almost looks fake. Where am I? What is this place? How do trees grow inside?

I step farther into the room, and my hair tosses back from my shoulders on a great gust of warm, moist wind. It pulses down from above in timed, gentle breaths. I look up. Pipes crawl the ceiling, steam purging from their pores, irrigating all the plants and trees below in a shower-like mist. Beyond the trees, three solid walls of lead-glass windows encase the room.

It's a garden! A room full of garden! A giant indoor terrarium!

I venture farther inward, keeping to the cobblestone walk, careful not to crush any plants. Strings of aether lamplights glow above the foliage like tiny bulbs of artificial sun. Everything looks shiny and vibrant, bathed in tropical dew. Or, at least, what I imagine tropical dew to be, from illustrations I've seen in science books.

My, it's warm in here. I fan myself, shoving the arms of my jacket higher. Sweat beads along the edges of my hair and coats my upper lip. I reach up, loosening the top buttons of my chemise. I swipe the perspiration from my brow. Such a major contrast from the weather out in the hall—yet the hall is only steps away.

How is this possible? How is any of this possible?

I drop my hands, dragging my fingertips over the tops of the leaves. Plants of every kind sprawl out on either side of me, row after row. There must be ten, twenty, thirty exotic species growing here! Some I've seen only in picture books.

I race up and down the rows, identifying them one by one. "Ginseng. Fennel. Hawthorn berry. *Shepherd's purse?*" I stoop and sniff.

"I can't believe it. Shepherd's purse hasn't grown in these parts for over ten years. And yet, here it is."

I turn. "And cinnamon. And nutmeg, too? And over here"—I reach—"peppermint!"

My eyes stretch across the room to the end of the plant bed, to a bush with prickly, emerald-coloured leaves. "Oh my goodness." I take up my skirts and rush toward it, plucking the fruit from its branches. "Olallieberries!" I shriek and pop them in my mouth, wincing at their sweet, tart flavor. "They've olallieberry bushes! No wonder the pie!"

I step back to get a better look and something stirs at my feet, causing me to jump from the path. Coos come up from the leaves, and all at once I'm laughing. "Quail?" A bird scuttles out of the plants and over my toes. Its neck juts in and out. "Of course, what else would it be?"

I turn, and my eyes set on something so unusual it brings me to my knees. I blink twice, thinking I must be dreaming. Raising the leaf of the very large hosta that hovers over top of it, I stare at the tiny plant. *"Chemodendryum charcoalreous?"* I gasp, reaching out, rolling its soft, fuzzy leaves between my fingers. If only I had my textbook to verify. Though my memory assures me it is what it appears. A classified medicinal plant, bred to challenge cancer—grown only in the official laboratories of the Commonwealth, at the Academy, for distribution among the wealthy. "How did the Babbits get access to such a classified plant? Where has all this come from?"

I lean, overcome by its scent. Or *is* it the scent that's affecting me? Growing dizzy, I sit on the ground, pull my legs up beneath me, and throw my arms about my knees. The room begins to spin.

"Oh no, not now. *Please* not now." I hold my breath and fight against the all-too-familiar tinge. It's the silver, not *charcoalreous* that creeps through my veins, determined to pull me under.

I tuck my head and will it away, but it's no use, it's not listening. I have no time for this. I need to get on with my journey. If I don't uncover my father's machine tonight, I may never have another chance.

The silver shivers up my spine, and the world around me starts to fade. I clutch the ground, trying to hold on. Please, no, I beg you, not here, *please* let go. I can't be found alone in this room!

The silver ignores me, biting its way slowly up the back of my neck. I cringe at the thought of losing control. Slowly, the room turns to shadow, variations of grey and black. My body begins to quake.

If you must take me, please have mercy.

Let this be a small episode. I beg.

I fall back, writhing against the wall, my hands flailing out at my sides. My fingers grope at the leaves around me, shredding them from their stalks, in a pointless effort to steady myself. Their aroma floods my nose: a sharp, musky smell, like the vinegar-mustard poultices my mother used to mix—only this one's gone rancid. It permeates my nostrils and worms its way to my brain.

I long to shake my head to stave off the smell, but I can't; the silver controls me now. The scent is so piercing it sends daggers to my head and stings my lungs. I must get away from it. Somehow.

With my last surge of energy, I throw my hands to my face and draw in a desperate breath, forgetting the leaves still gnarled in my fingers. Their scent bolts through me like a strike of bitter lightning. I nearly collapse.

My hands drop to my sides and I fight for air, but all I can smell is the leaves. I'm hot and cold all over; my throat begins to swell. It's as though I've been poisoned.

My heart gallops in my chest.

Just as the smell heightens to a point where I fear my brain will explode, the sensation suddenly lets go. I gasp as it drains from my senses, dragging the silver away with it, smoothing away every sharp nerve. My heart slows. Every cell in my body tingles. Slowly, colour pushes back into my world. The murky blacks and greys dissolve. The room comes alive with more vibrancy than it had before. All the sights and smells have been sharpened.

I drink in the beauty as, slowly, my body quakes to a halt. It's a few moments before I can catch my breath. My muscles lengthen and relax. My fingers stretch and let go. My jaw becomes unclenched.

I stand, prepared to leave, to rush from this strange garden—then pause and pocket a sample of the mysterious leaves before I go. I don't quite understand what's just happened, but whatever it was, I'm thankful.

*

Urlick's laboratory feels like I've stepped into a cave, its skylights swathed in trolling Vapourous brume. I move about the room quickly, igniting the gaslight sconces on the walls, trying to make myself feel better. They hiss to life in a trail behind me, making my skin crawl.

The hydrocycle chortles from under its tarp, causing my heart to skip. I stop what I'm doing and move across the room, approaching it cautiously. "It's okay," I whisper, pulling back the corner of its cover. "It's only me."

The cycle rattles.

"What's the matter, not exactly what you were expecting?"

It groans.

"I guess that makes us even, doesn't it? Kind of like the first time I saw you. I was expecting the Illuminator. Not some bat-winged bicycle creature."

The cycle whimpers.

"No offense, but you're not exactly a cyclist's dream."

It sighs.

"Can I count on you not to give me away?" I bend a little closer.

The cycle shudders, ducking aside.

"I'll tell you what," I whisper. "If you agree to not give me away, I promise to fix your wings before I leave here tonight."

The hydrocycle straightens.

"I knew you'd like that." I pat it on the handlebars. "Consider it done. But you must never, ever tell Urlick I was down here, do you understand?" I wag my finger in front of its bony face.

The hydrocycle shimmies.

"Good." I reach out, running a hand over its head. "I have a feeling you and I are going to become great friends before all this is through."

The cycle shudders, then exhales.

"Now, if you'll excuse me, I have a machine to unveil."

The cycle whimpers as I weave my way through the centre of the room, dodging this gadget and that, feeling rather stupid at just having had a conversation with a machine. I look back over my shoulder at it resting peacefully, wings rising and falling again to the floor. I still wonder how that's happening.

Turning, I dash at the square of curtains at the back of the room. Time is of the essence, after all. Excited to reach it, I throw aside the heavy velvet screen. "Aha!" I shout, then drown in disappointment.

Behind the curtain stands nothing.

Absolutely nothing.

Just a vast expanse of stone floor. A large square has been cut into the surface of it, as if marking where something once stood.

"It's gone." I step inside the square, staring in disbelief. "I can't believe it. He must have moved it. This afternoon, after he noticed my interest in the curtain." I run to the wall, testing to see if it opens, pounding my fists on the quarry stones. "Where is it?" I whirl around. "Where can it be? He can't have moved it far! The thing weighs a bloody ton!"

I race around the room, checking behind every partition, flipping over every box, every crate, pushing aside every bin. "It has to be here! Somewhere! It must be!"

The hydrocycle whimpers.

"You." I turn. "You know where it is, don't you?"

The cycle shudders, wincing away from me.

"Please." I race toward it, falling to my knees. "Please tell me. I need to know, where is it? The machine he stole from the market in Gears. Where has he hidden it? Show me, *please!*"

The cycle cowers at the tone of my voice, and I realize how frightening I must seem.

"Very well, then," I say, picking up a wrench. "Perhaps if I help you first?"

The hydrocycle brightens, then sighs.

Twenty-One

Eyelet

A scream trumpets from the ceiling, startling both the cycle and me.

My head shoots up, my heart drumming in my chest. "For the love of God, what was that?"

The cycle shivers as the scream goes off again.

I'm up and across the room in a flash. My eyes scan the ceiling, searching for the source of the noise, stopping under the apartment on the second floor.

Iris!

The scream rises again. A high-pitched, tortured howl. I drop the wrench. "Something's happening to Iris!" I snatch up my skirts and bolt for the stairs, activating them as I grab for a torch on the wall.

"Hold on, Iris!" I shout as I lunge out into the corridors. "I'm coming!"

*

I fly through the corridor and burst up the stairs, throwing open the back kitchen door. Racing up the main stairs, I cross the narrow passageway that separates the main house from the turret, and I throw my back up against the wall. The scream sounds again, raising the hairs on my neck. Whatever is happening to her must be horrible.

I suck in a breath and head for the stairs leading to the second floor, gasping when I reach the landing. The scream is so intense now I can barely stand it. Tears come to my eyes. The mournful sound travels up my spine and bites at the back of my neck.

My heart lurches hard in my chest as I try to decide what to do next. Where is Urlick? Why has he not come to rescue her?

I blink in the darkness, fighting off the tears, torchlight hissing in my hand. Another scream rattles the bones beneath my skin. Fear sloshes inside my stomach. I swallow hard, trying to muster the courage to charge up the stairs. What monstrous thing could be happening up there for her to scream so chillingly?

The scream rises again and I long to flee, but I can't. Iris needs me. Jittery-legged, I force myself around, gather up my skirts, and swallow hard before bounding up the flight, two steps at a time. I'm only halfway when I'm stopped cold in my tracks by the sight of something truly gruesome.

In the shower of aether light that shines down on the landing above stands a man the same height and build as Urlick—but it's not Urlick. Dressed in a gentleman's suit, top hat, and tails, his skin looks as though it's made of wax. His eyes are those of a nightmarish goon. They stare at me, transfixed, like the eyes in a painting. I gasp, pulling a hand to my mouth as my breath falls away.

In his arms he holds a child. A girl of ten, maybe eleven years. Her eyes are dull, lifeless, glaring at the ceiling as if she were dead. Her long hair falls over his arms; her legs dangle at his hips. In the shadows beyond, the feet from the basement appear, shinnying up the sides of the chimney behind the two figures.

I can't help myself: I scream.

Clutching my heart, I race from the stairs, around the corner, up the hallway to my room. My hands fall to the lock, trembling too much to activate it. "Oh, please, just let me in!"

"Eyelet?" Urlick appears, quite strangely out of nowhere, his white hand landing hard on my shoulder.

"Urlick!" I turn, falling into his arms. "Where have you been?" I tremble.

"What is it? What's the matter?"

"It's your father! He's torturing a child!"

"He's what?"

"Upstairs, just outside of Iris's room. You must have heard her screaming?" I furrow my brow at his lifeless expression.

He says nothing, just triggers the lock and whisks me over the threshold into the room. His hands feel tight as a vise on my skin. Why is he acting like this? What's the matter with him?

"There were feet," I tell him. "They shuttled up the chimney behind him. And I saw them before, down in the—" I stop myself before I give myself away.

Urlick ignores me, dragging me across the floor of the bedroom, kicking the door shut behind him.

"Please," I beg, struggling. "You have to listen to me. I saw your father on the landing with his victim in his arms."

"That's enough," he says through clenched teeth. He shakes me.

Another scream swells in the air above us.

"You see?" I shudder under the weight of it. "I'm not lying. He's hurting her." I twist, trying to break free of his grasp, bolting up on my toes, but he hauls me back. "Please, Urlick, you have to do something." I fall against his chest. "He may be killing her!"

He says nothing, just stares at me hard.

"What's wrong with you? Why won't you listen to me?" I try to pull away again, but he pulls me back.

"Because it's not what you think!" he says.

"What are you talking about? How can it not be? I saw her with my own eyes!"

He snaps me around by the shoulders to face him. His eyes are intense. "What you're hearing are the cries of the criminals and the Infirmed dying in the woods. That's it. Those sounds are not coming from this house—"

"That's not true and you know it." I scowl.

Another scream rakes the ceiling, throwing both our chins up to see.

"Don't lie to me, Urlick. Please tell me what's going on."

"Nothing," he snaps. "I assure you. There is no one else in this house but you and me and Iris—"

"And your father."

A muscle twitches at the side of his cheek.

A noise from the hall has Urlick looking panicked, as another scream rolls up our spines.

"Iris!" I shout, suddenly remembering, cranking my head around and back. "Where is Iris? What's happened to her?"

Urlick gasps. Looking as though he's harbouring a secret in his eyes.

"Where is she? I demand to see her *now*! *Iris!*" I spring from his arms and he reels me back, lifting my feet from the ground. I kick, trying to run, my heels meeting with his shins. *"IRIS!"* I scream. "Iris, where are you! Answer me!"

"Eyelet, please." Urlick tightens his grip, and I cough from the pressure. "Iris is in no danger, you have to believe me—"

"Then prove it!" I spin in his arms, trying to strip myself of his grip. "Produce her! Immediately!"

"IR-IIIIIS!" Urlick shouts. "Iris, show yourself, *please!*"

The bedroom door handle turns. The door creaks slowly open. Iris's round moon face appears at the side of the jamb, her sad-dog eyes gawking in at me, her expression riddled with guilt.

"Iris?" I say, giving up the fight. "Iris? Are you okay?"

She says nothing, just tightens her grip on the jamb.

"You see, I told you"—Urlick's breath is choppy—"Iris is perfectly fine." He lowers my feet to the floorboards.

"Iris," I gasp, my gaze shifting between the two of them. "Talk to me. Please, Iris. Tell me what's going on!"

Her lips part as if to speak, but Urlick interrupts. "Go upstairs and fetch the *comfort* tea." He flicks his chin toward the ceiling. "The medicinal one. From the room."

Iris's eyes grow big and desperate. Her grip tightens on the jamb.

"What room?" I wrench around, facing Urlick, then turn back to Iris. "What's happening here? Iris, speak to me—"

"Right away, Iris, *please!*"

"No!" I shake my head, thrashing up against him. "I'm fine. Honestly. I'll go back to bed and won't get up again, I promise. Please, just let go of me. Please. Just let me go to bed."

Another scream jags across the ceiling, sharp and ugly. My heart pulls to a stop. I stare hard into Urlick's eyes. "Why are you doing this to me? Why won't you tell me the truth?" My gaze pulls at Urlick. His jaw begins to drop.

"Iris, *please!*" He pulls his eyes away from me. "Go get the tea! NOW!"

Iris darts away, returning a moment later with a cup, steam rising like fingers from its rim.

"No." I fight. "No, Urlick, please!"

Forcing my head back into the crook of his arm, he parts my lips and thrusts the rim of the cup up against my teeth. "Drink this," he says.

"No!" I sputter and squirm.

"You must!" His eyes are sharp and mean.

Another scream rises as he brings the cup back up to my lips. "Please, Eyelet," he begs. "Just drink it. It won't hurt you, I promise, I'd never hurt you . . ."

I look into his eyes, not knowing what to think. What's happened to the Urlick I know? The one I spoke with last night at supper, the hurt little boy with the horrible birth story, the one who was kind enough to fix me a pie?

What's happened to him? Where did he go? Why is he doing this to me?

He brings the cup to rest on my lips again, and I purse them tight. His eyes beg me to drop my resistance. "How much do you trust me?" he whispers, and I gasp.

"What did you just say?"

"I asked how much you trust me."

As if I've just been pulled underwater, Urlick's features begin to distort, his face interchanging sporadically with that of his father, then my father, then back to him again. The room starts to spin, becoming a whir of wobbly shadows. The light dims to a grey veil. I smell burning bread, and all at once I realize it's the silver, threading its way up inside my veins.

Not now. Oh, *please*, not now.

He mustn't know. He mustn't see this.

I close my eyes, trying hard to fight the feeling, but the silver's toxic tentacles are far too powerful.

I can't allow this to happen. I can't fall into a full episode and writhe in his arms. I've got to find another way out.

Reaching out for the cup, I pull it to my lips, gulping down every last drop of its bitter contents. Then I push it away, planning to blame whatever happens next on the potion he's just forced me to drink, not the silver.

Twenty-Two

Urlick

I lower Eyelet to her bed, bringing the bedcovers up tight around her chin, and leave her room, weighed down by guilt as I stalk the hall toward my own.

I flop on my bed when I reach it, staring past my mobile of molecules at the ceiling, consumed with guilt. I reach out and spin the wheels of my origami hydrocycle model, knocking it from the shelf, and squint past my bat-winged chevron wallpaper at the portrait of Charles Darwin that hangs on the wall.

"I had no other choice, did I?" I whisper to him. "There was nothing else I could do. Perhaps Iris is right, I should have just told her. Perhaps Eyelet would have understood. Perhaps—*no*." I run a hand through my hair.

"She can't know. She must never know."

I turn my head and stare out the window at the Vapours swelling high and fat over the ridge. It won't be long now. They'll come tumbling down and swallow us. And she'll have nowhere else to go. If she were to find out now—before the Vapours set in—God knows what would happen to her. I can't risk her knowing, for fear she bolts. I couldn't live with myself if anything happened to that girl.

I swallow, forcing down the mix of feelings that have formed a wedge in my throat.

My bedroom door flies back, crashing into the wall, knocking Darwin dangerously off kilter.

A steaming Iris stands in the doorframe, her arms tightly crossed over her chest. Her lips as well as her brows are pursed. I'm in trouble.

She storms across the floor and hands me a note:

Do you really think that was necessary?

"Oh, I don't know." I sit up. "Don't you?"

The line of her lips grows even more severe. Her hands thrust hard to her hips.

"Okay, so perhaps that was a little harsh. But what was I supposed to do?"

Iris snatches away the paper, scrawls something else, and stuffs it back in my face.

Anything but that.

"Really!" I spring from the bed. "All right, go ahead, enlighten me! How would you have kept her from knowing the secret?"

Iris's gaze drops to the floor.

"Yeah, exactly." I tug at the points of my waistcoat and smooth back my hair. "What do you think is going to happen if she ever finds out? Hmmm?" I jut my face toward Iris's. "The jig would be up then, wouldn't it?"

Iris refuses to look at me. She purses her lips even tighter.

"You know we can't let her wander around in this place unchaperoned." I turn and pace. "You know what that could lead to."

Iris glances at me through seething, squinty eyes.

"Don't you look at me like that! You know she can't know—"

She scribbles, forcing a note on me again.

Why not?

"Why not?" I toss it back. "Do you really think we can trust her?"

Iris scratches another sentence down and flings the paper back.

You expected HER to trust YOU!

"Admirable point," I say, leaning back on my heels. The floor-boards squeak beneath them. "But it's one thing for me to ask it of her, quite another for me to offer her mine in return. Why, the girl's little more than a gypsy!"

Iris narrows her eyes. She turns on her heel and charges across the room, heading for the door. "You're a fool," she mouths on her way past me, balling up the paper and throwing it in the rubbish.

"Perhaps," I say. "But I'm a fool with his secrets intact!"

She storms out into the hallway and slams the door, not once but three times in a row—and then again, four more times even quicker than before. Iris's code for "You. Are. So. *Im-pos-si-ble!*"

"Me?" I shout after her. "You should make your own acquaintance some time!"

"Pffff!" I hear her huff from the hall. She takes to the stairs, stomp-ing her way up the treads to her apartment, slamming the door of her bedroom as well.

I fall back on the bed, listening to her shoes clomp about the room overhead. Perhaps Iris is right. Perhaps I could have trusted Eyelet. Perhaps she would have understood. My eyes drift again to the window. Or perhaps she'd just think me a madman.

A gust of wind slaps the glass, drawing my attention to the wave of Vapours building momentum on the horizon. I jump from the bed, checking the Vapour barometer mounted just outside my window. Its needle fluctuates between forty-seven and forty-eight parts per million. We've got about twenty-four hours—maybe more, maybe less.

I stare at the needle. We'll need supplies. Plenty of them. What, with an extra mouth to feed and an extra pair of lungs to keep breathing? I don't dare risk not having enough oxygen on hand. You never know what's going to happen when the Vapours set in.

I look up again at the dark clouds brewing atop the ridge.

I hate the thought of leaving her here, unattended. But if I don't go now, I go never.

Twenty-Three

Eyelet

I sit up and check my face in the looking glass. I've no thrash marks on my cheeks. No dried drool to chisel from the corners of my mouth. I don't look drained or weathered, my skin isn't sallow, and I've no dark circles under my eyes as I normally do after I wake from a grand mal episode. Which I was sure I was slipping into last night. It's as though I sank swiftly into the depths of a major seizure only to somehow be pulled from it, escaping the brunt of its storm.

But how? It's not possible. Once an episode begins, it can't be reversed. That's never happened before. Unless . . .

My eyes land on the empty cup resting atop my dressing table.

The *tea.*

Of course.

I wash, dress, pull my hair up into a twist, secure it with combs, and race down the stairs. Exposed or not, I have questions that need answering. Starting with what was in that tea.

"I demand to know what happened last night." I fill the entrance-way, letting him know I mean business, a barbed tongue my weapon.

"Good morning to you, too." Urlick sips his tea, staring at me through the steam.

"I know there's something going on in this house, and I intend to find out what it is." I circle him like a panther.

"Really?"

"Yes, really."

He flips open a copy of *The New Age*.

I disarm him of it. "Let's start with the noises I heard last night, shall we?"

"Noises? What noises?" He exaggerates the word like he pours his tea: high, then low, then high again. "I heard no noises." He throws a glance at Iris across the room. "Did you?"

Iris beats the batter relentlessly.

"Perhaps it was just a figment of your imagination." He returns to me. "You know, new room, strange place—"

"It was no figment, and you know it." I pinch up close. "Neither were the feet I saw trekking up the chimney."

He swallows, his Adam's apple bobbing up and down like a boat in bad weather.

"Stymied you now, haven't I?"

"You're sure you've not become afflicted?" he says, reaching out and laying a hand to my forehead as if I were sick.

I bat it away. "Don't play games with me!"

"I don't believe it's *me* playing the games." He reaches for the paper. I snatch it away.

"Oh, really? Perhaps then you'd like to explain to me what was in the tea you forced me to drink last evening!"

"What tea?"

"Don't tell me you're going to try to deny it!"

Iris breaks an egg too sharply over the edge of her bowl.

"You were never drugged." He peers at me through flustered, snow-white lashes. His hands clasp and unclasp the chair back.

"What do you call it then? Oh, that's right, you called it *comfort* tea, didn't you? *Medicinal*, you claimed, as you forced it down my throat."

Iris crumbles the shell of an egg.

"I'll not discuss this further." Urlick tugs at the points of his waistcoat and sidesteps me.

"And yet last night you begged me to trust you!"

He whirls around.

"How can I trust you, when you don't even trust *me* enough to tell me the truth!" I step toward him. "What is it, Urlick? What is so important you'd rather *drug me* than have me find out?"

His lips quiver. He sucks in a breath of air as if preparing to tell me something, then turns his head instead. "I'm going into town to the mercantile," he says to Iris, dismissing me altogether. "The Vapours will be upon us soon. I need to get supplies."

"What? Wait!" I give chase as he turns to leave, the soles of his shoes striking hard against the linoleum. "You *are* hiding something from me, Urlick, I know you are!" I reach for him and he pulls away.

"I'm sorry" is all he says. "If I'm not back by this afternoon"—he swallows, staring past me at Iris—"you know what to do." He shoulders his pack and heads for the door. "And cancel Flossie," he adds. "No need her coming all this way for nothing. I'll make up the lessons later." He grabs a gas mask from the hook on the wall next to the door, eyeing me like I'm a naughty child in need of discipline. "You are not to leave this house for any reason, do you understand? Iris, you are *not* to let her out of your sight."

Iris nods.

"Until then"—he turns, drawing open the boxcar door across the tracks, filling the room with its rumble—"stay put," he says, eyeing me hard.

He reaches up, activating a box labeled *Guardian* on the wall. "The Infirmed will be on the move already. Trying to find safe haven to weather the storm. And we don't need them in here with us." He presses a numbered code into a pad, and a small red light starts to pulse from the box. "This stays on until my return. Don't turn it off unless you're sure it's me." He looks to Iris. She nods like she understands.

I, for one, sure don't.

He steps across the threshold into the elevator and pulls the boxcar door across in front of his face. His coal-black curls flicker through the slats as he starts his descent, and for a sinking moment I worry I might never see him again.

I glance at the window, the Vapours' curious fingers already prying at its seals like the steamy cloud in the jar I demolished in the study. I need to find the machine, use it, and get out of this madhouse quickly. Clearly, I'm running out of time.

I turn to Iris, shaking the black, billowing creeper from my mind, closing the gap between us. "You'll tell me, won't you, Iris? You'll answer my questions."

Iris turns her eyes away.

"You know why I've come, don't you?"

She picks up a dish and busies herself, dunking it in the dishwater.

"I know you know where it is, just like you know what was in that tea."

Her eyes flash.

"Where is it, Iris? Where is the machine?"

She hunches her shoulders and scuttles away as if trying to hide in plain view.

"Look at me." I whirl her around. "Tell me the truth, about the tea, the screams, everything—"

She breaks away.

"Iris!" I run after her. "Iris, *please* . . . I know you know everything that goes on around here. You have to tell me what's going on!" I grab her by the shoulders and turn her to face me. "Last night, why did he act that way? What did he give me? What was in that tea?"

She twists her head.

"Iris, please! You've got to help me. You don't understand. I need to know what's in it!" She rolls her shoulders and bolts away. "Very well, then!" I race ahead, circling her. "Urlick brought a machine here, from the market in Gears. And I know you know where it is." Her eyes quicken. "Please, Iris. I need to find that machine, before Urlick comes back. My entire future depends on it."

She drops the plate she's holding. It shatters on the floor. She stares at me purse-lipped.

"What is it? What's *wrong* with you?" I shake her. "Why won't you speak? Have you got no *tongue*?"

She gasps. Her mouth flies open—and I fall back, bringing a set of trembling hands to my face.

"What's happened?" My chest heaves. "Who's done this to you?"

A severed stub of cauterized skin flails in the back of her throat—all that remains of a tongue. It's swollen and black—the work of some terrible madman.

You are never to enter my father's third-floor laboratory, no matter what sounds you hear. The words of Urlick play out in my head. "Urlick's father!" I clap a hand to my mouth. "He's done this to you, hasn't he? He's a madman, just as I suspected!"

Iris lunges at me, shaking her head.

"It was Urlick, then? *He* did this to you?"

She shakes her head harder, her eyes round and desperate.

"Good God," I gasp. "*He's* the madman, not the father."

Iris panics, shaking her head furiously now. Tears spring to her eyes.

"The machine." My heart races. "He's been using the machine to torture people, hasn't he? That's why all the secrecy. That's why he drugged me. That's what he didn't want to me to see!" My eyes move from her to the ceiling and back again.

Iris moans, shaking her head. "The girl." I grab her by the shoulders. "What have they done to the girl?"

She gasps and struggles, breaking away from me.

"Please, Iris, for the love of God, tell me what's going *on*!"

She turns her back and heads for the door.

Taking up my skirts, I bolt for the kitchen up the main stairs, leaping them two at a time. If she won't tell me, I'll find out for myself.

Iris turns and bounds after me, stopping halfway up the stairs, turning and clattering back down. A horrible noise pours from her lips as she sails across the kitchen toward the boxcar door. She's going to warn Urlick.

I've got to find the machine before she reaches him. I've got to put a stop to his madness. I cannot allow Urlick to abuse my father's science any longer. I will not stand by and see one more person harmed.

She trips the Guardian and the alarm squeals. Its high-pitched whirring sound roars after me up the stairs.

I scale the remaining three steps, arriving breathless at the top of the third flight, waving a shaky hand over the brass plate to open it. Throwing it back, I storm the forbidden laboratory door. A second alarm fills the Compound with its shrill scream.

*

The room is dark and smells of formaldehyde, methacholine, and humectants. A shockingly vile combination, enough to drive anyone away. I hold my sleeve to my face and push through it, dust swirling in my wake. The walls are covered in shelves lined with jars containing some of the darkest things I've ever seen. A complete smorgasbord of pickled body parts—brains, tongues, eyes, all standing side by side with murdered rats and foetal pigs.

I cringe. Pulling my gaze from the shelves, I lock onto a cabinet full of mixtures below. "Alkaline. Formalin. *Arsenic*." I rumble through the tinctures and jars. "Glutaraldehyde?" I pick it up. "Used for the preservation of anatomical *specimens*?" I read the label. "What's going on here?" I gasp, holding my chest. "*Arsenic* next to embalming fluids. What kind of madman am I dealing with?"

My head cranks around to the sound of shoes on the stairs. I'm running out of time. Throwing back another door, my heart pounds as a table of mechanical body parts is exposed, arms and legs made of wood and shackles. Robotic eyes stare up at me from the sheets. Fingers of a mechanical hand clamp down on my sleeve. I shriek and try to sling it away, but it clings to me, its fingers seemingly possessed, acting somehow of their own volition.

I scream and falter backward, shoulders hitting the mantelpiece hard. My head whacks the glass mirror above. I reach out, groping the air, trying to steady myself. Shoes tread up the stairs. My hand finds the mouth of a sculpted lion on the front of the mantel, accidentally plunging its chin toward the floor. The hearth suddenly spins, taking me with it—dumping me out into a dimly lit cavern on the opposite side of the wall.

Everything smells of worms and dirt. There are no walls, there is no floor. I stand in a room dug into the side of the earth. Tunnels spring from it, like the corridor we crawled through, when I first arrived, in order to access the elevator shaft to the main door. Torches flicker from metal casters bolted to the walls. Cobwebs sag from the ceiling. It's so cold, my breath crystallizes before my face.

"Eyelet!" I hear Urlick's muffled voice call for me. He pounds the wall at my back. I move from the hearth, afraid at any moment it'll swing around and he'll appear in front of me, angry and ready to attack.

Grabbing a torch from the wall as a weapon, I dart down one of the corridors to hide. Hearing the rise and fall of another's breath, I turn, knees knocking, to find nothing but an old wooden surgical bed pushed up against the back wall of a cave. The bedding is ruffled, the pillow worn. I gulp, step forward, and throw back the sheet. The face of Urlick's father peers up at me.

I shriek.

It's the same eerie face with dull portrait eyes that peered down at me from the top of the landing last evening. Not one face, but ten of them, all in a row. Strewn across the mattress, each exactly the same. "Good God." I suck in a sharp breath, my hands trembling. They're masks, death masks, made for the living to remember their loved ones after death. I touch one and pull my hand back, chilled by its feel.

"Oh, Urlick, what have you done?"

Death masks. Cast of paraffin wax, using the deceased's face as the mold, they're then tinted with colour to make them look lifelike, their cheeks injected with ink to make them glow.

Shocked, I lean in a little too close, and one of the mask's eyes springs open, rubber lids fluttering back. Its dull painted gaze leers up at me, and my heart turns cold in my chest.

Something gasps, and I wrench around, torchlight blazing a trail through the darkness. "Who goes there?" I shout, clutching my chest. My throat pulls tight.

On the floor in the corner lies the girl, the one from the night before. Her long, scarlet hair lies pooled around her head, drenched in the foam draining from her twisted mouth. Her legs are curled oddly up behind her back. Her hands are gnarled into a stiff pair of claws. Her eyes look dead. Locked in a frozen stare. I know that stare too well. *Seizures.* She suffers from seizures. Episodes—the same as I do. That's why the noise. The screams in the night. It all makes sense to me now.

She lets out a moan, and her body gyrates. Acidic fear splashes up my throat from my gut. Though I've experienced grand mal episodes many times, I've never witnessed one. How very different it is to be inside the skin of the afflicted, compared to watching the afflicted inside their own skin. My poor mother—I wince at the thought. All those times she was forced to watch me suffer. How terrified she must have been.

The girl lets out a shriek and my heart freezes. I want to help her, but I can't. My feet won't move, my hands are stiff. A shiver runs the length of my spine.

And then it hits me. Perhaps she hasn't always been this way. Perhaps she's the product of some mad experiment gone wrong. Perhaps Urlick knows my secret. That's why he drugged me last night. *This* is what he didn't want me to know.

I nearly vomit at the thought, and the twelve that follow, as my mind races through possibilities. Perhaps he only agreed to let me stay because he had plans for me. After all, what better specimen than a runaway?

I stumble backward as the girl screams again, dropping the torch-light in my hand. A face comes to light in the spiraling lick of flame. A man, squat in stature—with no arms, just legs. I shoot backward, bringing a hand to my mouth at the sight of him, as he creeps from the shadows to comfort the girl, raking her hair away from her face with his toes. Every cell in my body curdles.

He looks up at me through the darkness, and I can't help myself: I scream, imagining my own mutilated future. Turning, I fling myself at the mantelpiece, pounding and shouting for it to turn. Father's machine or not, I need to get out of this madhouse while I'm still in one piece!

At last my hand connects with the lion's jaw. I plunge it toward the floor. The mantelpiece spins, hurling me out on the other side. Urlick stands in the door. I crawl forward, gasping, stumbling onto my knees and from there to my feet, snatching the poker from its stand.

"Get away from me!" I shout, spearing at him through the air. "Get back! Or I *swear* I will cut your throat wide open with this."

"Eyelet, *please*, let me explain."

I swing the poker, lofting the pointed end at his head.

Urlick jerks back, avoiding the blow, and I dash for the door, bursting from the room and down the stairs, past a stunned-faced Iris, back pasted to the wall of the kitchen.

"Wait!" Urlick shouts, chasing after me.

I trigger the lock and throw back the boxcar door.

"You can't go out there!" Urlick screams. "Eyelet, you'll die!"

I roll the door across the tracks and pull on the throttle, clinging to the wires inside as the platform descends, Urlick's pleas fast becoming a distant memory.

Twenty-Four

Urlick

I chase her into the forest, my hand clamping down on her shoulder. She twists away from me, falling back up against a tree.

Shattered.

Breathless.

Screaming.

"Get off of me. Let go of me!"

She fights.

She sinks her teeth into my hand.

"*Eyelet!*" I shake her off, her image veiled by thick mist. "Eyelet, *please*. It's not what it seems."

"It's not, is it?" She kicks and bites. Vapours roil atop the hills. "You've an explanation for Madness, have you?" Her heel connects with my groin and I groan, buckling. Eyelet slips from my grasp, shrouded instantly in mist.

"*Eyelet! Please!*" I hobble after her, glancing up at the Vapours crouched atop the escarpment, ready to pounce. "Eyelet! Let me explain!"

She runs on, charging through the forest toward the Vapours. I don't think she even realizes.

"Eyelet, look up!" I shake off the pain and chase after her. "Look where you're going!"

Her chin swings up and I dive after her, catching her by the arm and throwing her back up against a tree, harder than I intended. Her eyes pop as she smacks her head.

"I'm sorry," I breathe. "I didn't mean to—"

"You're a murderer!" She scowls. "A murderer who wears the mask of his victims!"

"What?"

"Don't insult me by lying to me anymore." Her lips tremble. "I saw them, up there, in your secret room. Your collection of masks. Like the one you wore last night on the stairs." I gasp as she heaves for breath. "Tell me, what kind of a monster kills his own father and then masquerades around in his face?"

Oh Lord, what is she thinking?

"Eyelet, please. It's not what it seems—"

"What else could it be? I found her, you know! The girl you held on the stairs. Up there, stashed away in your secret lair. I saw what you did to her. And that other poor creature, whatever you did to him! You're a monster! A horrible monster!"

She brings her knee to my gut and breaks away, arms flailing at her sides.

"Eyelet, *please* . . ." I sprint after her, clearing the Vapour-laced mist from my path. I strip the gloves from my hands and place them over my nose like a mask. "Eyelet?" I shout, seeing just the ruffles of her skirts bobbing through the mist. "Please, Eyelet, let me explain!"

She ignores me, racing deeper and deeper into the forest. Vapours hang dangerously close to flooding over the ridge. I hear her cough, and my heart jags in my chest. I'm running out of time to convince her. I've got to make her understand. If we don't turn back soon, it'll be too late. She coughs again, and I lunge in that direction, pulling her down to the ground when I reach her, the two of us rolling to a stop in the dry grass.

"Let me *go*!" She pounds at my chest as I pull up onto my arms. "I'd rather die here alone in the Vapours than at the hands of your Wickedry." She arches her neck and spits in my face. I pull back, astonished. She can't mean this. She can't possibly believe what she's saying. How can she think so ill of me? What have I done?

Frustration has me catch her hard by the wrists. I force her arms to the grass. She winces at me like she's expecting to meet her death. "Listen to me!" I shake her. "You have to listen to me!" She stops struggling, her eyes watching the spit snaking down the side of my purple cheek. "My father killed himself! I had nothing to do with it! You have to believe me! I am not possessed with Wickedry!"

"Just as I'm to believe you never drugged me last evening?" Her eyes pinch tight. "You asked me to trust you last night, Urlick, and like a fool I did—"

"You were not a fool." My heart sinks. Iris is right, I should have told her. I should have told her everything long before now.

She wrenches herself to one side and I pull her back. "Please," I whisper. "Just listen. It was an accident! I had nothing to do with it. My father died the Night of the Great Illumination. The result of a bungled experiment. *His* experiment. I had nothing to do with it. I am not his *murderer*. I could never murder anyone."

"But you have no problem with mutilation, do you?"

I furrow my brow. "What are you talking about?"

"Iris! I saw what you did to her! How could you do such a thing? You cut the tongue from that poor girl's mouth—"

"No. That's not what happened—"

"Then what did?" Her neck juts toward me.

"Iris has been tongue-tied since birth. Her parents brought her to my father, desperate for his help. They begged him to try and fix her, so he tried. But then infection set in and threatened her life, and he had no choice but to remove her tongue." She makes a face. "There was no other way. You have to believe me—"

"Why should I? The man who lies about everything? Himself. His father. The source of the screams."

I pull back, stung by her venom.

She narrows her eyes, stares at me hard. "What's wrong? Didn't you think I was smart enough to put that together?"

"Eyelet, I'm sorry, but you have to believe me—"

"How am I to believe you now, with the lies you've been telling?"

I take a breath, not knowing how to fix this. Not capable of making things right. I've lost her. The only girl I ever believed could understand me.

"Is there anything else you'd care to lie to me about? Perhaps the armless man in the attic? Have you a story for him?"

"No," I say weakly. "No stories, just the truth, from here on in, I promise you." I bring my hand to my chest, crossing my heart with a finger.

She purses her lips, turns her head away.

The stench of the encroaching Vapours burns in my nostrils. I know she must be feeling their grip.

"He showed up at the door a few years ago," I explain to her as quickly as I can, "an escapee from a travelling freak show. He wore shackles around his ankles and a chain around his neck. He begged Iris and me to let him take refuge inside our house, just until his show master gave up his search for him and left town. When we did, he told us of his long journey through the woods, being hunted by dogs. How a friend who'd escaped with him was torn up by one. He shared how he'd been born without any arms from the shoulders down, and how his father, fearing he'd be of no use for farmwork, sold him to the freak master for a loaf of bread at the age of ten. Since that day, he'd been forced to perform three shows every day, receiving beatings with a whip if the crowds weren't big enough.

"Later that day, when the freak master came knocking, Iris stood by while I lied, telling him I'd found a dead body in the forest, and handed over his shackles and chains. He's lived in seclusion with us ever since. That's the honest truth, Eyelet. So help me God." I cross my heart again.

She blinks up at me, and I can tell she's considering what I've said. "And the girl," she finally says.

"She's a specimen. Donated by your precious *Academy* to my father's lab for the purpose of experimental surgery. She arrived at two and a half. My father was to take apart her brain in an effort to isolate the root cause of her mental affliction, in the name of science, without even so much as a drop of anesthetic." Eyelet swallows. "But as cruel as my father was, he couldn't bring himself to do it."

A look of terror floods Eyelet's ochre eyes.

"After his death, when the Academy came knocking, Iris and I again lied. We told the headmaster she died in surgery years ago and produced a fake death certificate my father had forged for just such an occasion."

"Does she have a name? The girl, I mean?"

"Yes. Cordelia."

"And the man?"

"Ernest. But he prefers to go by his old stage name, Crazy Legs. On account of the fact he can do most anything with his toes that normal people can only do with their hands." She almost laughs. "As for the masks, you're right: I *have* been masquerading as my father since his death. But I assure you it was for good reason. In the mask, I can walk the streets of Gears freely, collect his pension, sell our wares, and pay the bills. Without it, I would be treated like a leper, possibly even jailed, a constant source of ridicule. By masquerading as my dead father, I've been able to keep a roof over our heads and food in our stomachs. Otherwise, we'd surely have perished by now. It's not something I wanted to do, but rather something I had to do. A choice I had to make."

I take Eyelet by the chin and stare deep into her eyes. "You're right. I have been telling a great many lies to a great many people. But I hope you can see now, it was all for good reason."

She stares at me, tears in her eyes. A warm smile bridges her lips, but she quickly bites it away. "And the machine. Why did you lie about the machine?"

I suck in a breath and hold it, my mind a muddle of worry. I can trust her. I can. I must. I let out the breath and begin. "You're right, I did steal a machine from a warehouse in Gears. And I've hidden it from you all this time. But I did so in an attempt to help the people you've discovered, not to hurt them. You must believe me. I thought if only I could locate my father's machine, I could use it to right what was wrong with them—"

"*Your* father's machine?" Eyelet's eyes light like flares. She sucks in a trembling breath.

"That's right. The one he was experimenting with just before his death."

"His death?"

Her pulse quickens inside my fists.

"That is not your father's machine." Her voice is a whisper. "It's *my* father's."

"What?"

"The Illuminator? It was my father's last invention. The machine you stole from the warehouse that day. My father built it. I, too, sought to find it. That's why I commandeered a ride in your carriage that day."

I pull back, a million arguments running in my head as she bites her lip. Her eyes look so convincing as she continues. "He built the machine for a specific reason"—she hesitates, as if something catches in her throat—"but for some reason he sold it instead." Her eyes shine with tears. "He, too, died the Night of the Great Illumination. Somewhere here in the Follies, on a business mission he never returned from. Clearly, whomever my father sold the machine to sold it to yours. Or perhaps my father sold it directly to him."

"Either way," I start, "someone from the Academy came and confiscated it the afternoon of the Night of the Great Illumination. He claimed to work for the Academy, insisted he'd been ordered to store the machine until further notice. He produced official papers from his pocket. Iris and I let him in, and he hauled it away. We were to tell my father, but he died that night."

The wind picks up at my back. I turn and see the Vapours cresting on the ridge, stalking rattler-like through the forest toward us, their metallic stench a brazen intruder.

Eyelet's hair spirals about her shoulders. Her arms flinch at her sides.

I jump to my feet. "The Vapours," I say. "They're cresting. We're running out of time." I offer her my hand.

She hesitates. Her gaze darts between the forest and me. Vapours spill down the hillside, thick and black as oil.

"Please, Eyelet," I shout over the howl of the wind. "Please, take my hand."

"It's no use, we'll never get there." She gasps.

"We will," I say, taking her chin in my hand. "How much do you trust me?" I say.

Twenty-Five

Eyelet

As much as the stars and the moon and the pesky ol' sun . . .

I sink my hand in Urlick's. We run. Like I've never run before, my feet barely touching the ground, my body propelled solely by Urlick's determined force.

The Vapours rush down over the escarpment in an angry wave, swallowing trees and rocks and hillside behind us like the grim reaper wielding his scythe of death. My head twists back and forth, gauging its distance from us. Terror swamps my soul as its force closes in.

"Don't look back!" Urlick hollers to me. "Think only of the door on the Compound and getting through it!"

I twist my head back around and squint to focus. "I don't see it! I can't see it!" I panic.

"Neither can I! You just need to believe it's there!"

He tugs my arm, and I stumble along beside him, believing I see it, imagining that the door to safety lurks just beyond the next patch of trolling fog, battling against the demons in my mind that say otherwise, Vapours roaring up behind us.

The black rock that forms the escarpment at the back of the Compound finally appears. Jagged pieces of its face pierce the cloud cover, and my heart swells with hope. Dark smoke roils up from the bottomless pit that lies between the rock and the Compound's edge. The one I peered into from my bedroom window the night Pan discovered me.

Pan. Where is she now?

I wrench my head around, catching a glimpse of the overhanging turret through the thick, black, rising smoke of the pit. "Where are we going?" I shout. "This is not the front!"

"That's right!" Urlick shouts, yanking at my hesitating hand.

"But there is nothing past the rock. I've seen it. It just drops off. The turrets, they stand half over the edge of a bottomless pit. If we continue this way, we're sure to fall into it!"

"Embers," he corrects me.

"What?"

"It's called Embers, not a pit."

"Embers!" I gasp. "As in proverbial Hell?"

"That's the one." He turns to me. "But there's nothing proverbial about it."

My feet instinctively slow.

The steam map was right. The Compound not only sits at the very edge of the Earth, but hovers over the very end of existence. No wonder Urlick told me there was nothing beyond his home but death. His home teeters over the threshold to Hell. No wonder the Commonwealth chose *here* to dispose of their discards. Could there be a more fitting place?

But the map. It claimed the Follies used to be part of the Commonwealth. How could that be? My legs seize at the thought. Urlick hauls me forward.

"Don't worry." He squeezes my hand. "I've no intention of diving in."

"Then how—?"

He turns to me, eyes like beams of red hope in an otherwise blackening world. "How much do you trust me?"

My heart warms in my chest.

We push on, and I begin to choke. My vision blurs. My head starts to spin.

"Here!" Urlick reaches up, tearing the sleeve from his shirt. "Cover your nose and mouth with this." I press his sleeve to my face and try to keep running, my legs like rubber beneath me, clutching his bare arm with my other hand, the Vapours gaining on us like an angry, roaring tidal wave.

Urlick turns and scoops me up into his arms, then speeds through the trees. I have no idea how he knows where he's going. One misstep and our lives could end. His heart lurches in time with my own. I cling to him, staring over his shoulder at the rolling froth that threatens to devour us, praying the pit doesn't swallow us first. How has he survived in such a place all these years? Perched on the very doorstep of evil, on the very hearth of Hell.

I close my eyes, overcome by dizziness, my eyes no longer feeling like they're my own, instantly haunted by images of my mother's face as she hangs in the gallows, my father as he lies asphyxiated on the road. Does a similar fate await me? Will I die here, now, with Urlick?

The Vapours pick up speed as Urlick surges forward, bidding me to hang on as tight as I can. I feel the muscles in his legs strain to carry me. Breath chugs from his lungs. I close my eyes and beg the world to let us make it. Moments later Urlick slows and drops me to my feet.

"Where are we?" I gasp, turning my head.

"The Compound." He falls, breathless, against a door.

"It has a back door?"

"Two, actually." He palms the centre of my back, pressing me toward him. "Be careful." He flips his chin. "Don't want to step back too far."

I turn to see the heels of my boots straddling the lip of the pit. Black steam rises at my back. One false move and I'll go over. I swallow and lean toward Urlick, steadying myself against his chest, not caring if it's improper.

He curses, his arms around me, as he tries to unlock the door.

Vapours spiral toward us, deathly black. We're running out of time.

"What's the matter?"

"I don't know. It won't open." He slams his fist against the door. "Blast it! The seal!" he remembers. "I told Iris not to break the seal until my return!"

"What do we do now?" My lips tremble.

"Iris knows we're out here," Urlick says. "She wouldn't give up on us that easily. We'll just have to get her attention somehow!" He turns and pounds at the door, the two of us screaming, kicking it with the toes of our boots.

The squeeze of the Vapours pinches my lungs and hitches my breath. I feel lightheaded again, woozy. I bend at the knees, melting down Urlick's side. He rescues me, his hands clasped tightly about my waist. "I don't think she's coming," he whispers. "We're running out of time."

"She's coming," I say, refusing to give up faith. I let my head fall to his shoulder, burying my face in his neck, fighting to maintain my thoughts against the Vapours' encroaching breath.

At first I'm convinced it's a dream. Iris's moon-round face in the porthole window of the door, eyes wide with panic. But it's not, it's really her. A couple of clanks and bangs and a shoulder later, the door finally flies open, exhaling a rush of cleansing, salty steam. Urlick launches me through the doorway, the two of us coughing just as the Vapours rush the gates. "The *seal*!" he screams to Iris as he slams the door and activates the lock.

My legs give way and I crumple to the floor, feeling the cleansing steam working hard to pull the Vapours' poison from my lungs, as Iris runs at the panel. The alarm squeals. The Guardian lights glow. The Vapours rush the side of the Compound, causing the floor to quake, colliding with the Guardian in a mighty explosion that curls them up and away from the door.

"Don't worry," Urlick shouts. "It'll settle down in a moment." He flips a look out the window. "Or it won't." He bends. "You okay?"

"Mm-huh," I gasp. "And you?"

"I've been better." He grins, still heaving in breaths. "But better now we're on this side of the door." He looks to me, eyes shining like red stars in the night sky, and I can't help but think how wonderful they are.

"You." He stands, reeling Iris in tight to his chest, planting a big fat kiss on her forehead. "Thank God for you!"

Iris pushes him off, disgusted, turning red as her dress.

"Can you stand?" He reaches out for me. "If you can, I'd like to show you something."

I reach up, and he pulls me to my feet. I still feel wobbly, but my eyes have finally landed. I'm no longer as woozy as I once was, though my lungs still burn a bit.

"Get the others and meet us in the kitchen, will you?" he tells Iris.

Her eyes grow big as teacups.

"It's all right," he assures her. "Eyelet knows. I've told her everything."

An expression of unmistakable relief comes over Iris's face, followed by her first genuine smile.

"We'll meet you upstairs in a bit," he says, grabbing me by the hand. "Come on," he says, skipping forward. "I've got a surprise for you."

"I'm not sure I'm ready for more surprises from you." I stumble along behind him up the dark tunnel corridor, toward his lab. He stops, pulls me close, his eyes soft in the torchlight. "I doubt this one will surprise you." He smiles.

I'd like to stay in this moment, but he bounces away, linked to me only by the fingers of our threaded hands. Seconds later we arrive at the scaffold stairs that lead to his laboratory.

*

He trips the stairs, and they begin to descend noisily.

"It can't be possibly be down here—I looked everywhere," I say.

"Oh, not everywhere." He grins. "But you were close."

"How do you know?"

"A certain Bertie told me."

"Who?"

"Bertie"—he flips his chin—"my hydrocycle."

"You've given your cycle a name?"

"What of it?" He tugs his waistcoat.

"Nothing."

I bring a hand to my mouth to hide the giggle that bubbles up inside of me as the stairs rattle down to rest on the floor.

Jumping from the treads, he pulls me to the left, around a corner to the back of the room, toward the curtain. "Traitor," I say as we pass the hydrocycle. It rumbles beneath its tarp.

"You stay here," Urlick says, twirling me around. "And close your eyes. Tight."

"I thought the plan was no more keeping secrets."

"No more secrets, I promise." He pushes a finger to my lips. "But I never said anything about surprises."

Reluctantly, I close my eyes.

His breath pulses a warm trail across the hollow of my neck, he stands so close. My skin flares.

"When I drop the drape, you may open your eyes," he whispers.

"How will I know when you've dropped it if I'm not allowed to look?"

"Your ears still work, don't they?" His breathy voice sends a chill down my spine, prickling the hairs on my arms. I bite my lip; my pulse races at the excitement welling up inside me.

He turns and sashays across the room, and I envision his lithe and gentle movement. I hear his hand run down the curtain, and the hairs on my neck pull to attention.

"Don't peek, now."

"I'm not."

His head ducks out from behind the curtain, red velvet crushed up around his chin.

"I can see you peeking."

Caught, I pinch my eyes shut.

"Are you ready?"

"Ready."

His shoes clatter across the floor behind the curtain and then, with the rip of a cord, the curtains drop, plopping into a puddle on the floor. My eyes spring open as behind it stands . . .

Absolutely nothing.

"Is this a joke?" My hands land on my hips.

He smirks and trips a button on a cord in his hand. A spin of turbines gives way to a creak of gears, and the pattern in the floor breaks apart, shifting and moving into a series of plates. Slowly they shuffle to one side or the other, exposing a giant, dark hole. Drawing back, the plates disappear one by one beneath the floor. In their place, a platform rises up. On top of the platform sits the Illuminator, shimmering in the aether light of the room.

I gasp at its appearance, drawing my hands to my face. Tears press at my lids. The glass-and-wood cabinet housing the giant spinning glass disks; the snaggled wires that run from the cabinet to the mighty glass Crookes tube, resting in its brass stand next to it. I stare up at all the pieces of the machine, remembering the path of the lightning as it jumped from the wires to the long needle-nose tip of the Crookes tube in its stand. The mighty flash as the arc hit the glass. The smell of the wires as they crackled and sizzled. The whir of the glass disks as they spun inside the cabinet with such force, I swore they'd break loose.

I step toward it, remembering the acrid smell of my father's laboratory as we descended the stairs. The bite of the cold metal gurney against my back. The spiders. There were so many spiders. The sound of the wires as they crackled and popped. The sizzle of the current jumping between the big brass conductor bars mounted to the front. How afraid I was that I'd be electrocuted.

"Well?" Urlick's hands fly up from his sides, the Illuminator towering at his back. "Is it as you remember?"

I don't answer; I'm still deep in thought.

"Is this the machine your father invented? The one you were talking about?"

My father's words come rushing back to me from that day long ago in his lab. The two of us, alone, preparing to shoot a picture of me. The only one he ever took.

You must hold completely still, do you understand? You can hold still for me, can't you?" He smiled, and I remember the fear in his eyes.

I must have nodded with mine, because the next thing I remember he was turning the crank. The noise of it made my innards squirm. The more he turned it, the closer the needle-nosed tip of the Crookes tube came to my head, closing in on me like the stinger of a bee. "Must I smile?" I remember asking as his shoes whisked away, falling silent at the back of the machine.

"No, darling," he said. "Just hold perfectly still."

And I did. And that's when the walls came alive with green lightning streaks, crawling the walls of his laboratory like the legs of a hundred erratic green spiders. I remember wanting to cry.

Giant glass plates then began to whirl inside cabinets. Friction vibrated the room. Wires popped. Circuits crackled. The smell of burnt sulfur shifted to that of burning bread.

"Do you smell that?" I remember asking my father.

"Smell what?" Father shouted over the chaos.

"The bread," I shouted back. "You're burning it."

It was the first time I remember connecting the smell of burning bread with the feeling of the silver rising in my veins. After that, it would become my warning sign. My only signal.

But my father knew. He fell on the wheel, cranking it ever faster until the ominous green glow filled the room. Arcs of green lightning sliced the walls and darted across the ceiling, and then—there was a *flash*. A plume of light so bright it blinded me, illuminating even the darkness I'd been dragged into by the episode I'd fallen under.

"Well, is it?" Urlick interrupts my reverie.

"Yes," I finally say. I step forward, running a hand over its lens. "But it seems to have shrunk since I saw it last."

Urlick laughs.

"You know how things are, when you're a child you seem to remember things bigger than they really are." I judge it to be about twice my five-foot-five height. I suppose to a child of five years, maybe six, that would seem large.

"For some reason I thought you'd be happier to see this." He scowls, his enthusiasm reduced now to a smouldering frown.

"I am," I say, trying to reassure him. "I'm delighted, really." But really, I'm not. I circle the machine, running my fingers over the Crookes tube, emotions running hot inside me. All my life I've longed for this moment, believing if only I could unearth my father's machine, I'd at last have the chance at a normal life. But now, as I stand in the presence of it, a part of me is afraid to have found it. What if it doesn't work? What if it doesn't cure me? What then? What if it's all just been a lie? Without the dream of the Illuminator curing me, I have nothing left. No other way to fix myself.

It has to work.

"You all right?" Urlick steps toward me.

"I'm fine," I lie, then change the subject. "I just realized I've never asked: what exactly do you intend to do with the machine?"

He drops his gaze. "I intend to fix things with it."

"Like what?"

"Like *me*." He scowls.

"I beg your pardon?" I blink, not believing what I'm hearing. What exactly does he mean by *fixing* him?

"Don't play stupid with me. You know exactly what I intend to do."

And then it hits me . . . I'd been so focused on my own needs, I'd forgotten to look outside myself. The carny's words that day at the carnival flood over me, reciting the Illuminator's list of other "uses." *Removes scars, pits, blemishes. Unsightly birthmarks, consider them zapped.* He's not thinking. He can't be thinking of exposing himself to the light for *that*.

"Tell me you're not serious," I gasp aloud.

Urlick throws me a dark look. "Would you deny me the opportunity to rid myself of these *hideous* marks, the chance to live a normal life?"

"No, that's not it—"

"*How dare you*, knowing full well all the things the machine can do!" He glares at me through slatted eyes.

"But that's just it, it can't. It's a lie—"

"How dare you say such a thing! You'd rather I remain a freak, unable to face the world without persecution?"

"No, of course not!" I shake my head. Then shake it again, horrified at the thought of confirming him as a freak. "That's not it. It's none of that!"

I stand there gasping, staring, not knowing how to say I like him the way he is. I've never thought of Urlick needing to be *fixed* before now. I'd grown to think of him as perfect.

"I should have known you wouldn't understand." He storms past me, then turns back. "How could you? Perfect as you are!"

My lips part. If only he knew.

I should tell him, I should let him know the truth. But I can't. "Wait!" I chase after him, my hand falling softly on his back.

He hesitates, turning to face me, pink eyes glistening.

"Those things they say the machine can do. I'm not sure they're true. They are not the reason my father built it—"

"Then what is?"

I turn away, a million thoughts running through my head. If I tell him the reason, I'll have to explain my secret. And if I do, there's a chance he'll think me Mad. "My father designed it to look inside of things" is all I say. "Not to zap things with."

"How do you know that?" he snaps. His eyes are mean.

"I just do. All those other claims were made by the carnival carnies who were paid to peddle the prototype."

"What?"

"Mini-Illuminators. Prototypes. My father was commissioned by the Academy to make a dozen of them, to be sold to the public. For fund-raising purposes. It was the brainchild of a professor at the Academy named Smrt. The idea was to raise funds for cathode-ray research and bring awareness of its wonders to the community. My father was against the idea. But he lost out. In the end, the prototypes were sold, as well as the main machine."

Urlick drops his head.

"There is no solid science to back the carnies' claims, Urlick. There never was. It was all just a farce to raise money."

"You're lying." His chin snaps up. "You just don't want to see me cured!"

"Why would I do such a thing?"

His lip quivers as he considers it a moment.

I continue, gently. "I'm only telling you this because I don't want to see you hurt."

"What happened to the prototypes?" he snaps. "Where are they now?"

"I don't know for sure. Why?"

"Then how do you know they're not capable of doing what they said they did?"

I go to speak, then shut my mouth.

"Don't you see?" His voice shakes. "This machine is my only hope."

His words cut deep into my skin, oozing like blood into my soul. I know what it is to hold out such hope. More than he will ever know.

"Does it work?" I ask.

"No. I can't seem to get it to run. I've tried everything. It's as if something's missing." He turns and strokes the side of the cabinet.

"You're right. Something *is* missing." I walk past him to the front of the machine, tapping the pewter lid of one of the glass containers perched on either side of the cabinet. "You've no silver dust." I pluck the container from its perch and toss it to him. "*This* should not be empty. And neither should this." I tap the second one. "Without these, nothing works. That much I know. You need fairy petrol or your plans are nixed."

"Fairy petrol?"

"Yes, that's what my father called it. The powder that goes inside of these. When the powder's stimulated, an arc jumps between those two brass bolts mounted on either side of the front of the frame"—I point to them—"creating a charge like a lightning bolt that then jumps to that Crookes tube over there." He looks. "Without a Crookes tube to jump to, the whole thing's euchred. And without silver powder, you can't even get started."

"How would you know?" His brows arch. I know he knows I have more to share. "You've witnessed this?" he pushes.

I swallow, realizing my mistake. I must answer him in a way that doesn't broach the truth. Which I'm not yet prepared to share.

"Sort of," I hedge, biting my lip as I think. "I saw prototypes demonstrated at a carnival once," I blurt. "I would think their working principles are the same, wouldn't you?" His brows furrow. "It was actually quite frightening." I keep talking, hoping to divert his suspicions. "Everything within twenty metres of the machine glowed an eerie shade of green. Even Mrs. Benson, the carny's assistant, glowed green—and her eyes glowed red."

"Really?" His brows perch.

"Yes, even after the picture was taken. She didn't stop glowing for quite some time."

I see the muscles at the sides of his jaw churn furiously. I'm not sure he believes me. "This so-called fairy petrol, where do we get some?"

"That's just it, I don't know."

He throws me a look.

"Fairy petrol's just what my father and I called it. I don't know its real name."

"Fantastic." He turns his back again. "That ought to be easy to order at the mercantile. One sack of fairy petrol, please." He reaches out, replacing the canister on its perch. "I was a fool to think I could ever get this thing up and running." He runs a frustrated hand over the white dash in his hair. White on white—such a strange combination. "You're sure you've no idea?" He looks to me.

"Well, there is one place we could look for an answer." I swallow.

"Go on."

"But I'd have to be able to trust you, implicitly."

"And you don't, yet?" His brows rise.

"I mean, I'd have to know we were in this together. That whatever happens, we'd both be responsible for it. And you'd have to promise me that if the safety of either one of us were in jeopardy, we'd stop what we were doing immediately. And that we won't use my father's science for other than what was intended."

"But that doesn't include—" He looks worried.

"With the exception of trying to remove the marks from your face, but no other."

He brightens.

"Have we a deal?"

Urlick moves toward me, placing his hand in mine and giving it a firm shake. "Deal," he says.

"My father. He kept journals. Scientific ones. Detailed entries of the work he did with this machine. Whatever fairy petrol is, it's sure to be outlined inside his journal. That, and specific instructions on how to operate it."

"Where are these journals?"

"Well, that's the tricky bit." I bite my lip and stare at my shoes. "Somewhere back at the Academy."

"Somewhere?" His brows rise.

"Yes. I'm afraid I don't know where, but if you're willing to go back with me to Brethren, perhaps together—"

Urlick pulls me in, hugging me like he did Iris earlier, minus the kiss. "We'll leave as soon as the Vapours retreat."

Twenty-Six

Eyelet

"Excuse me, sir."

Urlick tosses me aside, startled by the new voice in the room. At the side of the curtain stands the man with no arms, only legs—the one from the tunnel off Urlick's father's room.

I can't help it: I gasp at the sight of him.

"Sorry, mum, din' mean to intrude." He tips his head. His eyes are painfully crossed. "It's Miss Iris." He rolls his toes together. "She's asked me to come down 'ere 'n fetch yuhs. Says to tell yuh the soup's gettin' cold." His *S*'s whistle through the spaces in his rotted teeth.

"Eyelet, this is Crazy Legs. Crazy Legs, this is Eyelet." Urlick's hand sweeps between us both. "I'd hoped for you to meet in the kitchen, but—"

"Pleased t' meet yuh, mum." Crazy Legs bows his head to me, bringing a dramatic hand—*foot*—to his chest, as if I were royalty, then holds a foot in the air for me to shake like a hand.

My heart skips a beat. I flush, not wanting to take it, then finally accept, warily, feeling horridly guilty. It's warm and dry, much like a hand, though I don't know what else I was expecting. His grip is mighty, nothing at all like Flossie's floppy palm. It almost makes me laugh. "Pleased to meet you," I say with a shiver, marveling at how balanced he is, standing on only one leg.

"Oh, the pleasure's all mine, believe me, mum." He grins, a dubious twinkle in his eye. "Yuh can call me C.L.," he adds. "All me friends do."

I can't help myself: I laugh just a little.

He grins again, and I grin, too. "I feel just terrible about running away from you earlier."

"Nonsense, mum." He waves my words away. "Not like it hasn't happened before. Oh, and"—he nods toward the staircase—"Cordelia says to tell yuh she's right sorry for scaring yuh away. She feels right badly about it, mum."

Something stirs on the stairs, like a mouse, only bigger. My eyes track the sound. A little girl appears from behind the chain rail, her eyes as round and blue as planets. Long scarlet hair falls in crisp curls down to her hips. It's the girl from the hidden room, the one who suffered an episode. She's dressed all in white, like an angel, an emerald bow in her hair. She blinks innocently, looking up at Urlick like she's waiting for permission to join us.

"Hello, *Cordeeeelia*," he says, bending his head.

The child smiles but says nothing.

"This is Eyelet. From this morning."

Her fingers move in a tiny wave.

"Is there something you wanted to tell her?"

Cordelia blinks.

"Come on over here, then." Urlick motions, but the child doesn't move. "It's all right. She won't bite. I promise."

Cordelia sucks on her lip a moment, then bounds across the room, all legs and arms like a brand new puppy, stopping just short of colliding with me. She slings her arms behind her back, though it looks like she'd rather throw them around my waist in a hug, and stares up at me with big round eyes. She's a tiny waif of a thing, with sunken cheeks and dark circles under her eyes. How long, I wonder, has she suffered from my same affliction, with no mother to comfort her, to help her cope with the ordeal?

"I'm sorry," she whispers in the thinnest, sweetest voice. "I don't mean to scare people."

My heart melts. I bend toward her. "There's no need to be sorry." I run my hand through her hair. "Such a pretty bow." She grins. "And what's this you're wearing?" I touch the locket she wears around her neck. Silver in colour, with an angel's wing etched into the front of it. "A gift from a secret admirer?" I tease.

"No," she giggles. "It's Iris's. It used to be her sister's."

"Her sister's?" I look to Urlick.

He drops his chin. "Iris had a twin," he says. "Her name was Ida. She passed away last spring."

"I'm so sorry." My hand floats to my chest.

"Don't be. It happens to everyone, eventually," Cordelia says matter-of-factly, followed by a broad grin.

I look back at Urlick, a lump in my throat. "Yes, I suppose it does, doesn't it?"

"She was born with spina bifida," Urlick continues. "From which she suffered terribly. Her passing was something of a blessing in disguise."

"Oh, I see."

"She spent most of her time in her chair," Cordelia says, opening the locket, flashing a photograph of her my way. Ida's features are those of a motion-picture star.

"She was beautiful," I say, ashamed at the shock in my voice. "Could she speak?"

"Aye." C.L. laughs. "Quite the chatterbox, that one. Good day if yuh could get a word in edgewise." He winks.

"Iris must miss her terribly," I say.

"Oh, yes, mum," C.L. speaks up. "We all do." His grin fades.

Urlick lowers his head and twists his hands together. I sense his pain without even seeing his face. Ida must have been very special to all of them.

"Iris is going to be upset if we spoil her soup," Cordelia sings, breaking the mood. "It's not half as good when it's cold." She reaches up and takes me by the hand. My heart beats warmer in my chest.

I grin and squeeze her fingers in mine, and we head for the stairs, my life richer than it was when I woke this morning.

Twenty-Seven

Eyelet

We pop through the back door of the kitchen like corks from bubbly bottles of champagne. But our happy mood is short-lived. The Vapours bear down on the house even harder than before. The noise is enough to stop your heart. No rain. No lightning. Just furious wind. Moaning and clashing against the sides of the Compound like incarcerated luna-tics against the bars of their pen.

Nothing could have prepared me for this . . . this spiraling hur-ricane of all-consuming death. I never could have imagined anything so raw, so powerful, so unstoppable—it makes no sense. It's horribly unnerving the way the winds come from all directions at once, slam-ming different sides of the Compound. There's no pattern to their assault. It's random. We can't prepare ourselves.

Everything's so dark and seamless; not even a slice of light to take the edge off the terror. It's as though the house has been wrapped in the undertaker's shroud. Smothered in it, really.

I feel my way along the chairs into the centre of the kitchen, shuddering at the thought. The blackened window over the sink that once seemed so forbidding is a welcome sight to me now.

I turn my face to it, staring through the black abyss of the room, and hug myself, imagining the giant booms at the edge of Brethren working furiously to protect its people. Growing thick with toxic muck as they hold back the destructive fumes of the Vapours from all those lucky enough to live behind them. My heart aches to be back in Brethren, safe within our apartment, held tight in the security of my mother's arms. Her graceful fingers looping through my hair the way they used to when she'd soothe me. The warmth of her eyes. The breadth of her smile. The creamy pattern of her voice as she'd comfort me.

I should have said more often how much I loved her. I should have told her how much she meant to me. It's a horrible thing when you lose the chance to express your love, and you realize how much time you wasted.

Urlick strikes a match, and I jump at the scratch. He reaches up, steadies the aether chandelier in the centre of the room, and lights it for the third time. He lets it go and it swings, flickering, slowly igniting into a weak, uncertain glow.

"You all right?" He moves toward me, his eyes wide and sympathetic. "I know it's hard to stay calm the first time."

The winds pick up, rushing the walls, rattling the dark window in its pane. I'm somewhat glad I can't really see what's going on out there.

"How long does this insanity last?" I shout, cupping my ears to block out the roar.

"Hard to tell! It could last a week, or it could be two months!"

An explosion rocks the hillside, jolting the floor beneath us, and I'm dropped to a knee. Urlick steadies himself on the back of a chair.

"Two months of this?" I shout as he helps me up. I grab for the table as another ripple shimmies the footings of the house. The aether chandelier sputters and spits, then slowly flickers out.

"Two months is better than two years, isn't it?" Urlick grins, striking a match and lighting it again. His face glows ghostlike in contrast to the rest of the dark room. The sight of it makes me shiver. "They say the very first time the Vapour storm hit, it lasted two years."

"Two years!" I swallow, bringing a hand to my chest. "I can't fathom tolerating this madness *that* long."

Iris shifts to the centre of the room, looking startled, her eyes two giant agates bursting from their lids. I don't think I've ever seen Iris so far off her game before. Not even when I nearly lopped off her thumb.

She tries to serve the soup with a trembling hand, her head cranking back and forth, monitoring the activity beyond the blackened window. The look on her face implies she senses something even worse is about to happen.

"What's the matter?" I say. And then it happens. Another explosion hits, and Iris launches the soup. It douses out the swinging chandelier; the lamp's dripping crystal droplets slap hard against the ceiling. Iris's gaze snaps up, chin wagging.

"Well, at least now we don't have to worry about it getting cold," Cordelia shouts, gripping the table.

"Don't worry, mum, by the second day yuh'll be used to it," C.L. assures me, reading the expression on my face.

"Or, if you're like Iris, you never will," Cordelia chirps. C.L. scowls down at her. "Well, it's true," she defends herself.

Something flares on the hillside. The first streak of light we've seen through the window in hours. A shot of steam follows, travelling straight up into the air. Iris's near-empty soup pot leaps from the stove to the floor.

A pair of hands hits the window and my head snaps around. First one pair. Then others follow.

"What is that?" I reach for Urlick.

"The Infirmed." He pulls me close. "They've scaled the rock. They're trying to get in."

"But they can't, can they?"

"The Guardian's activated. We should be safe—"

"Should?"

Another pair of hands hits the windows. Nails claw at the glass. Iris screams, burying her head in her arms.

"They're circling the Compound." Urlick leaves me and dashes across the room. "As long as the light stays on"—he checks the Guardian—"we're fine."

"And them?" The room fills with the sounds of nails and slaps and screams. Iris lets out a gruesome wail. I throw my hands over my ears to drown out the sound, willing them away. "They won't survive it, will they?"

"Some don't. Some do," Urlick says, returning to my side. I reach for him, my fists full of his biceps. His wide hands fall warm across my ribs.

"How?" I pull back. "How could anyone survive this?"

"No one knows, exactly." Urlick pulls me back. "They're known as the Turned. The ones that survive. They emerge from the fog at the end of the storm, like forgotten ghosts on the tails of the Vapours. Forever genetically altered. It is *they* we fear the most, *they* we designed the door locks and the Guardian system to keep out. *They* who are doomed to spend eternity feeding off others' souls."

"Souls?" The word escapes my mouth before I even know I've said it. I see the pit beyond the footing of the Compound in my mind.

"Yes. Once turned, they are transformed into Vapour-like, wandering, lackwit souls, camouflaged by the rolling cloud cover. Cannibalistic killers on a never-ending quest to suck out the brains of the living, in an attempt to replenish their damaged minds. They feed off the Infirmed and the criminals dumped in the woods, but they'll feed on others, too, if they cross their path. Some believe the officials of Brethren intentionally discard the dregs of their society here, to keep them from wandering into the city to feed. That way, the Turned remain a threat only to those who live in the woods. In the annexed part of the Commonwealth."

My eyes shoot to the map in the study. He must know more about it than he's let on. I pull back, staring up at him wide-eyed, my heart pounding in my throat. "And the Turned, how long do they live?"

"Forever." I swallow. "That's why we don't dare break the seal of the Compound until well after the Vapours have retreated. Until we hear the whistle of a steamplough delivering new Infirmed and criminals to bait the woods. No one must leave the Compound until the Turned have had a chance to feed, or we risk becoming their dinner." He lifts my chin and stares into my eyes. "That's why I was so intent on you following the rules."

I lay my head on his chest, breath heaving, thinking how close I came to risking it all when I ran away.

"What do they look like? How do you know they're there?"

"Some say they look like mist. Others describe them as smoke. Some claim to have seen their faces, while others say it's only a mirage."

The winds pick up, stripping the clinging hands from the window-sills. I wince at the sound of their screams as they fall away. I cling to Urlick, bones trembling inside my skin, considering myself lucky to be alive.

"What do you say we try to take our minds off of things?" Urlick says, raising my chin.

"How on earth are we going to do that?"

"We dance," Cordelia says, appearing between us.

"We do what?"

"She's right," Urlick says. The corners of his lips curl up into a smile. "There's nothing better than music to drown out the sound."

He crosses the room in two quick strides, his gait almost as giddy as Cordelia's laughter. "And to lift the spirits."

He presses a button on the wall, unveiling a secret alcove with a shelf holding a phonograph. He affixes the horn and cranks the handle on the side. Even Iris breaks a smile when he sets the needle down on the cylinder.

It crackles at first, then finally breaks into song. The soothing sounds of string instruments permeate the kitchen, softening the horror outside.

Urlick steps across the room as lyrics begin. The singer's voice spreads like sunshine across the room.

> *After the ball is over, after the break of morn,*
> *After the dancers' leaving, after the stars are gone,*
> *Many a heart is aching, if you could read them all—*
> *Many the hopes that have vanished, after the ball . . .*

C.L. reaches for Cordelia and they spin around in an animated circle, C.L. hopping, Cordelia shrieking. The excitement is high. C.L. lets Cordelia go and moves on to Iris, leaving Cordelia to giggle, launching Iris into an unsuspecting dip at the end of the verse. Iris fans him off, laughing, as she returns to her soup.

"Will you do me the honour?" Urlick appears beside me, his eyes glinting in the fractured aether light. He tucks his arm across his chest and bows to me, and I melt. Never before has anyone danced with me. Never before has anyone even asked.

"I can't," I say. "I don't know how."

Urlick smiles and nods his head. "Not to worry," he says. "I'll lead."

Another explosion rocks the floors, sending me toppling into his arms. His breath pulses down over me, twisting with the scent of sweet vanilla and his favourite peppermint tea. My favourite, too, now. He presses a firm hand to my back and we're away, his heart beating over mine. Together we spin in tight, safe circles, inside the storm, as if nothing else in the world existed.

Part Three

Part Three

Twenty-Eight

Eyelet

The Vapours lasted only a few days—thank goodness.

I don't think I could have stood more.

We wait another two weeks, until the day after the first steam-plough whistle fills the night, delivering a fresh batch of discarded humans—sacrificial lambs from Brethren dropped off as food for the Turned—before solidifying plans to head off for the Academy in search of my father's journals.

I can barely sleep that night, haunted by the ghostly voices of the Infirmed who survived the Vapours, howling up through the trees as they devour the brains of those who were cast from the steamplough. I shudder, imagining their shadowy bodies disguised by fog, attacking without warning. I turn my head and bury it in the pillow.

Urlick says once they feed, they'll be satisfied for a short while. Then, and only then, will it be safe for us to travel the woods. If we leave too soon, we risk becoming their dessert. Too late, and the Turned will be hungry again.

The thought of meeting up with a Turned terrifies me. But some-how we have to get back to Brethren. I trust Urlick to know what he's doing. He hasn't let me down yet.

Another moan belts through the trees. I sit up, unable to sleep, and pull my father's notebook from my boot. *Lumière.* I run my finger slowly over the writing on the front, then flip it open and scour the pages again. Finding nothing more than I did the first time I perused it. Page after page of detailed ledgers—compilations of scientific data, none of which I can interpret, nothing whatsoever about how to oper-ate the machine. Though I'm sure such a journal must exist somewhere back at the Academy. My father was a very meticulous man.

I sigh and curl the notebook enough to shove it back down the side of my boot, when my eyes catch on something peculiar. Along the edges of the pages of the notebook is a drawing, an etching done in ink. I release the curl and the drawing disappears. It's only visible when the pages are fanned. I curl them again and gasp at what I see. A building made of smooth, white walls surrounded by forest. A cone of light shines up from its highest point, far beyond the cloud cover. I have no idea what this is or what it means. I've never seen such a build-ing before. But I do know that my father drew it. It looks just like the rest of his sketches in the book. But why? Why is it here?

I pinch the pages into a tighter curl, and words appear in tiny print below the drawing:

Find me.

*

"We leave now," Urlick greets me on the stairs the next morning.

"Now?" I swallow, trying to look pulled together, a mess of worry and doubt roiling in my chest. "But I thought you said it'd be another day, maybe two, before the Vapours completely cleared."

"I did, but then the steamplough came last night; did you hear it?"

"I did." I swallow.

"You know what that means."

"I do."

"We'll just have to carry gas masks and risk it. I'd rather risk Vapour residue than Infirmed who've freshly Turned. How about you?"

I nod in agreement. "So, now, then? This very second?"

"Well, you can have breakfast first." Urlick grins. "Don't worry," he says and squeezes my hand. "You can trust me, remember."

I grin back.

He turns and trundles back down the stairs. "Iris, have we any eggs left?"

"I can do this." I follow him down the stairs, smoothing the sweat from my hands onto my skirts. "I can."

*

"Where do you think you're going with that? To battle?" I say, confiscating a strange-looking pair of tin snips from Urlick's grasp as we pack.

"Perhaps." He snatches them back. His midnight brow arches over a suspicious eye. I love the way he makes his face so animated.

He turns and stuffs the tin snips in his pack along with several more of his crazy-looking homemade gadgets.

"I thought you said we needed to travel light." I strain to pick up his pack. It clatters as I shake it. "Only pack the things we really need."

"Precisely," he says, adding a combination peeler/ice pick/switchblade to the mix.

I pull it out and wag it at him. "You'll never get past the Security Sorcerers with this."

"Security Sorcerers?"

"Edgar and Simon. The security-system ravens that watch over the gates of the Academy." I toss it aside. "They're trained to detect all weapons."

"Watch-guard ravens?" He almost laughs. "Who thought of that bit of silliness?"

I whirl around. "My father did."

"Oh." He bites his lip.

I glare at him as he deflates. "This would be much more useful, don't you think?" I say, stuffing a bedroll into the pack instead.

"You plan to sleep? On a major mission."

"We'll be gone for three days, won't we? Don't you?"

"Not while we're in the woods, that's for sure." He turns his back. "And that's at least forty hours' venture by cycle."

"Cycle?" I race around in front of him. "You plan to take the cycle through the woods to Brethren?"

"Well, we can't very well show up in Brethren by coach and expect to go unnoticed, now can we?" He stares at me. My face flushes red. "What's the matter?" He leans onto his pack. "You have a problem travelling by cycle?"

"No," I answer too quickly.

"Then why the panicked look on your face?"

"What panicked look?" I dab the perspiration from my brow, disguised behind a nonchalant wave. I hadn't planned on Urlick seeing the cycle again quite yet, let alone him using it for this purpose. I'm not sure we should rely on it to function properly on such a dangerous mission, but I don't know how to say it. Good Lord, why must I always meddle in things? I turn heel and head for the pantry, wringing my hands, hoping he'll drop the subject.

"Is there something I should know about the cycle?" He chases after me.

Boulders. It figures he wouldn't leave it alone. I throw myself around, chin up, trying to look confident. "Don't be ridiculous," I say, feeling the edge of my lips quiver. "What would I know of the cycle?"

Urlick lowers his brows and stalks even closer until our bellies nearly touch. "You're sure there's nothing you want to tell me? Considering where we're headed." He stares into my eyes.

I struggle to swallow, imagining the worst—the Vapours, the criminals, the ghostly Turned. "No," I rasp, my throat dry. "I'm confident everything will be fine."

Urlick's eyes narrow; he says nothing. A heavy silence hangs between us.

"Food would be a good thing to pack, don't you think?" I say. I turn my back on him and my attentions to the provisions, ignoring the well of doubt swelling in my mind. Perhaps I should say something? I should probably say something. No. It'll be fine. I reassure myself, stocking my pack with breads and canned meat.

Urlick steps closer, filling the space behind me. The light in the pantry grows dim.

I turn and scowl at his shadow blocking the doorway. "I can't really see." Urlick shifts, but he doesn't move.

Instead, he crowds ever closer, all but closing the gap between us. What on earth has got into him? The pantry is small enough without two bodies in it.

"I said, the light, it's not getting through." I point past his head.

"Don't worry about the light." Urlick grins.

His Cheshire Cat smile ignites a frazzled fire of nerves in my belly that slowly tingles throughout my limbs. Flustered, I turn and toss a final tin of deviled ham into my pack, then try to squeeze past him. Urlick steps to the side, blocking my path.

"Can I help you?" I say, growing more and more anxious, the hairs on the back of my neck prickling.

"I dunno"—he whispers—"maybe?" His lips sneer into an awkward sort of smile, and the fire in my belly surges. He pinches up even closer, his hot breath falling in lazy sweeps across my chest. What is this? What's he doing? Why is he acting so loony? He's never stood this close to me before, not even in the elevator shaft, when clearly there was a need to. Clearly, there is no need for him to do so now. I swallow.

"Are you all right?" I say, bosoms heaving.

"Never better." Urlick smirks. The heat between us grows unbearably delicious. Perspiration dots my brow.

Urlick reaches back and kicks the door shut, and my stomach lurches. My heart skips a beat. My skin tingles as though I've been brushed all over by a feather. I'm both queasy and exhilarated at the same time. He reaches for me, cradling my face in his hands, and my blood thickens, coursing like sugary syrup through my veins.

"What is this?" I say. "What do you think you're doing?"

"You talk too much, you know that?" he whispers.

"I wha—"

Palming my back, he pulls me to him. My breasts mash to his chest. He's going to kiss me. Kiss me. Me. My pulse flashes in my wrists.

Bending his head, he parts his boysenberry lips and I gasp, breathing in the sweet scent of the peppermint tea that lingers on his breath as he lowers his mouth toward mine . . .

And then, just as suddenly, his head snaps back.

Light blinds my eyes.

A frazzled Iris appears in the space over his shoulder, pantry door thrown open wide.

"What do you think you're *doing*?" Urlick shouts. He tosses me aside, embarrassed. I smooth out my clothes and primp my hair, hoping she can't see the colour of my cheeks, which I'm positive are the deepest shade of red.

Urlick tries to step from the pantry and Iris pushes him back, swinging shut the door and locking it.

"Iris!" Urlick rattles the handle. "Iris! What is this?" He peers at her sternly through the slats in the shutter door. She looks panicked.

A second later, the door pops back open just long enough for Iris to toss Urlick's pack in at our feet. She brings a finger to her mouth as if to say *Be quiet!* and then slams the door again and falls hard up against the front of it, concealing our whereabouts.

"I demand you hand her over!" Flossie's shrill voice barrels into the kitchen.

"What's *Flossie* doing here?" Urlick whispers.

"Iris!" Flossie's voice pelts off the kitchen walls. "There you are," she growls at the sight of her, back pinned to the pantry door. "Where are they?" she demands, grabbing at Iris. "Stop playing stupid! I know you know where they are!" She pinches Iris by the chin hard until she yelps.

Urlick's fists curl at his sides.

"Fine. If that's the way you want it, I'll go find them myself." Flossie releases Iris, shoving her across the kitchen. Iris falls backward, stumbling through the chairs around the table, but her eyes warn us not to move.

"Urlick!" Flossie's voice fills the corridor. "Urlick, where are you?"

Flossie's boots strike the floors in a circle, stomping through the kitchen, then into the study and back again. Iris follows. "I'm not leaving without her." Flossie's angry face reappears through the slats in the door. She turns on Iris. "You either hand her over, or I'll tear the place apart until I find her myself! The lying little tramp." She turns, stripping the gloves from her hands, pacing the floor like an angry tiger. "I knew something was wrong the second I laid eyes on that girl. I knew she was no cousin of Urlick's."

"What's she talking about?" Urlick whispers to me.

"I don't know." I shake my head.

"Half of Brethren is out looking for your little houseguest." Flossie pulls a poster from her jacket pocket and stuffs it up in Iris's face. "She's a fugitive, on the run! A sorceress! Accused of Wickedry!"

"Accused of what?" Urlick mouths.

"Her mother was hanged and dipped for the very same thing!"

Urlick gasps. Iris's eyes pop. She stares at me through the slats in the cupboard. I shake my head, hoping she can see me, my expression begging.

Please don't believe Flossie, Iris.

"They've even put a price on her pretty little head." Flossie points to the poster again. "Eight thousand junipers for her safe return."

"My *safe* return!" I straighten, shocked.

"You're a fugitive?" Urlick hisses. "Accused of Wickedry?"

Flossie's head spins like a cobra in our direction, and I freeze. My blood ripples cold beneath my skin.

Iris panics, hurling a plate at the floor. It shatters, drawing Flossie's attention back to her. "You lackwitted, graceless dolt!" Flossie shouts. "Clean that up at once!" Iris bends, and Flossie starts away. "I'll find Urlick on my own. *Urlick!*" She stalks past us into the back kitchen. I wince as her shadow flits past the pantry door. "Urlick! Is that you?" Her voice fades as she enters the hallway, buying us a small window of time.

"I thought you were in danger." Urlick turns on me. "I thought you needed my help when we met!"

"I was. I did. I do," I stammer. "I've been wrongly accused. You must believe me."

"Urlick!" Flossie's voice returns.

I cling to Urlick's arm. "How much do you trust me?" I say.

"Unhand me, you puddinghead!" Flossie shouts, shrugging a tugging Iris from her arm. She clatters through the hallway toward the kitchen, her heels a crackling storm. "I refuse to leave here without her!" She slaps at Iris. "She's wanted. And dangerous! Can't you see?"

She gawks in Iris's face. "Do you know what happens to people who harbour fugitives?" Iris gulps. "They go to jail right along with the wanted!"

Iris backs away.

"Now produce her at once, or pay the price." Flossie glowers mean. When Iris doesn't move, Flossie clucks her tongue. "Very well then, we'll just have to tear this place apart. Coachman!" Flossie shouts, flinging her head to the side. The coachman—henchman—appears.

I shudder at the sound of his breath exhaling so close to the pantry, his fingers curled into fists.

"Search the basement!" Flossie growls his way. "I'll head up the stairs. You're not to stop until one of us finds her. Have I made myself clear?" The henchman nods.

He starts away, Iris clawing at his sleeve. The coachman turns and knocks her to the floor. Urlick drives forward, nearly giving up our hiding place, but Iris's glare stops him, her eyes demanding he stay put.

I gasp as she scrambles to her feet and lunges after the coachman, throwing the door shut and triggering the lock behind, swinging back the pantry door. Wide-eyed, she shoos us out and stuffs us under the canning table, tossing a cloth over the top to hide us. She throws a stern finger to her lips and then she races away. C.L. appears seconds later.

"'Urry, sir." His head pops in under the cloth. "We've got to get y'outta 'ere whilst the gettin's good." With his foot he tosses each of our packs in under the table. "Grab those and let's be gone, shall we?"

"Wait!" Urlick grabs for his shirt as he turns. "But what about the hydrocycle?"

"Not to worry, sir, Bertie's all gassed up and ready to go. I took the liberty of preparing 'im as soon as I saw the carriage pull up. Loaded two extra canisters of hydrogen in yer saddlebag, too. All yuh need is a couple of gas masks and yer good to roll." He sprouts his familiar toothless grin. "Now come on, shall we? Iris can't distract them dunderheads forever." C.L. turns to go.

"I guess this is it, then." Urlick turns to me. He sucks in a tight breath, and I realize it's the first time I've ever seen him frightened.

"URLICK!" Flossie's voice crashes down the stairs, causing me to jump. I smack my head on the underside of the table. Urlick grabs my hand.

C.L. whisks us out from under and pushes us toward the door. "Yuhs two go on a'ead," he whispers. "I'll meet yuh at the cycle."

"What?" I blurt.

"I've just remembered something I've forgotten." He winks at me as if to calm my nerves, but it doesn't help.

Uuuuurlick! Flossie's voice rifles up the hallway.

My stomach tightens like a fist.

Urlick lunges forward, yanking me with him, snatching a couple of gas masks from the limbs of the hall tree. Together we bolt across the kitchen, the two of us disappearing seconds later behind the main cattle-car door.

*

Together we dash across the yard, using the fog as cover, making our way to where C.L. said the hydrocycle would be. "Bertie," Urlick gasps when we find him under the trees. "Oh, Bertie, our trusty steed." Urlick pats him on the handlebars. Bertie groans, then shudders. I swallow down the purge of sick that leaps from my stomach. I should tell Urlick what I've done, but what good would it do now? We've no other way out of here.

He takes the seat in front and helps me on behind him, and then we sit and wait. My head swings every time a branch creaks in the trees. My heart bangs in my throat.

"You all right?" Urlick reaches out, taking my hand to comfort me, squeezing it in his grip. His skin is soft, yet he's so strong. I love the way his hand swallows mine.

C.L. darts out from behind a sheet of fog and I nearly scream.

"'Ere," he says. He's out of breath, his pockets loaded down with gear. "Yuh'll be needin' this." He passes Urlick a couple more gadgets and then a mask, one of the ones I found in the laboratory upstairs, the wax replica of his father's face. I turn my eyes away, unnerved by the sight of it. I know it's necessary, but still.

"Can't risk appearing in Brethren without that on." C.L. smiles, trying to soften the moment. "And for yuh . . ." He pulls a second mask from his pocket. I look down, perplexed, at the face in his hand. The image of a young girl stares up at me. Her eyes flutter open, and my heart departs my chest. It's the girl, Ida, the one from Cordelia's locket. Iris's dead twin.

"I only 'ope it's 'ad enough time to 'arden," C.L. says. "I only just poured it last week. Iris urged me to create it for yuh." I look at him. "After we all formally met."

"But how did—"

"She must 'ave 'ad an intuition yuh'd be needing it."

I stare down at Ida's face in his hands. "I'm sorry, but I can't."

"Please, Eyelet." He pushes it toward me. "Iris insists. It's the only way yuh'll be safe to travel the streets of Brethren."

Just a few days ago I cursed Urlick for stealing his father's identity in order to survive, and now here I am contemplating doing the same. What a hypocrite I've become.

"Take it," Urlick says and kick-starts the cycle. "And hurry up about it."

Bertie sputters, then purrs.

I accept the gift, weighed down by guilt, and tuck it in the side of my pack. "Thank Iris for me, will you, please?" I say, leaning forward. Urlick's feet hit on the pedals and we're off, jerking bumpily up the road toward Brethren, the two of us nearly clacking heads as he switches from foot power to motor. A breath later, he veers off the main road into the forest.

Bertie shudders.
I shudder, too.
Something creepy chatters in the woods.

Twenty-Nine

Urlick

I can tell Eyelet's never ridden second-rider on a cycle before by the way she's jostling around behind me. Even her breath feels nervous at my back. Truth be known, I'm nervous, too. I've never been out in the Vapours this soon after their retreat. I'm not sure what to expect.

"Shouldn't we stick to the main roads?" Eyelet's timid voice drops in my ear.

"Not unless we *want* to get caught."

I shift into high gear, and the cycle groans. "Enough, Bertie," I say. "You know the drill." Reluctantly, he settles under us. He's as worried as Eyelet is about my decision, I can tell. But honestly, it'll be only a matter of time before Flossie figures out we're gone and comes after us. Taking the main road, we'd be caught for sure. At least through the woods we'll have a chance.

"But what about the Turned?" Eyelet insists. "Don't they roam these woods?"

"Along with the criminals, yes."

"I thought you said they strung the criminals in the trees—"

"They do. Trouble is, they don't always stay put."

Eyelet's body stiffens. "Don't they die in the Vapours?"

"Some do. Some don't. According to the locals, the ones that don't take refuge in the old abandoned coal mines up in the hills. If they go underground far enough and block the entrance, they're able to survive. After that, they travel the woods in bands, slightly deranged and hungry, killing all in their path. Feasting on humans if necessary."

Bertie shudders.

"So essentially, they could be anywhere, is that what you're saying? Both escaped criminals and the Turned."

"That's correct." Eyelet swallows and tightens her grip. "But we have a cycle and they're on foot," I'm quick to add.

"Well, there's that, I suppose." She exhales.

I reach back, take her hand and squeeze it gently. It's cold and clammy. "Don't worry, I don't plan on stopping very often along the way. A canister of hydrogen lasts a long, long time. When we do stop, I'll be sure to refuel in a clearing, in plain sight. The criminals don't like it out in the open."

I glance over my shoulder at her panicked eyes. They sweep the forest, her gaze darting from one snakelike crevasse to the next. Fiery black steam belches up from their jagged lines. Glowing molten rock oozes from the scores of potholes that flank either side. Tar-like sludge bubbles from smaller cracks like blood from punctured veins.

"What is all of this?" Eyelet whispers.

"The aftermath," I say. "This is what happens when the Vapours retreat."

"Will it stay like this forever?"

"No. Eventually the molten rock will stop glowing and the holes will dry up and everything that's scorched will turn to ash."

"Then what?"

"Rebirth. The forest is resilient. Much more resilient than man. There'll be foliage again here in the spring. Not much, but some."

Bertie groans, then chokes and sputters. "We'd better mask up," I say. "If Bertie's coughing, the air's not safe for us."

I slow, reach around, pull a gas mask from my pack, and slip it over my head, tightening the straps before helping Eyelet find hers. "How's that?" I ease it carefully down over her face, secure her straps, and turn both our oxygen packs from filter to purify. Her eyes look like a bug's through the lens of a microscope in the bubble-eye visors of the mask.

"What's that?" Eyelet points past my shoulder, her voice muffled by the regulator, her eyes bigger than they were before.

I swing around, somewhat frightened.

Hot, gassy steam shoots up from a hole in the ground about twenty metres in front of us. Bertie stalls, lurching to a halt. I throw down my feet to steady us, staring up at the sky. "It's a geyser," I shout.

Steam careens skyward for a good thirty metres before spiraling back to earth. It smells of rotten eggs and unlaundered stockings, even through the mask. The pressure of the surge throws Eyelet's hair back at her shoulders and scorches the exposed skin on my brow.

"Geysers?" Eyelet shouts over the rumble of the spray. "We have to dodge geysers, too?"

"For about a month after the storm retreats, yes."

"I thought all the explosions ended when the Vapours retreated."

"They did. These are new. Every time the Vapours pour down over the escarpment, they disrupt the atmospheric pressure of the Earth, creating a drag on its surface when they retreat. The drag wreaks havoc with the Earth's geothermal balance, causing it to erupt in this way. Mix that with a hundred years of man poking holes in the ground to mine coal, and whatever went on the Night of the Great Illumination, and voilà!" I stretch my hands to the forest. "We get the toxic cocktail you see before us." I drop my arms. "Or at least that's my theory."

Black clouds rise from fumaroles to our left; mud pools gurgle to our right. A smouldering, fast-running river of dark-red sand weaves through the centre of the forest, bathing us in incredible heat. It smells of rotting flesh and ripe sewage.

From charred limbs in the distance, a few criminals dangle—or what's left of their corpses.

Eyelet turns her eyes away, her bottom lip quivering. "So how will we know when we're upon a geyser, then?"

"We won't. But Bertie will." I reach down and activate the gadget attached to the inside of the cycle's bottom rib. "He's equipped with a sensory seismometer," I say, setting the dampened pendulum, immersing the arm in oil. "This should pick up any low frequencies of oscillation from now on, alerting us with a sharp bell at any sudden movement in the Earth's surface."

"Should?" Her eyes are wide.

"Will. Come on." I kick the cycle into gear and pedal on. "We'd better keep moving." I throw open the throttle, hoping I'm right, as a tree liquefies in the path—draining like oil into a slick swamp on the ground. Bertie swerves to miss it. "Good boy, Bertie," I say, popping it into the next gear, fishtailing around the hot, lapping pool—don't want to melt a tire—and keeping my eyes open for more of the same.

I ride the ridge from then on, trying to keep to the cooler rocks on top. I don't want to frighten Eyelet any more than she already is, but if we have to stop now to change a tire, we could be goners.

We push on for what seems like an eternity, trees dissolving, mud pools festering, crevasses sizzling all around. Bertie does his best to alert me to things, but still, we have a couple of close calls.

"Look!" Eyelet nearly jumps from her seat. Bertie shudders and slows. A massive plume of dark black smoke rises from beyond a hill a short distance away. It fills the skies overhead, drowning out the clouds. It looks like there's a fire, but there's no smell of smoke.

"What is it?" Eyelet breathes.

"I don't know." I pull up to the base of the hillside and stop. Bertie trembles beneath us. "You two stay here." I dismount. "I'll work my way up the rocks and take a look."

I lunge, scaling the rock face in a couple of giant steps, startled at the top by the niggling presence of Eyelet's warm fingers lacing through mine. "I thought I told you to stay with the cycle." I swing around.

"You should know by now, I don't take orders well." She grins. "Now, let's go see what this is, shall we?" She takes up her skirts and hikes up in front of me, charging to the top. "Good God!" She gasps and pulls back. "The earth. It's gone." She turns to me, clutching her heart.

I leap the rest of the way up and stare over the edge into the roiling mire. The sight is daunting, I must admit. Smoke belches from a seemingly endless pit, a swirling cauldron of black ash and steam. It's as though someone's taken a knife and cut away the earth. It's the biggest crevasse I've ever seen.

"Where's the other side?" Eyelet says, squinting.

"There isn't one."

"What do you mean?"

"It's Embers. Not a crevasse."

"Like at the back of the Compound." Her head swings around. "It extends this far?"

"Disturbing, isn't it?" I raise a hand to my eyes, squinting through the trolling fog. "I hadn't thought it, but it must skirt the entire countryside."

Eyelet swallows as she leans out over it, face engulfed in its smoke. "Do you suppose it skirts Brethren now, too?"

"May well."

She looks up at me. "What do you think is down there?"

"Nothing good."

"Where do you think the land has gone? Do you think it's possible the earth could have broken off and floated away, up beyond the cloud cover?"

I wrinkle my brow. "Don't be ridiculous." I lean forward, nose to the pit. "It's far more logical that it would sink."

"Says who?"

"Says me, that's who." I straighten, seeing her squint at the sky. "You're not seriously looking for the missing piece of land, are you?"

"No more than you were leaning over just now, peering into the pit to see if it was there." She scowls, then bites her lip. "Have you ever heard of a place called Limpidious?" she adds sheepishly.

"Only in fantasy books," I say.

"So you do know," she says. My turn to scowl at her. "You don't think—"

"Of course not," I snap.

Her cheeks flush red.

I throw out a quick arm and drop into a crouch, pulling Eyelet down with me, my heart racing.

"What is it?" she says, clutching my sleeve. "What's the matter?"

"Shhhhh!" I whisper. "We've got visitors." I point out the movement in the trees. Eyelet gulps and pulls in close to me.

Horses whinny inside gas-mask regulators, sounding more alien than horse, their feet stamping in the gravel. Voices stream over the edge of the rock, the hard drawl of working-class men. Through the cloud cover I make out a row of trolley carts hooked to flatbeds, each backed up to the edge of the pit, about a hundred metres away on the opposite side of the hill.

Eyelet crouches beside me, silent, as I squint through the heavy fog. "Who are they?" she whispers.

"I'm not sure."

A workman yanks on a cord, and one of the flatbeds mysteriously rises, unloading the cargo from the cart into the mire.

"What are they doing?" Eyelet hisses.

"Dumping, by the looks of things. Disposing of garbage from some factory, it looks like." Sheets of metal, rusty gears, springs, and old machine parts tumble and clank through the fog as they fall over the edge of the ridge. The noise is deafening.

A second worker raises another flatbed.

"Where do you think they're from?" Eyelet shouts.

"Some factory in town, I guess." I try again to make out the name of the company on the sides of the carts, but the shifting fog's too thick for me to see.

The mire belches as the debris tumbles in. Eyelet chokes. One of the workers' heads jerks in our direction.

"You there!"

"Oh God," Eyelet whimpers.

I yank her down flat onto the rock.

"Show yourself!" the worker shouts.

I hold my breath and pull Eyelet tight to my chest.

"What?" A second worker laughs. Stones crush beneath his boots. "Yuh calling on a criminal, are yuh? Better check them gauges of yers. I think them fumes are getting in."

"Naw, I thought I saw a girl."

"Out 'ere in the middle of no-man's-land." He laughs and biffs the worker. "Come on, back to work, yuh ol' fool." He rips another cord, and more garbage dumps, drowning out their conversation.

I wait for another shift in the cloud cover, then yank Eyelet to her feet. "We'd better get out of here," I say, pushing her down the rocks. "Before we end up in that pit."

Thirty

Eyelet

"The beggar's breeches!"

Urlick shakes out his hand, then sucks on his thumb. He's hurt himself. Bertie's blown a tire, despite our best efforts, and we've had to stop to change it, against our better judgment.

I'm supposed to be keeping watch on the woods while he repairs the balloon, but a part of me feels like I should give him a hand. Especially since he's having such a time of it. It seems we have no spare. Only a patch, which isn't exactly cooperating— *"Blessed blunder!"*—at all.

Urlick relights his torch a little too close to his face, and when it bursts into flame it singes the ends of his eyelashes. The already vapid air swells with the stench of sulfur and burnt hair.

Bertie chortles.

"Perhaps I could—" I lean over.

"Go back to keeping watch!" Urlick eyes me hard.

"Very well, then." I straighten. "Have it your way." I take a few steps, then double back. "You do know you've got the balloon in upside down, right?"

His hand slips from the wrench, grazing a knuckle.

"I'll just wait over here," I say, moving away.

He stands, yanking the points of his waistcoat, as Bertie lets out a monster sigh.

"Ouch!" I shout, bringing a hand to my head.

"Now what is it?"

"Something just struck me in the back of the head." He rolls his eyes. "I'm not kidding." I run my fingers through my hair. "Oh, good Lord, it's a beetle." I try to pluck it out, but it sticks. "There's a beetle running in my hair!" I dance around, flapping my hands. "Come help me get it out, will you *please*!"

Urlick laughs, drops the extinguished torch to the ground, and stalks toward me. "Relax," he says, fishing an object out of my hair. "It's just my Insectatron."

"Your *what*?"

"My mechanical Coccinellidae." He flings it under my nose. "You know, a ladybird? Cute, don't you think?"

"Not really." I scowl.

"It's a mechanical messenger, like a carrier pigeon. Only it's in beetle form."

I reach to stroke it, and the mechanical ladybird scuttles to the other side of his palm.

"Inside here is a homing device that doubles as a timepiece to keep its secret." He shows me, getting its wings to flutter open, revealing the face of a watch. "It must have mistaken the face of your chrono-cuff for the lens of my pocket watch when it tried to land. There's a magnet buried deep inside the belly of my timepiece that's designed to attract it." He eyes the sterling timepiece affixed to the metal cuff on my wrist. "Perhaps there are magnets inside your piece, too, and it became confused."

"You said it acts as a homing pigeon—but only one way, then?"

"No. Just like a pigeon, if I were to let it go it would return to Iris's duplicate base back at the Compound."

"I see," I say, watching him release a tiny brass latch at the rear of the bug, deploying a spring-loaded arm. The round face of the time-piece then lifts up, revealing a secret chamber. The space is filled with tiny mechanical gears and levers, all shifting this way and that. In the centre sits a miniature cylinder wrapped in a thin sleeve of tin, like those found in the heart of a music box.

"See this?" He pulls a tiny, skewer-like pin out of the rear of the bug. It holds a row of miniature brass cubes, each speared through the middle. "Thirteen cubes containing everything necessary to send a message," Urlick announces, spinning them around. "See here? Two sides of each cube are inscribed with the letters of the alphabet, while the third is etched with the numbers zero through nine. The fourth and final side features either a commonly used letter, a vowel, a period, an apostrophe, or a blank."

"Why, you've just thought of everything, haven't you?"

"I have."

"R, S, T, L, N, E," I chant, touching each letter on the final side. "I see. Just in case you need to double a letter."

"Right." Urlick nods.

"But suppose you need to use a letter more than twice?"

Urlick frowns. "Then you pick another word." His eyebrows jump. He tugs at the points of his waistcoat, as if pulling himself back together, before carrying on. So easily this man comes undone. "Next, you spin the cubes around on the skewer like this, you see?" He demonstrates, twisting and shuffling the cubes one by one. "Until the message you desire clicks into place."

"HELP." I read.

"Then you plunge the skewer back up into the beetle's body, this way"—he reinserts the pin into the rear of the bug—"and it stamps your message onto that tiny tin scroll wrapped around that cylinder, there. You see?" He shows me.

"You mean it imprints it?"

"Yes. The same way a stamping does."

"I get it, now."

"Once the word is stamped, the cylinder automatically shunts to the right a tenth, providing a clean bit of slate for the next word."

"And at the end of a sentence?"

"It rotates up a tenth."

"How clever." I smile. "How many words can a message hold?"

"Anything up to one hundred and forty characters."

"That's it?" I make a face.

Urlick's face falls. "Isn't that enough?"

"Well, *I'd* have at least rounded it up to an even one-fifty." I fold my arms.

"Would you, now?" He scowls.

I smile.

Urlick lowers his head. Unraveling the small, scroll-like message from the tiny cylinder, he reads it. His face grows uncharacteristically serious.

"What? What is it? What does it say?" I launch up onto my toes.

"It's from Iris." He looks up. "There's been a problem. Seems someone's broken into my laboratory."

"Let me see."

LAB COMPROMISED. SECRETS BLOWN. FLOSSIE
AWARE OF YOUR PLAN. SENT WORD VIA
LADYBIRD AHEAD OF YOU TO ACADEMY.
COULDN'T CONTAIN HER. TURN BACK.

"What does she mean, *Sent word via Ladybird*? Does Flossie have one, too?"

"Yes." Urlick rakes a worried path through his hair. "I gifted one to her last Christmas."

"You and Flossie exchange Christmas gifts?" I trip over the words, they come out so quickly. I must have misread their relationship. I'd not have taken them as sweethearts. Have I been a fool?

"Not exactly," Urlick breathes, and strangely I'm relieved. "It was more of a gift of necessity. The Academy threatened to cut off my studies last fall when the Vapour activities increased. Unless there was a way Flossie could be in constant contact with them, they were no longer going to allow her to venture so far into the Follies. Out of desperation, I created the Insectatron and gifted it to her at Christmas. The match of it was sent to the Academy. That's how she could send the message."

"But I thought you said she lived in the Follies. I thought she was an itinerant."

"I did, and she is, but she has family connections back at the Academy."

"What?"

"Her parents. They're both professors."

"Oh my . . ."

"Rumour has it, Flossie is the illegitimate love child of some high-ranked professor and his married professor mistress. In order to protect both their images, Flossie was sent away at birth, to be raised by an aunt out here in exile."

I knew I'd recognized those eyes.

"We're jiggered!" Urlick turns and pounds his fists on a tree. "It's only a matter of time before they catch us now."

"Perhaps not." I fling myself around. "Perhaps her Ladybird didn't make its destination?"

Urlick scowls, angered at the thought of his gadget not succeeding.

"All right, then." I swallow. "Perhaps we can still outrun them? It might not have landed yet."

"We'll have to," Urlick snaps, staring off into the distance as if he's calculating the Ladybird's arrival. "We've no other choice." He races over to the cycle and drops to his knees. Bertie groans as he forces on the tire.

"Get your pack," he shouts to me. "We're leaving."

Thirty-One

Eyelet

Urlick veers onto the main road for the last few clicks of the journey, slowing from time to time. He pulls a Dyechrometer from his pocket and activates it, scanning our surroundings for feral heartbeats, checking for intruders. The sonic sound of its beep makes both Bertie and me jump. My blood runs cold until the sound switches to a dull gong, the signal for all clear. The device hasn't detected any other heartbeats but the two of ours within a hundred-metre radius.

We're safe.

For now.

Urlick flips shut the lid and pockets the Dyechrometer. "Better don the masks anyway."

"Why?"

"We're almost at the entrance to Gears." His eyes wander the horizon. "Another hundred, maybe hundred-fifty metres. Though we're not going to use the entrance. Best not to take any chances." He looks to me. "You being wanted and all."

"About that . . ." I lower my head. I should tell him. But how? How do I explain what happened to Mother and why I'm wanted, without explaining my affliction?

I look up to see him gazing at me sympathetically. "You can tell me later."

Bertie sighs.

I reach into my pack, pluck the gas mask out, and pull it down over my face.

Urlick laughs. "Ride into town with that on and you're sure to draw unwanted attention. Here." He reaches into my pack and pulls out the wax replica of Ida, the one C.L. gave me before we left. "The idea is *not* to stand out."

"Of course," I say, accepting it reluctantly, holding the thin, waxy replica of Ida's face in my hands. A chill sneaks down my spine as I look into her eyes. Crazy Legs's last words swirl in my head. *"Please, Eyelet. Iris insists. It's the only way yuh'll be safe to travel the streets of Brethren."*

Iris. Thoughtful, kind Iris.

Urlick pulls his father's death mask from his pack, rakes back his hair, and slips it into place. Its gelatin-coated backing sucks to his skin in a noisy slurp. I shiver. The idea of walking around in someone else's likeness curdles deep in my belly. It's not right. None of this is right. But *oh* so necessary.

Urlick rubs his hands over his fake skin, pressing out every groove, every line, securing every dart-like wrinkle. Slowly his father's face comes to life, adhering securely to his own, and I can't help but think how wicked that seems.

Carefully, he centres the fake pale-pink lips of the mask over his own purple ones, pinching them down into place. From another box he pulls two shiny, circular translucent skins, lifts up his lids, and places them over his eyes, blinking, until at last his eyes adapt to their new painted veils. He turns and looks at me through the same ghostly eyes that stared down at me before, from the landing of the stairs—and I shudder, unnerved by their empty, glazed-over stare.

His whole face looks so strangely unnatural; I can't imagine how it's going to fool anyone. The skin is a jaundiced-peach in colour, mixed with the stark white of his natural skin beneath. The mulberry birth stain on his cheek—he's tried to disguise it beneath layers of extra wax injected with dark-brown ink—has turned out looking more like a glob of raisins than the mole he intended. His painted blue eye-skins blend with his own vibrant pink, turning his irises a deep shade of inhuman violet blue. I tremble, biting my lip to keep him from seeing my reaction, casting my eyes to the ground.

"What's the matter?"

"Nothing." I look away, then back. "It's just shocking to see you this way."

"You find *this* shocking?" Urlick almost laughs. "Over my face before!" He turns away, shaking his head. "You are a very strange girl, Eyelet Elsworth. A very strange one."

He tucks the box and tools back into his pack, and when he turns around, I notice the mask has warmed to his face; the colours have become more realistic. But still, he's not himself to me.

"Your turn." He motions toward the mask in my hand. "Just hold it close to your face; the mask knows what to do."

I look down at the mask in my hands and think of Ida, whether or not she'd approve of me borrowing her face. My mind drifts to my father, and I cringe at the idea of someone donning a wax replica of him without his permission.

"Come on, Eyelet." Urlick touches my shoulder. "We need to get going."

Bertie groans.

I reach up, anxious, and place Ida's likeness over mine. The jelly-like lining springs to life when it makes contact with my skin, eerily drawing me in. A moment later, it's a part of me, moving as I move, grinning when I grin, grimacing as I grimace.

Urlick helps me smooth down the bumps along the edge of my hairline, coaxing my bangs to drop naturally down over my forehead again. Pressing out the bubbles over my cheek, he caresses away the wrinkles from my chin.

I look up, feeling sick yet weirdly grateful. Without her cover, there's no question I'd be recognized in Brethren. "How do I look?"

"Pretty good." Urlick grins. "How does it feel?"

"Okay, I guess." I lick my lips, no longer my own, repulsed by their chalky paraffin taste.

"And now for the finishing touch." Urlick walks to his pack and back again, producing a brush and a tin of stage makeup. He stands back, dipping the brush in the tin. "Try not to smile," he says, dusting my face in a layer of powder. I choke under the screen of dusty smoke, waving away the excess with a hand.

"Now me," he says, passing me the brush. "And make sure you cover everything." Wax crinkles at the corners of his mouth as he talks. I reach up and work out the imperfections. He returns the favour, using his thumbs to get rid of stress splits in my lips, pressing each crevice delicately into place. His touch is so tender; so wonderfully caring. It's hard to believe he raised himself.

"There." He finishes. "Now how about that makeup?"

I reach up. My breath catches in my throat. The hairs on the back of my neck nettle as I dust his cheeks and coat his chin, the eyes of his father watching me the whole time. I try not to think of it, but it's not his gaze—and the one that stares at me makes my skin crawl. It's Urlick, I tell myself. It's not his father; it's him. I close my eyes to make it easier, imagining the real Urlick beneath the mask, trying not to think of the one I wear. "There," I say when I'm finished. "All set." I turn away.

"Listen." Urlick catches me softly by the arm, his voice soothing. He raises my chin until our eyes meet. "I don't like this any more than you do, but it has to be done. You know that, right?"

"I do."

His eyes dart gently over my face, and for the first time I see a hint of the warm Urlick I've come to know, behind the imposter's eyes.

*

We abandon Bertie—much to his dismay—at the edge of the quarry on the outskirts of town, hiding him among the boulders on the far side of the tracks, and cross, unnoticed, at the checkpoint. Then we slink through the streets of Gears, an easy labyrinth under Urlick's swift and skillful guidance, and dart up the back of the hillside toward the Academy, arriving breathless at its gate. Our fingers are numbed by the cold, twisted iron of its sprawling ivy cage.

We're alone, thank goodness. The streets around the school are empty. Only a few widows, on their way to the market for high tea. Everyone else is consumed by daily duties. We've arrived at the perfect time of day.

"What now?" Urlick looks at me through a veil of painted aspiration.

"Now to get past the keepers." I point.

Urlick's eyes follow my hand down the hillside to the front of the school, stopping on the pair of mechanical ravens that tower above the entrance about fifty metres away. "Simon and Edgar?" he says, returning his gaze to me.

"In the flesh. Or should I say metal."

A blanket of fog rolls between us, rendering the Academy and Urlick briefly invisible. The skies overhead come alive with the sound of real ravens, their cries slicing through the air. Urlick looks up, alarmed by the shrillness of their voices.

"There must be a dozen of them." Urlick squints to see them.

"No, there should only be nine." I look up.

"What did you say?"

"Pan, and Archie, and seven more," I say, grinning.

"How do you know this?"

"They're friends of my mother's," I say.

"Friends?" Urlick looks troubled.

I swallow, worried that I've said too much. But he's bound to find out sooner or later anyway, and by the look of the approaching flock, it's going to be sooner for sure. "My mother was gifted a raven as a child," I continue. "It was a very different time then. She taught it to talk, and they've been inseparable since."

"Your mother taught a raven to speak?"

"Yes." I look up. "For which she was hanged in the square."

He swallows.

"Some of the townspeople caught her talking to the bird and had her arrested. She was unjustly accused of being a Valkyrie, possessed of Wickedry, and thus she was disposed of—but it wasn't true." My voice increases. "It was all a lie. She wasn't any such thing. My mother was a gentle, honest soul. She hadn't a wicked bone in her body." I lower my head.

"And you?" He raises my chin. "They believe you're one, too, don't they? That's why they're after you."

"I'm afraid so, yes." I bite my lip. "I was fleeing Brethren for that very reason, the day I jumped your coach."

"I thought you said you were searching for your father's machine."

"I was. As the authorities searched unjustly for me." I bat back the tears that warm my eyes, remembering the moment.

The flock of ravens above drops from the clouds, breaking the tension between us. They hover in a tight circle around my shoulders, chattering in my face, and for the first time ever I'm not annoyed.

"Archie!" I reach out and stroke his neck. "Oh, Archie, you have no idea how glad I am to see you."

Urlick ducks and shoos them away. I laugh at how flustered he appears.

Archie caws, and Urlick bolts back. "Don't worry." I stroke Urlick's arm. "He won't hurt you."

Urlick stares at the bird, and then at me, and I'm afraid I know what he's thinking. He's judging me, just as everyone always has all my life.

I so hoped he'd be different.

"This is your mother's constant companion?"

"No." I laugh. "This is just Archie." I turn back to the birds. "Where is Pan?" I ask. "Why isn't she with you?" I hold my breath, terrified of Archie's answer, knowing the last time I saw her how close she winged to death.

Archie caws, tipping his wings to the park on my left. Through a gash in the cloud cover a black shadow appears, weaving its way through a skeleton of trees. "Pan!" I shriek and race down the hillside. "Pan! It's you!"

Urlick trundles after me, looking bewildered.

Pan swoops in, fluttering close to greet me, rolling her head and feathers up against my cheeks. "Oh, Pan, I was so worried about you." I giggle, bending my neck against her tickling feathers. "I'm so glad to see you again."

Pan lands gently on my shoulder, snuggling her head up against my neck, and I catch a glimpse of Urlick looking sorely perplexed. "Oh, how rude of me," I breathe. "Pan, this is Urlick. Urlick, this is Pan. My mother's bird, the one she taught to speak." I gesture between the two of them.

Pan nods her head, then curtsies, one wing outstretched.

Urlick can't help himself: he laughs. "It's as if she really knows what you're talking about."

"Of course she does. I told you, my mother taught her to speak."

"Teaching a bird to mimic a few human sounds is one thing, having it understand what's being said is quite another."

"Well, I assure you, Pan does both." His brows rise. "Are you calling me a liar?"

"No. Not exactly . . ." He tugs at his waistcoat.

"You think Pan's nothing but a common house parrot, don't you?"

He yanks on the points of his waistcoat again.

"What would you say if I told you she can talk on her own? Without prompting?"

"I'd say you've snorted in a few too many Vapours."

"Really? Say something to him, Pan." Pan says nothing—just stares. "Go ahead, you have my permission, tell him what you think." She cocks her head but remains silent.

"This is ridiculous," Urlick says. "She's not going to speak unless you speak first. There's no magic to it."

"There's no what?"

"You heard me." He pulls a hand through his hair. "All this nonsense about brilliant birds and floating worlds!"

Floating worlds? I never said anything about a floating world.

"Come on. We've got an Academy to break into, or have you forgotten?" He turns and stalks away up the hill.

"*This* from a man who crafts enchanted teapots, winged messengers, and a bewitched coach that can park itself?" I call after him.

He swings around, his lips pursed. "Those are inventions. That's completely different—"

"How so?" I poke my nose out at him.

"It just *is*."

"You know what I think?" I move toward him. "I think you're afraid. Just like all the cowardly professors at the Academy, unwilling to acknowledge there might be powers at work in this universe that science can't explain."

"You know what I think?" He whirls around, wagging his finger. "I think you a fool—"

"Really." I gnash my teeth. "Well, I think you insufferably closed-minded!" Pan lifts from my shoulder as I turn and stalk away.

"Eyelet!" He hesitates. "Eyelet, wait, *please*." He chases after me. "Eyelet, I'm so sorry! I didn't mean—I'm sorry." He lowers his head. "It's just that"—he paces—"if magic really did exist, I would never have been born looking like this, and my mother wouldn't have died giving birth to me. Ida and Iris would have been normal and Crazy Legs would have arms, don't you see?"

I swallow.

"I can't tell you how many times I've called upon the powers of magic in my life to right the wrongs of it," he continues. "To save my father, to spare Ida, to silence Cordelia's screams! And—just as reason would dictate—it never *once* worked!" He bares his teeth. "Because *magic*. Doesn't. *Exist!*"

Pan takes to the air, swooping above our heads, startled and cawing, as Urlick turns his back.

"That's not true, Urlick," I call after him, my voice wavering. "And you know it. A little bit of magic exists in everyone's heart. Even yours!" My words tug at his step. "Otherwise you could never have designed a cycle with wings, in the hope that one day, the two of you could fly."

He turns briefly, a hesitant look on his face.

Pan jumps from my shoulder and wings through the trees.

"Where is she going?"

"I don't know." I look up. "Pan!" I chase after her. "Pan, come back!"

She circles with something in her bill, swoops down, and drops it at Urlick's feet.

"What is it?" He turns to me.

"I'm guessing it's a bit of magic," I say.

Thirty-Two

Urlick

Eyelet races over, snatching up the small cotton pouch from the ground. She loosens the ribbon that binds the top.

"Should we be opening this?" I say as she dumps the contents into her palm—a fat package with distinctive markings—and then passes me the empty pouch. I'm almost afraid to take it from her. All this talk of Valkyries and tongued birds has me on edge. I'm not even sure I know who she is anymore.

"Careful," I say, as she breaks the wax seal. "That looks rather official. Even royal, perhaps."

"Relax." She smirks. "It's my father's."

"Your father's? But how's that possible? I thought you said he was dead."

"He is. This is from his royal stash."

"His *what?*" I spin around. "I knew it. I was right. I've gone and kidnapped royalty! I *am* both a kidnapper and a thief—"

"Please, don't flatter yourself." Eyelet laughs. "My father was only the Royal Science Ambassador of the Academy, serving under

Brethren's Ruler. So technically, you've only kidnapped the daughter of a royal slave."

"Oh, well, that makes it *so* much better."

I check over my shoulder to make sure no one's watching. Though trees hide us, I'm still worried we'll be discovered. And now with the royal pot.

"Not to worry, my father was stripped of that post shortly before he passed away," Eyelet continues. "Besides, you've kidnapped nothing. If anything, it was *I* who commandeered *your* coach." She grins, eyeing me hard.

"Here, hold this," she says, turning her eyes skyward, rolling the contents of the pouch around in her hand.

"Why? What are you doing?"

Pan swoops in again, dropping a second item. I duck. Eyelet laughs. I swear the two of them are enjoying this.

The item billows down on the breeze, its gilded edges glinting in the grey of the day, coming to rest in Eyelet's hands.

"And what, *pray tell*, is that?" I snatch a roll of parchment paper, tied in a red velvet ribbon, from her hand.

"A smudging," she says, snatching it back.

"A what?"

"A magical message—"

"Why, of course."

She pinches me. "Ouch!"

She casts off the ribbon and unrolls it.

"A magical message that says"—I hover over her shoulder in heightened anticipation—"*nothing*." I rock back on my heels. "Well, there you have it. What a brilliant bird, she's dropped you a blank piece of paper."

"To the naked eye, yes."

Eyelet throws her hand out in front of my face, catching another pouch from Pan.

I watch as she struggles to loosen the knot on the top of the pouch's drawstring. "If it's magic, shouldn't it come with a wand or something?"

She smirks. "Here," she says, finally tearing it open. "Shut up and strike these." She hands me a couple of dark rocks. "But not until I say." She stops me from rolling them together. "And whatever you do, don't drop them."

"Why not?"

"Because they won't light if they're wet."

"Light?"

"They're flints," she says. I scowl. "To make *fi-re* with." She mocks me.

"Oh, yes . . . yes, of course." I tug at my waistcoat, feeling a bit daft, confident that was the object of her game. "And that?" I nod to the herb in her hand she's busy twisting around the end of a stick. "What is that?"

"Mugwort," she says plainly, as if it's something you come across every day. *Of course. Mugwort. What else would it be?*

I check again over my shoulder as she bites off the end and spits.

"Bitter." She excuses her unladylike behaviour.

I've never seen this side of Eyelet before, and I must say, I kind of like it.

"Mugwort's used to stimulate psychic awareness and prophetic dreams"—she turns to me—"which, of course, you'd know nothing about."

I smirk. "And this?" I hold up the small bit of root she asked me to hold, from the first bag.

"That's osha. We're to burn it after the smudging to rid ourselves of any evil influences."

"Of course." I roll my eyes.

"Perhaps I should wrap you up in it, instead?"

"Funny." I crinkle my nose.

"Strike them, will you?"

"What?"

"The *flints*."

"Don't you think lighting a fire might bring attention to us?"

"Just strike the flints, will you, please?" She coaxes me with her chin.

I take the flints in my hands and strike them hard. Eyelet raises the herb end of the stick up to the sparks. The aged mugwort bursts into an inferno, comparable to that of the Great Fire of 1766. "Good Lord!" I panic, jumping back. The flame burns high and quick, from orange to black in seconds. A sweet mare's tail of charcoal smoke pours from what remains of the withering nest.

"Hurry!" she shouts. "Get the scroll!"

I stumble into action, swooping for it.

"Now *quickly* roll it out over top!"

I do as she says, and Eyelet steps forward, passing the smouldering stick under the page. She works her way from the bottom to the top corner of the paper. Smoke slowly penetrates the paper's pores, releasing a hand-scrawled message into the air.

"It's from my father," Eyelet gasps. "I recognize the writing. Quick!" She launches to her toes. "Help me decipher what it says!"

Each puff billows up into fat, swirling, spiraling letters that hang for a moment and then sizzle into ashes, dissolving into nothingness before our eyes.

She breaks away, leaving me to hold the paper, etching the message with what's left of the stick into the dirt at her feet.

> *Inside a tortoise, wisdom waits,*
> *At the spin of a velocipede, or two.*
> *Heed the underpinning of the raven's troubled wing,*
> *For beneath it hides the master key.*
> *Inside a spoked and circular tomb,*
> *You will find the treasure you seek.*
> *Tucked away beneath the stars, a moon,*

And a shimmering sun.
But beware the knowledge that lies within,
For once known,
It can never be forgotten,
Only unearth it,
If prepared to protect it,
For in so doing,
You become the guardian of both destiny,
And doom . . .

"What's that supposed to mean?" I glance at her nervously as the message turns to embers and sails off over my head.

"I don't know, exactly." She stares, unblinking, then yanks up her skirt, exposing her white cotton petticoat below.

"What are you *doing*?" I gasp and pull my eyes away.

"Solving the riddle." She tears off a piece and I flinch at the sound, doing another check over my shoulder, terrified we're going to be caught this way. Me stealing glances, and her with a torn petticoat and skirts about her neck. My face flushes twelve shades of red. I am hot and cold and a little shamelessly excited. I loosen the collar at my neck.

"Heed the underpinning of the raven's troubled wing." She dabs her finger in the soot and records the riddle on the swatch of cloth. My eyes fall again to her snowflake-white thigh.

"Perhaps he's talking about your mother's raven?" I swallow, tearing my eyes away again. I tug at my waistcoat and smooth back my hair.

"No, not my mother's." She springs to her feet. "He means his own!"

"He means *what*?"

Her eyes shine. *"For beneath it hides the master key.* That's it! Come on!" She grabs me by the hand.

"Wait!" I shout as she pulls me forward, the two of us lunging back up the hill, toward the gates, through the trees.

"What about the osha?" It's as if she doesn't hear me. I look back to see it blowing off in the wind.

Thirty-Three

Eyelet

"There they are." I point.

Urlick staggers to a stop beside me, just shy of the Academy gates. He drops his head between his knees and gasps for air—a runner he is not. "There what are?" he says, glancing up at me. I clutch his sleeve and drag him in behind some bushes to hide.

"My father's birds." I point again. Robotically the birds bow from their posts. "The one on the left has a bum wing," I add.

"How do you know that?" Urlick crinkles his brow.

"I've always known it. I just never knew it was important until now."

He glares at me out of the corner of his eyes.

"Heed the underpinning of the raven's troubled wing . . . For beneath it hides the master key," I say. "Near as I can figure, there it is." I nod toward Simon. "The troubled wing. His left wing's always been wonky. If I'm right, under that wing we'll find what we need to unlock my father's treasure, which I'm hoping means his journals. But first, we

need to get past them"—I point to the birds—"and through those gates. Or, should I say, *you* need to." I turn to Urlick. "*I* won't be recognized."

"I beg your pardon." His brows dip. "Isn't that the whole idea? *Not* to be recognized?"

"You'd think so, but not in this case. According to ol' Simon and Edgar over there"—I point to the mechanical ravens sitting atop either side of the entrance gates—"if they can't register a solid identification for you, you're not getting into the place. In fact, if they don't recognize you, they'll kick up a fuss and call Security in to have you arrested. But if you're recognized, you can pass without incident. Therefore you must be recognized." I give Urlick a shove.

"Me? Why me?" He resists, falling against me.

"Because *my* register has likely been stricken from their mental memory plates. Not to mention, I'm currently posing as a dead girl who's never even attended the school. At least you have a fighting chance." I push him out and he balks again.

"What do you mean, *mental memory plates*?" he whispers.

"Each raven has a permanent collection of memory-recognition plates stored in its head. Tiny metal stamped images of every person who's ever been permitted to pass through these gates. When someone stands before them, they scan them from head to toe, shuffling through the library of possibilities until they find a match."

"So what makes you think they're going to recognize me? I'm borrowing the face of a dead man, too—"

"Exactly. The face of a former Academy professor. See the difference? At least he should be somewhere in their memory banks."

"But he's dead." He lifts a cocky brow.

"I know." I lift one of my own. "The Academy has a strict policy about never deactivating the memory plates of one of their own. It's considered shameful to cast out the memory of a serving professor. Therefore, their plates remain untouched, marking their existence like tombstones in a graveyard. To remove them would be like spitting on the casket of the dead."

Urlick winces.

"So you see, of the two of us, *you* have the better chance of being recognized. Now, get out there." I nudge him again.

He licks his waxy lips and presses a hand to his mask. "Simon and Edgar, you say?"

"That's right."

He takes a step out and I catch his sleeve, yanking him back. "Oh, and one more thing. Act casual. The birds can sense if you're nervous."

"Fantastic."

"I'll stay here, out of range, until you're recognized. And then I'll make a run for it." I wink.

"Great plan." He swallows.

"Ready? One, two . . ."

He springs from the hedge before the count of three and saunters toward the gates, whistling horribly off tune.

"Good thing they're deaf," I hiss after him.

He wags his head and shoos me away.

Simon and Edgar ruffle on their posts, their heads tilting side to side. They nod, greeting him—*so far, so good*—their cathode-red lantern eyes spurred on by the hiss of methane, activating from lights to beams. My heart creeps to my throat as I watch them scan Urlick from his toes to his head, hesitating at his shoulders.

Edgar lifts his wings. What's wrong? What's happening? I hold my breath. *Come on, come on, put them down, keep going.* Simon's mouth falls open. My heart drops to my stomach like a stone.

"No!" I stumble out of hiding, race at the gates, and tackle Urlick to the ground. Simon's head jerks up. "Move!" I shove Urlick toward the hedge. "MOVE! MOVE! MOVE! MOVE! MOVE!" I crawl behind him as fast as I can, keeping my head low, out of the range of the ray.

"What are you doing?" Urlick shouts.

"Just keep moving!" I slap down his head. "Go! There! Back behind the hedge!" I tuck and roll in behind one of the stone pillars at the base of the gate. Urlick scrambles for the hole in the hedge.

The ravens keep searching, tracking our movements with their beams.

"Why aren't they giving up?" Urlick gasps.

"Something's wrong." I swing my head out around the corner of the pillar. "They sense we're still here." If they don't stop scanning soon, our plans of ever getting in the school are all but knackered. Somehow, I've got to get them to stop. "Wait here!" I scramble to my feet.

"What?" Urlick shouts. "Where are you going? *Eyelet!*"

I lunge from behind the pillar out into the centre of the beams. "Simon, Edgar!" I wave my arms. Urlick gulps behind me. The ravens flap their wings, and their mouths fall open, prepared to shriek. *"How much do you trust me?"* I scream.

Urlick gasps. My heart freezes. For a long, agonizing moment, nothing happens. Then, simultaneously, the birds' beaks hammer shut. Their wings drop to their sides. Their red-beam eyes fade from red to black. Behind them, the gate pops open as if nothing were awry, hinges sorely complaining.

Urlick races from the hedge, joining me. "What just happened? How did you do that?" He stares at the birds.

"I overrode their program."

"You did *what?*"

I stick a boot into the ivy latticework of the gate and pull myself to the top of the post. "My father"—I huff, lifting Simon's bum wing—"he installed a safeguard sentence deep in their memories, in case I was ever denied entry to the Academy when I was small. They're both trained to recognize me by voice when I say it."

"Then why did you send *me* up there?"

"'Cause I only remembered it just now?" My voice lilts.

Urlick claps a frustrated hand to his head.

"*Aha!*" I shout, pulling a long, slotted pin from under Simon's faulty wing. "No wonder it never retracted properly. See this?" I hold it up for Urlick. "*This* is our key!"

I slip it down the side of my stockings until it reaches the heel of my boot, hitch up my skirts, and jump down. Simon shifts on top of the gatepost, his wing settling into place for the first time in his life. I grab Urlick by the hand and tug him through the gate.

"Any other magical surprises you'd like to share with me, before, *oh*, I don't know . . . we get caught and hauled off to the *stone jug*?"

"No," I grin, stuffing him through the side door of the Academy. "Not yet anyway."

Thirty-Four

Eyelet

Urlick follows close behind me as I drop down the first flight of stairs, then make a sharp right turn. Entering the grand hall, I lunge forward, scurrying across the open floor, heading for the professors' west wing.

"What are we doing out here in the open like this?" Urlick hisses over my shoulder, his gaze swinging this way and that. His boots slap hollowly against the crisp alabaster floors. A master sleuth he is not.

"Making our way to my father's old office. Now will you please shut up before you give us away?"

"Do you think this wise?" He catches me by the shoulder.

"Do you know a better way? Now come on." I shrug his hand from my shoulder, and he reins me back by the sleeve. "But why your father's office? Why not somewhere else?"

"Because that's where the professors keep the shimmering sun."

He squirrels up his face. "What are you talking about?"

"*You will find the treasure you seek. Tucked away beneath the stars, a moon, and a shimmering sun.* The riddle, remember? Each of the professors' offices at the Academy features a different astrological oracle embedded in its floor. My father's happened to feature the sun. I used to sit on it and play as a child while I waited for him to finish his work. My guess is 'the treasure we seek' is beneath it."

"And if you're wrong?" Urlick's voice ripples throughout the room, bouncing off the alabaster walls.

"Have you a better idea?" I glare at him.

He cowers, lowering his head.

"Now come on, before we get caught and thrown in the jug for trespassing, will you?" I tiptoe on through the next doorway, the sculpted-plaster ceiling pressing down above our heads. Clearing the next flight of stairs, I push on through the ballroom and up the corridor, where I'm frozen, midstep, by the sound of hard-soled shoes clattering over granite.

My heart thunders in my chest. I reach out and throw a hand across Urlick, slapping his back up against the wall. "Shhhhh." I bring a finger to my mouth. "Academy headship." The cluck of dark voices creeps up the hall toward us. "We've got to find somewhere to hide, and quick," I say.

Urlick's Adam's apple jumps. His eyes scan the premises. "Over here." He lunges, yanking me across the hall, pulling me in behind a huge marble statue of Aphrodite just as the Academy headship round the corner. The ancient stone chafes my shoulders as he pulls me close, wrapping his arms around my middle. His heart drums at my spine. It's all I can do to keep my mind on the moment, the warmth of his body an utter distraction, his hot breath falling at my neck.

"Sir!" I gasp at the sound of the lone voice hustling up to join the rest.

"This better be urgent, Radcliffe." Shoes shuffle to a stop in front of us. "I've an important meeting to attend."

"This won't take but a minute of your time, sir. I promise you."

"Go on."

"I may have just witnessed a breach in security. The ravens at the gate, they were about to summon the guards, when suddenly they gave up and stood down."

"You've stopped me to report a false recognition by a pair of mechanical gatekeepers?" The man's voice is annoyed, heavy.

"No, sir, I've stopped you to report a potential break-in."

My heart jerks in my chest. Urlick stirs behind me. His hands grow sweaty. Or are those mine? I swallow. He couldn't have seen us—could he? If so, why didn't he come for us immediately? How could we have got this far?

"A *potential* break-in? Or a *successful* one?" the man barks.

"Well, that's just it, sir. I'm not sure," Radcliffe says. "When I first looked and the ravens were prepared to call in the guards, a strange-looking man stood before them. Then a drape of fog passed over, and when it cleared, a young woman stood in the man's place."

I suck in a breath and hold it. Behind me, Urlick's breath grows ragged. In the window on the other side of the hall, a small flicker of diamond-like light glints at the edge of the beveled pane of glass.

"It was because of *her* the ravens stood down, sir," the man continues. "Yet I did not recognize her face."

"And you profess to know everyone at this school, do you?"

"I *am* the record keeper. It is my job to recognize the entire student population. And I can assure you, the girl I saw does not attend this school."

"I see." The second man pulls at his chin. I cringe at the sound of his beard beneath his fingers. "The man? Did you recognize him?"

Urlick squeezes my hand, crushing my knuckles inside his grip. The light in the window fades.

"I believe this to be him, sir." The sound of a metal plate passes hands. Fingers trace over the etching. "Though the ravens stopped short of recognizing him, by my own eye, I believe he was once a business partner of yours?"

The professor hesitates, his breath sharp as he returns the plate.

Urlick's heart pounds at my back. I gasp.

"Initiate full lockup. Search every hallway, every room, every nook and cranny of the Academy from top to bottom; place a guard at every exit. See to it that this intruder doesn't leave the premises. Do you understand me?"

"Yes, sir. And when we catch him?"

"Bring him to me."

Thirty-Five

Urlick

When I'm sure the hallway is clear, I spin Eyelet around to face me. "What do we do now?" I say, my hands clamped to her arms.

"What we came here to do," she says. "Nothing's changed."

Though she appears unaffected, I know it's not true by the distinct quiver in her lip.

"*Nothing's changed?*" I hiss. "Did you hear what they said? Don't you know what that means?"

"Of course I do, I'm not *stupid*." Her brow furrows.

She pulls her arms loose from my grip. "What would *you* have us do, hmmm?" She pinches her hips. "Turn around now, after we've come this far, we're this close?"

"Of course not, *no—*"

"Well, then?"

I pull a worried hand through my hair.

"There, you see, we've no other choice but to go on with the plan." She turns and flits away.

"You don't even know if what we're after is where you think it is!" I hiss after her.

"Then there's only one way to find out if I'm right, isn't there?" She hesitates. "Are you in?"

I stare into her less-than-confident eyes. "I'm in," I say, grabbing her by the hand.

We speed off down the hallway together, treading softly to silence our steps. "What did he mean by 'business partner,' do you think?" She turns to me on the run.

"Your guess is as good as mine."

At the end of the hallway, she hangs a sharp left, then another right at the end of that hall. Zigzagging our way past another stand of statues, she leads us down a dark, narrow corridor, and then off into a separate wing. Her shoes skid to a stop outside an office door, second from the end of an abandoned hallway. "This is it," she says. "My father's old office."

I lurch to a stop beside her, waving dust motes away from my nose. Everything smells of mildew and mothballs. "Are you sure this is it?" I look around. "It doesn't look like anyone's been down this hall in years."

"They haven't," she says, fussing with her skirts. "They abandoned the entire corridor after my father's death. Headmaster's orders. His office has been kept like a shrine. That's why I've never been able to get near it."

"Why is that, do you figure?"

"My guess is, the headmaster feels guilty about betraying my father."

"Either that, or about what's hidden behind these doors."

She flips up her skirt, exposing her entire thigh, and I nearly faint at the sight.

"What?" She pulls the notched pin from the raven's wing out of the top of her stocking.

"Nothing." I choke on my breath. Hot roses bloom in my cheeks. I shuffle in place, trying to compose myself. I swear if she doesn't stop with these drapery antics, it'll be the end of me.

"Brace yourself." She pushes me aside, threading the notched pin slowly into the lock on the door. She thrusts it heartily in and out of the hole, and the lock pops opens, gasping as if relieved. The door creaks open wide.

"How did you know to do that?"

"I didn't." She flits in past me. "But it worked, didn't it?"

"Yes, I suppose it did."

"Now if I could just be right about the room being the crypt for the treasure, we're all set." She slips into the room.

I follow, closing the door behind, turning the handle back slowly so it doesn't clunk, then turn, shocked to find the room in complete disarray.

"Looks like someone may have beaten us to the treasure," Eyelet says, standing in the middle of the room, long faced. I've not seen her this close to tears since the day she ran off in the Vapours.

Boxes are overturned, papers lie strewn about the floors, and chairs are tipped, as if somebody's already ransacked the place.

"Hogswaggle," I say, crossing the room in a few staggered strides. "Looks to me like whoever was in here before us left pretty frustrated." I turn over a broken cup. "Besides, whoever it was didn't have the benefit of your father's magic message, now did they?" I cup her sagging chin in my hand.

"No, I suppose they didn't." She smiles.

"That's right." I drop her chin and dust off my trousers. "Now, I believe we've got a riddle to solve. Where's this blooming sun you've been going on about?"

"Over here." She grins. "Can you help me with this?" She stalks over to her father's desk and takes hold of the edges. "It should be under the rug beneath."

Together we hurl her father's desk aside, reach for the carpet, and throw it back. A shimmering oracle of the sun appears embedded in the floor. Each ray of sunshine forms a separate spoke in the wheel that surrounds the intricate drawing.

"Well, I was right about one thing." She falls back to admire it. "It's just as I remember."

"Now what do we do?" I bend at the knees.

"Solve the rest of the riddle." She paces. "As fast as we possibly can. Let's start with the tortoise." She wrings her hands. "We need to find the tortoise."

"You work that side of the room and I'll work this. Once we find it, we'll move on to the next clue."

"Good thinking." She scurries to the opposite side of the room and dives into a stack of papers.

I lower my head and start digging, too. "Oh God," I hear her gasp.

"Everything all right?" I turn around in time to see a rat cross over the end of her boot. The skin on the back of my neck crawls a little. I shudder, shaking off the feeling.

"I'm fine." She clutches her heart. "Just wasn't expecting that."

We return to our search, her tossing over boxes, me combing through stacks of paper.

"This is futile." She slams her fists down over the lid of another box. "I don't even remember him having a tortoise."

"Perhaps he didn't." I step toward her. She glares at me. "I mean, perhaps he didn't mean a *real* tortoise. Like he didn't mean a *real* bird. Perhaps he meant something *like* a tortoise, or some representation. He was talking in the text of a riddle."

"All right." She charges across the room, her eyes fixed on something in the rubble. "So, perhaps something like this?" She holds up a shadow box. Inside is a relief drawing of a mechanical tortoise. Its shell is made of scrap widgets and gadgets, with gears pasted below to form its legs. Some sort of wheel sits embedded in a hole in the middle of the tortoise's scrap-metal shell.

"Precisely," I say. I'm across the floor in a blink, letter opener in hand, and use it in one smooth movement to break the glass, throwing a towel over the top first to muffle the sound.

Eyelet can hardly contain herself. She reaches in, twisting the wheel-like ornament in the middle of the tortoise's back. Nothing happens at first, and her face falls in disappointment—then we share an astonished glance as the wheel suddenly spins in the opposite direction and sinks into the depths of the shadow box. A moment later it pops loose from the box altogether in a dramatic puff of silvery steam.

Eyelet grabs the abandoned wheel piece, pokes her finger through the centre of it, and holds it up for me to see. "This is it." She spins the wheel off the end of her finger. "Get it? *At the spin of a velocipede, or two.* The answer to the second clue. This makes one—"

"So there must be another one somewhere." I dash across the room, prepared to search.

"What was that?" Eyelet freezes. Her eyes are twice their normal size.

A creak in the floorboards sends us scuttling off into the corner like bedbugs, hiding behind her father's desk. Eyelet reaches up, clutching her necklace, concealing its flash within her palm. I pull her close and wrap my arms around her, preparing for the worst.

The tick of the clock on the wall by the door echoes throughout the room, challenged only by our racing breath, nothing more.

"Whatever it was"—I swallow, peeking out around the leg of the desk—"it appears to be gone." I creep out slowly.

"Urlick." She stares past my shoulder. "What is that?"

I turn, half afraid to, tracking her hand to where she points. Across the room, in the corner behind the door, stands a stack of timber crates. Leaning against the wall behind them is an object hidden by a blanket. Just a sliver of its rusty rim is exposed.

I'm across the floor in a breath, tossing aside the crates. Eyelet follows, yanking away the blanket once I've cleared the way. Together we gasp at what we've found. "The second wheel," Eyelet exults. "We found it!"

"Now the question is, what do we do with it?"

Eyelet pulls out her petticoat message.

"Heed the underpinning of the raven's troubled wing, for beneath it hides the master key," she reads. "The master key—" She throws up her skirts, pulling the pin again from her stocking. "This is it! The master key!"

"Inside a spoked and circular tomb," she continues. *"You will find the treasure you seek.* Spoked and circular." Her eyes land on the giant wheel. "Help me with this, will you?" She bends to pick it up.

I lunge to help her, and it nearly takes me down. I can't believe the weight of it. Together we drag it across the room, to the emblem of the sun beneath her father's desk. "You see," she says, pointing to it. "It's a match. An exact match."

"It is, too," I marvel, dropping the wheel to the floor on top of the sun, amazed at how the rim is exactly the same size and shape as the circle that surrounds the sun in the design on the floor.

"Stand it upright, will you?" Eyelet turns as I do and jabs the slotted raven pin through the wheel like an axle. It clicks as it passes through, then locks into place halfway.

"Now, toss me the small one, will you please? I have an idea."

I grab the small one and lob it her way. She holds it up, and sure enough, the circle at the centre of the sun's design is the exact shape and size of the smallest velocipede wheel. She slips it over the top of the pin, just like the first one, and pushes it down. It, too, clicks into place.

"I knew it!" She grins. "Now for the *spoked and circular tomb . . . beneath a shimmering sun.* Steady this for me, please." She motions for me to take hold of the pin. Her gaze drops to the floor. She bends, picking at a metal cover at the oracle's centre.

"What are you doing?" I say.

"Looking for a keyhole." The metal cover pops up, exposing a thick brass ring. She loops it in her fingers and pulls. "It's stuck." She looks to me.

I drop to one knee and give it a yank, steadying the pin-skewered wheel in my other hand. The ring gives way like a stopper from a tub. I crash backward into the glass cabinet behind. Beakers and instruments rattle and jump and shatter on the floor around me. "Now we really need to hurry," I say, leaping to my feet, kicking bits of broken beaker beneath the cabinet legs, trying to cover our tracks.

"Ready," she says, lifting up her side of the wheel.

I race to lift up my side. Together we hover over the centre of the oracle, feeding the rod of skewered wheels—the mostly unlikely key— into the plug in the centre of the floor.

It drops squarely into place with a generous click.

"Inside a spoked and circular tomb, you will find the treasure you seek." She grins. "Let's hope so. Ready?" She grabs the smallest wheel, I grab the larger. "Turn!"

She spins hers one direction and I spin mine the other. When nothing happens, we switch directions and try again. Sure enough, a pulse of steam begins to rise from the seams in the floor. Jumping back, we hear the grind of a piston shunting, and then the floor begins to peel back. Each ray of the sun, in a neatly cut triangular section, curls upward from the floor like the individual petals of a flower extending in the heat. Cool clouds of steam waft out of every section of the oracle, filling the room in white, billowing mist.

Eyelet gasps, as do I; below each and every section of spoke appears a slot in the floor, a tiny crypt containing one hidden journal, twelve in all.

Thirty-Six

Eyelet

I've found them. After all the years of searching, they're really here. My father's journals. I can't believe it.

I sink to my knees and run a finger down one of the spines of the red hardcover journals. "*Volume One—Rayon.* That's French for *ray*—this one has to be connected." I yank it from its crypt and start leafing through the pages. Drawings of parts of the Illuminator appear. Urlick drops to his knees beside me. "Do you know French?" I say.

"Some, why?"

"It appears my father's coded the journals. Look for words like *cathode ray*, or *particulate matter*, or *radiate*. Only in French." Urlick looks up at me through queried brows. "Oh, and anything that means *light* or *lightning*, or *illuminate*. We can leave the rest and come back for them later."

Urlick rolls up his sleeves and busies himself, pulling journal after journal out of the ground and sorting them. "So, yes to *Foudre* and *Un Éclair*, but no to *Sang* and *Cellule*?"

"That's right."

"What about *Noir*?" He holds it up. "Another one of your father's riddles, perhaps?"

I frown at the volume. "Pass it here."

He tosses it over, then continues to weed through the rest, stopping to thumb through the volume that sits in his lap.

I open *Noir* to the table of contents and drag my finger down the list. Just seeing my father's penned words affects me. The way he looped his *m*'s, his exaggerated *s*'s. Seeing them again brings me to tears. I recall his hand, how swiftly he moved it across the page. The way he dunked his nib into the inkwell twice for luck before beginning a new line. I swallow, remembering how he'd let me help hold the pen as he wrote his final nightly entries. The smile on his face when we finished.

A ball of emotion lodges in my throat.

I fight through the tears that come and continue my search, flipping page after page, looking for relevant entries, but I can't understand a one. Though penned of my father's hand, they seem to be in a language I can't understand. An expertise only *he* understood.

Particulate radiate matter readings higher than the highest reading last month. Soil clearly contaminated. Abundant traces of radiate matter found in human hair? Equal trace amounts detected in the plaster of the walls?

What does this mean? What is he talking about, particulate radiate matter?

I suck in a splintery breath.

I turn the page and a letter slips out of the centre of the journal and drifts into my lap. I pick it up, examine it. The letter's never been sealed. Nor sent.

I open it quickly and pull out the contents, smoothing out the yellowed three-page letter over my knee. It's in my father's handwriting but is not part of his journal. It appears to contain his last will and testament, dated *March 5, 1892*, one day prior to his death.

> *It is in the express interest of the Commonwealth I record this information, out of love for my fellow man and country.*
>
> *Though I'm confident my science has been placed in the hands of an equally capable scientist, I have my reservations about his sanity, as well as his integrity. And I worry about the future of my machine.*
>
> *Though his papers claim he's a doctor of neurological science, as am I, he seems disproportionately obsessed with the mechanical workings of the apparatus itself, showing little to no interest in the human case studies I put before him, referring to their importance as secondary in nature. Furthermore, he refuses to acknowledge my documented findings and ignores me when I speak of the dangers of the machine. Referring to all the data I've gathered regarding the negative effects of exposure to the Ray as nothing more than controversial hearsay . . .*

The Illuminator. He's talking about the Illuminator. He has to be. I turn the page.

> *Repeatedly, he inquires about the range of the machine and its potential potency, speaking nonstop about his plans to modify both. He appears to be more concerned with interplanetary exploration than for the science for which the machine was intended.*
>
> *In a private meeting, he expressed to me his plans to use the Illuminator to ferret out the exact location of an alternate universe—which he believes exists beyond the cloud cover— where the dead still live. With the help of the Illuminator he*

seeks to navigate the heavens to verify this world's existence—
so he may join his dead wife there.

It is for these reasons I fear the newly appointed pro-
fessor suffers from some kind of degenerate brain disorder.
Some strange malady he's acquired since the tragic death of
his beloved wife, who passed while giving birth to their only
child—a son of whom he never speaks. Insanely, I'm told that
he blames the child for the death of his wife.

Urlick. I glance his way, remembering the things he told me
about the night of his birth, about the Illuminator ending up in his
father's lab.

This scientist. It's Urlick's father. It has to be.

I drop my eyes and return to the page.

I fear the harm that may come to our society if the
cathode-ray program is left in this man's hands. He cares not
about the patients, referring to his clinical trial subjects as
specimens, not people. It is as though his heart's gone cold,
made of stone.

Even more disturbing is the close business association this
man holds with Professor Smrt.

Smrt? Oh, God, no . . .

Between the two of them, I fear the worst for Brethren
and the Commonwealth at large. If they succeed in manipu-
lating the machine as they've indicated, any number of things
on Earth could be affected: from the soil, to the air, to the
water in the rivers.

Despite my recent findings to convince the Council oth-
erwise, Smrt appears to have the upper hand. He continues

to dismiss all pertinent data I lay before the Council—proof that the dangers of this science far outweigh the benefits—as nothing but the ravings of a madman.

Using my interest in Limpidious, he has been able to paint a picture of me as a failing scientist whose capacity is questionable.

That's why my father was demoted. It wasn't because he was failing. It was Smrt. He made my father out to be crazy, to gain access to his science. The machine. It was taken from him. He didn't give it up. He didn't give up on me.

In the absence of support, I've decided I must take matters into my own hands. I leave this morning for the Follies, to try and stop my successors.

May this letter (and the research contained within this journal) serve as record of my findings, should anything happen to me.

God be with me.

And with the future of humanity if I fail.

He knew. He knew something bad was going to happen. He knew and he went out there anyway . . .

Addendum: Let the record also show that in recent research, done since the completion of this journal, I have detected trace amounts of radiate particulate matter in both the urine and hair samples of a particular female subject whom I exposed to the Ray, up to a full month after she was photographed. Furthermore, her cells show signs of irreparable damage, to which end I've been feverishly working to create an antidote. I have divulged this information to both Academic parties named herein, as well as the Scientific Council of the Commonwealth, all of which have ignored me. I did not, however, divulge the name of said subject, but will now, out of fear, should I not return.

Said subject is none other than my very own daughter—Eyelet.

Eyelet? I gasp. The letter drops in my lap.

That's why he stopped. That's why he never cured me. Not for the lure of money. But out of the fear that he was hurting me.

I bite my lip. My heart rushes in my ears.

That day at the carnival. The business he had in the Follies. The look on my mother's face when I caught the carny with father's machine. He didn't give up on me after all. He stopped in order to protect me—

"What is it?" Urlick looks up. "Have you found something?"

I stare. "It's nothing," I finally say and drop my eyes to conceal the tears. "Just an old letter my father wrote my mum."

Thirty-Seven

Eyelet

"I should have known you'd know exactly where to find them."

Urlick's head shoots up at the sound of the voice. My gaze follows his. Professor Smrt stands before us, beady black eyes leering down at me, his shadowy features glimmering into view through the veil of leftover oracle steam. The hiss of it must have masked his approach. Neither Urlick nor I heard him coming.

I tremble as he steps through the steam, closing the tiny gap between us, the hem of his dark professorial cloak swaying to a stop over Academy-issued red-soled shoes.

"Whose face do you wear? Because I know that's not your own!" He lunges forward, tearing the mask from my face.

My hands spring to my cheeks to quiet the sting. I wince under the familiar stench of his sour, curdled breath.

"This is brilliant, really." He touches the eyes on the mask, his hand jerking back when the lids flutter shut. "It really is the perfect untraceable disguise. That is, if you don't mind wearing the face of the dead." He tosses the mask aside. It hits the floor with a soggy thud, too far away for me to retrieve it. "I knew you'd return," he hisses at me. "No good having the machine if you don't know how it works, is it? And you—" He turns on Urlick. "Who might you really be?"

He rips the mask from Urlick's face, then stumbles backward, aghast. "Unbelievable. Winston's son's come home to roost."

"What are you talking about?"

"The prodigal son of Professor Goddard shows up at last. I knew you had to be out there somewhere—"

"How do you know who I am?" Urlick stumbles to his feet, stunned.

"I've always known, I just didn't know you were still alive, not for sure. Though I had my suspicions. I suppose it would have behooved me to have tried to find my property sooner."

"What are you saying?"

"You're mine. You've been mine since birth."

"What?"

"Your father. He signed you over to me. You're a registered specimen." He reaches into his pocket and produces a document. "It's all right here. You're property of the Academy. Missing property, presumed dead. A little charade your father obviously tried to play. I had Radcliffe dig it out of the archives on a hunch when I heard we had a mysterious intruder . . . who looked an awful lot like your father."

Urlick lurches, snatching the document from Smrt's hand.

"Go ahead. Read it."

Registered specimen 29663.

Male: 8 pounds, 13 and one half ounces.

Distinguishable markings: Port-wine stains on face and neck, pink eyes, albino-like pigmented skin.

Category: Severe deformity affecting mental stability.

Prognosis: Extermination.

Donated by Sir Winston Goddard Babbit. February 27th in the year of our Ruler, Eighteen Hundred and Eighty-Three.

Urlick looks up. Shocked. Breathless. His hands tremble.
As do mine.

"That is the day of your birth, isn't it?" Smrt rolls his hands.

"It's not true! It *can't* be true!" The muscles at the sides of Urlick's jaw clench. "My father signed me over to the nursemaid, not you!" Urlick spits.

"The nursemaid?" Smrt's eyes jump in their sockets. "I was told you were lost to the Vapours in transport." His brows rise. "I guess that confirms we've *both* been lied to, haven't we?"

"If it's true, then why did my father accept me when I was returned to him? Why didn't he just turn me over to you?"

"Good question." Smrt circles Urlick, eyeing him like a racehorse at market. "He was in clear violation of the law. Perhaps he had plans of his own for you. Can't blame him, really, seeing you now." He reaches out, stroking Urlick's cheek. "You are a very special one, aren't you? Pink eyes, white skin, dark hair . . . *mostly* . . ." He flips the one stray lock of white hair away from Urlick's eyes and grabs him by the chin. "You truly are a freak of nature. The lab will be so thrilled."

Urlick jerks his chin away. "You're a liar! You just made that paper up!"

"How could I, when I didn't know, until moments ago, that you even still existed? Besides, who could deny those tattered edges?"

Urlick looks down at the card in his hands, then back up.

"My, my, my," Smrt tsks, sizing up Urlick's face. "You really are the spitting image of your mother under all that nastiness, aren't you? She was a good-looking woman, your mother. Course, you'd have no way of knowing that."

Urlick's fists ball at his sides. I reach over, taking one of his fists in my hand.

"What's this?" Smrt notices. "How charming! The pink-eyed monster has a love interest. Though I can't say my daughter will be impressed. Radcliffe!" He snaps his fingers and the other voice from the hallway appears, producing a struggling Flossie from behind his back. He holds her tightly by the arm.

"I believe you've met my daughter?" Smrt grins, rolling an Insectatron around in his palm. "Also known as my messenger."

"I knew it," I breathe.

"Seems the arrival of your so-called *cousin* here"—he flips a look at me—"tweaked my little Flossie's jealousy antennae enough to contact her dear old dad. After a brief exchange of information"—he holds up the Ladybird—"I realized what a fool I'd been, believing her story about her needy little student in the woods." He glares at Urlick. "Lucky for me, her love for you pales in comparison to her desire to gain her estranged father's approval. Always the way, isn't it?"

Urlick glares at Flossie across the room. "How could you do this? I trusted you!"

"I didn't mean for this to happen!" Flossie shrieks, struggling against her captor. "You have to believe me, Urlick! I only brought you to his attention to try to protect you. I had no idea who you were! I didn't know *any* of this before today!" She sobs. "I thought you were unwittingly abetting a dangerous fugitive! I was only trying to save you! I didn't want to see you go to the jug!"

"*Liar.*"

"Oh, come now, Urlick, you mustn't blame the girl." Smrt laughs. "Fool that she is, she's been keeping your secret for years. Fearful that I'd disapprove of the looks of her *love interest*, she had me believing the 'special student' in her charge out in the Follies suffered from a hole in the heart. She lied for you. Never gave me a description. Never even told me your address. If she had, I'd have found you years ago. In fact, if it hadn't been for the memory-plate match to your deceased father at the gates, I might never have put this all together. But I have."

Urlick swallows.

"I win. You lose." Smrt turns and snaps his fingers. "Radcliffe. Call the guards. Let them know we have a specimen that needs locking up—"

"*No!*" Flossie screams.

"You can't do this." Urlick lurches forward. "You'll never get away with it."

"I don't see how you're going to stop me. This is not the Follies. There are *laws* in this part of the Commonwealth. In Brethren, a man is due his *property*, and those who take it from him go to the jug. Not only are you legally my specimen, but I have it on good word"—he flashes a smile at Flossie—"that you have something else that belongs to me. A certain machine . . . hidden in your basement."

He turns toward the door. "Radcliffe!"

"Wait!" Urlick stalls. "If you knew we were coming, why didn't you just arrest us the second we got through the gates?" I can see by the look in his eyes he's cooking up some kind of plan.

"Come now, what fun would that have been?" Smrt smiles. "Besides, I needed to give you enough time to make the discovery." He eyes the journals on the floor. Bending, he scoops one up. "You have no idea how many times I've gone over this room in search of these." He stares at me coldly. "I should have known to employ your skills sooner—"

"I never would have employed them for you."

"You'd have done whatever I told you!"

He closes in on me. Anger burns in his eyes. "The moment your mother passed away, you became a ward of the Commonwealth, property of the Ruler, to do with as he sees fit."

"What are you talking about?"

He leans. "Things have changed in your brief little stint away from Brethren. Let me catch you up. The Ruler of Brethren is dead, and I've taken his place."

"How is that possible?"

"Anything's possible in a world where you can write your own laws. And where the Ruler leaves no male successor."

I swallow as Smrt grins.

"As law would dictate, upon his tragic and unexpected death, in lieu of an heir, all the Ruler's powers transferred to me."

"Who arranged that?"

"Who do you think?" Smrt reaches for his palsy puffer, inhales, and slowly lets it seep out through his teeth.

"How convenient," mumbles Urlick.

"Seems the Ruler contracted some form of toxic disease," Smrt goes on. "Despite all his efforts to keep Brethreners safe. Poor man, passing as quickly as he did, and in such an agonizingly horrible way. He died the same way poor Mrs. Benson did." He looks at me. "You remember Mrs. Benson, don't you? I believe you were given the first picto-ray of the coins in her purse, at the carnival?" He stares.

Those eyes. Smrt's dead-lark eyes. It was he. The carny. The one peddling the prototype of the Illuminator at the carnival that day. *My* Illuminator.

Not *his*.

"Oh, how the Ruler loved to get drunk and take photographs of himself with his little miracle machine. More than a hundred picto-rays were found taken of his lungs alone, I'm told. Not to mention all those he took of his *brain*."

I suck in a nervous breath, thinking back to the words of my father's letter. "You killed them," I whisper. "You killed the Ruler, didn't you? You set it all up to take his place. You killed them all. Mrs. Benson, my father, too—"

"I never killed your father, he killed himself!"

Out of the corner of my eye I see Urlick reaching for something. A flicker of light passes over the mirrored glass. I turn just in time to see him crack a beaker over the sideboard. Shards of glass rain to the floor.

Urlick wheels around, the jagged remains of the beaker in his hand. "Don't move!" he shouts, swinging it up under Smrt's chin. He swipes the journal from Smrt's hand and lofts it to me across the room. "Run!" he shouts. "And don't look back!"

"But—"

He reads my mind. "I'm right behind you."

I catch it and scoop two more up off the floor before bursting out the door, knocking Radcliffe to his arse along the way.

*

I race up the corridor and into the next, taking refuge behind Aphrodite to catch my breath, hoping Urlick will think to find me there. Before he can, I hear boots and I'm off again, racing up the stairs to the second floor.

"There!" A voice jolts me to a stop, and I race the opposite way up the hall, rounding a corner, journals clutched to my chest. Someone's breath falls hard at my back.

Fingers thread through mine, then fall away, and I nearly scream at the touch of them. "This way," someone shouts. It's Urlick. He's caught up. He reaches out. "Give me your hand."

I do, and he whirls around another corner.

"After them!" Smrt's voice charges up the back stairs. His henchmen leap them two at a time.

I turn my head. Guards charge from all directions. "They're everywhere!" I shout.

Urlick slows, locking our fingers, and flings me around another corner. "Don't stop!" He pushes me ahead of him. "Keep running! No matter what happens, just keep running and don't look back!"

I surge forward, twisting up two more corridors, wondering if he's following. At the last turn I'm relieved to hear him drop from the banister behind me, shoes landing hard in the hall. "I may have bought us some time," he says, racing up beside me. "At least I hope I have."

He grabs my hand and we race down the next corridor, sliding to a stop at its end.

"What now?" I gasp, staring at the window. "How are we going to get out of here?"

"Like this." Urlick pops the latch, and the towering garrison windows swing open, revealing a small balcony overlooking a monstrous tree.

"What are you doing?" I cry as Urlick grabs me by the arm and stuffs me through, leaving me to teeter on the ledge.

"See that drainpipe there?" He points. "I want you to swing your leg over it and shinny down."

"You want me to *what*?"

"Listen to me." He grabs my chin.

"But—"

"No buts. You're going down."

"But Urlick—" I gaze at the ground. My stomach lurches up.

"I'll meet you at the quarry where we left the cycle. Do you remember how to get there?"

"No." I shake my head.

"Call your magic bird." He grins at me. "I'm sure she'll help you find the way. Now go!" He pushes.

"Wait!" I cling to him. "What about the windows?"

"I'll lock them behind you."

"And Smrt?"

"He'll never suspect a thing."

"What about you? How will you get away?"

"Don't worry about me." He twists. Combat boots thunder up the hallway. "I'll find a way. Now go!"

Voices fill the corridor. Urlick's head jerks around.

"Oh, and Eyelet—" He pulls me back in. His lips graze the side of my cheek as he speaks. "If I'm not there in thirty minutes, leave without me."

"Never," I say.

Urlick grins.

I disappear through the window, swing my leg out over the drainpipe, and shinny down, my feet meeting hard with the grass.

A symphony of shouts pour through the cracks in the stone wall. Gunshots ring out, jerking my head back to the window.

Oh, Urlick. Please be safe.

Thirty-Eight

Urlick

I lock the window behind Eyelet, race up the corridor, and slip between the pillars into the next hall. Smrt's guards converge on the landing, blocking the stairs completely. Blast it! There's no other way out.

I lean, seeing another set of guards closing in from the opposite end, and yet another charge filling in the opening in the hall below. I'm surrounded. Literally surrounded. Nowhere to go but up.

I tip my chin, searching the ceiling for possibilities. A chandelier. I grin.

Wasting no time, I sink my feet into the carved leaves at the base of the pillar I'm hiding behind and shinny up it, reaching for the wrought-iron curls of the massive chandelier hanging overhead. My arms looped through the curls, I unlock my legs from the pillar and swing out over the heads of my pursuers, crystals droplets tinkling.

"There he is!" a guard shouts as I sail past. I drop from the fixture into the ballroom below, scramble to my feet, and run.

Smrt's henchmen follow close behind.

I round the corner to the lower set of stairs, leaping over the shocked head of a rogue guard, ride the banister, and spring arch-backed from the bottom.

"Stop him!" the guard shouts, turning and galloping down the stairs.

I bolt through the lobby out into the great hall and then up a dark corridor—where the barrels of two armed and ready steamrifles confront me. Guards peer over their ends.

"Don't move." One of the guards cocks his gun. "Or your little sweetheart will never see you again."

My shoes stagger to a halt.

I stand there a moment, gasping for breath, my eyes searching for a way out. In a flash of glass I see an opening. Like lightning, I double back, skipping over bullets, and launch myself through a doorway, skittering headlong through the back of a kitchen, toppling rack after rack of pots and pans in my wake. Cooks, scullery maids, and servants scatter, wearing looks of horror on their faces. A barrage of screams erupts.

I crash through a set of swing doors at the back of the room and gallop through the ballroom and up a slim corridor, and I throw open the doors to a pantry, where a small boy startles and gasps. The stockpot of steaming water in his hands falls to the floor, metal pot yowling as it conks the stone. Scalding water slops forward, lapping the toes of my shoes. The boy's chin wags. He screws up his face, prepared to bawl.

"No." I wave my hands. "Don't, please, I beg you."

But he wails anyway, letting out an ear-puncturing screech. I dive at him, throw my hand over his mouth, and drag him with me backward into the cupboard, slamming the door behind us.

"If you promise not to scream again, I promise I won't hurt you." The whites of the boy's eyes bulge in the dark pantry. "Do we have a deal?"

The boy snivels and nods.

"You're sure? You promise you won't scream if I lift my hand from your mouth?"

The boy nods again.

Slowly I lift my hand, expecting an eruption, pleased when one doesn't come. "Do you know what this is?" I say, reaching, pulling a gadget from my pack.

The boy gasps. He looks at me, confused, worried, serious. "A peeler," he says. His voice quivers. His eyes plead with me not to stab him with it, and I realize I may have just made things worse.

"It's not just any old peeler," I whisper quickly. "It's a magical one." I click a mechanism on its side and it coughs up a blade. The silver glints in the din of the closet. The boy smiles, elated.

He reaches for it and I pull it back. "Ah ah ah . . ." I say. "First you have to help me get out of here. Deal?"

He smiles.

"You see, I'm playing a little game of hide-and-seek with the guards, and so far I'm winning. You don't want me to lose, do you?"

The boy shakes his head.

"Good, 'cause I don't want to lose, either. But I'm going to lose if they find me in here. I need to find another way out. Do you know another way for me to escape without using the door?"

The boy frowns.

"Come now, surely a curious little boy like you knows some secret passageway. Another door, maybe? A hole in the wall?"

The boy bursts into a smile. He scrambles to the back of the closet, revealing a dumbwaiter inside the wall, behind a cupboard door.

"Well done!" I ruffle his hair as I climb in. "Now," I whisper, the sound of boots approaching. "I want you to count to ten, then open the door *very slowly*. Do you hear me?"

The boy nods.

"You can count to ten, can't you?"

He nods again.

"Good, here you are." I drop the peeler into his hand, and his eyes light up. Boots scuffle outside the door.

"Now don't forget," I say, lowering my voice, "a full count of ten, then step out with your hands raised. That's very important. Don't forget that bit. The guards don't like it if you don't play by the rules."

Shoulders crash against the door.

"Ready?" I crawl in on the shelf and cross my legs. "One." I pull on the rope.

"Two." I launch myself up inside the brick-lined chimney inside the wall.

"Steamrifles ready!"

"Three . . ."

"Come out or we're coming in!"

"Four . . ."

The boy throws open the door.

"Don't shoot!" one of the guards shouts as I ascend the chimney as quickly as I can.

"What do you have in your hand, boy?"

"A peeler," he says.

"Where did you get it?"

The boy hesitates. "From the nice monster, getting away in the closet," he says.

*

I spill from the dumbwaiter on the third floor, literally tumbling out of it. Dashing over the turquoise tiles in the room, I sail out into the hallway, clambering up the hardwood to the balcony at its end. Throwing open the garrison windows, I step out onto the ledge, greeted by a massive tree. I can barely see through it to the ground, its leaves are so thick. *Perfect.* Likewise, the guardsmen patrolling the grounds won't be able to see me.

Just beyond the tree, the mechanical ravens lurk, presiding over the gates through which we entered. Just a few metres separate me from the end of the nearest branch. Though flimsy, it'll have to do.

My head cranks around at the sound of voices barreling up the stairs. The snouts of steamrifles flash. "I'll check the second floor, you head up to the third!"

I swallow. Here's hoping the branch holds me. I turn back, sink my hand into my pack, and search for my rod, pulling it out by the telescope end. Steadying the wheel on the side, I hurl the rod up and over my shoulder, then fling it forward out the window like a fishing pole toward the tree, just as I did out over the table that day with the bacon, in the biggest cast I've ever attempted.

The fingers at the other end clamp down around a branch, and I jump, hanging off the end of the rod. My knees pulled tight to my chest, I swing apelike out over the yard, skimming the heads of the guards, and disappear into the leaves.

Thirty-Nine

Eyelet

I weave through the city, lost, my mind consumed with Urlick. Did he get out of the Academy safely, or have Smrt's men captured him?

Will they capture me?

I struggle to remember the way back to the quarry, Brigsmen following close behind. I've no idea which way to go, what roads to take. Nothing looks familiar. The first time, Urlick led the way.

Reaching up, I touch my face, startled by the feel of skin. The mask of Ida lies on the floor at the Academy. No time to retrieve it. Only time to run. My eyes fix on the "Wanted" poster nailed to a pole on the opposite side of the street. My stomach curls. The face on the poster is mine. I suck in a sharp breath, realizing there'll be others posted all over town. If I'm discovered, I'll be jailed—or worse, locked up in the asylum. I cannot risk being seen.

I flip my hood up over my head and duck off the main street into an alley. "Pan!" I call to the sky when I think it's safe. "Pan, where are you! I need your help! Pan! Where are you, please!"

A steamplough whistle shrieks in the distance, jerking my spine to its full length. I clutch my chest. A steamplough. I must be close. There was a steam yard right next to the quarry. Urlick stashed the cycle among the boulders. The whistle sounds again.

I pick up my skirts and dash toward it, hurdling a hedge, landing stiff-legged in a farmer's garden. I trip through a tangle of carrot tops and shabbily kept peas, clear a goat, and springboard over the arse of a mule before I'm through, darting in and out of fruit trees and around the corner of the barn, only to end up where I've already been.

"Blast!" I swear, for the first time ever. A filthy habit I've picked up from Urlick. "Oh, Urlick, where are you?" I spin in circles, pinching the stitch from my side. "Pan! Urlick! Someone! *Please . . .*"

A steamrifle shot rings through the trees. I scramble for cover behind a hedge, crouching low and silent, cupping my pendant in my hand to hide its pulsing light, terrified it'll give me away.

"Over there," I hear a voice say. Boots rush forward, then off in the opposite direction. I breathe a sigh of relief. After a count of ten I step out from the hedge, only to be sent scuttling back as a streak of black clips the edge of my draperies and then rises up into the clouds. It descends again moments later, cawing.

"Pan?" I squint at the blur in the sky.

She wings back around, appearing through the cloud cover, her red beak shining like a beacon of hope through the grey. "Oh, thank God it's you! The quarry, Pan, I have to get to the quarry."

She caws, signalling for me to follow. I bolt after her, eyes fixed on the sky. "Lower!" I shout, following glimpses of her black feathers through the cloud-choked sky. "You have to fly lower! I'm losing you!"

She lowers herself, twisting through the streets. I burst after her, my heart thundering, my boots crashing against the cobblestones. Before I know it, we've reached the dancing mechanical fence line that separates Gears from Brethren. The one I passed through the first time, when I entered Gears alone.

"The hole!" I shout to Pan in the sky. "You've got to help me find the hole!" I gulp as she dives, winging her way through it, soaring into the sky on the other side.

"Well done!" I shout, racing after her, stopping to toss Father's journals through the hole ahead of me. I lunge headfirst, my chin scraping the dirt, collect the books on the other side, and run, following Pan's lead through the backstreets of Gears as Brigsmen pour through the formal gates.

"This way," Pan calls, her voice strained and gravelly.

"You spoke!" I gasp, stumbling forward. "Your voice! It's returned!"

"So it has." Pan nods her head. The surprise in her eyes is as big as in mine.

Another steam whistle sounds, this time very close.

Pan's wings catch on a stream of air that tips her to one side. She almost falls from the sky. Regaining her balance, she veers sharply left, swooping low between two buildings. I follow. She wings out over the city's square, and I panic. "What are you doing?" I slow. "You're going the wrong way!"

Pan loops around and swoops down in front of my face. "Follow me," she orders, staring at me firmly, like she's my *mother*, her eyes flecked blue and green.

"I can't!" I shake my head. "There are too many people. If I enter the market, someone will recognize me."

Pan hovers in place, holding her gaze. "How much do you trust me?" she says, then wings away.

I gasp, hearing my father's words, my mother's voice in hers. Perhaps Urlick was right. Perhaps she is nothing but a common household parrot, picking up on words and phrases my parents have said. No. I shake my head. Pan is much more than that. Look at all the things she's done for me. Her loyalty alone proves she's more than a dimwitted, mimicking parrot.

I stumble on, following Pan through the low, rolling fog around a corner, into the centre of the bustling market square of Gears. My likeness hangs on every signpost, at every corner. The terror of that reality worms through my head. A flash of me dangling from the gallows haunts me, followed by another of me caged in an asylum with Smrt holding the key.

I'll die before I let that happen. I swear I will. I shake off the images and push forward, flipping my hood up over my head.

"Posies?" I slam into an old peasant woman, not looking where I'm going. She stuffs a half-dead bouquet under my nose.

"No, thank you," I say, pushing them away.

"Don't I know you from somewhere?" Her pupils dance. Her prying eyes linger dangerously on my face.

"No," I breathe, rushing past her, my knees knocking beneath me.

Her eyes dart to a poster and back. She sprouts a toothless grin. "I have seen you. You're the girl!" she calls after me. "The one on the poster!"

Heads twist in my direction.

Pan shrieks, diving down from the sky at the woman. "You nasty lot, get outta 'ere!" The woman shoos her off. People scatter on the street.

I run ahead, blind to where I'm going, veering off the main street into a corridor. Pan joins me, and I breathe a heavy sigh of relief.

"I told you that wasn't a good idea."

We weave through the backstreets. Four tight turns later, the fog lifts just enough for me to make out the skeleton of a station. Loading docks loom to the left; steamploughs rest on the tracks to the right. The quarry falls over the edge behind.

"We've made it!" I cry, smiling up at Pan. "Now to get to the cycle!"

I race forward under the disguise of the cloud cover, falling back up against the side of the steamplough engine, hiding myself inside its waft of steam.

"Brigsmen," I breathe.

Men in black leather boots and steely suits patrol not only the steamplough yard but the rim and the basin of the quarry as well. They swarm like flies over a withering corpse, steamrifles at the ready. Every inch of the quadrant has been staked out, not a rock left unturned.

"How did they know we'd be coming here?" I whisper to Pan as she lands on my shoulder.

"I don't know." She shrugs.

"What are we going to do now?"

I lean out around the front of the engine, searching the premises for signs of Urlick. "Do you see him?" I whisper to Pan. "I don't see Urlick anywhere."

The steamplough sounds its horn, giving my heart a start. Steam chugs from between the boxcar's wheels. My eyes catch on a Brigsman standing next to the boulders where Urlick stashed the cycle earlier. My heart thrashes wildly inside my chest. He jams his billy club in and out of the rock crevice, peering between the boulders.

"Don't move, Bertie," I whisper to the air. "We need you. Don't reveal yourself."

At last the Brigsman gives up and I let out my breath, relieved, as I watch him stalk away.

"Pan," I say. "Will you take a look?"

She nods, lifting off of my shoulder. I hold my breath again as she slowly circles the entire yard, scanning the ground from left to right. She dips into the basin, flying in low lines up and down the belly of the quarry before returning to me, a look of despair on her face.

"Nothing," I say.

She shakes her head.

"Do you suppose he's been caught?"

"Could be."

I twist my hands together. *If I'm not there within the half hour, leave without me*, I hear Urlick say. I check my chrono-cuff. It's been over three quarters of an hour. Something must be wrong. I wasted time, lost. But Urlick knows the way.

"I'm going back for him." I turn to Pan. "Will you help me?"

*

I slip on a puddle of street grease and slide past the corner out into the middle of the market. Mouths fall open, staring. My arms paddle-wheel backward in a furious attempt to regain my balance, drawing even more unwanted attention.

Pan panics, circling around, swooping low, creating the diversion I need. I dash from the street, falling in behind a makeshift wall at the back of the market, next to a balloon-maker's shop.

I peer through a knot in the wood at the shrouds of sackcloth lining the mud floor of his stall, cut into slices a hundred times the length of an arm. The vendor sits in the middle of the stall, a deflated balloon at his feet. He threads the needle on his sewing machine, pumps the throttle, and begins stitching on a patch. It's nearly as big as he is—though he's not very big—but only half his width.

Mounds of varnished taffeta lay billowed in the opposite corner, sky blue in colour, adorned with painted planets and constellations, as big as frescoes on a wall. He finishes stitching the canvas and lays the balloon in a perfect flat circle on the road. Attaching its ropes to a basket, the vendor lights a fire in the basket's canister. Slowly the balloon swells to life. The bluest of blue taffeta creeps to the sky, drifting up from the earth. On its side is a whimsical drawing of our long-lost sun.

A scuffle breaks out on the other side of the wall. My heart jumps to my throat. An angry voice pours through a crack in the mortar. I throw my ear to the knot in the wall and listen.

"I *saw* yuh take it. Now *'and* it over, yuh grimy little thief, yuh!"

"I ain't got it, *honest* I ain't."

The second voice sounds small.

I press my face to the bricks and peer through a hole into the vendors' lot beyond it. A brute of a man with a bristly beard holds a small boy up by the scruff of his neck. The boy's spindly legs are kicking. He's trying to connect with the man's shin. Something metal glistens from the boy's pocket.

"I *din't* take anything from yuh, I swear, *I din't.*"

"Yuh lying little sod, yuh!" The man shouts. "That's the third time this week yuh've pillaged from me! And I tell yuh, it'll be the last!" He drops the boy to the ground and grabs him by the ear. "Maybe some time in the orphanage will keep yuh from robbin' me blind!"

"Ooooow!" the boy yowls as the man tugs him forward. "Yuh can't do this!"

"The *'ell* I can't!" The man yells.

"Pleeeeeease," the boy fights. "Me mum, she's not far. She'll be looking for me." He wrinkles his face. "Yuh can't put me in a 'nage wiff parents—"

"Oh, can't, can I?" The man stoops to get a better grip, dragging the boy up the alley. My heart burns listening to the boy holler. I swallow as they draw near. My eyes move again onto the balloon in the alley, nearly half-filled.

All at once, I have an idea.

"There yuh are, Roderick." I step boldly from my hiding place, praying my plan is going to work.

My knees tremble as the man comes to a halt in front of me.

The boy looks up, sniffs.

"I've been looking everywhere for yuh," I say, trying to sound convincing, tripping a bit on my fake cockney accent. My gaze shifts from the ear-pinching man to the boy and back again. "I see you've found my little brother." The boy goes to open his mouth, and I flash my eyes at him, signalling for him to keep silent. "Me muvver and I been lookin' everywhere. What's 'e done this time?" I return my eyes to the man. "Pinched something again?" I put my hands on my hips and try to look cross. "How many times has Muvver told yuh not to steal! Yuh'll have to excuse 'im, 'e takes after our no-good father. 'E left us, 'e did, a long ways back."

The boy blinks at me and grins.

The man clears the choke from his throat, releasing his grip on the boy's ear just slightly.

"'E's got real sticky fingers, this one," the man says. "Made off with a 'ole lot o' me best tinkers, he did. And it's not the first time 'e's done it, either."

"Roderick!" I say, turning to the boy. "Return the man 'is tinkers." The boy looks at me, shocked, confused. "Yuh 'eard me." I shoo him with my fingers. "Go on, empty yer pockets."

Slowly, the boy dips his hand into his trouser pocket and pulls out the shiny object I saw before. "Now the other," I say. Reluctantly, he turns his second pocket inside out and several more trinkets fall to the ground. "There yuh are," I say.

The man snatches them up in his palm, using a dirty, fat finger to sort through the lot.

"'E won't do it again. I promise." I step up and rest my hands on the boy's shoulders. "I'll see to that meself."

"Yuh'd better. Or yuh'll both be finding yerselves in the orphanage." He wags his filthy finger in front of my face. Slowly he narrows his eyes. "Say"—he leers at me—"don't I know yuh from somewheres?" His lip grows a curious stitch.

My heart stiffens in my chest. "We'd better get going," I say to Roderick, dropping my gaze to the pavement to avert the man's. "Muvver'll be worried sick." I push the boy ahead of me up the alley, shuffling as quickly as I can behind.

"Wait a minute . . ." The man shouts after us. "Yer that girl! The one from the posters!" I break out into a run. "Get back 'ere!" the man shouts, sprinting.

The boy reaches back, grabs me by the hand, and wheels me around a sharp corner. The two of us fly up the alley into another. "'Urry!" The boy flits up the cobblestone. "Over 'ere!" He ducks in behind a trash bin and signals for me to join him.

I race the last few steps, fall in behind him, and crouch down.

The man thunders past the opening to the alley and out into the market square, hollering.

"Guess I owe you one," I gasp, looking at the boy once it's safe.

"I'd say we're even." He smiles at me. "Sebastian." He sticks out a grimy hand for me to shake.

I hesitate, then shake it begrudgingly. "Pleased to meet you, Sebastian."

"Yer Eyelet, right?" The boy grins.

"How did you know?" I snap.

The boy laughs. "Yer face is all over them posters."

"Saw them, did you?"

"Who could miss 'em? They's everywhere."

I lower my head.

"Don't worry, miss. I ain't gonna tells no one I see'd yuh. Yuh 'ave me word." He crosses his chest.

"Thanks," I say.

I look up, checking the skies for Pan. I seem to have lost her. "Don't suppose you know a safe way for me to get back to Brethren."

"Not for the likes of yuh, miss." The boy sucks his lip. "No offense, but with yer mug's all over the poles, yuh'd 'ave to travel by rooftop not to get arrested."

I tap my chin. "That's it!" I launch to my feet. I grab the boy by the sleeve and drag him up the alley.

"Where are we goin', miss?" he hollers.

"How do you feel about helping me steal something?"

The boy grins.

I haul him around the corner of the balloon-maker's stall. "What is it?" he asks as I hold him up to peek through the knothole.

"My rooftop ticket to Brethren."

Forty

Urlick

The thought of Eyelet standing alone at the quarry makes my stomach roll. I never should have sent her ahead without me, down a drainpipe and out into an open yard full of guards and Brigsmen. What was I thinking?

I *wasn't* thinking. Or I'd never have let us get separated.

I burst from the trees across from the Academy, twisting my way through Brethren's streets, hoping to lose the two Brigsmen who've now joined the guards in their search for me, snapping like dogs at my heels. Lucky for me, they're old and out of shape, huffing and puffing and easy to hear.

I dart down an alley, losing the Brigsmen altogether, or so I believe. I'm just about to rejoice when an angry dog appears in their place—ears flat to his head, teeth bared. Slobber flops from his chops.

"Easy, boy." I hold out my hands.

The dog curls his lips.

I turn and run, and he stalks me like a panther, his teeth nipping at the backs of my calves all the way. Racing to the end of the alley, I suck in my breath and leap sideways, slipping between the building and the fencepost, relieved when only the dog's head pops through after me, his shoulders too broad to fit.

I turn and run, grinding to a halt. Dead end. I look both ways. No escape. The dog still yaps through the hole in the opening. I have no choice. The only way out is up. I gulp, scaling the fence at the end of the alley—only to come face-to-face with a Brigsman. The same one who forced me into the forest at the beginning of my run. He aims his steamrifle directly at my head. "I knew it would only be a matter of time," he says, grinning.

I drop off the fence, choosing dog over Brigsman, only to find myself facing four more guards in the alley. They cock their guns and take aim, prepared to blast my head from my shoulders. I've got to do something, and quick.

Luckily for me, the dog decides to make the first move. Twisting his body sideways, he pops through the opening and charges, snarling, into the alley, capturing the Brigsmen's attention. Their heads swing sideways just long enough for me to boot the dog into the other Brigsman and squeeze my way back through the hole in the fence.

I race through the alleyways, catapulting over fences, toppling garbage cans behind me as I go. I'm just about to drop down from another fence top when a voice behind me yells, "Stop!"

A Brigsman appears out of the cloud cover like a ghost. I look down the barrel of a steamrifle into a set of angry eyes. His jaw is set. His finger, twitching.

"*Stop!* Or I swear I'll blow a hole straight through your *ticker.*"

He's young. Barely nineteen, if that—just a year older than I. His chin is covered in a soft layer of manly dust, not even enough to be bothered to shave. By the looks of how hard his hands are trembling, my bet is he's never shot a man before. Let alone blown a hole in someone's ticker.

Banking on that, I drop from the fence and start running, my backside disappearing over another before he's had the time to think.

"Bloody *hell*!" He hurdles the fence and chases me, his shoes striking the cobblestones like gunshots. I fly down another alley, gauging my speed ahead of the roar of his breath—again, blocked by another fence. This time a brick wall with a flat cement top, stretching a good foot over my head.

"Blast!" I swear, leaping, barely hurling myself onto the top edge, my organs groaning as they collide with the bricks. *Certainly not as much give to this wall as there was to the wooden ones.* I pull to a stand, coughing. Teetering tightrope-like over the narrow cement top, I race sideways, seeking safety between two buildings. A bullet takes out my right heel, knocking my leg out from under me. I spin around, fighting to regain my balance.

"Get down from there or you're dead." The boy shows his teeth. "I've orders to kill you on sight—and trust me, I will."

"I doubt that," I say, my heart lurching in my chest, "as you've already had your chance and haven't." *That's it, taunt the man with the gun. That's always brilliant.*

"Get down," the boy growls, pulling the hammer back on his gun.

"Halt!" Another Brigsman appears in the alleyway behind me. I glance over my shoulder to find at least five more. Brigsmen fill in the streets on either side of me. I'm surrounded. Smrt appears out of the fog. "Shoot him!" he snarls through gnashed teeth.

The Brigsmen on either side raise their guns.

I scan the fence line, my stomach in my throat. *If only I could make it between those two buildings.* I track the fence line through the middle of them onto the next street. *If I ran and turned sideways perhaps . . .* "Wait!" I shout, buying myself some time. I throw my hands in the air. "I don't think you really want to shoot me! Not with this strapped to my chest!" I reach down, slowly, and throw open the front of my coat, exposing the covers of three red journals. "I don't think they'll be very legible riddled with steamrifle bullets, do you? Not to mention spattered with my blood."

Smrt's face morphs into indignation. "Shoot him in the head!" he says. "Straight through the eye, so there's less blood!"

"Wait!" I say. "Wouldn't you rather I pass you the journals first?" I swallow, hoping he takes the bait. Nothing goes down, my mouth is so dry. My hands are shaking.

"Very well, then," he smirks. "As you please." He reaches out to take them.

I act as though I'm about to pull them from my waistcoat, but instead turn, high-stepping it across the top wall, clutching the journals as I go.

"Shoot!" Smrt shouts.

Rifle shots pitch past me—one skins the heel of my shoe.

"Good God, good God, good God," I chant. "If you're listening, I could use a little help down here!" Bullets sing, chipping holes in the cement behind me. One nicks the crease from the leg of my pant. Another sweeps past my ear.

I spin, almost falling, and dart between the two walls of brick, shoulder thrust sideways to allow me to make it. Another barrage of bullets pops off the walls behind me. I pour on the speed, sidestepping across the middle as fast as I can, to the next street.

"Urlick!" I hear my name and my head shoots up.

"Urlick, up here, it's me!"

A head appears through a part in the cloud cover, wreathed in a ring of steam.

"Eyelet?"

"Yes!" she shouts back. She peers at me over the side of a basket, tethered to a hot air balloon. "Here!" she says, tossing me a rope. It unfurls a good click from my hands.

She hauls it back up and throws it out again.

I race for the rope, but it slips through my fingers. "Jump!" she shouts.

Another bullet grazes my shin.

Brigsmen round the corner, surrounding the fence.

"Hurry!" she shouts. The basket rises.

I cross my chest in a ritual I've never believed in, close my eyes, and leap off the end of the fence. My hands grasp for the rope, a flurry of bullets lighting up my coattails.

Forty-One

Eyelet

I breathe a sigh of relief as Urlick's hands meet the rope, then cringe when his shoulder pops under his weight. "Hang on!" I shout, bullets winging my ear. I drop back into the basket for momentary cover.

"I'm trying!" Urlick's voice cuts through the rifle fire.

I look down again to see his tucked-up bottom swinging over the heads of a growing crowd of Brigsmen. I yank the controls of the balloon, trying to get it to rise, unsure of what I'm doing. Four controls later, something happens. The basket surges upward, rope running through Urlick's hands.

"Urlick!" I scream, afraid I'm about to lose him.

"It's okay!" he shouts, grabbing hold. "I'm okay!" He wraps his foot around what's left of the rope and starts to shinny up, one hand chasing the other, bullets zinging past his thighs as he climbs.

I tug on the lever, releasing more steam. The balloon climbs again, taking Urlick with it this time, saving him from a fresh onslaught of bullets, but then he slips. A bullet passes through the fleshy part of his upper arm.

The rope spins. Blood spews in a spiral from his sleeve.

"UUUURLICK!" I nearly cast myself over the side of the basket without thinking. The basket careens to one side. I look down, spinning, swallowing down what comes up.

Urlick winces below me in pain.

"I'm coming!" I shout.

"You're what?"

"Just hold on!" I grab the rope and lean out of the basket, stretching a hand out to reach him, but I can't. I try again, stretching farther, and a bullet zips past, grazing my cheek. I suck in a breath, imagining what it would be like to be earless, or brainless, should it hit. No time for this. Urlick needs saving.

Threading the toes of my boots through the weave of the basket, I make sure they're securely hooked, then launch myself backward off the bottom edge, swinging upside down by the toes of my boots.

My hair rolls out behind my head like a flying caramel carpet. *"Ohmilord, ohmilord, ohmiLOOORD!"* I scream.

"What are you doing?" Urlick shouts.

"Saving you?" I gulp as I swing past. "What does it look like I'm doing?"

"Have you lost your mind?"

"No, not yet. But soon, I suspect." I swallow, trying to hold the contents of my breakfast down. *Up, rather.* The ground looks like a drawing of a map from one of my textbooks. We're up so high, the Brigsmen look like tin soldiers from here.

Another flurry of bullets swoops past us, and one grazes my calf. "Ooooh!" I scream, noticing the hole in my stocking. "Better hurry," I say, twirling the rope around my arm, reaching out, and clutching the sleeve of Urlick's bad arm.

"When I pull, you shinny past me up the rope, understand?"

He nods as bullets sing past our ears.

"On the count of three. Ready?" A bullet clips the top of his ear. "Threeeee!" I scream, wrenching him upward.

"Again!" I shout, repeating the process. Slowly, I manage to tug him up parallel to my waist, basket bent almost sideways in the air. "One more time," I say. I shove him up the rope. His hand meets the bottom of the basket.

"Oh, no," I rasp, feeling the tinge of silver slinking through my veins.

"What is it?"

"Nothing," I lie, the two of us dangling upside down, and right side up. "Just climb, before one of us ends up with a bullet in the brain!"

I'm running out of time, and I know it. I can tell by the haziness of Urlick's face. The silver is on the move. My boots slip. "Hurry," I shout as he struggles to swing up onto the basket. One-armed, he drags himself over the side. The balloon jerks under the weight of his fall.

"Eyelet?" he calls to me.

"I'm coming," I shout. With the last fight I have in me, I hinge at the hips and thrust myself upward, my fingers groping the air in search of the basket. By the grace of all there is in Heaven, somehow they touch. Digging my fingers into the weave, I hurl myself upright— silver slithering through my shaky veins, the world around me turning black—stab the toes of my boots into the side of the basket's thatch, and I climb, blindly, to the top.

"Eyelet! Oh, thank God," Urlick breathes.

I hear him but I cannot see his face.

I lean, tumbling over the side into the basket, dropping down alongside him. The smell of burnt bread overcomes me.

"You all right?" Urlick's face appears as a dark circle above me. "Eyelet!" His fingers stroke my cheeks. "Are you all right?"

I want to say yes, but the answer is no. No, I'm not all right. Not at all. And I never will be.

"Eyelet?" He shakes me. "Talk to me. What's happening?"

"I commandeered a balloon," I finally manage to say. The words echo inside my head like they were never spoken. "I commandeered a balloon to come and save you."

"That you did," he says.

I shudder as the silver drags me under.

Forty-Two

Urlick

"Eyelet?" She's shaking.

Shock, likely, due to all the excitement.

The basket lurches to one side, threatening to expel us both, catching on the top branches of a tree as we float by. We're too low. I've somehow got to pull us up.

"Eyelet!" I shake her. "Snap out of this, I need your help!"

She's unresponsive, lying there with her eyes open, locked in a ghostly stare. I don't want to slap her, but I fear I must. It's the only way to bring her out of this shocked state. God knows it must have taken all her courage to hang from that basket the way she did to save me. But if we don't gain some altitude soon, I'm afraid we'll need saving again.

"Eyelet?" I tap her cheek lightly. She doesn't respond. "Eyelet?" I try again. "Eyelet, wake up, please!" For a moment I worry she might be dead, but then, she's trembling, so she can't be. Corpses don't move once they're dead.

The basket tips to one side and I scramble to the other, trying to keep it balanced as I tug on the ropes. I stand and adjust a few levers, but nothing happens. "Eyelet, please, I don't know what to do." Finally, I pull something and it works. The balloon jerks upward, causing my stomach to jerk with it. My cheeks flush warm as sick jumps to my throat.

I yank on another lever and the flame pulses. The balloon sucks gently upward inside a healthy dose of steam. "That's better," I say, falling back against the side of the basket. At last, we're camouflaged by thick cloud cover and out of rifle range. I reach up, backhanding the sweat from my brow. "Now to figure out how to land this bloody thing."

I look down and realize I'm bleeding. The bullet, yes, I'd almost forgotten. I strip off my overcoat, rip a strip of fabric from my sleeve, and tie it into a tourniquet around my arm above the wound. Grabbing the ends with my good hand and teeth, I pull and knot it tightly. "There, that should do for a bit."

I return my attention to Eyelet, bending my face to her ear. "Eyelet, can you hear me?" She continues to tremble. It must be the altitude. I roll her to one side, worried she'll gag on her tongue. She moans when I do this, not unlike Cordelia when she's transfixed in a state of—

I gasp in a breath. No. It's not possible. Is it?

I shake my head. No. This is not as awful as what happens to Cordelia. She's not calling out or crying in pain. She's shaking, yes, but this is different. Different altogether.

I lay my coat over her, tucking it in around her chin. Perhaps if I keep her warm, whatever this is will pass. "It's all right," I tell her, smoothing the hair from her face. "Everything's going to be all right." I stand, perplexed by her condition, hoping I'm right.

The basket bumps up again, slipping through a seam in the cloud cover, exposing us in the sky. I hold a hand to my eyes, surveying the horizon. An array of farmland, roads, and hillsides spill out before me. I strain my eyes, searching for the gaping maw of the quarry. I need to figure out a safe place to land our floating ship—close enough to it, but far enough away not to be seen.

Something hisses above my head: a gentle whine at first, then it gets stronger and stronger until it becomes a wind-flapping roar. I look up to see a small hole in the balloon's fabric. The loose edge of a patch whipping in the wind.

"Eyelet!" I shake her. "Where did you get this balloon?"

Something pops above my head. Stitches rip. The patch blows loose from the side and slowly drifts to the earth.

The repair shop in Gears—I clap my head—she must have pinched it from Hammad. God knows that old man never fixes anything well.

The balloon begins to drop, plummeting toward the earth, dropping down beneath the camouflage of clouds. I seize the ropes, trying to hold our position. They burn the skin from my hands. It's no use: whether I like it or not, we're going down.

"Eyelet!" I nudge her with my foot. *"Eyelet, wake up, please!"* I yank back on the ropes, struggling to nurse the last bit of flight out of our wounded balloon, ground rising at a furious pace. "For the love of *God*, Eyelet, PLEASE, WAKE UP!"

The balloon balks and jerks in the wind. The ropes cut my hands. We've no choice: we're going to have to bail if we're to survive this. I look over the side. There'll be nothing left of this basket when we crash. "Eyelet!" I shout again.

A set of tracks comes into view. Beyond them I spy the quarry through the cloud cover. It's lined with Brigsmen holding guns. There have to be at least fifty, maybe sixty of them.

Even if I could land this thing in one piece, we wouldn't stand a chance. We'd be shot the second we crawled from the wreckage. A steamplough whistle sounds to the right. Its shrill shriek ripples through the air.

My eyes fix on the long black locomotive snake slithering toward us through the grass. *That's it.* "Eyelet, we've got to go now."

I let go of the ropes and take her by the arm. "Eyelet"—I shake her—"our ship is sinking! We have to bail!"

The steamplough whistles again, drowning out my voice. A sharp popping punch follows. The balloon's sprung another hole. Eyelet lurches forward into my arms, blinking, gasping, her hands shooting up over her ears. "What was that? What happened?" Her head twists up. "Where am I?" She looks petrified. Her cheeks flush red. Her eyes are wide and reaching.

"It appears we've just blown another tire," I say.

"A what?" She looks up, bewildered, at the wilting balloon folding down around us. I can tell by the change in her eyes that she gets it now.

"We've got to bail. And fast!" I say, yanking her to her feet.

"Bail? As in jump?" She gasps.

"That's correct." I rest a foot on the side of the basket. "Ready?"

She clings to me, her eyes springing even wider when she realizes how close we are to the ground. Her gaze moves from there to the Brigsmen lining the ridge.

"But what about them? Won't they shoot us as soon as we land?"

"Not if they think we're already dead."

"What?" She scowls at me.

"As long as our balloon gets hit by that steamplough"—I point—"there's no way they'll believe we survived."

"But—"

"Don't worry, I've got this." I lunge for the rope and yank one last time, sending us careening into the steamplough's oncoming path.

"Urlick!" she gasps, burying her face in my chest.

The steamplough's whistle lights up the air, its wheels thundering hard up the tracks. We're so close now, the force of its steam rocks the bottom of the basket, knocking our balance out from under us.

Eyelet turns to me, panic in her eyes. "Take my hand," I say, gauging the steamplough's speed. "When we hit the ground, start running and don't stop until we've made it to the cycle. Do you hear? Head straight for the tracks and don't let go of me."

"But the steamplough! What if we're not fast enough?"

I take her face in my hands. "How much do you trust me?" I say. "Now jump!" I turn and spring from the basket, squeezing her hand in mine. She leaps behind, our hands entangled as we fall, twisting and turning through the air, bouncing hard off the ground when we hit, the two of us rolling into a battered heap. Scrambling to my feet, I'm off, stumbling forward through the furrowed field, dragging Eyelet along behind.

The steamplough screams. Smoke purges from its stack. I bear down and charge at the tracks.

"We can't!" Eyelet shouts.

"We will!" I scream.

My shoes hit the rails—whistle shrieking. I spin, yanking Eyelet across the ties. The steamplough's cowcatcher shears the lace from her skirts as she falls into my arms on the other side.

Brakes bite the air in a metallic squeal. The engine disappears inside a plume of gold and blue canvas balloon, ropes shredded under its metal wheels. I look back just in time to see the basket burst into flames, lit by the engine's stack. The Brigsmen stand frozen in place, guns lowered at their sides, staring at the wreckage in disbelief.

Forty-Three

Eyelet

"You all right?" Urlick asks when we finally reach the boulders. He drops my hand and brushes the hair from my face.

"As good as one can be after one's just been hit by a train," I say, mustering a quivery grin.

"Good." He smiles and yanks the hydrocycle from its hiding place. "How about you, Bertie?" Bertie shakes, knocking the dust from his bones. "Fantastic, let's get out of here then, shall we?" Bertie groans.

Urlick gives me a hand to help me on, then throws his leg over the cycle. Seconds later, we're pedaling at high speed through the woods. A herd of Brigsmen swarms the tracks in search of our remains, just as Urlick predicted they would. I look back at the smouldering wreckage, our balloon a ball of fire, realizing how close we just came to death, gasping as Urlick pedals on.

It's then I realize I've misplaced some time—the time between falling into the basket and jumping out of it. Then I remember: *the silver.* It took me down. But for how long? How much did Urlick see? He's said nothing. Absolutely nothing about it. Perhaps it wasn't as bad as I think?

I look down, shocked to find the heel of one of my boots is missing—the only victim of the tragedy, thank God. It must have got caught and yanked off as Urlick hurtled across the tracks. Without him I never would have made it.

I lean forward and wrap my arms around his middle. Grateful to be alive. Grateful for Urlick. Grateful we made it away together.

"Do you still have the journals?" Urlick turns his face to me.

"One," I say, pulling it from my jacket. "Have you any?"

"Three." He grins. "The most important ones, I'm hoping."

I close my eyes and take a breath, hoping he's right. That couldn't have been all for naught. When I again open my eyes, I realize I've only saved the journal marked *Noir*. The other one—the one Urlick tossed to me before I ran from the room—I seem to have lost somewhere on my journey. I shudder to think what might happen if it ends up in the hands of Smrt. Secretly, I pray I dropped it as I crossed the steam-plough tracks and it's burning in the wreckage right now. I'd rather that than let Smrt have his way.

I close my eyes, praying the missing journal is not the one we need to run the machine.

Urlick slips off the main road into the forest, looping cross-country through the underbrush. It's bumpy and hard to keep my balance on the back of the bike. Thistles whip my legs. Branches pelt my arms. Thickets yank at my skirts. This part of the forest seems rougher than before.

I lean and bury my cheeks in between Urlick's shoulder blades to protect my face. His coat smells of rosewood and cinnamon, just like the day we first met, which seems so long ago now. For the next few clicks, I concentrate on nothing but hanging on, trying hard not to think about what lurks in this part of the forest. I can't believe we're here again.

Urlick suddenly swings out of the forests onto a mucky secondary road. Surprised, I look up. "I thought you said using a road was out of the question."

"It is, but we were getting nowhere fast travelling through the woods. Besides, no one uses this road anymore. It's been abandoned for years, because of flooding. We'll stay on it as long as we can, to get a head start. Otherwise, I don't know if we'll be able to outrun them."

"I thought you said they'd think we were dead."

He's quiet a moment, then swallows. "On the chance I'm wrong, I want to make sure we're well ahead of them. There'll be no stopping to hide in these woods."

I lower my head, remembering the criminals. He's right: if we get stopped out here, it won't be Smrt we'll have to fear. I squeeze his waist a little tighter and sink back into place.

He shifts into fourth gear, and mud flings at our back as the cycle buzzes silently up the road.

*

All at once, Urlick slows to a stop. I become a quick, stiff line in the seat behind him. My spine aches, I'm holding myself so tight. "What is it?" I whisper. "What do you see?"

Urlick leans off to one side. Up the road, through the fog about a hundred metres, a couple of Brigsmen stand watch over a makeshift blockade.

"I thought you said no one used this road anymore."

"No one does," he whispers. "Smrt must not believe we've perished. He's ordered a blockade on every road out of Gears, passable or not." Urlick cranks his head around. "We're going to have to travel by woods. We have no choice." He pops the cycle back into gear and wheels it around, concealing us behind a patch of sumac at the side of the road.

"I'm going to need your help now, Eyelet," he says.

"How do you mean?" I swallow.

"A while back I saw a gang of criminals."

My stomach lurches.

"And they weren't hanging in the trees." I dig my fingers into his sides. "I turned off onto the road for that reason. I didn't want to tell you because I didn't want you to be frightened—"

"Too late for that," I gasp.

"But now, I'm afraid I'm going to need you to keep a close eye on the woods for me as we pass through them. Warn me immediately if you see anything, *anything at all* that looks suspicious. The tiniest red glow along the edge of the road could be the eyes of a criminal reflecting off the hydrocycle's headlights. It'll be the only warning we get. One flash and that's it. If we wait to see faces, it'll be too late, understand?"

I nod my head, shuddering inside as he pushes the cycle off the road with his feet and starts off into the underbrush of the forest.

"Hang on tight." He stands up to pedal, and my stomach jumps up with him. Never in a million lifetimes could I ever have imagined this. The two of us alone in a forest full of criminals, with virtually nothing to defend ourselves with.

I lean, wrapping my arms tight about his middle when he sits back down, my teeth chattering at his back. I'm trying to be brave, but it's hard, knowing if I miss a sign we could be eaten alive. The stakes are far too high.

"How much longer, do you think?" I say after a while.

"Just keep your eyes peeled on the forest," he says. He shifts gears so clumsily we clack heads, and I realize the terrain is getting muckier, harder to maneuver through. Oily pools linger to the right of us, fumaroles gurgle to the left. We're entering the part of the forest destroyed by the Vapours.

Twice I think I see red circles glinting up from the edges of leaves at the side of the road. Twice I almost say something. It's hard to know if it's just my mind playing tricks, or if it's really happening, and I don't want to alarm Urlick if it's not. Perhaps I should say something. My eyes fall to the mucky terrain. What'll happen to us if we stop?

Two little lights flash like luminescent drops of blood from a bush at the side of the road. Just as quickly as they come, they're gone. It's like they were never there at all. I concentrate hard on the spot in the leaves, but nothing reappears.

"Urlick?" I say, wondering if I'm crazy. "Urlick, I thought I saw something back there in the bushes." I stare over my shoulder at the spot again. Something flashes. Only this time it flashes slightly over to the left. A pair of eyes. And then another. I'm not crazy, I'm sure of it now. "Urlick." My voice pulls thin. The flashes move, then move again. "They're jumping around us—"

"I know. I see them." His breath grows uneasy. "Keep your eyes on them, will you, please?"

He keeps his hands steadied on the wheel, veering off the path to the right. We drop down into the thicker part of the woods, and right away I sense we're in trouble as he stands, struggling to push the cycle harder. The tires pinch and snap against stones and sticks beneath us. The muck turns into silt.

When he sits, his heart pounds through the sides of his ribs into my hands. Sweat breaks on the back of his neck.

I'm empty, cold, and hollow inside. It's as if nothing remains of me but a beating heart. It thrashes inside me at such a speed I fear it may explode, destroying me before the criminals even have a chance to appear.

"It's all right, we're all right." Urlick grabs my hand and pulls it across his middle, squeezing it hard inside his own. He must have sensed I was afraid, so very afraid, my breath rushing over his shoulder. "We'll be fine as long as we keep moving. Isn't that right, Bertie?" he adds. He grinds his teeth, and I'm not sure I believe him—the muscles at the sides of his jaw tense.

Bertie shudders beneath us.

I bury my face in Urlick's back, praying he's right, my heart now bursting in my ears I'm so frightened. Oh, *please*, let us make it through this part of the woods. Please, don't let them stop us.

We travel less than thirty metres—tires gripping then spinning, becoming bogged down in the muck then freeing again—when we become stuck, axle-deep in swamp gunk, engine sputtering and choking. Bertie strains trying to get us out, but it's no use. Urlick's not able to get us out, either. The hydrocycle gasps between attempts.

"Bertie's going to burn himself out," I say.

"I know." Urlick dismounts for what feels like the umpteenth time so far and pushes, only to sink into the bog himself. "Get off," he shouts. "Quickly." He's up to his knees in the bog. "Stand over there." He points to firmer ground about ten metres away, holding out his hand to help me from the bike.

I jump from the back and my boots become immediately stuck. I struggle to pull myself out, and something chatters in the trees beside me, less than a stone's cast away from the cycle. *Teeth.* It's the sound of criminals chattering their teeth.

Urlick sucks in a sharp breath. "Hurry," he says. "We haven't much time."

I try again to free myself, and my boot disappears into the depths of the bog, almost to my knee.

Urlick turns to me, mud-faced and panicked, struggling to save the cycle from a similar fate. "Keep moving, Eyelet, don't stand still. It's the only way to get loose!"

I lean back and yank my boot from the bog, only to have the other taken down by its grip. Lunging backward, I manage to dislodge both at once; a huge *suck* sound fills the forest. I stumble backward, and something strokes the side of my face. "Urlick?" I say, reaching out for him through the cloud cover, threading my fingers through his. I pull back, shocked by their Siberian feel. "Urlick?"

The clouds lift long enough for me to see a man strung up by his neck, dangling in the trees.

"Water." He reaches for me. "Water, please."

I gasp, falling back, every nerve in my body screaming, and rebound off yet another. His arms are lopped off at the elbows. An *X* is prod-ironed into his chest. Flesh hangs from his bloodied bones as if wild animals have feasted on him. His head flops over, revealing a skull without eyes. Blood surges from their empty sockets. A barbed-wire noose cuts deep into his neck. "Help me," he chokes. "Please, help me."

A bolt of horror rifles through me. I whirl around, facing a barrage of bodies all cobbled together and left to twitch on the ends of barbed wire. A graveyard full of them hangs all around me. Some dead. Some alive.

I turn and race away, fighting the urge to puke. "Urlick!" I scream. "Urlick, where are you?"

Other voices sift through the trees, begging for water, shouting to be freed. Their hands grope the air in search of me. Fingers rake my hair. Hands brush my cheeks. "Urlick!" I shout, hurtling back through the forest. "Urlick! Answer me, please!"

"Over here!" he shouts, appearing in my path.

I slam into his chest, falling slack and shaken into his arms.

"What?" he says.

"Criminals," I gulp. "Dangling from the trees. There were criminals, everywhere."

He brushes the tears from my cheeks, leaving a trail of sand on my skin. "It's all right." He embraces me, dragging me soft-kneed back toward the cycle. "You're all right."

I look down at Bertie. His gears are covered in clumps of mud. I can't imagine how he'll work.

"Get on," Urlick says, falling to the ground to claw it away.

I throw a leg over the cycle and freeze. "Urlick," I whisper, trembling. "Turn around." Two tiny red dots burn through the fog-laced foliage just beyond his head. They're too low to belong to anything I saw strung up in the trees.

Urlick's head swings up, sensing the movement around us. His eyes bug out wide.

The lights grow in number. Two sets, three, then four appear. Accompanied by gnashing teeth.

He throws a leg over the cycle and pops it into gear. "Hold on!" he shouts, shifting gears madly as we speed away, fishtailing through the mucky woods.

My head swivels left to right. More and more sets of eyes surround us. "Urlick!" I shout over the chatter of teeth.

"I see them!" he shouts back, pushing Bertie's motor to its limit. It sputters and coughs and threatens to fail.

"No, Urlick!" I try again.

"Please, Eyelet, not now!"

"But Urlick—"

"Eyelet, I'm going as fast as I can!"

He revs the throttle. The cycle launches up and over the trunk of a fallen tree, hanging in the air before slamming back to earth. I land—hard—on the seat behind him; my stomach is lodged in my throat. Thankfully, he hasn't lost me.

"Urlick, *please*," I shout as he speeds up the path. "Listen to me! We don't have to outrun them!"

"What?" He hits a stump and loses control. Bertie jerks to one side. We skitter from the path and fall down the rock face onto another path—a narrow switchback that skirts the edge of the escarpment.

A wall of rock ascends to our left; the escarpment drops off to our right. Urlick stands the cycle almost on end as he brakes to avoid what's blocking the path in front of us. Our back wheel drops down over the edge of the switchback when we finally come to a stop.

"Good God in Heaven, save us," I breathe.

In front of us stand two criminals, bloodied and beaten. They form a human chain across the road. Their necks are still bound in their broken barbed-wire nooses. One has open wounds still gushing where he struggled to get free. The other is missing an eye. It looks as though it's been plucked from his head.

"Ain't much use calling on 'im. He don't show 'is head much round these parts." The eyeless criminal laughs.

"May as well give up," the other one says. "You're trapped."

"Like rats, backs to a corner," says the other, chattering his teeth.

I swallow down a spiked clump of fear. My heart thumps in my throat.

The eyeless one tracks Urlick's gaze. "Thinkin' of jumpin', are ya?" he says. "Even if you were to make it, there's eight more of us down there."

The second one starts chattering again. I throw my hands to my ears to block out the sound.

Urlick digs his toes into the dirt and tries to back us up.

"And ain't no bother backin' up, either. 'Ave a look." The criminal's eyes flicker.

I whirl around. Three more criminals block the path, stalking toward us. "It's true, Urlick," I say, turning back.

Urlick eyes a small shelf of rocky ledge above us, running along the inside of the escarpment. We can't possibly reach it without building up speed enough to make the jump. What is he thinking?

"Don't do it," I say, leaning forward, whispering in his ear. "There's another way."

"What are you talking about? It's the only option left—"

"No it isn't."

Urlick's head snaps around.

"How much do you trust me?" I stare into his eyes. "Now I need you to turn around and pedal straight at them, as fast as you can, do you understand?"

"That's ridiculous—"

"Just do it, will you please?"

He turns back, and I wrap my hands around his waist and lock my fingers. "Now," I say.

Urlick leaps onto the pedals, pushing Bertie harder than he's ever pushed him before. Bertie gulps in air as we hurtle up the narrow path toward the criminals.

"*What the—?*" They fall to the side, their hands snatching at the air all around us as we pedal past.

"What now?" Urlick shouts as we reach the end of the cliff.

"Press the button!" I shout.

"Do *what?*" Urlick panics as we sail off the end.

I lunge forward and plunge a fist down on the mechanism myself.

To his amazement—to *my* amazement—wings spring out of the sides of the coffer box and flap wildly in the wind.

"By *Jove!*" Urlick rocks backward in his seat, astonished. "It's blinding!"

"Isn't it, though?" I smile. "But I can assure you, it had nothing to do with Jove."

Bertie circles, filling his lungs with air, making one more pass to taunt the criminals, then flaps off over the ravine toward the Follies.

Urlick twists around to face me. "Nice work," he says. "For a girl, that is." He grins. His lips graze the side of my cheek.

Then, as if some otherworldly force has come over me, I raise my hands to his face, and I pull him to me, engaging him in a long, mind-tingling, heart-trembling kiss.

Forty-Four

Urlick

Did she just—?

She did just, didn't she?

She kissed me.

She did!

I gasp, steering Bertie out over the treetops toward home, my whole body an excited, giddy mess.

Eyelet lays her head on the back of my shoulders, her cinnamon breath rolling sweetly past my neck. I take her hand in mine and place it over my chest. Her heart strums musically up and down my spine.

For a long time we just ride in silence, Bertie cooing beneath us. But then the winds change. And the sour, foul stench of the Vapours ripples up through a rip in the cloud clover, through the trees. "Better don the gas masks again," I say.

Reaching back, I secure Eyelet's mask to her face first and check her gauge. She's running low on oxygen. I flip mine over my head, noticing my gauge is running low, too.

We'd better get home soon.

*

We arrive at the Compound to find it surrounded by Brigsmen. I should have known he'd send his troops ahead when I saw the blockade. I pull Eyelet close, crouching behind a thicket of trees at the edge of the forest, Bertie parked out of sight a short distance away.

"So what now?" Eyelet looks to me, her eyes worried.

"I don't know," I say.

In the distance, Iris stands face-to-face with a Brigsman, her body wedged between him and the front door of the Compound.

"I'm only going to ask you this one more time." The Brigsman's voice cuts through the trees. "*Where* is the master of the *house*?"

Iris makes a face like she doesn't understand; her eyes dart all around.

"What is she doing?" Eyelet whispers.

"Playing deaf and dumb, I believe."

Iris's head cranks around at the sound of my voice.

"Oh, no!" Eyelet gasps, a little too loudly.

The Brigsman's head jerks around.

A bullet from his pocket drops into the stream. Iris's shoulders bounce.

"You lying little sod, you!" The Brigsman closes the space between them. "You've heard me all along!" Iris drops her gaze, immediately realizing she's given herself away. The Brigsman strikes her across the cheek, and I nearly bolt from my hiding place.

"No!" Eyelet yanks me back. "You can't! They'll shoot you! You're no good to either of us dead." She stares up at me, a frightened child. "Not to mention Crazy Legs and Cordelia. How will they survive without you? How will *any* of us survive?"

I unclench the fists at my sides.

"As much as I'd like you to kill the man, now is not the time." She grits her teeth.

Iris screams and our heads shoot up. The Brigsman has knocked her down. She claws at his boots, trying to detain him, glaring at me. Her eyes beg for us to run. Brigsmen pour from the porch, over the bridge, out into the forest.

"They know we're here." I turn to Eyelet. "Somehow they've figured it out."

"How?"

"It doesn't matter. What matters is, we've got to leave. *Now*."

I turn my head, searching the forest for options, straining my mind for somewhere else to go.

"What about the back door—?"

"They'll search the Compound."

"Then where are we to go?"

My eyes fix on the remains of Moncton Gate—the entrance marker to the road leading to my father's old secret laboratory.

"I've got an idea." I push up onto my feet. "I know of a place. Deep in the forest. A sort of second compound, called the Core. It's my father's old laboratory. No one knows about it outside my family. We could go there and hide until this blows over."

"When will that be?" Eyelet stares at me, and a part deep inside me crumbles.

"I don't know," I say. "But it's the only shot we've got. We either stay here and surrender or take our chances out there in the Vapours. What do you say, Eyelet? It's all I've got."

Eyelet's gaze shifts to Iris and back again. Brigsmen filter closer through the trees.

"Let's go find the Core," she says.

I grab her hand and run, under cover of cloud, back to Bertie, screeching to a halt when we reach him.

"What are you doing?" Eyelet gasps, watching me tear open the saddlebags. "Aren't we just going to get on and fly?"

"So they can shoot us down in the trees?" I tear open the laces. "I don't think so. Besides, Bertie's almost out of gas."

"C.L. said he packed a second canister."

"Which I don't have time right now to change. Not with the Brigsmen on our heels. Here, take these," I say, tossing gadgets at her one by one.

"What do we need these for?"

"Protection." I check back over my shoulder.

"How am I supposed to protect myself with this?" She holds up an eggbeater.

I reach over and click the button on its side. Long spinning blades snap out from its centre. "Any more questions?"

She swallows.

"And you didn't want me to bring these." I grin, dropping another device in her hand.

"Not just a bee smoker, I presume?"

"No. That one doubles as a mustard-gas bomb."

"And this?" She holds up a long, skinny rod with dual prongs.

"Cigarette holder, also known as flamethrower."

"Let me guess." Her hand trembles as she holds up the next one. "Miniaturized pipe organ turned deadly explosive?"

"Close." I flip it over, showing her the groove. "Envelope sealer turned heat-seeking missile with a button-activated trap."

"Because every household needs one of those," she says.

"On second thought"—I snatch the missile from her—"you'd better be in charge of these instead." I hand her three innocent-looking but not-so-innocent darts. "Be careful with those. They're poisonous."

"What?"

"Only once they've been deployed—"

"Of course." She rolls her eyes.

"Oh, and take this, too." I pass her a tiny, flat piece of steel.

"What's this?"

"A nail file." I turn, filling my own pockets with gadgets of my own.

"Yes, but what is it really?"

"Nothing," I say. "Just a nail file. But perfect for close-range retaliation, though, don't you think?" I demonstrate, pulling a finger across my neck. She retches. I tuck the nail file in her coat's breast pocket and pat it.

Her eyes grow wide. Her breath quickens.

"I'm sorry," I say. I jerk back my hand.

Eyelet turns and reaches for her pack.

A stick snaps behind her.

Stiffly I turn around.

Brigsmen lurk not twenty metres away, backs to us in the trees.

"Time to go," I whisper, grabbing Eyelet by the hand.

"What about Bertie?" she breathes.

The cycle creaks forward as if intending to follow. "No," I snap at him. "You stay here. And make yourself scarce. Quickly."

I burst forward, dragging Eyelet behind me, the two of us drifting quiet as quail through the steamy underbrush, leaving Bertie behind to whimper like a spoiled child.

Forty-Five

Eyelet

Brigsmen converge on the space in the forest where Urlick and I just stood. The sound of their boots tamps up my spine as Urlick and I charge away up the road. Or what's left of the road.

I'm pretty confident that the Brigsmen can't see us for the rolling cloud cover, for at times I can't even see Urlick's face in front of me. But still I feel their eyes burning at our backs, never far enough away.

"We just need to make it to that ridge over there," Urlick pants.

"And then what?" I gasp as we run.

"That's where things get exciting."

"What do you mean, exciting?"

Urlick huffs in a breath as he turns to me. "That's where we have to scale down the side of the escarpment."

"We have to do *what*?" My feet grind to a halt. "What about the road? Why can't we stick to the road?"

Urlick jerks to a stop beside me. "It's gone. It fell away in the explosion, the Night of the Great Illumination."

"Explosion?" My mind leaps back to the night of the flash; to the many other things it destroyed.

"Yes." He catches his breath. "It knocked out the road. The only way to get to the Core now is to scale over the side of the ridge there." He points.

"Embers? Your plan is to descend into Embers?"

"Not exactly. Just to descend onto the fringe."

I gasp. "You're mad. You've gone mad." I turn to leave.

"Eyelet, please." He yanks me back. "I promise we won't be down there long. Just long enough to cross the old ravine to the other side."

"What old *ravine*—"

"The one we have to cross to get to the Core!"

I swallow. "And then what? Assuming we survive the drop and find the ravine, where do we go from there?"

"I believe it's to the left."

"You *believe*?"

"That's right, I *believe*." Urlick runs a worried hand through his hair. "I've only been there once—"

"Once!" I whirl around. "Why didn't you tell me this before we left?"

"Would you have come if I had?" he shouts.

I narrow my eyes. I can't decide if I'm angrier with him or with myself for following him.

Teeth chatter in the trees.

I swing around.

"Come on." Urlick grabs my hand and pulls me forward, his eyes like crimson lanterns burning through the fog. "Best not dillydally in this part of the woods."

*

He's the first to drop over the side when we reach the edge, hanging by his hands from an exposed root at the top of the ridge. "Your turn." He looks up at me. "Just ease yourself over until your feet reach mine."

"Surely you jest," I say.

I peek over the edge at him, toes teetering on two jagged rocks protruding from the smooth rock face. "This doesn't look at all safe to me, Urlick," I say, trembling. "In fact, this looks downright ludicrous."

The thought passes over me: *what about my episodes?* What if I lower myself over the ledge and an episode hits? They tend to rear their ugly head in times of stress, and *this*—I glance over the ridge again—I'd say this qualifies as stress. "I don't think this is a good idea, Urlick." I bite my lip.

"Don't worry, it'll be all right," he says, and his foot slips, sending the rock he's been standing on crumbling down into the ravine. For a harrowing moment he swings out, dangling by one arm off the cliff, then kicks his way back to the side. "You see?" He looks at me, eyes wide. "Everything's fine."

"Yeah, splendid."

Criminals moan again in the trees. I gulp down the terror rising in me.

"Come on, Eyelet." Urlick reaches out. "We've got to get going."

I turn around, trying not to think of what I'm about to do, and lower myself slowly over the side. My boot slips almost instantly and I fall, skittering down the rock face in one quick, stomach-sloshing jerk.

I swing down in front of Urlick, hem caught on a root. "See?" Urlick grins, his broad hand trembling at my back. "Nothing to worry about. I've got you."

"I see that," I say.

I move again and slip again. Urlick catches me, his arm wound tight about my waist.

"See now?" His nervous breath sweeps past my ear as we dangle from the root together. "That wasn't so terrible, was it?" His lips graze my earlobe.

In a small way, he's right: this isn't so terrible. It's quite divine, actually. My back pressed up against his chest, his heart beating a vibrant concerto at my spine. All the blood in my body tingles. Not in the cool, metallic way it does when I'm falling into an episode, but warm and cursive, like fancy handwriting over fine parchment paper, all loopy and beautiful, seeping in and out of every pore.

We hang there, catching our breath, and I wish this moment would never end. But reality dictates if we don't move soon—the root creaks—we'll be falling instead of rappelling the rest of the way.

"Ready?" Urlick whispers in my ear.

"As I'll ever be," I say.

One shaky-legged hold at a time, we descend through the cloud cover into the belly of the ravine. My mind races with what might lurk within its frothy, black, boiling mist. Images of criminal corpses and gape-mouthed spirits shudder through me. I shake off the thoughts and try to concentrate on the footholds instead. By the time we drop down onto the ledge, I'm feeling winded, light-headed, and mushy-limbed. The fog is so thick down here it's dizzying. My lungs sting when I try to breathe.

Perhaps it's due to nerves, or the drop in altitude. Or perhaps this is just the plight of entering Embers.

I stagger forward, hoping upon hope it's not an episode. It can't be, or I'd feel shaky as well. *Please don't let it be an episode.* I suck in a breath and immediately cough.

Urlick's head snaps around. "What is it?"

"I don't know." All his edges are muted. As if he were a vision in a dream. Yet there's no hint of silver rising in my veins; no familiar stench of burning bread. It's not the same feeling. This is completely different. More like the oxygen down here's been traded in for lead.

"You all right?" He stares into my face.

I cling to him, soft-kneed and out of breath, our fingers laced as if my very survival depends on it. "Are we floating?" I say.

"Oh, no!" Urlick drops my hand and rifles through his pack.

I stagger beside him, dangerously close to the edge.

"Hold on!" He reaches up and steadies me, yanking a gas mask out of his pack with his other hand. He suits me up, turns the valve to purify. "Blast!" he shouts, frantically tapping the gauges.

"What is it? What's wrong?"

"Breathe slowly," he cautions. "We haven't much left."

I nod, telling myself not to panic, my thoughts already clearer after only a few short breaths.

"I'm all right," I say, pulling the mask away.

"You're sure?"

"Positive," I lie.

Urlick shuts off the valves and pockets the mask. "I'll keep it right here in case you need it again."

Good plan, I think as I stumble along behind him again.

We follow the ledge around a bend in the escarpment. "Shouldn't be long now," Urlick says.

"What exactly are we looking for?"

"A bridge made of boulders."

"Up here?"

"A suspension bridge. More like a crossing, between this ledge and that." He points, and through a faint hole in the cloud cover I see what he means. A second ledge runs parallel to the escarpment, past a notch in the sidewall, like a canyon, only no water runs through it and it's not very deep. It's as though someone took a giant knife and cut a wedge out of the side of the escarpment in the shape of a piece of pie, and left it to stand off on its own.

"So, it's sort of like an island, the piece where we're going?"

"Exactly." Urlick pulls to a stop. "That's strange."

"What is?"

He moves away, leaving me to shiver in the cold wind, racing up and down the ledge. "It should be here. Right here." He paces.

"What should be here?" I steady myself against the rock wall, my eyes still a little swimmy.

"The logged path leading to the stone bridge." He twists one way and then the other. "It should be here. There should be a logged path leading to a bridge connecting this piece of land to the piece where my father's laboratory is."

"Don't worry. We'll find it." I bite my lip.

"We *have* to." He drags a hand through his hair. "There's no other way in."

I gulp down the thought, scanning the ridge through dotted clouds. "Perhaps it's just a little farther up?"

"It better be." He shields his eyes and squints. "By the looks of things, we haven't much ledge left."

He takes my hand and we lunge forward through the coiling mist, my heart a drum in my chest. I heave in a breath and choke on it. Urlick's head jerks around. "It's all right," I say. "Carry on."

His eyes linger on me a while before he turns. The ledge becomes narrower and narrower with every one of his steps. Mine are shaky at best. I focus hard on where to place my feet as Urlick urges me onward. I can tell by the way he's glancing back at me he's worried, both about me and about where we're headed. What are we to do if there's no bridge?

My foot connects with a rock, and it breaks away, pulling me down with it. I sink to my knee over the side of the cliff before Urlick yanks me back onto the path. My pulse gallops in my wrists. My hands are cold and clammy. "Perhaps we should go back," I say.

"To what? A forest full of Smrt's men?"

He has a point, but this, *this* is ludicrous, just as I said. This path is leading nowhere.

"You stay here." He steadies me against the escarpment wall. "I'll go on ahead and see if it's there."

"And if it isn't?"

"It has to be here." His eyes are stern.

"Urlick!" I say when he turns to go. "I don't think we should separate."

My lips start to quiver.

He looks at me, his eyes soft. "I'll be back, I promise."

I lay my head against the rock and concentrate on his steps. Short and hollow, they ring out—the only sound in the ravine—reverberating through the dense and eerily quiet fog. The stillness shudders through me.

He rounds a corner, and I can no longer hear him. My heart jerks in my chest. The air rolls bitter as absinthe in my throat. I close my mouth and breath through my nose, but it pinches. It tastes sour, sourer than before.

Something's wrong. I feel it in my skin.

A slow, cold howl ripens overhead, dropping down around my shoulders from a strange, writhing cloud.

My head snaps, tracking it. "Urlick?"

The howl swoops past us again, splitting into several haunting voices, then circles back. *"Urlick!"* I scream.

"What is it? What's the matter?" He appears through the grey, misty mass now hanging over the ledge.

"Listen."

A low groan slithers up behind him, coiling about his legs. Urlick bolts forward, pulling me tight to his chest.

"Is it what I think it is?" I say.

"I'm afraid it is, yes."

"The Turned?"

"I'm afraid so."

The groan breaks into a chorus of maniacal laughter.

All the nerves in my body stand on end.

"We've got to get out of here." Urlick looks to me. "We can't waste any time. If they surround us, we're finished."

"Where are going to go?"

"The bridge. I saw it. It's just up ahead. We can make it, if we run."

The howls swoop past us again, poking us, prodding us, crooning in our ears. I throw my hands to my ears to block out the sound, my eyes tracking their every movement.

"No!" Urlick shouts, taking my face in his hand. "Whatever you do, don't look at them. Don't let them in your head. They'll steal your mind if you do."

Throaty cackles break out overhead, and my chin swings up.

"Listen to me!" Urlick yanks my chin back down. "The Turned create illusions out of your dreams and desires and present them back to you as a mirage. That's how they lure you close enough to feed off your brains. Don't look at them. Don't listen to them. That's how they confuse you." Urlick stares in my eyes. "Concentrate only on me."

"I will, I am, I promise," I say. I pinch my eyes shut, trying to force their sardonic howls from my head. Their moans gnaw at my spine.

Urlick grabs my hand and yanks me forward, around the corner, up the narrow slope, his feet moving at an incredible speed. I stagger along behind, unsure of my footing, my breath quickening as I slam into his back.

"What is it? What's wrong?"

"Shhhhh . . ." He throws a hand out in front of me, pasting my back to the side of the escarpment.

Shadows roll in front of us, intertwined with the mist, swirling inside curls of grey smoke. Their shimmering silver faces appear one moment and disappear the next, as unpredictable as the Vapours themselves. A group of at least twenty Turned hover across the path in front of us. Their white-flame eyes burn holes through the mist.

Urlick swallows so loudly I hear it inside my head. Or maybe it's me; I can't be sure.

They swirl toward us, twisting and turning snakelike through the air. Ghastly mouths open, yowling—others laughing, filling the canyon with their demonic sounds.

"We're going to have to make a run for it."

"What?"

"Straight through them."

"Have you lost your mind?"

"It's the only way. We've got to get to the bridge."

"But—"

"They don't like sound. So we need to make a lot of noise. And whatever you do, don't let go of me." Urlick squeezes my hand.

"Not a chance."

Without Urlick's hand in mine, I swear I'd have turned to stone from fright by now. I couldn't let go of him if I wanted.

"Ready?" He braces his feet. "Let's go!" He barrels forward, screaming and shouting. I follow, doing the same, shrieking so loudly I nearly go hoarse.

The Turned swoop in circles around us, faces darting in and out of the mist. Urlick bats at them and they disintegrate into ash, only to float up and re-form again.

"They come back!" I shout.

"Don't look at them!" Urlick screams. "Just run!"

I tuck my chin and pour on the speed, the rock face crumbling beneath me.

"We're almost there!" Urlick shouts.

We round another corner and I see the bridge, waffling into view through the cloud cover. Two pillars of stone tower over a long expanse of the same. On the other side is the slice of escarpment we've been searching for.

My heart pounds as hard as my boots hitting the log path leading onto the bridge, our boots then snapping against stone as we race to the other side.

"They're gone," I say, twisting back as we pour from the bridge out into the forest. "They've left us alone."

"Don't be so sure," Urlick breathes.

I track his gaze and gasp. The Turned plummet from the treetops, their wraithlike bodies twisting and coiling all around us. There must be a hundred of them. Their chants vibrate inside my ribs. "What do we do now?"

"We're going to have to take a stand, that's what." Urlick drops to a knee. He riffles through his pack, pulling out weapon after weapon.

"I thought you said they were spirits. Apparitions. How do you expect to kill something that's already dead?"

"I don't," Urlick shouts. "The Turned hate light. The only chance we have of surviving this is to try and frighten them away. Take this!" He tosses me the envelope sealer, which I know is not just an envelope sealer—

"And deploy it now!"

Spirits whistle past, their misty, shroud-like clothing dragging over my back. My gaze dashes about the forest, tracking their stealthy movements.

"Throw the bloody thing, will you?"

I turn and launch it in the direction of the voices, handle spinning turbine-like through the air. It hits the ground and explodes, embedding shrapnel into the trunks of the surrounding trees, but has little effect on our attackers.

"It's not working," I shout.

Urlick tosses me the flamethrower. "Try again."

I turn to launch it and an old man's face appears in front of me, glowing a translucent white. He snaps his chin toward me, mouth open wide.

"NO!" I scream.

Urlick whirls around, snatches the flamethrower from me, and launches it at him like a spear. The face screeches and then evaporates, turning to dust in midair.

"You all right?" Urlick reaches for me.

"Yes." I nod.

"Good. Take this." He tosses me an ornate-looking doorstop before stepping forward to launch another bomb. A piano finger-stretcher sails through the air, which of course is not just a stretcher. It illuminates the skies—along with several gruesome faces of the Turned—as it explodes.

I fall back against a tree, gasping in a petrified breath, paralyzed by the prospect of having our brains sucked out, the sight of their faces having made it so real.

"Eyelet!" Urlick shouts, snapping me back to reality. I step up, ready to lob the doorstop underarm like a cricket player would a ball, when Urlick snags my arm.

"Not like that, like this!" He twists my arm up over my head. "Like a sword thrower intent on beheading his assistant!"

I let it go and am astonished when, midflight, a flap pops open, revealing a fire-cracking pinwheel of knives.

The apparitions scatter.

"Sound and light, the perfect combination," Urlick says. "Too bad I haven't another. Quick." He yanks me closer to him. "Prepare to run." He scoops up my pack and tosses it to me. "You have the journals?"

I check. "Yes."

"Good. When I throw this, I want you to lose yourself in those trees, you hear me? Follow the path of the light."

"What about you?"

"I'll be close behind. Ready?"

I'm not really, but I guess I have to be. I clutch my pack to my chest.

Urlick steps forward, releasing the cigarette-holder-slash-flame-thrower like a javelin through the trees. It bursts into flames, lighting up a clear path for me to follow.

"Go!" He shoves me forward. "Go go go go go!"

I burst forward, the fog abuzz with chants overhead, dashing this way and that through the trees. A cold hand falls on my back.

"Urlick?" I turn. Severed heads float in front of me, their eyes white-hot and shifting. Their centres spinning like ever-changing kaleidoscopes, hypnotizing my mind.

"You can't escape," the creatures hiss. "You belong to us now."

"No!" I shriek and race on through the trees.

They swoop and circle, their laughter rumbling through me like the tail of a thunderstorm. "Urlick!" I shout. "Urlick, where are you?"

"Urlick! Urlick!" They chant. *"He can't help you now!"*

I cover my ears and push deeper and deeper into the woods. The air is thick with the stench of Vapours. It wends a toxic path to my brain. My mind becomes muddled. My gait falters. I stumble. Lost. Surrounded. Staggering . . .

"Urlick? Where are you, *please* . . ."

"Eyelet!" I hear Urlick's voice.

"Urlick!" I scream.

"EYELET!" The voice comes again, only this time clearer. He sounds frantic. "EYELET! Come *quick!*"

I charge toward the voice, breaking through the trees into the clearing. *"Urlick!"* I shriek.

He lies at the bottom of a heap of criminals, barbed wire wound about their necks. Hands pummel him, broken chain hanging from their wrists. "URLICK!" I shoot forward, leaping onto the back of the top brute, and pound at him with my fists. The criminal rears up, shocked to see I'm a girl, before dumping me to the ground. I fall, dizzied from the blow.

A second criminal pulls himself from the heap, holding Urlick's pack. He reaches in and tears out a gas mask.

"Oh, no you don't!" I scramble to my feet, jumping and snapping a branch from the tree over his head. It falls, cracking hard over his back. The criminal grunts and melts to his knees. The gas mask drops from his hand.

"Eyelet!" Urlick calls.

Before I've had the chance to catch my breath, the criminal's on me. He knocks me to the ground, his hands around my throat, choking me. I gasp and gag, trying to pry his bony fingers from my neck, but it's no use. He's much bigger than I am.

"Eyelet!" I hear Urlick scream, the criminal drooling over me like a rabies-stricken dog.

Then I remember.

The darts.

I plunge a hand into my pocket, fingers forming a tight grip around a dart. There's only one. I must have lost the others in the struggle. *This better count.* I thrust my arm up in a surge of determination and stab the dart into the side of the criminal's neck.

The criminal hollers. His eyes flash. They roll to the back of his head.

I gasp at the air as he scrambles to his feet, staggering off into the bushes, disappearing among the foliage.

"Eyelet!" Urlick chokes.

I roll to see him still pinned to the ground, a makeshift knife made of stone at his throat, about to break the skin. "A little help here!" he gurgles.

I stand, lurch forward, grab a handful of the criminal's hair, yank back his head, and draw the blade of the nail file across his throat, tearing open the skin. Blood gushes from the wound, pooling around my feet. The criminal gags and collapses to his knees.

"Good Lord," I gasp, bringing a hand to my mouth, watching the life drain from his eyes. "What have I done?"

"What you had to." Urlick draws in a badly needed breath. "Now come on." He crawls to me, clawing his way to a stand. "Let's get out of here before the one you stuck with the dart comes back." He scoops up a journal that's fallen from his pack. His face morphs into a blur.

"Eyelet?" He looks at me. "What is it?"

The forest floor spins. Trees turn themselves on end. I reach up to swipe my brow, and my arm falls away.

"Eyelet!"

I melt backward into Urlick's arms. "I can't move," I say.

Grass prickles against my cheeks, replacing the warmth of his skin. Treetops swim above me. Perhaps the silver is rising again, or perhaps it's already risen. I'm shaking so badly it's hard to tell. My head feels stuffed with cotton, and it hurts to breathe. Yet I smell no burning bread.

The Vapours. It must be the Vapours. The silver doesn't sting.

"Eyelet!" Urlick falls to his knees beside me. "Eyelet, can you hear me?" He presses his mouth to my lips. "Breathe!" he shouts. His voice sounds muffled, distant. His face is a whirlwind of spiraling features funneling away from me.

I gasp and my lungs seize, stilled by the sharp, breath-stealing stench.

"Come on, Eyelet, breathe for me, *please*." Urlick presses his cool lips to mine again and again. Something canvas falls over my face. "Breathe! *Blast it!* Breathe!" I hear him say.

I'm trying, Urlick. Honest, I'm trying.

"Again!" he shouts. "And again!" He pounds my chest. I wince under the pain.

"Concentrate!" he shouts.

I suck in a breath. It burns. I suck in another. Slowly the black veil begins to lift from my eyes, the stinging pressure lifts from my chest—until at last Urlick's face appears again before me, that glorious chalky-white skin of his, those sweet mulberry lips. He stares at me through eyes as pink as cotton candy.

"Hi," I say, pushing the mask from my face.

"Hi yourself." He grins, brushing a dead leaf from my cheek. "You just scared the *shite* out of me. You know that, right?"

"Good. You'll be lighter to travel then."

He grins. He whisks me up into his arms and tosses me over his back. "I wish I could say the same for you."

I slap him, and break out into another coughing fit. Urlick glances back at me, worried. "Come on." He launches forward, adjusting me on his shoulder. "Best get you to the Core, before anything else happens."

Forty-Six

Urlick

I race toward the Core—or at least where I think the Core is supposed to be—carrying Eyelet on my back, weaving through heavy, rolling fog and a forest of half-dead trees. I stop only to buddy-breathe air from the gas mask from time to time. Eyelet is fading fast.

I'm frantic to find the pathway leading to the door. It's made of white stones, I remember, white stones. It doesn't seem to be here anywhere. I circle around, then double back. Nothing seems to be here.

I stop, heave in a breath, and lay Eyelet gently in the soft grasses at the edge of the path, up against the side of the rock for cover. I pull out the gas mask and secure it over her face, rummaging desperately through Eyelet's pack for the second.

It's gone.

The criminal must have made off with it before Eyelet could stop him. We've only this one left to share. I tap the gauge. It's running low. In fact, it's almost out. We can't stay out here too much longer in the Vapours without oxygen. We won't last.

I roll a hand through my hair, feeling the pressure of the Vapours in my own head—a sharp, gnawing pinch above my temples. I yank a handkerchief from my pocket and tie it around my mouth to breathe through. It's not oxygen, but it'll filter some of the toxins away.

Where is the path?

I check on Eyelet to see if she's all right. She isn't. I can tell. Her breathing is irregular. I remove the mask and am stunned to see her lips are blue. Her skin is turning grey. The Vapours are getting the best of her, despite the oxygen. If I don't get her to the Core soon, I'm afraid I'm going to lose her.

I drop my head. *Please, Eyelet, don't leave me.*

I stand and suck in an icy breath. It shivers through me like a storm. What have I done? What's wrong with me? Leading us all the way out here on a whim? So far away from the Compound, so far away from everything, without even being sure the Core still exists. It could have perished the Night of the Great Illumination for all I know. In the explosion that destroyed so much of our landscape—creating crevasses where there were none, toppling trees, burning forests. Leaving us teetering on the brink of an ominous, frothing pit dividing our world from all others.

What made me think anything out here could have survived that? I drop my face in my hands. How could I have believed the Core could withstand such a thing? How could I have been so stupid?

Eyelet gasps, and I drop to my knees, brushing the hair from her face and replacing the gas mask. *Please don't let me have dragged us all this way just to surrender us to the Vapours.*

I look up into the coiling mist. "The Core has to be here somewhere," I gasp. The bitter tinge of Vapours blisters in the back of my throat.

I launch to my feet and pace the pathway, squinting through the fog, looking for any kind of sign. The building was white, that much I remember, made of white stone—alabaster. The curtain of fog parts for a second, and across a clearing I see the crevasse. Black mist rises from its belly. I had no idea we were wandering blindly so close to the brink of Embers. I swallow, imagining our fate if I'd taken one misstep. I draw in another uneasy breath. Desperation rattles my bones. Something flickers to the far left of me, high on the ridge, glowing alabaster through a charred stand of trees.

Backlit by the roiling smoke of Embers . . .

Stand the cornerstones of a building.

Abandoning Eyelet, I race up the hill, galloping the final few strides, falling to my knees on the overgrown stone path that had eluded me—

"It's gone," I gasp, shuddering. "My father's lab is gone."

Only the front pillars and the cornerstones remain. The rest of the building lies scattered about the ground like the ruins of Stonehenge. To the rear, Embers froths, its black guts belching sour smoke into the air. A vile combination of pungent Vapours, crisped earth, charred wood, and scorched stone.

"No!" I slam my fists to the dirt. "This can't be happening! It can't be true! *Please!*" I shout to the sky. "*Something* has to be here! Something *has* to be left!"

I launch forward, stumbling through the brush, my knees weak, my muscles quivering, searching the site for something, *anything*, any form of shelter, any protection from the Vapours. "*Please*, let there be something left."

Using all my strength, I shoulder aside the slabs of broken alabaster wall, searching the ground beneath them for a tunnel, a hole, a hidden hatch maybe. And then it hits me . . .

My father's constructions always included an underground bunker. Built to soothe his irrational fears of toxic war. Always kept stocked and readied to support life within them for up to ten years should his worst nightmare materialize. Surely he would have built one here as well.

Eyelet coughs, and my head swings around. A shadow sifts through the trees. One at first, and then several. I swallow. Gooseflesh prickles my neck.

I turn and race to Eyelet, gathering her up in my arms. "Hold on," I whisper, travelling the same path back to the Core, laying her down on the soft ground beside me. I lean, pressing my lips to her cheek. "Hold on, Eyelet, *please*."

Covering her with my coat, I scan the grounds for any indication of the bunker's lid, clawing at the dirt, rolling aside the larger rubble and digging beneath it. A dark mass of cloud cover closes in on me from behind.

I swing around, catching it out of the corner of my eye. "Blast it!" I gasp.

The Turned.

They waft in and out of the shadows of the rubble, so close I taste their sour stench. They must have followed us, tracked us somehow through the woods. Something howls, and I crank my head around. More waft toward me through the trees on the opposite side. We're surrounded.

My gaze drops to Eyelet, lying lifeless on the ground. I've got to get her out of here before they take her from me.

I lean over, scooping her up into my arms, folding her close to my chest as I paw at the dirt. *"Please!"* I beg. "Please help me find a way in."

The Turned swoop, dragging their atrophied fingers over Eyelet's cheeks, knocking me in the back.

"No!" I swing at them, whirling around, curling Eyelet under me. "You will not take her from me! I will not let you!"

Laughter, chatters through the trees. Fingers comb through Eyelet's hair.

"It's over," one whispers in my ear. "She's ours now."

"No!" I swing. The spirits bend in the air.

"*It's no use! You're surrounded! We've won!*"

They cackle.

"No, you haven't! You never will!"

They laugh again, and it rolls down my spine. I lower my head and claw at the earth, fingers bleeding. "Come on, come on."

The Turned swirl closer, their voices worming like a disease into my head. I close my eyes, trying to shut them out.

"*She's ours!*" they hiss. "*You're ours. Give her to us!*"

"NEVER!" I twist, shielding Eyelet.

Their ghoulish eyes sear through the mist. They warp and curl, their spiny fingers pulling at her shoulders.

It has to be here! I cradle Eyelet in one arm and dig with the other. Somewhere! Let it be here! *Please!*

The face of a spirit appears at the back of Eyelet's head, shimmering silver through the dark cloud. Its jaws stretched wide, teeth gleaming.

"No!" I backhand the spirit into ash and yank Eyelet to the other side, groping at every dent and pebble in the earth until—at last—my fingers catch on something solid, something gold in a sea of beige earth.

A ring, glinting in the darkness. I clear the dirt and find a solid brass ring, big enough to fit the nose of a bull. I pry it upward and yank it back hard, finding it attached to a latch. Another tug engages the lever beneath. The ground beneath us shudders.

Spirits swoop and scream overhead as the earth begins to shake. Gears creak and turbines tumble, giving way to a trapdoor buried just below the ground's surface. A siren screeches, driving back the Turned, as the long, thin door rumbles open. Launching to my feet, I throw Eyelet over my shoulder and stumble down a set of stairs through a blinding waft of steam. The hammered fingers of the Turned claw at my arms, my face, her clothes, as we descend.

Sweaty and breathless, I roll the door closed over our heads and fall to the stairs, shaken and gasping, the bitter voices of the Turned still screeching overhead.

"We're safe, Eyelet. At last, we're safe."

*

I drop Eyelet softly down on a bed and run to the storage room in search of oxygen, feeding it to her straight from a tank I find among my father's stash, hoping the supply is still good.

"Please," I whisper, rocking her. "Please, Eyelet." I stroke her forehead and press my lips to her brow, over and over again. "Please come back to me. Don't leave me now, *please*, Eyelet." I lift the mask and kiss her lips. "I can't go on without you . . ."

I replace the mask, stroking her hands. Her nail beds are blue. Her skin is the colour of stone. I'm losing her. I weep inside, adjusting the flow on the pump to pour a steadier stream, unable to breathe myself.

Come on, Eyelet . . . Come on, please . . .

She sputters, then coughs. Her eyelids flutter.

"Come on, Eyelet!" I breathe.

Slowly, mercifully, colour seeps in, pinking her cheeks. Her eyes roll before finally popping open, looking glazed and groggy, but alive.

I suck in a breath as she scans the room, her gaze finally settling on my face.

"There you are," she says. I smile and she smiles back. The most beautiful smile I've ever seen. I take her hand in mine, squeezing the warmth back into her fingers. Slowly they turn from grey to pink.

"What's this about you not being able to go on without me?" She grins. The warm toffee centres of her eyes sparkle in the room's flickering aether light.

"Oh, Eyelet." I fall forward, crushing her to my chest, lost in her scent, our hearts beating wildly. "Promise me," I breathe at her neck. "Promise you'll never, ever leave me—"

"Never," she whispers, her lips grazing the side of my raised purpled cheek. "Promise you'll never leave me, either?"

I pull back, taking her face in my hands. "Oh, I promise," I gasp.

She reaches up, pulls me closer, her lips hovering over mine. Her warm, cinnamon breath wakes a part of my soul I never knew existed. Every cell in my body illuminates, as though she were the light I've yearned for all these years. Surging forward, I drop my lips over hers, engulfing her in a kiss so deep, and so long, it's electrifying.

Her hands caress my hair, my face, my chest. Lacing her fingers behind my neck, she urges me to lower myself over her on the bed. The heat between us burns hot as white coals.

"Are you sure?" I whisper, our lips tightly pressed.

"Aren't you?" She breaks away, looking forlorn.

"Of course I am," I breathe into her mouth. *God knows I am.* "I just want you to be—"

"I've never been more." She lurches forward, peppering me in savage kisses, kneading my arms, my shoulders, my chest. Slowly she unbuttons my shirt, yanking its tails from the top of my britches, and peels it back—exposing my bare chest.

I sink into the moment, her mouth on my mouth, her hand on my hand, guiding it beneath her skirts. The touch of her thighs, so soft and warm—then all at once she pulls back.

She's changed her mind. Thought better of me . . .

My heart falters in my chest. "What is it? What's the matter?"

"Shhhhh!" She scowls, pressing a finger to my lips. "Don't you hear it?" Her head cranks around.

"Hear what?"

"That sound. In the wall. What is it?" She clings to me, frightened, as the sound of churning gears increases.

"I don't know." I shake my head. "I've not heard it before."

"It's getting louder." She looks panicked.

"You stay here." I push up onto my arms over top of her. "I'll go find out what it is." I launch myself off the bed, about to leave.

"No." She grabs my arm and hauls me back. "I'm coming with you."

"Eyelet, I don't think—"

"You just promised never to leave me, remember?" She sits up, her lips quivering.

"Very well, then," I say, and she breaks into a smile in that precious way she does. "We'll go find out together." I collect her in my arms and start down the hallway, the sound getting louder. It leads us to a massive set of black iron doors at the far end of the Core. The doors fill the wall from side to side and floor to ceiling. I've never seen anything quite like it. A jagged sawtoothed joint runs vertically through its middle. That must be how they open.

"Where do you suppose *that* leads?" Eyelet whispers over the chug of gears that roll inside. Her eyes are wide and fearful.

"I don't know." I drop her feet to the floor. "You all right to stand?"

"I think so." She nods, though she's still a bit wobbly. I reach over, threading my fingers through hers. She steadies almost immediately.

"I thought you said you've been here before." She turns to me.

"I have. Once. I've just never been inside."

Slowly, I drag my hand down the sawtoothed joint that runs the length of the middle of the doors, laying my ear to the jagged crack. The churn of gears inside grows stronger. Eyelet steps forward, placing her ear at the door as well.

"Look," I say. Her necklace is levitating.

Eyelet's eyes are wide, shocked by the sight of it—the chain standing horizontally, the vial at its end pointing toward the crack in the door.

"What on earth?" She turns to me. "Why is it doing that?"

"If you have no idea, I surely don't." I reach out for the necklace and it hovers away, tracing the crack between the doors.

She tries to pull it to her chest, but it just floats back up as if it has a mind of its own.

"Has this ever happened before?"

"No. And it's never flashed as brilliantly, either." She loops the chain from her neck and lets the vial go. It dances mysteriously up and down the crack in the door. Emerald bolts of lightning streak like rays between the vial and the jagged opening, bursting into a searing flash of light when the vial finally reaches the floor. It releases and rolls to her feet.

A buzzer sounds and the door wafts apart, engulfing the hallway in a violent gust of steam. We jump back, coughing, as the steam fountains up from the floorboards to form clouds in the hallway, and the doors shimmy the rest of the way open. They roll back, then disappear completely into a set of hidden pockets carved into either side of the doorway.

"Where did you get that?" I gasp, swooping to pick up the necklace.

"From my mother." She takes it from me, looping it again round her neck. "It was my father's. He asked my mother to keep it for him the day he left for the Follies and never returned."

"And you never knew what it was? You had no idea it could do this?"

"No." She shakes her head. "My mother told me it was the key to the future. Mine and everyone else's. But I never understood what she meant."

"The key to the future." I scowl, coughing, waving off the smoke that lingers in the hall. "Well, shall we go see?"

Eyelet takes my hand, and we step across the threshold through a warm veil of steam, her hand trembling inside my own. Buzzers sound. Sirens scream. The floors vibrate, shaking the walls.

"Perhaps we'd better go back," she gasps, squeezing my hand.

"There's no going back now," I say.

We carry on into the centre of the dark room, following the low, pumping churn of the gears.

"Look!" Eyelet's head pops up. She sucks in a sharp breath.

I follow her gaze to the ceiling.

The walls of the room stretch up much higher than they did in the hall. They must extend thirty, maybe forty metres. A solid stained-glass dome of windows crowns the top, featuring scenes of gods and their worshippers from the sacred book.

In the middle of the room, the floor sinks into a circular well, which I'm certain adds to the height. Inside the sunken circle sits an array of extendable telescopes, high-powered eyes, and looking glasses used to explore the planets.

"It must be some kind of underground observatory," Eyelet whispers, creeping away from me.

"More like a planetarium," I say.

"Strange, don't you think?" She turns. "To keep such things underground."

"Very." My head twists, taking in more details, my eyes locking on several large, rectangular windows cut into the sides of the glass dome, apparently designed to roll open, allowing the nozzles of the great ocular guns to project through.

"Good merciful Heavens," Eyelet gasps, clutching her heart. She turns. Her face is the colour of ash.

"What is it?" I race over, tracing her gaze.

"The Illuminator," she stammers. "It's grown."

Forty-Seven

Eyelet

"It's as big as the entire room." I let out a breath, albeit a very shaky one.

"It is indeed." Urlick bursts forward, delighted.

In the centre of the room, on a raised platform—now exposed through the dissipating cloud of steam—sits a giant replica of the Illuminator, several times the size of the original.

I gasp and stumble backward. How can he see this as anything good? It's a monster. A monster-sized machine. "This is terrible." I shake my head.

"What are you talking about, *terrible*?" Urlick jerks around. "This is wonderful! Look at the size of that thing!" He throws his hands in the air.

Turning, he trundles up a metal staircase on the side of the platform that leads to the base of the great machine. A starter throttle protrudes up through a hole in the grates. Urlick takes hold of it, and I shiver.

"Just imagine its power! Imagine its ability!"

"I am. That's why I'm worried." I swallow.

"What are you talking about?" He turns, almost laughing.

"That's a giant cathode-ray lens looming above your head. You do realize that, don't you?"

"What of it?" He frowns, furrowing his brow.

"What *of* it? Are you *kidding* me?"

"Don't you think you're being just a little bit silly?" He holds his fingers up as if he's about to pinch salt. "I mean, we wanted to find the machine, and now, *well . . .*" He turns, looking dreamily up at the massive Crookes tube perched high above the machine in a giant copper stand. "We certainly have." He smiles at me. "Don't you see? With a machine this size we could affect far more than we *ever* thought possible."

"That's just the problem." I bite my lip. "I think it might have already done just that."

He scowls. "What are you saying?"

I have to tell him.

I have to tell him everything.

About the journals. The letter. His father.

Everything I know.

I lower my head and suck in a shaky breath.

"Go on, tell me." He nods his head.

I hesitate, suck on my lip, then blurt it out. "In my father's journals, back at the Academy, I found some information I don't think you're going to like."

He looks offended, and yet I've barely started.

"There was a letter tucked in the middle of the journal you passed to me. It was penned by my father's hand. Inside it, my father wrote of your father and your father's connection to the machine, and how he feared what might happen to the world at large if his Illuminator was left to your father's sole discretion. In short, he didn't trust him."

Urlick's demeanor grows cold, but I must continue. He has to know the truth.

"According to the letter, your father was obsessed with interplanetary research. In particular, he had a lifelong desire to confirm the existence of an alternate universe beyond our own—where the dead still live. He sought to find it in order to join your dead mother there. He was ill, Urlick. Your father was ill."

"Stop!" Urlick raises his hand. "You're making this up!"

"I wish I were, Urlick. I truly wish I were." I swallow, rolling my hands inside each other. "But it appears the death of your mother sent your father over a brink . . . from which he never returned—"

"Enough. I will not listen to this."

"I'm sorry, Urlick, but you have to know. You deserve to know the truth. My father tried to warn your father about the machine—of its dangerous side he'd only just found out about—but your father refused to listen to reason. Obsessed with finding this alternate world, he pushed on with his plans to manipulate the power and scope of the Illuminator and use it to search the heavens."

"What are you saying?" Urlick scowls. "Be clear."

"I'm saying my father feared your father's plan so much, he came out here the last day of his life to try and stop him."

"Are you implying my father's responsible for your father's death?"

"Look up, Urlick. Look at the Crookes tube." I lift my eyes. "It's pointed toward the heavens."

Urlick's gaze swings between the Crookes tube and me. "No." He shakes his head. "It's a lie. You *lie*. It can't be true. My father may have been a lot of things, but he was *not a murderer!*"

"Think about it. It all makes sense. The letter. The claims. What's happened here. Look around you, Urlick. Don't you see? Together our fathers created something that ended our world as we knew it. Or, at least, changed it forever—"

"Are you saying they were responsible for the *flash*, the Night of the Great Illumination?"

"Look at it, Urlick. Look where we are. What other explanation could there be?"

"You have no proof this machine was ever detonated."

"That's where you're wrong." I produce the notebook journal labeled *Lumière* from my boot and hand it over to him. "Hold it out with the spine away from yourself." Urlick turns the thin notebook until the pages face him. "Now fan the pages just slightly." He does. "What do you see?"

"A miniature drawing." Urlick gasps. "Of the Core—" He stares at me. "Who drew this?"

"My father."

"Why?"

"Fan the pages again, only squeeze it tighter."

He squints. "Find me," he reads.

"I discovered it as I stuffed it in my boot back at the Compound, but I had no idea what the drawing was or what it meant. Until now."

He looks at me, astonished. "Go get the other journal. The one that contained your father's note."

Forty-Eight

Eyelet

I disappear into the hallway and race to the bedroom, pulling the journal labeled *Noir* from the depths of my pack, and fly back up the hall.

"Let me see." Urlick fans the pages as I stare over his shoulder. A drawing of the Illuminator appears—the small one at first, then the giant one next to it. Bolts of lightning connect them. In between the machines, the hands of two men struggle over a giant key. Beneath are the words *God be with me.*

I gasp at the sight of them. My father's words. From his final note. It's true. What I believed is true.

"That's what my nursemaid meant," Urlick utters, his eyes fixed forward on nothing in particular, "when on her deathbed she told the lawyer I wasn't to be returned to my father because he'd come undone." He looks up at me, tears in his eyes. "He was Mad. That's why he hated me so much. It wasn't me. It wasn't my fault. It was his."

I place a hand on his shoulder, and he shrugs it away. He turns, a new light in his eyes. "This is why Smrt didn't shoot us back in Brethren."

"What?"

"*This* is why we're not dead." He shakes the journal. "Smrt knew if he just waited long enough, we'd solve the puzzle and lead him to the prize possession he's been looking for all these years: *this* machine. Not the one in the warehouse in Gears! This one!"

An envelope falls from the centre of the journal, drifting slowly to the floor. I bend to pick it up, shocked to see my name written across the front of it. *For Eyelet*. Written in the hand of my father.

I rip it open and read it aloud:

In regard to my recent findings—the discovery of residual amounts of radiate particulate matter lingering in the hair and nail samples of the human specimens I've exposed to the light, up to a month after their exposure. I have feverishly been pursuing an antidote, in the hope of deradiating my victims. The formula for which, you will find encrypted here on the final pages of this journal.

I look up, and Urlick frantically flips to the final page, running a finger down the equation.

It should also be noted, large sums of radiate particulate matter were found in the wall and floor sample scrapings of the laboratory where I took the photographs. I also found readings far above acceptable levels in the groundwater and earth surrounding my laboratory, as far as twenty metres out in all directions.

Urlick looks up.

"No wonder he so feared your father's plan," I say.

Though I've not yet had the chance to test the serum, I believe it to be of sound and trustworthy science. Unfortunately, to date I've only had the chance to produce a single vial, enough to deradiate just one human subject. You will find the vial in the possession of my wife, one Lila Isadore Elsworth.

"My mother." I take a breath.

Should anything happen to me, I hereby solemnly request the vial be used for the preservation of my daughter, Eyelet Emiline Elsworth, who ranks among the afflicted.

I gasp.

"Afflicted?" Urlick stalks toward me. "What does he mean, afflicted?"

I ignore the question and keep reading.

The vial is infused with a de-ionized arc from the cathode ray, vacuum-packed under glass. It doubles as a key to unlock the doors behind which you will find the machine.

"The pendant," I say. Urlick's gaze falls to my neck. "No wonder it behaved the way it did. It *is* the key to my future. To everyone's future. Just like Mother said."

"What?" Urlick says.

"Those were the last words she said to me as she lay dying. She told me never to give it over to anyone for any reason. Now I understand why."

"And your father, why did he insist you take the serum? What did he mean by 'afflicted'?"

I bite my lip and fall silent, studying the toes of my boots. "I've wanted to tell, I was just so afraid—"

"Tell me what?"

I twist my fingers in my hand. "I suffer from mind struggles, Urlick. A form of mild insanity. I'm troubled with seizures. Much like Cordelia. Only mine are not quite as severe. Sometimes they're very small, but other times they're large. I start to shake and then I'm taken under. That's what happened to me the other day, in the balloon. That's why you couldn't wake me up—"

"Is that all?"

My chin springs up.

"What do you mean, is that all? Isn't that enough?"

"Why, it's nothing." Urlick laughs, tucking the hair behind my ear. "Just a minor imperfection."

"It is?"

"Certainly." He grins.

"So it doesn't matter to you?"

"Why would it?" He reaches for me, cupping my face in his hands. "You're perfect, Eyelet, just as you are."

"You're serious?" I say.

"Have I ever been anything else?"

I laugh and fall against his chest, my arms wrapped tightly about his waist. He strokes my hair and kisses the top of my head, and I feel as though a weight has been lifted off my heart—an anchor I've carried since birth. I cling to him, letting the years of heartache melt away, his hands stroking my back. How many years had I believed I would never be loved, never accepted, all because I was different? And now, our differences have brought us together. I couldn't be a luckier girl.

"Your father." Urlick pulls back, concern in his eyes. "How many times did he expose you to the Ray?"

"Just the once. When I was very young. Never again," I say. "According to his note, he realized his mistake and ceased experimenting on me immediately. Which, I realize now, I misinterpreted as abandonment. I've hated him, you know. All these years, I thought he'd betrayed me. When in truth, what he did, he did out of love." I pinch my lips together, fighting back a sob.

Urlick wraps his arms around me, pressing another kiss to my head. "It's all right." He thumbs a tear from my cheek. "You were young, you didn't know. But now that you do"—he picks my necklace up off my chest—"you need to do as he says and drink this immediately."

"No." I snap back, shaking my head. "I can't."

"What do you mean, you can't? You heard what he said. You could die otherwise. You've been exposed to the Ray."

"I couldn't live with myself knowing I drank the only antidote. You heard him. He said there were others."

"But—"

"I promise you I'll drink it, as soon as we find a way to duplicate the formula."

"And if we can't? What then?"

"Don't talk like that, of course we can. Look at all the things we've done together." I take his hand in mine, the necklace clasped tightly between our fingers. "Think about it. If it takes one vial of serum to deradiate a human, what could a thousand, maybe a million vials do? Perhaps we can produce enough antidote to reverse the effects the Night of the Great Illumination has had on the rest of our world."

"Such an arresting premise."

Our heads snap around to the sound of his voice. Smrt emerges from the shadows, pistol in his hand. He cocks the gun and points it at us.

"Too bad it'll never have a chance to come to fruition."

Forty-Nine

Eyelet

Urlick steps out in front of me. Smrt closes the gap between us. The sides of his trench coat flap as he stalks toward us, ebony buttons glinting silvery-white.

Flossie trots along behind him like the dog she is, her gaze stretching up and down the frame of the Illuminator in fearful, giddy awe.

"How did you know where to find us?" Urlick breathes.

"You weren't difficult to find." Smrt grins. "I simply followed the bread crumbs you left for me." He pulls the remains of one of Urlick's arsenal gadgets from his pocket. "Ingenious, really. It'll be a shame to waste such a brilliant mind. Though not brilliant enough to realize he shouldn't leave a trail of these." He spins the gadget on the end of his finger. "Not to mention the dead bodies. Oh, and the cycle was a rather nice touch. You *are* aware the silly thing follows you around like a dog?"

"*Bertie,*" Urlick mumbles.

Smrt smirks, then inspects his nails. "At any rate, it all made for wonderfully easy tracking. The bridge was a bit of a trick, I must admit, but then the cycle sniffed out this." He holds up my torn piece of petticoat. The one I scripted my father's message on with ashes. It must have dropped from my pocket as we fled the Turned. "Now"—he balls it in his fist—"shall we get down to business?"

Urlick's eyes are wild, his teeth clenched. "Go ahead, tell us. What is it you really want?"

Smrt snorts, jutting his neck out over the stone floor. "What I've always wanted." He lowers his voice. "Power. *Ultimate* power."

His eyes flick to the centre of the room. He spins on his heel, charging toward the Illuminator, tossing his gun off to Flossie along the way.

She fumbles with it, then points it at my head, her hands trembling.

Smrt strips his gloves from his hand, running an adoring finger over the rim of the machine's giant lens. "It appears I have it now, don't I?" Smrt turns and grins. "And to think your father *was* right, Eyelet." He leans back, elbows on the rail, and flips his chin. "His father *was* a madman." Urlick's body tenses next to me. I squeeze his hand to hold him back. "But an incredibly fine and innovative one, lucky for me!" Smrt laughs.

Flossie's eyes move over me, and her finger twitches on the pistol's trigger.

"Ironic, isn't it?" Smrt's eyes flash. "How everything in science created for the purpose of *good* ends up having an equally ill-intended use? Case in point: your father creates a seemingly harmless picture box"—he nods at me and then turns to Urlick—"which *your* father then turns into the ultimate killing machine."

"How dare you speak that way of his intentions?" Urlick scowls.

"Oh, come now, you've read her father's notes. I know you have. I listened." Smrt clatters back across the room. "Your father's intentions may not have been purposely malevolent, but he sought power just the same. What is the saying? Ultimate power corrupts absolutely, or some such silly thing. Nevertheless, here we are and there it sits." He tosses a hand back toward the machine. "Just imagine the price nations will pay to get their hands on a weapon of such massive destruction."

"You've known all along, haven't you?" I step around Urlick. "How dangerous this science is." I grit my teeth. "You knew and you did *nothing?*"

"Wrong." Smrt grins. "I knew and I did *everything.* Everything in my power to preserve the science, while your father fought to have it put to bed."

"You're the reason he was demoted."

"Your father was the cause of his own demotion, the *nizy* fool! Always bringing to light the machine's harmful side instead of championing its endless possibilities."

"Because my father had a conscience!"

"Oh, you think so, do you?" Smrt snaps. "Your father promised me a cure for my palsy if only I helped to finance his machine. I handed over the money, but no cure ever came. Instead, he paid me off in prototypes, telling me I could keep the revenue from their sales. I took the money and planned to build a bigger one, a better one, something stronger, more capable of mastering a cure. But then my *daft* assistant Mrs. Benson up and died and ruined everything! Rumors spread across the countryside, claiming she died of her repeat exposure to the Ray. People began calling for the Academy to abandon the science, for all the machines to be destroyed. So I volunteered to perform Mrs. Benson's autopsy, hoping to quell the gossip, during which I realized your father had been right.

"The tumor that stilled Mrs. Benson's lungs was, in fact, due to exposure to the machine. A giant mass of particulate radiate matter the size of a baseball lay lodged in her lungs. The machine was in fact *killing* people.

"Imagine my delight when I found out that in my hands I held such *power.* What was once billed as the world's miracle machine"—he raises his arms—"was, in truth, a silent killer.

"People flocked in droves and paid great sums of money to lie beneath the Ray, believing it would cure them, when actually it was nothing but a cruel joke. The Ray wasn't saving them, it was slowly killing them.

"And now, not only will I possess the power to decide who lives or dies, I'll hold the secret to the antidote, too. Just think how much people would pay to cure themselves, once they realized they'd been such fools."

"You'll never own it," I say. "I'll never give it to you."

"You'll give it to me"—he pulls another gun from his pocket and cocks it next to Urlick's head—"or I take his life."

"Don't give it to him, Eyelet," Urlick shouts. "He won't shoot me! He's too much of a coward!"

"Shut *up*!" Smrt smacks him in the head with the gun.

Blood bursts from Urlick's temple.

"Hand it over, or he dies."

"Don't do it, Eyelet! He's only bluffing."

I gasp, my head swinging between the two of them.

"Your choice." Smrt moves his finger to the trigger of his gun. "Your pendant in exchange for your boyfriend's life. Or death for the both of you."

"Wait!" I shout. I unloop the chain from my neck and toss it across the room.

"No, Eyelet! *Don't!*" Urlick screams.

The vial lopes, tumbling slowly through the air, too far to the side for Smrt to be able to catch it. My plan all along.

Smrt lunges for it. Urlick leaps on his back. They spin, Urlick clawing at Smrt's eyes. "Shoot him!" Smrt shouts.

Flossie's gun goes off, grazing Urlick in the leg.

I race at her, heart pounding, and kick the gun from her hands.

"Eyelet!" Urlick screams, Smrt on his back driving punches into his side. "The journals!"

I turn to see Flossie racing from the room, my father's journals pressed tight to her chest. I hitch up my skirts and charge after her. "Urlick!" I turn back at the door.

Smrt's hands are on Urlick's throat. Urlick's back is draped over the controls. The Illuminator's panel is flashing—red.

"I've got this!" Urlick shouts. "Go after the journals!" He throws a solid left into Smrt's jaw.

Fifty

Eyelet

I turn and race up the stairs, out into the Vapours, no time to search for a mask, and chase after Flossie through the splotchy fog, hurdling logs, tree trunks, and bushes. It soon becomes clear I'll never catch her—Flossie's got too much of a lead. I slow, my eye catching on something glinting in a stand of trees on the outskirts of the Core. White bone wrapped in brambles.

"Bertie?"

The cycle whimpers, his frame shuddering. He rears and bucks but can't get loose. Someone has tangled him up in the thicket and left him to fight his way out. "Smrt," I grumble as I race toward Bertie, "it had to be him."

I reach the base of the trees in seconds. Thorns stick me as I try to part the branches. "Hold on," I say to Bertie, yanking the nail file from my pocket. I hack and slice at the branches with the file's edge.

Bertie jounces, breaking himself free, spilling breathless out onto the path.

"Good boy!" I say, patting his handlebars. "Though I'm positive Urlick told you to stay put," I whisper in his ear, leaning over, "I'm glad you don't listen to him either. You up for a little chase?" Bertie trundles. "Good, because we can't afford to let her get away."

I throw my leg over the seat and jump on the pedals, guiding Bertie off through the woods at a magnificent speed. Steering through the tangled underbrush, maneuvering past rock and tree, through the blackening fog.

I give a fleeting thought to the Infirmed, but then erase it. Whatever it takes, I can't let Flossie get away.

Within seconds I have Flossie in sight, spotting her sapphire coat shimmering through the foggy drape. Gaining on her, I pull up to a stand, pedaling harder, pushing Bertie to his limit. Using a rock as a ramp, I yank back on the handlebars, launching Bertie and myself up into the air over her head.

Flossie cranks around, her face awash with panic.

I lean out from the cycle, and I jump.

Her skirts pulled high, Flossie pours on the speed.

I pounce, catching her by the knees. My chin bounces off the ground as I haul her to the earth, journals spilling from her hands. We roll in a tight ball of tangled arms and legs, journals scattered across the forest floor, pages fluttering in the wind.

When at last we stop, I punch her hard in the stomach and scramble to my feet, lunging after the journals. I stuff them down the front of my jacket—then I hear the cock of a gun.

"You don't know when to give up, do you?" Flossie seethes.

I whirl around to find her behind the snout of a lady's silver pistol. Her eyes are small and mean. Twigs sprout like wires from her hair. Muck streaks her sapphire coat. Her harelip is torn and bloodied.

"Stubborn little bitch, aren't you?" she spits.

"I could say the same of you." My eyes narrow.

"But you won't, because in a moment you'll never speak again." She stalks toward me, closes in, pistol wobbling in her shaky hands. "Pity Urlick isn't here to see this." She squeezes one eye shut, sizing me up over the barrel of the gun. "I so wanted to see his expression as I put a bullet through your *heart.* Or perhaps I should wait and kill you both together, like the traitors you are. So much more Romeo-and-Juliet that way, don't you think?"

"I don't know what you're talking about."

"Don't play stupid with me. You know very well what you've done. Before *you,* Urlick and I were perfectly happy." Her brows dance wickedly over her eyes. "All my life I've wanted only *one* thing. Someone to love me. I always thought that someone would be Urlick—until *you s*howed up and ruined *everything*! *You* and your *pet* name and your *fancy* face and your *whorish* way of dress!" Her eyes traipse up and down my frame, stopping to judge my short skirt in the middle. "Everything was fine between us until *you* came and *stole* his affections from me."

"I stole nothing. You never had them—"

"That's not *true*!" Her bloody lip quivers. "You know nothing of him! Nothing of me! Nothing of us—"

"I know that even with me out of the way, he will never love you, because he never *did.*"

"*Shut up* and hand over the journals, you filthy, lying wench."

"What do you want with the journals? I thought you only wanted me dead."

"Stop talking and hand them over." She cocks the hammer of the gun.

Behind her head something rustles in the trees. I swing my gaze in that direction. Lights, like eyes, glow white through the darkness. A knot of fear chokes off my breath. I search the trees overhead and see more fiendish eyes peering down, tracking our every move.

There's a sudden swoop, and a thick grey cloud forms behind Flossie, rising above her shoulders like a wave out of the fog. Gnarled fingers curl and reach for her. Lizard-like tongues lick the air.

"Flossie," I say, breathlessly. "You need to listen to me—"

"I've heard enough from you *already*!"

"Please." I swallow. "It's the Turned. They've tracked us—"

"And why should I believe you?"

"Because I speak the truth."

A low, throaty moan spirals past her, splits into two at the end of the clearing and doubles back, swooping low over Flossie's head. She jerks out of the way, tracking the sound, her eyes the size of walnuts.

"We can't let them surround us." I shiver. "We need to move or we're dead."

"How do you know this?"

"Because I do. Now drop the gun so we can run."

The moan shrieks past us again.

"And if I don't?"

"We'll both be eaten."

Flossie raises a wobbly gun and prepares to shoot me. "Or perhaps just one of us will."

Flossie's eyes flash as a hand lands on her shoulder. Laughter breaks through the trees. Before either of us can draw another breath, the mist behind her comes alive. The faces of twenty or more gape-mouthed ghouls swoop and swirl about her head and mine.

They cackle and howl, poking us, taunting us, like cats worrying mice before a feast. Flossie screams, punching at the air, dropping the pistol to the ground.

I lunge for it, sending a warning shot off above my head to clear the air of spirits, and turn to run, but Flossie drags me back. I've no choice. It's either her or me.

Turning, I throw my hands into her chest, saving myself—sacrificing Flossie to the Turned.

A look of horror etches across her mole-ridden face as I turn to run. Bertie catches up with me by the end of the clearing. I throw a leg over his frame and ride away as fast as I can, haunted by the sound of Flossie's screams as they drag her off across the forest floor to feed.

Fifty-One

Eyelet

My feet are as wobbly as jelly beneath me. It's all I can do to pedal. I push on for the Core, praying Bertie's got enough wind left in him to get me there. We don't dare stop. He takes over quickly, sensing my exhaustion, doubling our pace through the trees.

"Thank you," I whisper, leaning over him.

Bertie groans, then sighs with relief.

He zigzags his way through the forest, avoiding stumps and slicks. I'm thankful he knows where we're going. At least I hope he does.

The air suddenly grows too hot, too thick, too hard to breathe. The lining of my lungs burns. The forest is steadily growing hotter, yet there's no sign of fire. I don't understand what's happening.

I pedal on, the lace trim on my skirts withering to nothing in the infernal wind as if they've melted off the fabric's edge.

"Bertie!" I shout. "What *is* this? What's happening?"

Bertie shudders, struggling to breathe, the lacquer peeling from his handlebars.

I look up to see a green beam of light radiating through the trees, shooting up from the ground in a perfect circle. It cuts through the dense fog, illuminating the heavens above in a ring around the Core—or what's left of it—creating a halo around the rubble. Heat emanates in waves from its sides, scorching out into the forest.

"Oh, no," I gasp. "No. No, no. This can't be happening. We've got to get there, Bertie. We've got to stop this, quick!" I jump on the pedals, leaning out over the handlebars, my skin bubbling from the heat.

A churn of gears, and the earth on either side of the door to the Core tears open, revealing two giant holes. The Crookes tube appears through a third, in the middle, just behind the door. The earth cracks and breaks all around it. The ground trembles as the Crookes tube rises up out of the burrow, cradled in its metal stand, the needle-nosed snout aimed at the heavens. "Good God," I gasp.

I race harder, Bertie wheezing as I pour on the speed. The closer we get, the more the sulfuric stench of the Vapours turns metallic, stinging my nostrils and pulling away my breath.

Tree limbs steam and smoulder. Voltage jumps.

"Oh, God! It's happening!" I fall back on the seat. "The machine, it's been activated!"

The ground shakes beneath, throwing the cycle's tires into a wobbly mess. I nearly lose control. From out of the slats in the earth around the entrance to the Core rise two gigantic mechanical arms. Massive hands stretch from the ends of them, reaching creakily skyward. Each holds an enormous brass bar—a conductor—like the ones mounted on the front of the original Illuminator. Circular canisters of silver powder appear next, as long and tall as rooftops.

"Fairy petrol," I say in disbelief. "Hundreds of thousands of pounds of it."

I bend my head into the scorching wind, driving Bertie forward. My hair blows back from my shoulders, from the force of the massive spinning disks as they rise. *The Illuminator.*

We're running out of time.

Wires crackle at the sides of the disks. Sparks leap. Lightning jumps the length of the wires onto cables connected to the main structure.

"Urlick!" I power the cycle forward in a burst of speed. "Urlick! *Get out of there!*"

Bertie balks as we approach the rim of green light. I leap from the cycle, dashing through it alone. "URLICK!" I scream, searching for him. *"URRRRLICK! NOOOoooooo!"*

My eyes land on him struggling with Smrt near the edge of the ravine, backing slowly toward the frothy black cauldron of Embers.

The machine zaps and crackles.

Sparks fly.

Electricity jumps.

The conductors sizzle overhead.

A flash of lightning slinks snakelike up the sides of the metal toward the top of the structure. If it jumps from the bolts to the tip of the Crookes tube, it's over. We're all goners.

I can't let that happen. *Won't* let that happen.

Snaggled wires wince and seethe.

I turn and race for the stairs of the Core, fling open the door, and fly down them, bursting into the back room, the floor bouncing beneath me, the Illuminator quaking.

Another arc of lightning cracks, shooting through the holes in the domed ceiling, up the structure toward the conductors.

I sprint for the machine, voltage jumping beneath my skin, and lunge at the controls. Wrapping my hands tightly around the lever, I pull with all my strength.

Nothing happens.

The lever's stuck.

It doesn't even budge.

Anchoring my feet, I try again, throwing all my weight behind it. "Please," I shout at the sky, arcs flashing all around me. "Help me, please. *Don't let this happen.*"

The giant Crookes tube tilts slowly into position, and I gasp. Arcs jump all around. I hold my breath and release the lever. It's too late. I can't stop it now.

Unless—

If there wasn't any Crookes tube—

It would produce a harmless flash!

I abandon the lever and race up the stairs, out of the Core, and back through the beam.

"Bertie!" I shout over the howling machine. "Bertie! *Come quick!*"

Fifty-Two

Urlick

I see Eyelet disappear through the beam, running toward the Core. *If anyone can stop this, she will.* Smrt connects with my jaw.

I stumble backward, my boots teetering over the edge of the ravine. The heat of the Embers burns at my back. Smrt winds up in front of me. He catches me with a quick clip to the jaw and wrenches my neck to one side. "You've outlived your usefulness," he sneers, crushing my windpipe with his thumb. "It's time for you to die."

"After you," I hiss, prying his fingers from my neck. I wrap my hand around his. Hate bulges from his beady black eyes as I strengthen my grip. "One thing you should learn about me. I *never* give up."

I throw a jab to his gut and he buckles to his knees.

"Hand over the vial," I breathe through gritted teeth.

"I'll die first," he gurgles.

"You'll die, all right." I curl up my fist, delivering another right to his cheek. His head bobs left, then right. Blood splatters in a trail to the very brink of the ridge.

"Hand it over." I shake him, hauling him up by the scruff.

"I can't." He spits blood through his teeth. "I haven't got it."

A sinking thought pours over me. Perhaps he lost it in our scuffle. Or perhaps Flossie made away with it, too. She couldn't have. There wasn't time.

"You lying bastard!" I shout, pounding him again.

Smrt leans to avoid my blow, stumbling sideways, the heel of his shoes hooking on a rock. He tumbles backward, falling hard to the ground, landing on his rump. The vial pops from his breast pocket.

It skitters across the dirt, heading toward the lip of the ridge.

I lunge, grasping for it, falling over Smrt. He dives beneath me, reaching for it as well. The vial bounces past me, dancing on his fingertips.

My heart stalls in my chest.

"Noooo!" Smrt screams as the vial trickles through his fingers, over the side, tumbling length over length into Embers.

All the blood in my body turns to ice.

I hover over him, frozen.

Sparks fly up from the ground all around us. Lightning bolts snap overhead.

Adrenaline pulses through me like a drug. I clutch him by the throat and drag him to his feet, suspending him in the air.

"No, *please!*" he rasps, kicking his feet, clawing at my wrists like a frightened animal. "I can help you. We can make more!"

"I don't need your help!"

"Are you sure?" A wicked light burns in his eyes. "Don't be stupid. Don't cost Eyelet her life."

"Which life?" I seethe. "The one you would have gladly taken from her?"

I tighten my grip and swing him out over the ridge, my arm trembling under his weight.

"No! *Please*," he wheezes, clinging to my wrists. "I beg you. *Spare me!*"

"As you spared so many others?" I shake. "Tell me"—my eyes narrow—"how does it feel to be on the wrong end of power?"

He gurgles, feet twitching. I close my eyes. Let out a breath. And release my grip.

Cringing as he slips through my fingers.

His haunting screams ratchet up my spine.

As he sinks below the mist.

Spiraling to the bottom.

The endless bottom.

Of the nothingness.

The *Hell*.

That lurks below.

Fifty-Three

Eyelet

A boom shakes the earth. The ground snaps out from under my feet like an unruly child has flicked a blanket. I'm tossed in the air like a rag doll. I land metres away in a bruised heap. Heart pounding, I hike up my skirts and stumble forward, trying to remain upright in the aftershock.

"Bertie!" I scream. "Bertie, please! Hurry!"

He races up, and I jump aboard. "I need you to fly!" I shout above the roaring machine. "Like you've never flown before!"

Bertie shudders as I dive on the pedals, bursting through the glowing green rim into the centre of the Core. I circle, trying to amp up our speed. Then, using the door of the Core as a ramp, I yank up on the handlebars and deploy the wings, praying.

Bertie sputters. His wings slap the ground first before he catches any wind. He flaps furiously, working hard to pull us up.

"Higher!" I shout as we circle the structure. Bolts of lightning graze his wing tips. "Hurry, Bertie! Hurry!" I shout as he climbs. The whir of the giant glass plates pushes him around. He fights against the friction, his hydrogen stores plummeting. The gasket gasps. The needle falls. The canister reads near empty.

Electricity lashes around my head, whipping to the top of the structure.

I tear at my clothes. The heat's unbearable. It radiates off the structure in an endless, burning wave. I wince as the hide bubbles from Bertie's bones.

My skin feels as though it's melting. Wires snap at us like angry dogs.

"Just a little farther," I push Bertie. "We're almost there!"

The Crookes tube glistens in its stand to my right. The point hovers close to my hand. *If only I could . . .* I reach out, my fingers brushing the glass. "Closer! Closer!" I shout.

Bertie balks, caught in a gust of wind. I lurch to one side.

"Hurry, Bertie! We're running out of time!"

He recovers, throwing himself into a turn. Tightening his rotations, he circles the structure, tipping his wings toward the tube. His hydrogen tank whisks dangerously close to the electric fire snaking around the structure.

A spark hits his wing, burning a hole in the hide. The elephant skin bursts into flame.

"Ten. Nine. Eight . . ." a countdown begins.

The Crookes tube shudders in its stand.

"Now, Bertie!" I shout. "It has to be NOW!"

Bertie swoops, making one last circle around the neck of the glass. I reach, pulling up onto my knees on the seat.

Everything is suddenly too loud, too bright, too charged with energy.

An arc leaps beside me.

"Five. Four . . ."

I let go of the bars.

Lean out over the seat.

And hurl myself at the Crookes tube.

A flash ignites at my back, knocking the breath from my lungs. The palms of my hands meet up with the smoothness of glass—the Crookes tube topples from its stand.

I fall, spiraling through the centre of the structure, my back to the earth, shards of broken glass bouncing up all around me in a twinkling storm, my eyes fixed on something glorious—

"Three. Two . . ."

Through the cone of green light parting the clouds, I see another world—another universe—floating on the wind. A series of tiny islands—chunks of land all tethered together by plank-and-rope bridges. Each one kept afloat by a huge, spinning paddlewheel. On top of each island sit the most glorious two-story thatch-roofed houses I've ever seen, on carpets of green grass, surrounded by white picket fences. Waterfalls spill clean water into private ponds. A yellow sun shines in a blue, blue sky dotted with cottony white clouds. I close my eyes and open them again, expecting it to be a mirage. But it isn't.

Limpidious.

It has to be.

It's everything Father described and more.

The flash begins to fade.

The ground comes heavy and fast at my back.

I close my eyes and think of Urlick . . .

His image spinning with me . . .

And I brace myself for the crash.

Fifty-Four

Eyelet

Something appears out of the darkness. Feathers strike softly against my skin. The voice of a raven chattering pulls me to the surface. *Where am I? What's happened?*

I reach up, pushing the gas mask from my face. How did I end up with this? My eyes spring open. Ravens loop in circles above me.

"Archie?" I try to sit up, but I can't. My limbs are too heavy. My mouth is dry. My tongue is thick, as if I've been drugged.

I run my hands over the makeshift bed of twigs I'm lying in. My head rests on a pillow of leaves. I'm still in the forest. But I'm not sure if I'm at the Core. The structure—it's gone.

I look around for the remnants of the building, but the cloud cover's too thick for me to see. The Turned. Have they taken me? Am I one of them?

Is this what my life is to be?

Archie spreads his wings, cawing over his shoulder, and I panic, thinking he sees the Turned. Instead, the rest of the flock arrives in a dither, swooping and circling, their chatter playing as musically as a zither in my head.

I sit up dizzily. The ground spins like a top. "Where am I, Archie? Am I dead?"

Archie shakes his head and caws—ridiculously loudly—and I wince from the pain.

This much I do remember: the sulfurous taste of the wind. The sound of the crashing glass at my back as I fell through the towers. And Limpidious. *Yes.* I remember seeing Limpidious.

If that was real?

"The towers?" I turn to Archie. "Where are the towers?" I look around. "Where did the structure go?" I try again to get up, but the ground refuses to let go of me. Archie hovers close.

I squint across the clearing in front of me, seeing two giant tears in the earth. A fire smoulders in between. "It's gone, isn't it? Did it burn? Or has it sunk back down into the Core?"

Archie squawks, then flaps his wings as if to lift off and leave me. "No, wait! I need to know what's happened! Where's Pan? She'll tell me. Where is she, Archie? Where is Pan?"

The flock divides, circling, and my heart drops heavy as a stone. The birds double back and then part in the centre, revealing a single settled bird. She sits atop the newel post of an old, broken-down gate. Her beak glints red through the spiraling grey cloud.

"Pan!" I breathe. "It's you!" I leap to my feet, nearly toppling over. The birds rush in, assisting me, steadying my arms with their beaks.

Regaining my balance, I reach up and find a goose-egg-sized bump on the back of my head—the cause of all my wooziness. I squint, trying to realign my eyes as Pan springs from the gate.

Her wings spread, she struts toward me through the amber grass, gradually increasing in both size and dimension. With every step her gait widens, grows more innately human.

I blink wildly. Is my brain playing tricks on me?

A blast of silver light bursts from her beak. I raise a hand to shield my eyes. It spins, silver streaks whirling through a black dust-deviling cloud. Feathers sprinkle off into the wind. A red steam twists, ribbon-like, through the cloud's middle.

I raise my arms to protect my face. "What *is* this? What's happening?" I turn to Archie. The forest around us leans to one side. It's all I can do to keep my footing. Archie and the rest are blown back.

The wind dies down. Something steps from the madness.

Not a bird, but a woman.

She's dressed in a bluish-black feathered gown. Her lips are painted garnet red. Auburn hair spills about her shoulders. She steps forward, her eyes flecked blue and green, beaming.

"Mother?" The word falls from my mouth. "It's not possible," I breathe.

I blink at her image, my logical mind working hard to imagine her away.

"I watched you die. In the square. In Brethren—"

"I know, my child," she speaks. Her voice is as steady and soothing as I remember.

"Is it you? Is it really you?"

She nods, and my breath falls away.

I don't move at first, afraid to close the space between us, for fear whatever spell's been cast will come to a crushing end.

"It's all right," she says and spreads her arms.

I rush into them, burying my face in her chest. Tears flood my eyes.

She wraps her arms tightly around me and kisses the top of my head. I'm overcome by the familiar scent of lavender.

"How?" I look to her. "How is it possible?"

"Pan," she says. Her eyes are wet.

"Where is Pan?" I pull back. "What's happened to her?"

"I am Pan." She reaches out and strokes my head. "She is I."

"What?" I shake my head, confused.

"Pan gave up her life so that I might go on living. The day you saw me dying in the square. Pan was a Valkyrie," she explains. "A shape-shifter. Able to transform from human one moment to raven the next. And now she's passed her powers on to me."

I gasp.

"I've always known it, since I was a little child. That's why I've always protected her. It was through those powers she was able to save me."

"But how? I don't understand. I saw you cut and dying."

My eyes fall to the scar on her neck.

"Exactly." She cups my face in her hands. "You saw me dying. Not dead, my dear. Pan accepted death in my place that day, bearing my punishment at the gallows. She entered my body and allowed me to inhabit hers, relinquishing *all* her powers to me. I became Pan, and she became me. That way you would never have to be without a mother. And *I* would never have to be without my child."

"So it was you?" I whisper through tears. "All along. You were with me?"

"That's right." She nods. "Thanks to her."

"Oh, Pan . . ." I fall into Mother's arms, sobbing. "No wonder you loved her so."

"I loved Pan, it's true, but never as much as I loved you, and your father." She runs a hand through my hair, pressing her lips to my fore-head. "It was because of Pan that your father and I brought you up the way we did—to believe that not everything in the world can be explained away by the theories of science. We knew better, your father and I. I had Pan, and your father had Limpidious. Together we believed in the mysteries of the world. And we wanted the same for you. Life is meaningless without magic in it."

"Urlick?" I pull back, remembering. "Where is he? What's hap-pened to him?" I'm frantic.

Where are the Turned? Why haven't they come? Did they—?

"Shhhhh, my child." My mother reaches for me. "He's not with the Turned." The look on her face sends my heart reeling. It must be something worse.

"Tell me." I step back. "What is it? What's the matter? What's happened to him? *Urlick!*" I scream and run at the ridge.

"He's not there," she hollers. I spin around. "Where is he, then?"

"They took him," she says quietly.

"Who?"

"The Brigsmen."

I suck in a serrated breath.

"I'm sorry, Eyelet. We tried, but we couldn't stop them. They arrived within moments of the flash. The ravens and I, we were barely able to drag you to safety. When we went back for Urlick, he was gone."

"Where is he now? What have they done with him?"

"None of us are sure. You have to understand, Eyelet, we thought you were dead. There wasn't time to follow."

"I need to go find Urlick. Bertie! Where's Bertie? *Bertie!*" I shout at the sky.

"It's no use," Mother whispers, pointing to the pile of smouldering ash at the base of the Core. "He's gone. He dove beneath you, breaking your fall. He gave up his life for yours."

I run to the site and fall to my knees. Bits of charred wings and scorched bone lie among the shattered glass. "Oh, Bertie . . ." I sob, running my fingers through the ashes. "I'm so sorry."

"You mustn't blame yourself." Mother swoops in. "It was not your doing. Not yours to be undone—"

"Yes it is." I pull back, tears in my eyes. "It's all my fault. Bertie. Urlick. Everything."

"What are you saying, child?"

"I lost the necklace, Mother. The one you told me never to lose. It's in the hands of the worst person possible. I've failed you, Mother. And Father, too—"

"You mustn't think that way—"

"But it's the truth." I shrug off her affections. "Whatever happens from this day forward, *I* will have been the cause. I lost the key to my future—to *everyone's* future—and I have to get it back. I have to change the course of things before everything, absolutely *everything's* destroyed."

I stand and start away. Mother pulls me back. "This came for you as you lay asleep," she says, dipping a hand in her pocket.

A brass Ladybird scuttles across her palm.

"How long ago did this come?" I say, snatching it from her.

"A few days back, I'm afraid."

I throw open the wings and extract the pin, peeling the slim tin foil from its drum. Carefully, I unroll it and read the message:

URLICK IN TROUBLE. NEEDS YOUR HELP.
ARRESTED. LOCKED UP IN BRETHREN. FACING
TRIAL FOR MURDER OF SMRT. SENTENCED TO
DEATH. COME QUICK. IRIS

I gasp at the vision that comes to me: Urlick hanging from the gallows next to my mother, the life drained from his eyes. My skin goes cold. My heart staggers.

"I've got to get to him."

Fifty-Five

Urlick

The old stone jug smells of urine and festering flesh. It's enough to make even the strongest stomach dump its contents. Then again, jail isn't supposed to be a holiday, now is it? Certainly this one is far from that.

I flop onto the straw-lined wooden cot that's to be my bed for a fortnight. I'm to be hanged in the city square on the fifteenth day. Found guilty of the murder of the Academy's beloved Professor Smrt—without even so much as a trial.

I let out a breath so big it startles my cellmate. The dragon tattoo on his forearm tenses its jaw. He stares over at me through his one good eye. The other is a nasty scar of pink-knotted flesh—the result of some brutal gouging, I suspect.

He sits whittling a piece of stone into a knife with another stone. The sneer on his lip warns me to stay clear of his side of the pen, or risk losing an eye of my own.

No worries, mate, I plan to keep my distance. The smell of him alone could kill me.

I pull my gaze from him and stare out the window. Iron bars separate us from the rest of the world. Each bar bears the scars of the failed attempts of those who tried to escape before us. A wry grin bubbles on my lips as I ponder how many of them were forced to spend their final hours with my cellmate. And how many of those were relieved to die.

He looks up. His good eye stares me down coldly. He grins, showing me his teeth. Two spotty rows of black-pointed spears appear where teeth should be. Another good reason to keep my distance.

This man is just a festival of fears.

I turn away from him, staring out over Brethren, wondering what's happened to Eyelet.

Where she is.

And if she's safe.

Or did they catch her, too?

Does she sit rotting in a cell next to me?

I resolve myself to believe she got away.

I wonder: if she did, will she come for me?

Does she even know I'm alive?

I close my eyes, draping my arm over top, trying to quiet my brain.

Something strikes the bars on the window, causing them to ring. My cellmate launches to his feet.

"You pesky rubbish pig, you!" he shouts, dragging his homemade knife across the bars. "Can't wait to peck me bones clean of me flesh, can ya? You horrid little Ketch's Helper!" He stabs through the bars at something black. It squawks and pecks at his hand.

"Pan?" I jump to my feet, shoving my cellmate aside, knowing I'll pay for it later. She turns her head, revealing her scarlet red beak. "Pan! It *is* you!"

I scale the wall, hanging from the bars. "What is it, girl? What have you got for me?"

She turns her head. Something glints in her mouth. *The Ladybird. My beloved Ladybird.*

I stick out a hand, and she drops it in. The brass legs of the Insectatron scuttle across my palm. "Good work, Pan!" I shout, closing my fingers over it just as my cellmate clocks me with a fist, knocking me from the window to the floor.

Quickly, I extract the Ladybird's message, seeing the six tiny words punched into its scroll. A smile warms my face as I read, then I duck my head, tuck my chin, and prepare to get pummeled, chanting:

"How much do you trust me?"

Dear Reader:

I can't thank you enough for selecting *Lumière* as your most recent read. You have no idea how happy you've made me. I hope you enjoyed reading it as much as I did writing it, immersing myself daily in the world of the Commonwealth, journeying along with Eyelet and Urlick and the rest of the crew. And I'd be thrilled if you'd include books two and three of the Illumination Paradox series on your "to read" shelves in the future.

In the meantime, I invite you to keep up with me at jacquelinegarlick.com, where you can sign up for my newsletter and be the first to hear about upcoming releases in this series, as well as others, and have the chance to enter exclusive contests, enjoy video blogs, and win bling and other prizes.

Again, let me thank you for spending a few precious hours in a world of my imagining. Please know that you hold a very special place in my heart.

Jacqueline

Are You Excited to Read On in the Series?

Enjoy this exclusive excerpt from the exciting continuation of the Illumination Paradox series from Jacqueline Garlick.

Noir

"What's all this?" I cough and choke, my lungs still purging Vapours. But Iris doesn't pull away—instead she squeezes me harder. "Iris," I say, peeling her off me. "Oh, my goodness." I catch my breath.

As I pull back, I see tears trickling down her cheeks.

"Iris." I pull her to me. "Oh, my." I pet her head and allow her to sob on my shoulder, tears starting in my own eyes.

"She was afraid you was never comin' back, mum," C.L. says, creeping out from the shadows of the stairway. He flashes me a welcoming toothless grin, and I smile, happy to see him in the shaky aether lamplight overhead.

"I must admit, I wasn't sure I'd be back myself." I squeeze Iris a little tighter.

"At any rate, you're *'ere* now," C.L. says. "And yer a merry sight, I must say." He drops his head. He reaches up with a toe and guides a tear from his cheek, and a soggy lump forms in my throat. How little time I've spent with these people, and yet, how much room they've made for me in their hearts.

Besides family, that's never happened to me before.

"Any word from Urlick?" I say, on the off chance he's been able to get them a message.

C.L.'s head droops. His smile erases, replaced with a wobbling lip of gloom. Iris pulls back from my shoulder, fear in her eyes.

"He will be back," I say. "Don't you worry." I cup Iris's cheeks, thumbing away her tears. "You have my word on that. Nothing's going to happen to him. Not as long as I live and breathe."

She half grins through her tear-filled eyes, as if she'd like to believe.

"I'm afraid it might be out of your power, mum." C.L. raises his head, a look of defeat in his eyes.

"Why is that?"

His lip quivers as he folds his feet. "We've gotten word. They've shortened his sentence. He's to be dipped in less than seventy-two hours."

"That's just three days."

"Yes."

"It'll take a full day, maybe more, just to cross the woods."

C.L.'s eyes grow watery as he stares at me.

"That's a Sunday. They never perform dippings on the Sabbath."

"Perhaps they've made an exception." C.L. hangs his head.

His words gnaw through me like a dull arrowhead.

My thoughts shift to Urlick sitting there in the stone jug, facing his end, feeling helpless, not knowing if help is coming for him. Those piercing pink eyes of his brimming with tears as he stares out between the bars. I close my own eyes, imagining us in a kiss. The kiss we'll share when he's free. I long to taste his mouth on mine again, feel the dart of his soft peppermint tongue brush against my own. To feel the strength of his warm, muscled arms envelop me. I can't imagine a world without that. I won't imagine one.

"Well, then," I say, sucking in a brave, jagged breath. "I guess we'd better get on with the plan, hadn't we?" I release Iris from my grasp.

Something lands with a thud at my knees, knocking me slightly off balance. I fall back, seeing a pair of tiny white hands clutching the sides of my skirts. Fiery red curls cascade down the back of a ruffled emerald dress.

"Hello, Miss Cordelia," I say, petting her head.

She looks up, her big brown eyes sparkling with tears.

"I thought you were dead," she whispers. Her voice is small and weak, as if saying the words louder might make them come true.

"A popular consensus round here," I jest, floating my gaze around the circle. Iris and C.L. grin. I bend at the knees. "Go on, now," I say, wiping the tears from her round pink cheeks. "Would I go and leave you alone in this world, after we'd only just met? What kind of a new friend would that make me?"

Cordelia looks up with a smile, and I take her tiny face in my hands. "I want you to promise me something. Can you do that?" She nods her curly head. I lean forward as if sharing a secret only with her. "I want you to promise me you'll never think that way again. All right?"

She nods.

"Thoughts are power, you know. They control the universe." I dart my eye up. "Whatever we think, it will come to be. So we must try *hard* never to think negative thoughts. Only positive ones. Do you understand me?"

She nods with a grin.

"Good." I tap her on the nose with a finger and pull her in for a quick hug. "Besides, the ones we love never die as long as we keep them alive in our hearts." I touch my chest. "Did you know that?"

She shakes her head and sucks in her lip.

"Well, it's true. It has to be. My father told me that. Now, don't forget it." I lean forward, planting a kiss on her forehead, and stand.

"Is Bertie with you?" she says in a soggy voice.

The look in her eyes shreds my heart. I hesitate before speaking. "I'm sorry, sweetie." I run a hand through her hair. I shudder, recalling the vision of Bertie, the glorious winged hydrocycle, lying charred among the ashes of the Core. "I'm afraid he didn't make it."

Her brown eyes brim with tears.

"Now, now." I bend and pull her in. "Remember what I just told you?"

She gulps her feelings back.

"As long as we keep Bertie alive in our hearts, he'll always be with us."

She sniffs.

"I'll tell you what," I whisper in her ear. "When Urlick gets home, we'll build another Bertie, in his honour—Bertie Junior, we'll call him. How does that sound? And we'll start with these." I pull back, digging Bertie's scorched headlights from my pocket and laying them in her hand. She looks down and smiles.

"About that," C.L. interrupts. "Not to throw a damper on the party, but 'ave you given any thought to 'ow you'll *get* back into Brethren without the *'elp* of Bertie?"

"I was rather hoping maybe you and Iris had a plan." I stand, my voice lilting.

Iris chews her lip, looks away. C.L. diverts his eyes.

"Well, then." I take in another laboured breath, rolling my hands. "We'll need to find some other way into town, won't we?" I turn away, my mind a flurry of thoughts—none of them viable. I pace, tapping my lips. "Some alternate form of transportation." I think aloud. "Some way to breach the gates of Brethren without using the ground." I turn and my eyes catch on something glinting on Cordelia's chest, hanging on a chain round her neck. *Iris's sister Ida's locket.* That's it.

I bend, hinging at the waist, and take it in my hand. I brush a thumb over the etching of an angel wing on the locket's front, a wry smile warming on my lips.

"We'll use Clementine," I say.

"Clementine?" C.L. staggers. "But you'll be spotted on 'orse for sure."

"On an ordinary horse, perhaps . . ." I swing around. "But not the kind I have in mind."

"I beg your pardon, mum?"

"Do you have some parchment and some ink handy?" I roll up my sleeves.

"Likely," C.L. says.

Iris races off to find what I need, returning quickly, passing me a pen while C.L. sets up the inkwell.

"What are you thinking, mum?" C.L. says.

"I'm thinking Urlick's not the only one who can make something fly."

Cordelia claps.

I stretch the roll of parchment out over a table at the end of the hallway, dunk the nib in the well, and start to draw. C.L. and Iris stand at my shoulder, hovering. A furious speed overcomes me.

"An armoured 'orse, mum." C.L. smiles as he examines my strokes. "You planning on storming the city in a Trojan?"

"Better than that." I add the finishing touches. "Have you ever heard of Pegasus?" I drop the pen and spin the paper around, stretching the drawing out for them all to see. "Now imagine Pegasus in an armoured suit and a set of mechanical raven wings."

"Oh, my . . ." C.L.'s jaw falls open.

Iris gasps.

Cordelia jumps up and down.

"We'll have to hurry, though," I say, turning back. "As you've mentioned, we don't have much time." I run my fingers over the drawing on the table again. "But I figure together we'll be able to finish the armour and wings by late tonight." I turn to C.L. "And then we can leave late tomorrow morning. I know it's rather tight, but it's the best we can do—"

"We?" C.L. swallows.

"Well, I was kind of hoping you'd come with me." I wring my hands. "I'll need a wingman, and I hear you're the best." I smile at him, remembering Urlick, how much he respected C.L.'s loyalty.

"Very well, then." C.L.'s eyes grow big. "Consider it done." He salutes me. "Anything for you, mum."

"Good." I take in a breath. "And Iris, you'll stay here with Cordelia in case, by the grace of God"—I cross my chest—"Urlick comes back on his own?"

She nods.

"If we need you, we'll call for you. Otherwise, you'll man the post. You, too, Cordelia." She grins. "Now"—I rub my hands together—"we should probably get started." I turn.

"Aren't you forgetting something?" C.L. says.

"What?"

"Once you're back in Brethren, 'ow are you going to disguise 'oo you are? We 'aven't any masks left. And they take at least three days to make new ones."

"Good point." I sag, defeated. "No use to the masks, anyway. We've already been made out." C.L.'s right. I'll be arrested the second I set foot in Brethren. "Wanted" posters of me hang everywhere. Even the Northerners will be looking for me by now. I hug my waist. I can't just waltz in as myself, now, can I? "We'll have to create some sort of diversion." I pace. "Elsewise, I'll be picked up immediately." I turn to C.L and sigh. "I'm afraid this is not going to be easy."

"Well, nothing worth doing ever is, mum," he says, scratching his head with his toes, then looks up with a devilish light in his eyes. "Unless . . ."

"What? What is it?"

"I think I just might know some people who'll 'elp, mum."

"You do?"

C.L.'s eyes light up. He dips a toe into his waistcoat pocket and pulls out a weathered advertising poster. He unfolds it and stretches it out over the table, pressing down the seams as he goes, revealing a full-colour illustration of a travelling freak show. The faces of five or more tortured individuals peer up from the page, staring out from behind the bars of the cages of a train. The one to the far left looks suspiciously like . . .

C.L. "Oh, my God." I bring a hand to my mouth.

"I know, mum." His eyes flash. "But they's *good* people, I know they is . . . If only we was able to commandeer the freak train on its way into Brethren, they'd be more than 'appy to 'elp us free Urlick."

"What are you trying to say?"

"The freak show's due to arrive in Brethren in two days' time. All we 'ave to do is commandeer the train 'ere in these woods"—he points to a remote part of the forest on the map—"then ride the train into the city—"

"You're suggesting we shanghai the travelling freak show, and then what? Tie up its master?" My voice squeaks.

"I prefer we kill him, but sure, we can do it your way."

"Have you lost your *mind*?"

"Can you think of a better diversion?"

I let out a breath and roll my eyes. "No, I suppose I can't."

About the Author

Jacqueline Garlick loves strong heroines, despises whiny sidekicks, and adores good stories about triumphant underdogs. A teacher in her former life, she's now an author of the very books she loves to read: young adult and women's fiction. *Lumière*, the first novel in her Illumination Paradox series, won the prestigious 2013 LYRA award for Best Young Adult Novel and an Indie B.R.A.G. Medallion. The book also received the title of B.R.A.G. Medallion Honoree. Jacqueline lives in a house with a purple wall or two, and dreams of one day having a hidden passageway that leads to a secret room.

Visit her website at www.jacquelinegarlick.com.